THE JANUS WITCH

I0608208

MICHAEL SCOTT CLIFTON

BOOKS BY
MICHAEL SCOTT CLIFTON

The Treasure Hunt Club
The Janus Witch

The Conquest of the Veil
(Coming Soon)

Book Liftoff
1209 South Main Street
PMB 126
Lindale, Texas 75771

Interior Book design by Champagne Book Design
Cover design by Simply Defined Art

Library of Congress Control Number Data
Clifton, Michael Scott
The Janus Witch / Michael Scott Clifton
Romance—Fantasy—Fiction.2. Paranormal—Romance—Fiction.
3.Paranormal/Fantasy/Fiction4. Urban—Fantasy—Fiction
BISAC: FICTION / Romance / Fantasy. | FICTION / Romance/ Paranormal.
2018946996

ISBN: 978-1-947946-42-2

www.michaelscottclifton.com
www.bookliftoff.com

DEDICATION

To Melanie, my wife, and my children, Brett and Holly, the three greatest blessings of my life.

ACKNOWLEDGEMENTS

Many, many thanks to my critique group, Lisa, Joy, and Galand. They have helped me to become a much better writer, and continue to be my go to touchstone for help.

"Are you a good witch or a bad witch?"
Glinda, The Good Witch of the South to Dorothy
The Wizard of Oz

ONE

THE CART ROLLED TO A STOP.

Wooden wheels squeaked and grated while settling on the dirty, uneven flagstones of the village street. A line of buildings stretched into the gloom of the night. Cobbled together in desultory fashion, no two structures appeared exactly alike. More than a few leaned precariously on their foundations as if ready to collapse at the first puff of wind.

Scattered torches sputtered, their dim light revealing a deserted, narrow thoroughfare along which the haphazard collection of shops, taverns, and dwellings were located. Stone gutters ran parallel to the road. Choked with refuse and debris, a sulfurous reek wafted into the air.

Warped from wind and weather, a wooden sign hung canted from a rusty lance bolted to the side of a nearby tavern. Creaking in the evening breeze, the cracked and peeling paint revealed the picture of an enormously fat soldier, his belly spilling over his belt. The soldier held a pike beneath which was etched, *The Potbellied Pikesman*.

A cloaked figure studied the sign from the padded bench of the cart below.

"You know how to pick'em, Morganna," a voice called from the back of the wagon. "Why must we always stay at pigsties and hovels in every village?"

Morganna ignored the comment and continued to study the sign. Blood-red lips were pursed in concentration, as she tapped the cart bench with her forefinger. A long, scythe-like nail grew from the appendage. Deep in thought, she scored grooves in the wooden seat with the razor sharp nail. Reaching a decision, she threw back the cowl of her cloak to reveal long, raven-black hair.

A pair of dark eyes glanced back into the cart's murky, canvas-covered interior. "Get out. We finish our business here tonight."

Groans greeted her command.

"Why here? Why must it be at this pestilent flophouse? Why can't we at least stay someplace where the bed lice aren't the size of rats?"

Morganna scowled. "I've told you before. We *must* keep a low profile. Witches cannot afford to bring attention to ourselves. The last thing we need is to leave a trail for the Hunters."

The hinged back of the wagon banged open, and two figures climbed out. A brace of sconces bracketed the scarred door of the tavern, their smoky light revealing two women of stunning beauty. One displayed hair the color of spun gold and eyes of deep blue, while the other, rich burgundy hair and emerald-green eyes.

Identical amulets adorned each woman's neck. The polished silver chains of each amulet held a pitch-black opal—no light was reflected or received by the gem. The surface of each opal rippled like water.

The three women, each taller than most men, stopped beside the tavern door to confer.

"Let me guess. Our disguise will be whores...again!" quipped the blonde.

"Of course, Argatha...and stop complaining before I turn you into a marsh toad!"

Tittering and cackling erupted from the women before Morganna brought it to a halt with a chop of her hand. "Enough! Tressalayne, get our implements from the cart. Argatha, follow me."

The burgundy-haired woman turned and rummaged in the back of the cart, while Morganna and Argatha approached the two scrawny horses hitched to the wagon. The lathered horses, sides heaving from the exertion of pulling the cart, appeared underfed, with ribs that protruded from tightly stretched skin.

The coven leader looked around, then mouthed a spell. She spread the fingers of her hands and the air shimmered. A thin halo of light rose from the ground to meet above the witches, then disappeared.

"The distortion spell will keep us safe from curious eyes. Anyone who attempts to look in our direction will see only dim shadows."

Morganna nodded at Argatha, and she touched the nearest horse. Immediately, a bright green light enveloped the animal and when it subsided, a man appeared. Gaunt and naked, he trembled on his hands and knees.

"Stand!" Morganna ordered.

The man rose on unsteady feet, the leather harness falling from emaciated shoulders. Vacant eyes stared, while saliva dribbled in a thin rope from the side of his mouth.

Using her scimitar-like fingernail, Morganna quickly drew it across her hapless victim's jugular. Blood spurted in a crimson stream from the severed throat which Argatha nimbly caught in a chalice tossed to her by Tressalayne. Embellished with arcane symbols, the amber-colored chalice never overflowed despite the torrent gushing into it. Within moments, the fountain of blood slowed to a trickle. Eyes rolled back into his head, the man toppled face first into the hard cobblestones. Ignoring the twitching limbs, Morganna repeated the procedure with the remaining horse-faux-man. The bottomless chalice welded by Argatha once again caught the hot, crimson stream.

Morganna picked up both bodies as if light as straw, and carried them to a dark, filth encrusted alley beside the tavern. Rats scurried from the witch to disappear in moldering piles of spoiled food and garbage. With an effortless heave, she sent the bodies flying down the narrow lane to land with a graceless *thud*. Wiping her hands on her dress, the witch turned back to Tressalayne and Argatha.

"Another advantage of these seedy inns is dead bodies rarely draw attention. A couple of men with slit throats in a back alley is more likely to elicit a yawn than any kind of investigation. I'll wager they'll lay there until they become so ripe the smell forces the innkeeper to remove them."

Quickly changing tack, Morganna asked, "Tressalayne, do you have the changeling powder?"

Tressalayne nodded and handed Morganna a blue bottle whose contents glimmered in the weak light.

With practiced ease, the dark-haired witch pulled the cork from the bottle while muttering words in a harsh, guttural, language few if any in the village, county, or even kingdom would recognize or understand. Arranged at arm's length from one another, Argatha and Tressalayne stood while she tapped a minute amount of powder in her hand. Blowing a portion of it, first on Argatha, then the next on Tressalayne, Morganna re-corked the bottle and waited.

At first nothing happened. Only the mournful creaking of the tavern sign relieved the quiet of the night. Then, like embers from a fire, sparks fell from both women. Sluggish at first then building in intensity until with a crescendo, the raging fire completely enveloped both women. With a *pop* the sparks disappeared, and in their place stood two shorter, scantily-clad women. Argatha wore a stained, blue gown opened to her navel and barely covered her straining breasts. Of a light, transparent material, it left little to the imagination. Tressalayne wore a torn and patched green gown. The garment contained a slit which ended at mid-thigh to expose milky skin and shapely legs, while her breasts threatened to fall out of the loose bodice. Cheap jewelry in the form of rings and bangles flashed from both witches' hands and wrists.

Scrutinizing them, Morganna, nodded, satisfied. She handed the bottle of powder to Tressalayne. "My turn."

Tressalayne stared at the bottle before comprehension began to sink in. "You—you mean—"

"Yes. You are ready. Its time for you to start using the spells I have taught you as my apprentice," the dark-haired witch said with a tight smile.

"But you haven't let *me* try transmogrification and I am older and more experienced!" Argatha protested.

"True," Morganna conceded, "but then Tressalayne is already a more skillful apprentice than you and I have no doubt, more powerful. Now shut up and let's get on with it."

Argatha opened her mouth to further protest, but a steely glance from the coven leader caused her to quickly swallow the comment.

Tressalayne fumbled with the cork and almost dropped the bottle. Fighting to keep her hand steady, she spilled some of the powder into it while repeating the spell spoken moments earlier. Finally, she blew the powder onto Morganna.

Time passed and nothing happened. Argatha chortled and Tressalayne feared she incanted the spell incorrectly. Just as she was about to ask for a second chance, sparks dripped from

Morganna's figure. A twisting tornado of sparks and flames roared to life until with a *bang*, it winked out.

Morganna stood before them, shorter and plumper in a worn, wine-red gown. Tight, it clung to her voluptuous figure, the gown cut low to expose the deep valley of Morganna's enormous bosom.

The coven leader examined herself with a critical eye and nodded in satisfaction. "A little overboard with the tits, but otherwise well done." Turning to Argatha, she said, "Get our 'guests.'"

Cackling, the young witch returned to the cart and stuck her head in the back of the wagon and commanded, "Come!"

Immediately, two figures climbed out and stood at attention before Argatha. One was a young man. Tall and slim with thick, curly hair falling to his shoulders, the handsome youth was clothed in an expensive tunic and breeches. The other half of the pair was a young woman. Lustrous blonde hair fell halfway down her back and framed a face of flawless perfection. A shimmering, light-blue dress clung to her youthful curves, the tight bodice molded to her modest bosom.

Both the young man and woman stared with blank, unblinking eyes.

Argatha reached into the back of the wagon, grabbed a canvas bag, and tossed the chalice in it. Then she pulled a wand from her sleeve and tapped the cart three times. It shivered like a leaf in the wind, began to shrink, and continued until it was a hand-sized object resembling a child's toy. Placing the tiny object next to the chalice in the bag, she closed it and motioned to the young couple. With wooden, jerking motions, they followed the junior witch as she returned to Morganna's side.

With a last look around to make sure they were unobserved, Morganna turned the iron handle of the door and they walked into the tavern.

Unlike the quiet of the darkened street, the common room

inside the inn was a maelstrom of noise, light, and commotion. A cacophony of voices assaulted the witches' hearing, some bellowing for more ale, others raised in argument.

In one corner, a half-dozen men in the rough, worn and stained clothing of drovers, herdsmen, and farmers engaged in a game of dice. Boisterous shouts erupted as one bald, grizzled farmer threw the dice, the roar from the winners mixed with the groans of the losers. Moments later a fight broke out over payment of the wagers.

Another corner contained a group of men throwing darts at a chipped and pitted board. A gap-toothed barmaid in an ale-stained apron struggled to negotiate her way through the knot of men. Slapping and in some cases, punching, the rough patrons whose hands attempted to grope and pinch her ample backside, the barmaid went about her business of pouring ale and picking up empty leathern jacks.

The smell of sour beer, smoke, and unwashed bodies was overpowering, and Morganna, had to stifle the reflex to hold her nose. Her sharp eyes spotted the tavern keeper wiping a worn and age-darkened bar a number of paces to their left. The rag the tavern keeper used looked little worse than the clothing he wore. Jug-eared, a thin sheen of perspiration covered his bald head. A sweat-stained leather apron covered his wide girth, while a thick growth of grizzled chest hair erupted from the top of the bib like a shock of wheat. He warily watched the three women approach.

Morganna stopped before the bar and purred, "We'd like a room for the night."

Running a critical eye over Morganna and her companions, the burly tavern keeper took his time answering. Finally, he said, "Ten coppers."

The coven leader bit back a retort. *Five* coppers would be more than a fair price at such a backwater inn! Instead, she reached into the canyon between her breasts and took out a small leather purse.

Before she could flip the coins to him, the innkeeper thrust his chin toward the young man and woman standing behind the three witches.

"And five more for your clients."

It took every ounce of self-control for Morganna to stifle the impulse to cast a strangling spell on the fat innkeeper. Her plan to smoothly arrange lodging and a quick exit from the common room was in jeopardy. The longer they lingered, the more attention they garnered...the last thing she wanted.

Many of the men in the common room pointed at the women. The less inebriated among them staggered to their feet and stumbled toward the witches, no doubt to inquire as to the price for a night's companionship. Quickly, the coven leader took a silver coin from the purse and pitched it to the tavern keeper. He deftly caught it in midair, and bit down on the coin. Satisfied, he reached under the bar and produced a sturdy iron key. With a smirk, he handed it to Morganna.

Morganna spun and led her entourage up a staircase some ten paces to the left of the bar. At the top of the steps, she waited impatiently, the *slap* of the key in the palm of her hand.

There was much work to do.

TWO

"HOW MUCH LONGER UNTIL WE REACH THIS ACCURSED village?"

Robert Lockstone cast a sour glance at the source of the voice. Although the light from the twin quarter moons gleamed weakly in the night sky, his preternatural vision allowed him to see the comment came from the mounted figure on his left. It was Edward, the Duke of Parmenter's son. For the hundredth time, he cursed himself for allowing greed to overcome his better sense when the Duke proposed his son and a few of his companions accompany Lockstone and his men on the Hunt.

"It will be good for the lads to get out and see more of the Dukedom," the old Duke said while he tossed Lockstone a fat bag of gold coins.

Now, he wished he had tossed the bag back.

Almost from the moment they crossed the moat to exit the massive keep at Parmenter, a nonstop litany of whimpering, complaints, and even threats issued from the young duke and his two companions.

Lockstone ground his teeth. "It is at least ten leagues...another four hours of hard riding."

"Four hours? That—that's unacceptable!" Edward sputtered. "My arse is already so sore I shan't be able to sit normally for weeks!" The young Duke's breath erupted in white, billowing clouds in the cold air of early spring.

"Then you'll be glad to know we will stop and camp a couple of leagues outside the village," Lockstone replied.

"You mean another night on the hard ground and cold air when we could be sleeping in a soft, warm bed? Are you mad?" Edward spat.

A hand snaked out from the rider beside Lockstone, restraining him from the angry retort that threatened to erupt from his lips.

"Careful," he cautioned in a low voice.

Lockstone glanced over to see, Emmitt, his partner and right-hand man, wearing a crooked grin. *He's enjoying this* the witch hunter thought. Emmitt—opposed to bringing the young lords—took every opportunity to remind him of this on the long trip.

Lockstone refused to take the bait. Instead, he grit his teeth and replied, "Best to take the witches at dawn, my lord. Their potency ebbs with daylight and they will be exhausted from their nocturnal permutations. By making our camp outside of the village, we can catch a few hours of sleep. Best of all, this will allow us to catch them by surprise."

"Father said you were the best Hunter in the realm. Seems your reputation is overblown if the night concerns you so that you must wait for daylight," Edward sniffed.

This time, Lockstone would not be constrained. He jerked the reins and turned his horse in front of the young lord. Grabbing the bridle, he pulled the horse toward him and leaned in so his face was inches from the lad.

"Listen, you pampered fool! I've been hunting witches since before you were shitting in your diapers. I've seen good men killed by careless mistakes, and I've seen them killed in ways you couldn't imagine in your worst nightmares. I agreed to this fool's errand, but enough is enough! You will do *exactly* as I command, when I command it, and without complaint. Otherwise, you can ride back to Parmenter and take the Duke's gold with you!"

Startled, Edward yelped and jerked his head back. His lips moved, but no words came forth as if he had lost the capacity of speech. Dazed, he looked past Lockstone toward his companions, imploring them for help. Neither friend moved a muscle. Eyes wide, faces ashen, they edged their horses away from Lockstone.

The Hunter was a fearsome sight. A giant of a man, he towered over the young Duke. A face that appeared chiseled from granite stared at the lord from behind flint-dark eyes. Lockstone flashed a carnivorous smile, white teeth gleaming in the dim moonlight.

"Have I made myself clear?"

Edward finally found his tongue. "Ye-yes."

Lockstone released the bridle and allowed the lad to rejoin his companions. Huddled together, they cast skittish glances at Lockstone like he was some poisonous snake preparing to strike.

Emmitt shook his head. "Was that necessary?"

"Yes! I couldn't listen to one more complaint from the rich bastard."

"So *you* get temporary satisfaction and *we* get no more contracts from the Duchy of Parmenter."

"There will always be a need for Hunters and I'll put my reputation ahead of any of our competitors."

"Ah, that's the point isn't it? Reputation? Who wants to hire a hothead?"

Lockstone bit back a retort. Emmitt was right, of course.

Unless he could do something to repair the damage with the young duke, he might have ruined their chances of doing more business in Parmenter. Worse, the old duke might talk to his fellow peers and cost them business in other parts of the kingdom as well.

"I'll do what I can," he conceded.

The witch hunter studied the land around them. "This place looks as good as any to make camp." Brooding, he dismounted and began to search for wood to make a fire.

His thoughts were more than a match for the darkness of the night.

THREE

"WHAT A DUMP." LIP CURLED IN DISGUST, ARGATHA pointed at the bed. "If I'm not mistaken, that's the remains of a custard pie moldering on the bed sheet."

The young witch lit an oil lamp resting on a scarred table beside the bed, then turned to watch roaches scurry from feasting on the pie.

Nose wrinkled, Argatha crossed her arms and tapped her foot. "Can we *please* get this over with? The sooner we're out of here, the better!"

"We've been in worse places, and you know it!" Morganna retorted. "But since you are so anxious to get things started, *you* can do all the preparations."

The expression on her fellow witch's face was such, Tressalayne couldn't help herself—she started to giggle. Argatha's face turned crimson, but before she could explode, Tressalayne held up her hands. "Don't worry, sister. I'll help you."

Pulling implements from the bag carried from the cart, the young witches arranged them on a table across the room. Shoddily constructed, some of the table legs had become warped over time and did not meet flush with the floor. With a snort, Argatha ripped pieces of dirty linen off the bed, wadded them up, and crammed them under the legs to level the canted surface.

Next, they placed black candles about the room in the four cardinal directions. In the precise center of the four compass points, Argatha drew a rectangular box on the floor with a blood-red wax stylus.

She stepped back to examine her work before motioning to Tressalayne. The apprentice witch took the chalice from the bag and handed it to Argatha. Both women turned and looked at the coven leader.

Morganna walked about the room and ran a critical eye over the set-up. She made small adjustments to the locations of the candles, then took the stylus from Argatha and touched up the lines drawn on the floor.

Satisfied, she turned and nodded. "Very good, Argatha. Prepare the first donor."

Face flushed with pride, Argatha disrobed the young man until he stood naked. A pail of water sat in the corner, and taking a clean rag, she washed him from head to toe. Frozen through the whole process, he stood unblinking.

"Walk," the junior witch commanded. "Step into the rectangle, but mind you do not step on the lines."

Obeying, the young man stepped into the box. Argatha turned and held the chalice out before the coven leader.

Morganna shook her head. "Complete the spell. You complained loudly enough about your sister. Let's see if your skill is a match for hers."

Licking dry lips, the young witch gripped the chalice. Making sure she stood completely outside the wax outline on the floor, she turned and faced the curly-haired youth.

Her hands trembled while she stroked the chalice and

chanted in the same harsh language used earlier by Morganna. A soft, amber glow radiated from within the vessel, becoming brighter as Argatha continued to incant the spell. Finally, a wisp of the ghostly light thrust upward from the chalice. Like a tendril from a plant, it grew and spread, urged on by her chant.

Drawn to the rectangle engraved on the floor, the shoots crossed the wax lines and onto the handsome youth, caressing his feet and legs. The tendrils crisscrossed and intersected to meet at the slack-jawed mouth of the youth. Now a solid cord of amber light, it reared back like the head of a snake.

Then struck with blinding speed.

Traveling into the hapless youth's mouth, the cord of light invaded and filled every inch of his body. For the first time, the young man showed a reaction. Gurgling as if drowning, his body shook in the grips of a seizure. This went on for some time until at some point, the gurgle turned into a low moan of incredible pain.

A soft sucking sound filled the air. The amber cord turned pink, then red before it reversed course and flowed from the youth's body back into the chalice. Within moments, the witches' victim began to age. His body shrank, his hair turning gray then white, then falling off in clumps. Skin became wrinkled and liver-spotted, the eyes rheumy and clouded with cataracts. When the amorphous fog finally retreated, an old man, bent and barely able to remain upright, stood before them.

Argatha shot a triumphant look at Tressalayne before she placed the chalice on the table and clapped with delight.

"I did it! I did it!"

"So it seems," Morganna concurred.

Seeing Tressalayne's expectant look, she wagged a finger at her. "One test is enough for tonight. You'll get your chance someday. Argatha, prepare the next donor."

Chortling, the junior witch ordered the old man to stand in

the corner. As he shuffled off, almost collapsing at one point, Argatha repeated the process, and disrobed and bathed the young woman while Tressalayne watched, arms crossed and fuming.

The woman was a beauty, with slim hips, a tiny waist, and small, pert breasts. Youthful vigor radiated from her like a beacon. As with the victim before her, she stood within the wax-drawn rectangle vacant-eyed and unmoving. This time, Morganna carried out the ritual. When she finished, an ancient crone stood before them. Toothless, the old woman had stringy white hair hanging from her scalp, her breasts reduced to drooping sacks of flesh.

The crone joined the old man in the corner.

Argatha rubbed her hands in anticipation. She reached for the chalice on the teetering table before a stern glance from Morganna stopped her.

"We need to let the potion steep. Patience is needed now— never a strongpoint of yours. Don't expect to lead a coven until you learn to curb your impulsive nature."

Red-faced from the rebuke, Argatha stepped back, her rage barely contained. Ignoring her, Morganna turned to Tressalayne.

"Tell me what you know of our client, the Earl of Bastrop."

With a smirk at her sister witch, Tressalayne crossed her arms. "He married a young woman twenty years his junior and has problems performing his duties as a husband. Childless, the Earl is eager to satisfy his young wife and to produce an heir. His Earldom is very prosperous, and he has the means to obtain anything he wants."

"Yes!" Morganna boomed. "*That*, is where we come in. The Earl is a fat, drunken fool, who by accident of birth, inherited the richest Earldom in the Southern Kingdom. He would pay *anything* to regain the vigor of his youth. We have been contracted to give him that means."

Morganna paused, picked up the chalice to sniff its contents, then put it back down. "What the fat fool doesn't realize is the *morlaga* potion only temporarily restores youthful vitality. The Earl will have a few months at best before he returns to the impotent husband he was before."

Argatha, regaining a portion of her good humor, picked up the thread. "Then he will want more of the potion, and we will be happy to supply him with more."

"Aye, but at a *much* steeper price," Morganna added.

The witches cackled and snickered while they danced and celebrated their good fortune.

FOUR

"**T**HEY'RE GONE."

An insistent hand shook Lockstone's shoulder. Groggy from sleep, the Hunter cracked open an eye. "Eh?"

"I said, they're gone."

Lockstone rubbed his eyes, then looked up to see Emmitt in the flickering light of the campfire, a concerned look on his face. "Who's gone? The Duke's brat and his friends? Good riddance I say. I hope he develops saddle blisters on his arse on the way back to Parmenter."

"That's the problem. He's not on his way to Parmenter. He's on his way to the village."

All sleepiness left the witch hunter in an instant. He sprang up from the hard ground and immediately noticed two horses missing. "Why? What do they plan to do?" he demanded.

"To kill the witches, of course."

The color drained from Lockstone's face. "How do you know this?"

His partner jerked a thumb over his shoulder to where a miserable, huddled form sat beside the campfire.

Three long strides took Lockstone to the fire where he

looked down at the face of Edward's remaining companion. He searched his memory for a name to match the face, then recalled Edward referred to him as Timlon. Further racking of his brain revealed Timlon to be the son of a minor lord within the Duchy of Parmenter.

Fear radiated from the boy's face. "I told them not to do it! I told them not to go!" he blurted.

The witch hunter grabbed Timlon and jerked him to his feet. "What do they plan to do?" he demanded. Eyes wide with fear, the boy's knees quaked. "Speak, damn you!" he growled, shaking him.

"Robert!"

Feeling a hand on his shoulder, Lockstone turned to see Emmitt.

"You will not shake the answers from the lad! Can't you see he is scared within an inch of his life?"

With a deep breath, Lockstone released the boy and stepped back. Through gritted teeth, he lowered his voice and said, "Tell me what happened. Leave nothing out…and be quick about it!"

Timlon stuttered, "Ed—Edward felt his honor was besmirched. He and Frederick decided if they captured and killed the witches, not only would Edward's good honor be restored, but, but…" the lad's voice trailed off.

"Go on. Finish, boy."

Timlon gulped and retreated several paces before he answered. "Edward thought if they killed the witches, he could convince his father your reputation as a Hunter was—was overblown. That—that you were a fraud!" He scuttled backwards and cowered, expecting Lockstone to cuff him.

The witch hunter turned beet-red, his breath leaving his lungs in an explosive rush. "The fools! That preening idiot is going to get them both killed! To go against a coven as if it were as easy as knocking on the door and demanding entry. They have no idea of what awaits them!"

Emmitt nodded. "Precisely why we have no time to waste."

Lockstone looked up to see their horses saddled, the supplies packed and ready. Emmitt wasted no time summing up the situation and preparing for their quick departure.

Lockstone leaped onto his horse, took the reins, and then turned to face Timlon. "Stay here. If you value your life do not follow us into the village!"

White-faced, the boy nodded.

Digging heels into their horses, the witch hunters thundered after the Duke's son.

FIVE

SNIFFING THE CHALICE AGAIN, MORGANNA SMZILED. "AH, THE potion is ready."

With a snap of her fingers, the bottomless bag opened and two small flasks floated out. Chased in silver, the slim objects were fluted with a bulbous base. Settling into her waiting hand, she put one aside and picked up the chalice. Upending the vessel, she poured a measured amount into it.

Amber liquid, thick and viscous, dripped in a syrupy rope into the flask. Morganna studied the dribbling stream, inhaled the aroma once again, and savored the bouquet like a master chef. She stoppered the potion with a cork, then repeated the process with the other flask.

Eyes bright, the coven leader could barely contain herself. "Not one but *two* decanters of the *morlaga* potion. And the potency! Just the scent caused my senses to sharpen!"

Morganna turned to Argatha. "You picked our donors well. A healthier brace I have rarely seen."

The junior witch flushed with pride. "They were so ripe for the picking. The lovesick fools wandered alone into the gardens during Baron Ralstaff's engagement celebration for his son. Half of the Baron's guests were already drunk, so it was easy to slip away under my guise as a serving girl and bewitch them."

At this, Morganna's ears pricked up. "Were they part of the Baron's entourage?"

Argatha shrugged. "What difference does it make? They fit our needs, a young male and female pair—perfect donors for the *morlaga* potion."

"I told you to pick donor's from among the serving staff—peasants whose absence wouldn't cause a stir or spur an immediate investigation into why they were missing."

"I chose donors who suited our purpose. You said so yourself. Why is this so important?"

Morganna reacted as if pricked by a knife. She cast about and spied the pile of clothes and belongings stripped from their victims lying on the rumpled bed. She jumped to the mound and began to dig frantically through the clothing until she came upon a ring taken from the young man. Her hand went to her mouth, and a gasp escaped her lips.

She grabbed the young witch by the back of the hair, pulled her close, and held the ring before her eyes. "Do you see this?" she hissed. "It is a signet ring. Do you see the sigil embossed on the crown? It is a coat of arms. The coat of arms for Baron Ralstaff's family. *You brought us the Baron's son and his betrothed!*"

Screeching, Morganna hurled Argatha across the room. The apprentice witch crashed into the wall and slid to the floor.

She staggered to her feet, her face twisted with pain and confusion. "Wh—what have I done wrong, sister?"

"*Don't* call me sister, you stupid bitch! You have imperiled all our lives with your impetuous act!"

Morganna's rage filled the room. Ozone filled the air as lightning crackled about her, her features metastasizing into a creature with razor-sharp incisors and talons. Pointed ears grew from her head, her eyes becoming catlike slits. Argatha cowered, her back grinding against the unyielding wall, while Morganna's other protégé, Tressalayne, retreated to the safety of a far corner, relieved it was not *her* who chose the donors.

With great effort, the coven leader regained her composure. Slowly, her features softened and returned to a human appearance.

Through gritted teeth, she said, "The Baron will leave no stone unturned in the search for his son and future daughter-in-law. When they are not found, he will suspect something nefarious has occurred. Those of noble blood are a suspicious lot, constantly infighting, so the Baron will reach this conclusion in short order. Then there will be an investigation, a *thorough* investigation, one which will reveal that a servant girl—*you*, Argatha—are missing as well."

Calmer now, Morganna paced back and forth talking as much to herself as to her protégés. "The court wizard will be summoned, your steps retraced. At some point, the wizard will inspect the gardens where the residue of your bewitching spell will be discovered. The Baron will know witches were involved, and he will summon the best Hunters his gold can buy."

Morganna stiffened, her face twisting in dismay. "Lockstone!"

At the mention of the name, the younger witches cried out. Among the Hunters of the realm, Lockstone was feared above all. Corpses of sister witches—having met their end at the hands of the great witch hunter—were scattered across the kingdom.

"Pack everything up. We're getting out of here now!"

Whirling, Morganna froze. Her sharp ears detected a noise outside the thin walls of the tavern.

The clatter of hooves.

SIX

MORGANNA FLATTENED AGAINST THE WALL AND MOVED TO the window. A finger pushed the moth-eaten drape aside. Through the dirty, dust encrusted window, the flickering torches by the tavern door revealed two young men. Puzzled, she pushed the drape open wider.

One was tall and slender, the other a shorter version of the first. Both wore expensive tunics and breeches, and looked barely old enough to shave. Even through the poor light and smudged window, however, there could be no mistaking the determined looks on their faces, nor the way they fingered the swords and daggers belted to their waists.

Suspecting a trap, Morganna scanned the roadway, buildings, and alleys in her line of sight. The sputtering torches left huge areas cloaked in darkness that even her preternatural vision could not penetrate. An army could be hiding in the shadows and she would be none the wiser. Besides, if indeed Lockstone hunted them, he would not send lads to do his job for him. He would lead, as he always did, in order to make the first kill. She had never faced a more fearless opponent.

"What do you see?" Tressalayne whispered, her caution over-whelmed by curiosity.

"Boys," Morganna replied, "and by the looks of them, not long separated from their mother's teat."

Wringing her hands, Argatha risked a peek through the sliv-er-like opening in the drape. "What are they doing here? What are we going to do?"

"The first question is easy enough. They are here to kill us."

Argatha moaned and cast about to seek a possible avenue of escape.

"Get a hold of yourself! Since when does a coven cower at the sight of two pink-faced lads?"

"We should find out how they found us and who sent them," Tressalyane said, boldness creeping back into her voice.

Morganna nodded and scowled at Argatha. "That's the first intelligent suggestion either of you has made."

A cunning glint appeared in the coven leader's eyes. "Get the donors dressed. Here's what we are going to do…"

The door flew open followed by Edward and Frederick who burst into the tavern. Dozens of pairs of eyes appraised them while they stood blinking at the edge of the common room. Their fine garments contrasted sharply with the rough, stained clothing worn by the patrons, and it soon became apparent they were out of place as pigs at a royal ball. For the first time, their determination began to waiver.

A cold knot of apprehension in his stomach, Edward swal-lowed and made his way to the bar where the tavern keeper stood watching them. Frederick followed close on his heels.

"Er, ah, do you have any guests that recently took a room at your—your establishment?"

The tavern keeper spat into a rag clutched in a meaty hand, then wiped and polished the boiled leather tankard he held.

Without a glance, he said, "Depends."

Confused, Edward looked back at Frederick who shrugged.

Turning back, the young duke asked, "Uh, what does it depend on?"

With a *thump*, the tavern keeper put the mug on a shelf beneath the bar. He placed both his large hands on its scarred surface and eyed Edward. "On what it's worth to you."

The young duke's mouth opened and shut as he processed the statement. "Oh. *Oh!*" Edward sputtered, the man's intent finally dawning on him. He fumbled for the pouch at his belt, then produced a silver coin. He placed it on the bar.

The coin disappeared in his hand, and the grizzled tavern keeper jerked a thumb at the stairs. "First room on the left."

Eagerly, Edward motioned to Frederick.

They swarmed up the stairs.

The knocking, tentative at first, turned into pounding.

"Coming," a thin, reedy voice exclaimed. "Goodness, who could it be this late at night?"

"We demand entry! Do not force us to break the door down!"

The sound of a bolt squealing filled the air, and the door cracked open to reveal an aged and wrinkled face. Hand on the door, Edward forced it wider. With a *hiss*, his sword left its sheath.

An old man stood there, an even older woman behind him.

Edward blinked and looked past the elderly couple. The single lamp on the table across the room left much of the room cloaked in shadow.

"Is something wrong, My Lord?" the old man croaked.

Thoughts raced through Edward's mind. Did the innkeeper

tell them the wrong room? Was he playing them for fools? Heat flushed his cheeks.

"Who are you? What are you doing here?" he blustered.

"Why, I am Roger and this is my wife Lilly. We are traveling home after visiting relatives in the next village, My Lord."

Frederick peered over Edward's shoulder. "I suppose we should at least search this pigsty."

His face now cherry-red, Edward wanted nothing more than to put this fool's errand behind him. With a curt nod, the young duke sheathed his weapon and stepped into the darkened room. Frederick took his position beside him, and both squinted in the poor light.

The door slammed shut, and out of the dark shadows came sudden movement. A sharp prick appeared at his throat as Edward reached for his sword. Abandoning the effort as too slow, his hand sped for his dagger. Pain flared from his neck, and he cried out.

"Careful my young lord. I wouldn't want to kill you…at least not yet."

$\mathcal{S}$EVEN

"**Y**OU WALK INTO A ROOM SEARCHING FOR WITCHES WITH A sheathed sword? If only all Hunters were fools such as you!"

Cackling erupted and a cold numbness began to creep up Edward's spine.

"Turn up the light. Let's see our catch."

The flame on the oil lamp flared, and the light revealed their captors to Edward's eyes.

The elderly couple stood off to the side, now blank-faced and silent. Two statuesque women—one with golden hair, and one with hair the color of burnished bronze—stood beside Frederick, their forefingers pressed to his jugular. The young duke shuddered when he saw why. An unnaturally long and curved fingernail grew from each like talons on a bird of prey. Razor-sharp, these talons glittered in the lamplight. He didn't need further inspection to know a similar claw pricked his own neck.

Edward's blood ran cold, and his bowels loosened.

Warm breath tickled his ear.

"Why are you here, young lord, and who sent you?"

"Don't tell them, Edward! They will just kill us anyway!" Frederick blurted.

Edward's eyes widened at his companion's outburst. Whether fear or courage caused this bravado, the murderous look in their captors' eyes left no doubt worse was in store for them. A squeak, fueled by terror, escaped from his lips. He clamped his mouth shut, and fought to keep his wildly beating heart from bursting out of his chest.

"Hmmm. Let's test this theory shall we?"

Hands shoved the young duke, and he stumbled forward. The two witches released his friend and caught him in the exchange. Held in an iron grip, the now familiar deadly jab reappeared at his neck. For the first time, he beheld the other witch. Beautiful like the rest, the witch—obviously the leader of the coven—possessed raven black hair with eyes whose darkness matched the shadows.

"Come here, dearie," she purred, placing the dagger-like nail beneath Frederick's chin. Eyes wide, Frederick had no choice. Like a hooked fish, the pain and pressure from the nail propelled him forward.

The witch chanted and held her victim's eyes with her own. The hair on the back of Edward's neck stood on end. He *felt* something, as if the shadows themselves moved and danced to the bidding of the witch. Trembling, he watched Frederick's eyes become unfocused and glazed.

With a step back, the raven-haired witch snapped her fingers. "Come here!"

Immediately, Frederick stepped forward.

"What you have seen, my young lord, is a bewitching. Your friend is now at the mercy of my bidding."

The witch studied Edward. "Is that doubt I see in your eyes, my young lord, or is it fear? *Hmmm*, it's hard to tell. Oh dear, I'm afraid a further demonstration is in order."

She moved to Edward's ear. "Normally, a bewitching such as this removes total consciousness, but since you and your friend interfered with my coven, I think I will add a twist."

She resumed her chant, and with a smile, pointed at Frederick. Blinking as though waking from a sound sleep, Frederick's eyes, empty before, now appeared sharp and focused. Deep within his chest, a moan erupted.

"Oh, yes. He sees. He feels. *He is my slave!*"

Cackling, the coven leader swept to the middle of the room.

"Come!" Without hesitation, Frederick moved and stopped in front of her.

"Take your dagger from your sheath and hold it high over your head."

Obediently, Frederick held the weapon with both hands, ready to make a killing strike.

"Walk to your friend."

Frederick pivoted, and stood before Edward, the dagger poised above his head.

"Kill him." The knife plunged toward the young duke's chest.

Screaming, Edward tried to pull away. The witches, demonstrating unnatural strength, easily held him in place.

"Stop!" the coven leader cried.

The dagger's sharp tip halted inches from Edward's chest. A warm, wet stain spread from his breeches, the battle lost to control his bowels.

The witch appeared at Edward's ear again. "It gets better my young lord. Watch this."

She pointed at Frederick. "Plunge the dagger through your own heart. But slowly, *ever* so slowly, dearie."

Frederick reversed the dagger's thrust and now held the tip above his own heart. His eyes pleaded with Edward while the tip drew nearer to his chest. Helpless to aid his friend, despair filled the young duke as he watched the blade reach Frederick's flesh.

"Stop! I'll tell you everything! I'll tell you anything you want to know," he cried.

The coven leader cackled and danced around Edward. "Oh, yes. I know you will, dearie."

The dagger met resistance at the breastbone, a *cracking* noise resulting from the blade's penetration. Teeth gritted in effort, the cords on Frederick's neck stood out as he strained to push the blade through the bone.

Frederick's eyes widened when the sharp blade suddenly pierced the bone and slid into his heart. He continued to push until the hilt stopped against his ribs. The young duke's companion stood motionless for several moments, blood gushing from the wound. His eyes lost focus and glazed over. Then, like a felled tree, he toppled to the floor.

When his screams stopped, Edward began talking.

CEIGHT

"I'D SAY AN HOUR. MAYBE MORE." EMMITT REMOVED HIS hand from the horse tied before the tavern, the lather already drying.

Cursing, Lockstone melted back into the inky shadow of the alley, joined moments later by Emmitt. They turned to face the night, the pink of dawn already edging the horizon. "Let's hope we aren't too late."

The words rang hollow, the witch hunter fully aware of the futility of the statement. An hour alone with a witches' coven was tantamount to a lifetime. The horrors that could be visited by witches on their victims in that time were too numerous to even consider. Likely, any action they would take now would be to avenge the Duke's son and his friend, not save them.

"Get our gear," Lockstone growled.

Unlike Edward and Frederick who boldly rode up to the tavern, the witch hunters chose not to announce their presence. They left their horses in a darkened alley on the outskirts of the village, then walked the rest of the way carrying what they needed.

With a grunt, Emmitt hefted a heavy tow sack and threw it over his shoulder. Following Lockstone, they came to the back door of the tavern. With an ear to the door, the big witch hunter listened. He nodded to his partner and took a long, thin, pincer-tipped wafer of metal from a pocket in his tunic. The flat piece slid into the crevice between the door and the frame, and he pushed it up until the open tip rested around the door's bolt. Squeezing the grip, it closed on the bolt. Lockstone wiggled the pincer, and was able to move the bolt back tiny increments at a time. Finally, the bolt squeaked open and the door cracked open with a groan.

The witch hunters jumped back and flattened against the tavern wall. Moments went by and the men held their position. When no alarm was raised, they approached the door again, each step taken with extreme caution. Lockstone pulled an enormous knife from a sheath at his waist, the blade a foot in length, and prodded the door open wider.

He could make out what looked like a kitchen, pots and pans stacked in haphazard fashion on a long table. The knife levered the door wider inch by inch until he was satisfied it was deserted. Moving in unison, Lockstone and Emmitt entered the kitchen.

The smell of congealed grease, smoke, and stale food assaulted the witch hunter's senses. Careful not to slip on the slick floor, he left the kitchen, Emmitt close on his heels, and entered the common room. Bustling with patrons hours earlier, it lay empty now, the farmers and herdsmen having gone home to sleep off the effects of cheap ale, with the tavern keeper having made his way to his own bed.

The embers of a dying fire burned in the fireplace, an occasional spark sputtered then flared. A lone candle, burned almost to its base, flickered in a puddle of tallow on a nearby table. Lockstone hurried over to it, and grabbed an object hanging from a leather thong around his neck. It appeared to be a compass, but this compass contained a bright red fluid, the directional needle float-ing and spinning on the scarlet liquid.

"Where?" Emmitt whispered.

"There," the witch hunter replied with a thrust of his chin at the stairs.

"Are you sure?" Emmitt asked, his uneasiness growing at a Hunt which had gone from bad to worse.

Lockstone tapped the compass. "Witches are murderous liars, but their blood always tells true."

The witch hunters moved in tandem up the stairs with pan-ther-like stealth. Careful to keep his feet wide to move up on the joists of each stair step, Lockstone avoided the worst of the creaks and groans produced by the warped stairway. Emmitt fol-lowed his lead, but, nevertheless, the ascent was not noiseless, as tiny groans and squeaks were simply unavoidable. Each time, Lockstone would freeze and hold his hand up at the sounds, lis-tening hard to see if anyone or anything would stir in reaction. When nothing happened, he dropped his hand and they moved on again. In this stop and go fashion, the witch hunters reached the landing, both men sweating and breathing hard.

Recovering, Lockstone straightened and pointed at a door to their immediate left. Emmitt flashed a thumbs up and began to remove implements from the tow sack.

He passed a crossbow to his partner, then pulled out another and placed it beside him. He flipped it over to check the brace of bolts clipped beneath the weapon. Emmitt pulled the bolts off to examine each sharp point, with Lockstone doing the same. A sticky substance—sap from a Witchwood tree—covered each tip. Harmless to most of the population, the sap was deadly poison to a witch.

Next, Emmitt pulled out a stoppered flask and handed it to Lockstone along with a small, horsehair brush.

An apothecary Lockstone trusted prepared the potion inside

the flask. Containing the powdered bones of slain witches, it also held a splinter from a witch's wand floating inside, along with a small amount of Heartstone. The gemstone was the key ingredient. Like the witches' bones, it had been ground to powder and mixed with the solution. In the presence of spells, potions, and the dark magic used by witches, Heartstone acted as a barrier, nullifying witch magic. In fact, it could cause explosive results harmful to both the witches and the Hunter if not used in a proper and careful way.

Which is why the witch hunter used *only* a trusted apothecary.

In precise amounts and when mixed by an expert, the potion remained a stable, neutral substance. If witch magic was used, the very air would carry the taint of it. When exposed to this, the balance within the potion would be breached, which in turn, activated the Heartstone and caused the solution to become corrosive—even to the point of eating through iron.

"Get the turtle ready," Lockstone whispered in his partner's ear.

With a nod, Emmitt removed a metal ball from the tow sack. The size of a small melon, knobby plates covered its surface much like a turtle shell. A hinge allowed the turtle to open and close, and popping it open, Emmitt inspected its contents.

Contained within were dozens of jagged pieces of metal, each piece coated with a dry, rusty-red substance. Satisfied, Emmitt snapped it shut and looked up at a grinning Lockstone.

"Like I said, a witch's blood always tells true," he whispered.

Lockstone took the flask, dipped the horsehair brush in the potion, and painted a large circle in the middle of the door. Then he repeated the process with the door handle and bolt.

He stoppered the flask and tossed it to Emmitt who placed it in the rucksack. The two grabbed the crossbows and took up positions beside the door. Wisps of smoke began to rise from the area he applied the potion to.

The Hunt was about to begin.

NINE

"**T**HEY ARE HERE. PREPARE YOURSELF."

Even before she saw the smoke seeping from the door, Morganna's sharp ears picked up the small, furtive sounds from the stairs. Clearly, the *real* Hunters had arrived.

All Hunters were dangerous, but the coven leader had faced more than her fair share down through the years and survived them all. Confident she could deal with the current lot stalking them, this assurance began to crumble when she considered *who* led them. If Lockstone led the Hunters outside the door, then none of them might live to see another day.

She needed to have an escape plan ready…just in case.

On one side of the room, Morganna used the blood-red stylus to draw what appeared to be the outline of a door on the wall. She stood by the diagram and motioned for the old man and woman to move beside her. They shuffled up to her and stopped while she pulled a wand from the sleeve of her dress. The polished wood baton—made from the blonde wood of the *Fiirch* tree—darkened near the narrow, pointed end, until it looked almost fire-blackened.

From memory, she chanted a spell to draw the last dregs of life from the ancient pair and into the baton. They collapsed at her feet, reduced to nothing more than bones and leathery skin.

The dribble of life essence did little to charge her wand, and Morganna cursed her hasty decision to kill one of the young lads. He would have been far more useful giving his life to the magic of her wand. True she still held one captive, but if things went badly, he might be needed as a hostage or a human shield.

A wide, smoking hole appeared in the door, the handle and bolt falling with a *clank* to the floor.

They were out of time.

A voice called from outside the door.

"Release the innocents you hold captive and we will insure your safe passage back to Parmenter for trial."

Lockstone! Morganna knew the voice only too well. Eyes closed in dismay, she snapped them back open moments later. Escape was no longer an option. It was the *only* option!

She needed time to complete the spell. Argatha and Tressalyane would have to buy her that time. Looking at both, she observed Tressalayne, her mouth drawn in a white line, but otherwise the young witch stood ready. Argatha was another matter. Her eyes darted about like a trapped animal, her body tense like a coiled spring.

She motioned them over.

"Hold your wands ready. Be sparing in your use of magic. The accursed Lockstone has an array of weapons and other implements which react to witch magic. All I need for you to do is delay and hold them off long enough for me to complete the transport spell. Then we will flee this place and start over someplace else."

Tressalyane nodded while Argatha, jaw clenched and rigid, gave a curt bob.

The two apprentice witches took up position and faced the door.

Morganna took one of the flasks containing the *morlaga* potion, pulled out the stopper, and placed the wand's tip into the vessel. Misty tendrils flowed into the wand. She almost wept over the ruinous use of the potion. Worth ten times its weight in gold, the potion would have set them up comfortably no matter where they fled to. Instead, she was forced to use it to charge her wand to enable their escape. At least they had one flask left.

And better to have only one dose of the potion and live than the alternative.

A voice from the other side of the door intruded on her thoughts. "I'm afraid you'll have to speak up. My hearing isn't what it used to be."

"Oh, thank you for your gracious offer," Morganna called out while willing her wand to absorb the potion faster. "But we have no captives, only guests which we are currently entertaining."

"By the beard of my grandfather! Is it you, Morganna? This *is* my lucky day!"

"Aren't you rather far afield, Robert? Shouldn't you be closer to home where the killing of helpless witches is more convenient for you?"

A mirthless chuckle bubbled from Lockstone. "I'll let you know—when and if I ever meet a helpless witch." His voice took on steel. "Now, I'll have to insist you release your captives."

The façade dropped from Morganna's voice. "I should have killed you when I had the chance!"

"Oh, but you tried. Don't you remember? You killed my mother while she fought to give me time to escape. A boy of ten eluded you, Morganna, the great witch, the coven leader all other covens look to for leadership. How that must have stuck in your craw."

Black anger boiled within Morganna.

"Your mother was a traitor to all witches. She left my coven and married a farmer. A farmer! My shame knew no boundaries. *No one leaves my coven without my leave. No one!*"

"She tired of all the killing, you merciless bitch! She wanted a normal life!"

"Spare me the sermonizing. It is *you*, her traitorous seed, hunting and killing witches, and *you*, a child of witch blood, who murders your own kind. My only regret is that I didn't kill her before you could be conceived in her womb."

"Liar!" Lockstone snarled. "I share no kinship with the likes of you, and I won't rest until I have exterminated every coven in the Kingdom!"

The witch hunter motioned to Emmitt to ready himself. Picking up the turtle, Emmitt waited for Lockstone to make his move.

"I'm afraid I've changed the terms of your surrender, Morganna. I'll offer a safe arrest and passage for trial to your coven, but not for you. The best I can do is promise you a quick death. Afterwards, I plan on cutting your black heart from your chest, and staking it and your head on a pike for the crows to feast on."

"Let's see. A trial which results in my coven being burned at the stake, and my head on a pike? Sounds like a fair offer. Let me confer with my sisters and we will let you know our decision."

The last of the potion disappeared from the flask, and relief washed over Morganna. After what seemed an eternity, her wand finally absorbed all of the *morlaga* potion. Engorged, it lay heavy and thick in her hand.

The coven leader turned and pointed the wand at the door outlined on the wall. Ancient words of power spilled from her lips as she chanted the spell. An intense light, concentrated in a rapier-like beam, erupted from the wand. Striking the wax outline, it spread like molten metal, until it completely filled the space. Wavering and shimmering, it solidified and coalesced.

The door stood open.

TEN

BEYOND THE DOOR, TREES SWAYED IN THE BREEZE. WOODED hills appeared as birds wheeled and chirped in the blue sky.

With a flick of the wand, Morganna caused a new scene to appear, this one a crowded bazaar. A vast array of goods lined the market, the displays picked at and scrutinized by kaftan-clothed shoppers, the air alive with the cries of vendors hawking their wares. Impatient, Morganna twitched her wrist, and a palm-covered island appeared. Surrounded by an azure sea, the tang of salt air drifted through the open doorway.

Then all hell broke loose.

Rolling on the floor, Lockstone took aim at the hole burned through the wooden door and let fly with a cross-bolt. The shaft struck Morganna in the shoulder. Shrieking, power pulsed uncontrolled from her wand and into the magical portal. A kaleidoscope of light exploded within the doorway, and images raced by faster and faster. Numbness spread from the coven leader's shoulder to her arm, the poison working quickly. Within moments, she could no longer feel her hand.

Her wand dropped from nerveless fingers.

With a screech, Argatha pointed her wand at the hole through which the bolt had traveled. A ball of green fire sizzled and struck the floor where Lockstone had been but moments earlier. The wooden floor splintered and exploded.

"Now!" Lockstone cried.

Emmitt tossed the turtle through the burned hole, the metal ball rolling into the room. Another bolt of green fire answered, pieces of the pulverized floor showering the Hunters.

Click.

The hinged top of the turtle sprang open, and sharp metal shrapnel rose from the hollow opening. Like feathers caught in an updraft, the pieces floated, then turned and oriented themselves—right at Argatha.

The young witch paused her onslaught against the Hunters long enough to turn and stare at the flotilla of metal pieces.

In the blink of an eye, the shrapnel homed in on Argatha, and streaked toward the witch. Her body shook, her flesh shredded by the sharp metal until it was reduced to bloody pieces. With a wet *thud*, the remains of Argatha's body hit the floor.

"*No!*" Morganna screamed in rage.

A booted foot kicked the door in, and the Hunters rushed into the room. With a howl, Tressalyane turned her own wand on the intruders. Lockstone dove to the left while Emmitt rolled right to avoid being incinerated. The witch hunters fired wildly, the air thick with bolts. Tressalayne kicked the table over and ducked behind it, Morganna joining her moments later. The thump of shafts striking the wooden barrier echoed in the closed space.

"We have to get out of here…*now!*" Morganna said, her face a pasty white from the poison's onslaught.

She cast about and spotted her wand. It lay beneath the magical door, less than six paces from her. It might as well have been in Parmenter for all the good it did her. The second she poked her head from behind the table, a bolt would skewer her like a suckling pig. Their bag of implements was closer, spilled an arm's length from her in front of the overturned table.

The coven leader ripped off one of the wooden legs and reached, one-armed, for the satchel. Snagging it, her improvised pole shivered while she pulled the bag to safety behind the table. A pair of stubby crossbow arrows festooned the table leg, proof of the Hunters' accuracy. Morganna tossed it aside in frustration.

Despair cloaked her. Without her wand, all Lockstone would have to do is wait. The poison would spread until she became helpless, and eventually, dead…if Lockstone even allowed the poison to run its course. She had no doubt he meant to keep his vow to cut her still beating heart from her chest. Tressalayne could forestall the inevitable, but in the end, she would be no match for the Hunter. Even now, her magic showed signs of waning, the incendiary balls hurled at the Hunters smaller and less intense.

Desperate, Morganna spotted the young lord standing statue-like in a darkened corner of the room. Bewitched into silence, he stood unnoticed by the Hunters.

And still under her control.

Hope bloomed in her chest as a possibility entered her mind. *A distraction. All we need is a distraction.*

"When I tell you, I want you empty the power of your wand at the Hunters. Don't worry about being accurate, just make them hug the floor."

Tressalayne cast a doubtful look at Morganna. The coven leader's fierce countenance, however, brooked no argument.

The apprentice witch turned and waited.

With an effort, Morganna stilled her heart, then concentrated. Across the room, Edward's hand moved to his waist. He pulled his dagger and held it by his side. Relief washed over

Morganna. *She reestablished her control over the young lord!* It was time to act.

"*Now!*" Morganna cried.

Tressalayne sprang to her feet and pointed the wand. Ball after ball of green fire shot from the tip, and the room erupted with explosions and flashes of light. The smell of ozone filled the air.

Edward took stilted steps toward a figure lying prone on the floor. It was Emmitt. The bewitched lord approached him from behind while the Hunter attempted to get a shot off at Tressalayne.

He never saw the young lord until the dagger plunged into his ribs.

Emmitt cried out and threw his elbow back. It connected with Edward's temple, the impact knocking him backward. The bewitched lord recovered and stalked the witch hunter again, the dagger raised for another strike. A bolt suddenly sprouted from his eye, and he pitched backward.

Lockstone cursed and lowered the crossbow. He killed the very person they came to save—not that the Duke's son left him any choice.

Morganna seized the opportunity.

She grabbed Tressalayne with her good arm, and leaped for the open doorway, the locations still whirling by like a color wheel, a blur of motion and color. A part of her mind knew the risks involved in plunging toward an unknown site. They could land in the crater of an active volcano or in the depths of the sea. However, when the alternative was to remain and face certain death, the choice became easy.

They disappeared through the door.

ELEVEN

FALLING.
Falling.
Falling.

Tressalayne plummeted like an anvil. Wind whipped by, howling past her ears like a wolf in winter, her eyes watering. At some point she became aware of her separation from Morganna. Unable to see or hear in the rushing wind, fear pierced Tressalayne at the knowledge her coven leader was lost to her.

Tressalayne knew enough about location spells to know something had gone wrong. When a witch stepped through a door created by a spell, the witch immediately located to the chosen destination…you didn't *fall*. When shot by the poisoned bolt, Morganna's wand released a tremendous amount of energy. Somehow, it corrupted the magic of the spell and in turn, the doorway itself.

Panic gripped Tressalayne.

Was she falling to her death, or worse, in some nether region, cursed to forever exist in some insubstantial domain?

Tressalayne swallowed her dread and noticed a subtle change in her descent. The whistling wind wasn't as loud and her headlong plunge had slowed. She risked a peek, cracked open an eye, and saw a speck far below her. As she drew closer, the resolution became clearer.

Another gateway.

The falling sensation became less pronounced, and Tressalayne drifted like a leaf toward the beckoning door. The open portal shimmered like a placid pool of water, and within moments, she arrived. Shadows moved and shifted on the other side, with the nebulous forms of trees and leaves undulating in the wind.

Then she was through the door, and her plummet resumed again.

Tressalayne screamed and held her hands in front of her while leaves and branches whipped her face and arms. She hit a limb, the numbing impact causing her to cartwheel while she plunged through the leafy growth. Stars exploded in her eyes when the back of her head connected solidly with another branch. Her ribs bounced off a stout branch, the breath driven out of her with a *whoosh*. With a *thud*, she landed, back first on the ground. Unbelievable pain enveloped her.

Her head hurt.

Her arm hurt.

Her ribs hurt.

She couldn't breathe.

Blackness overtook her.

Moisture trickled down her face. She licked her lips and tasted water mixed with blood. Opening her eyes, she panicked when at first, she saw nothing but darkness. Then a flash of light briefly illuminated a grove of trees. Thunder followed the flash. Relief filled her at the recognition of what her senses revealed.

A storm at night.

With a groan, Tressalayne sat up, the effort causing her head to spin. A wave of nausea gripped her, and she leaned forward and vomited. The solid bole of a tree next to her thrust upward into the rainy night, and she scooted back until she could lean against the rough bark. The effort left her weak and dizzy. Gingerly, she touched the back of her head to discover a large, bloody lump. When she tried to brace herself with her left hand to examine her aching ribs, excruciating pain coursed through her arm. Another flash of lightning revealed her limb bent at an odd angle.

Broken.

The wind picked up, and the rain beat down harder. Shivering, Tressalayne could feel heat radiate from her skin even in the cold downpour, the prelude to fever. She had to get out of the wind and rain.

Her back braced against the trunk, Tressalayne slid up onto her feet, unsteady and swaying. Planting one foot at a time on the wet, muddy ground, she cradled her injured arm to her chest and began to walk.

Progress was slow, and each step came with the price of enormous pain and effort. Tressalayne's knees began to buckle, and she realized she couldn't go much longer. Reckoning by the lightning strikes, she avoided colliding with other trees. Up ahead, she thought she saw a bright glimmer. Rubbing the rain out of her eyes, she looked again.

There! Like a beacon, a light glowed ahead of her in the blowing rain and darkness.

Tressalayne attempted to pick up the pace, and shuffled toward the light. Despite her best efforts, her progress remained slow, weakness growing with each step. The pain in her head grew worse, and she had trouble concentrating.

After what seemed like hours, she stood beside the source of the bright glow, a dwelling of some sort. The pain in her head felt like someone dropped a red hot coal on her brain, and she only vaguely remembered covering the final distance. Light streamed from large windows and revealed a porch with a door. Her head throbbed in a drumbeat of agony. Feeling faint, Tressalayne was obliged to lean against the doorframe for support. With the last of her strength, she lifted her hand and pounded on the door.

Nothing happened.

Spots appeared in her vision, and unable to remain upright, she slid downward. Without warning, the door opened, and Tressalayne pitched forward.

And then…nothing.

TWELVE

ORGANNA CLENCHED HER TEETH AND TOSSED HER HEAD, caught in the throes of agony.

Pain surged through her body like liquid fire, burning and scorching her from the inside out. It replaced the numbness from the poison coursing through her veins, and she realized if something didn't slow its spread, her death was certain. Like Tressalayne, she plummeted, but the howling, rushing wind was a mere annoyance compared to the torment within her.

Her lips moved, the enchanted words ripped from her lips by the hurricane-like wind. She forced herself into a meditative, hypnotic state. Her heart beat and breathing slowed to a near standstill. With her eyes rolling back into her head, she passed into semi-consciousness.

Karen Prescott drummed her fingers on the BMW's console. The wipers beat a staccato as she waited in the driving rain for the red light to change. Already late, she was meeting her husband and some of his clients at the country club for dinner. Pulling the visor down, she checked her appearance in the mirror. Satisfied, she dug her lipstick from her purse and touched up her ruby-red lips.

Thump!

Her windshield shattered, showering her with broken glass. A body landed in the seat beside her. Karen jerked back and stared in disbelief at the blood-streaked face of a woman whose head lay in her lap.

Raw, terror-filled screams filled the air.

"Are you insane? You're worried we might be sued? *The woman fell out of the sky right into my Beemer!*"

Drenched, Karen stood shivering in the emergency room, scarlet-tinged water pooled at her feet. Other than a few cuts from the flying glass, she was physically okay.

Her emotions were another story.

The sight of the woman's scratched and lacerated face in her lap scorched her memory. The horrifying image spooled over and over again in her mind…and her idiotic husband, Todd, was worried about being sued!

"What? No, I haven't called the insurance company!" Disconnecting on Todd in mid-sentence, she tossed the cell into her purse. Fuming, she calculated how long it would be until she allowed Todd to touch her again. She started with days and progressed to weeks.

She was now up to months.

Arms crossed, she stalked over to a police officer chatting to an admissions nurse. It was a slow night at Nacogdoches Memorial Hospital, and the two were deep in conversation. Karen cleared her throat. The policeman looked up.

"Can I at least go home and change? I'm soaked," Karen pleaded.

The officer, a young man with brown hair cut so short his scalp gleamed, shook his head. "Sorry, ma'am. We still need to hold you for questioning."

"I've answered all your questions. One minute I'm waiting for the light to change, the next, *boom,* a woman falls through my windshield."

"My instructions are to keep you here until we know more about the status of the victim. If she regains consciousness, we need her to tell us what happened."

Irritated, Karen tapped her foot.

Victim. Like it was her fault. Like she just drove around waiting for people to drop from the sky. Surely they didn't think she had anything to do with it!

The admissions nurse, a middle-aged woman wearing a blue and pink patterned hospital uniform, gave Karen a sympathetic look.

"They have the Jane Doe stabilized. We'll know more in a few hours."

Karen stared at the nurse. *How could the woman still be alive? How was that possible?*

As if reading her mind, the nurse said, "From what we can tell, the impact with your car caused no outstanding injuries. However, the Jane Doe was shot—the doctors think with some kind of poisoned dart or arrow. Removing it and finding a suitable treatment took some time. She has an excellent chance of recovering."

Karen threw her hands up. *Shot with an arrow...and a poisoned one at that? Could things get any weirder?*

A sudden thought struck her. "Wait. Why do you call her a 'Jane Doe'?"

The nurse looked at the officer, who replied, "Because she has no identification, nothing which would tell us who she is. We are running her prints, but that's a long shot. Unless she committed a crime, we'll have to wait for the lady to wake up and give us her name."

Karen closed her eyes.

Great. Just great! Probably an illegal alien. Maybe Todd was right about being sued. Lawyers might already be circling the hospital like vultures just waiting for the "Jane Doe" to wake up so they can represent her.

Karen spun on her heel and went in search of the hospital restroom. Turning the corner of the lobby, she spied it and shoved the door open. An antiseptic smell filled the air, and a sturdy mirror ran the length of the wall above the lavatory. She leaned on the sink and studied her appearance.

Her hair, styled at an exclusive salon, was in complete disarray, her make-up smeared and streaked. Her white cocktail dress, spotted with crimson stains and still damp from the rain, clung to her toned figure like a second skin, while her Jimmy Choo pumps, covered in blood and mud, were ruined. Although she just turned forty, she looked at least ten years younger, a testament to her personal trainer and a good diet. Todd, a high-end oil executive, pampered her, and the only serious work she was involved in during their fifteen-year marriage was in keeping her curvy figure.

Sighing, she dug into her purse to pull out her hairbrush and compact.

If I'm going to be interrogated, I'm going to look good!

THIRTEEN

LOCKSTONE CRADLED EMMITT'S HEAD IN HIS LAP.

It took no healer to know the wound inflicted on his friend was fatal. The dagger struck his lung, and the telltale wheezing became a strangled gurgle as Emmitt struggled to draw a breath. Coughing, bloody spew coated his lips.

Emmitt's eyes met Lockstone's, a mixture of embarrassment and resignation on his face.

"Survived all these years huntin' witches and then let a tadpole of a lad sneak up on me. What a note to end my life upon."

"Don't be beating yourself up. We were both dodging witch fire, and it could have just as easily been me on the receiving end of that dagger." Lockstone clenched his jaw in anger.

"Truth be known, it's my fault. The second I knew Morganna was among the witches we cornered, I should have known she would have some trick up her sleeve. I let my hatred for the murderous bitch blind me."

"No one blames you for feeling that way, Robert, least of all me. I know what she did to your family."

Tears began to leak from Lockstone's eyes.

"A better partner and friend I could never have than you, Emmitt. I'm sorry I let you down."

Emmitt patted Lockstone's hand. "Now, now. None of that. I knew the risks. Never a dull moment around you, Robert, that's for sure, and ridding the Kingdom of witches...well, someone had to do it. And we got our fair share, didn't we?"

A chuckle rumbled from Lockstone's chest. "Aye, that we did."

"Do you remember the time—"

Emmitt stopped, his eyes unfocused. One last raspy breath left his lungs, then his chest stilled. Lockstone looked down.

His friend was dead.

The witch hunter lifted his head and howled in raw, unrestrained anguish. He hugged Emmitt's head to his chest, tears streaming down his cheeks. Deep, racking sobs shook his body. Finally, Lockstone closed Emmitt's eyes and gently laid his head on the floor. Black rage boiled within him, replacing the emptiness over the loss of his friend.

Morganna scored another victim.

Hatred filled his mouth with a bitter bile. Emmitt *dead*, his name joined to a long list of the murdered whose blood stained her hands.

With grim determination, Lockstone stood, turned, and stalked to the gateway. He studied the magical door, his fists clenching and unclenching. The whirling images appeared to have stopped, frozen when Morganna and her protégé plunged through the door. He leaned closer but still found it difficult to see anything on the other side of the gate. It was dark, with flashes of light punctuating the darkness. He guessed it was storming, although it was hard to tell. He *did* know one thing, however.

He *would* kill Morganna.

There was no place she could run or hide. He would follow her to every compass point on the map, suffer whatever hardship necessary, even sacrifice his own life if need be, if that's what it took to end her life.

The magical gateway beckoned. Its outline rippled, insubstantial like mist or water. Hands before him, he tried to push through.

And struck solid wall.

The door would not allow passage for *him*.

Cursing, he paced about the room trying to think. The witchcraft which created the doorway came from Morganna. If such magic was common to her coven…

He spun, jumped to Argatha's shredded corpse, and eyed the amulet around her neck. On hands and knees, he studied it. Normally black as onyx, it appeared a dull gray. The lore of the Hunt had long held these talismans to be the repository of the souls of witches, a reflection of their true nature. If so, Argatha's soul had fled this mortal plane—and to a richly deserved level of hell.

Lockstone chewed his lip. Another fact widely known among witch hunters was that amulets shared a common thread of magic among all within the coven. If *he* were in possession of it, then the gateway might also permit *his* passage.

Of course, inherent dangers existed attempting to touch a witch's amulet. The enchantment of the talisman served only the witch and other members of the coven. It would not allow others to possess it. He witnessed other Hunters snatch these lockets from a witch's neck—with disastrous consequences. A hand or arm might be blown off if they were lucky, the loss of their life if they were not.

However, *those* witches still lived, while *this* one was stone cold dead!

Argatha's soul no longer connected to the amulet so the magic protecting it should be dormant…*in theory*.

Whatever course of action he decided upon, he needed to

do it soon. The gateway continued to fade, the witchcraft which created it losing its potency.

She killed my mother, my father, and now she's killed Emmitt.

He reached for the talisman.

His hand paused—then plunged downward to grasp it.

Nothing happened. Rivulets of sweat streaked his face, as relieved, he discovered his hand still attached to his body.

He yanked the amulet from the dead witch's neck.

"Wha—what's going on here!" a voice demanded.

Startled, Lockstone looked up to spy the innkeeper in his nightshirt, a candle held aloft and squinting in disbelief at the ruins of his guest room. Blackened, charred, and splintered wood covered the floor and walls. Seeing the bodies lying on the floor in pools of blood, he jumped back almost dropping the candle onto his nightshirt in the process.

"Th-those—"

"—Are a dead witch, a pair of dead lads, and my companion," Lockstone finished for the stammering innkeeper.

Taking two gold coins from a pouch at his waist, Lockstone pitched one to the innkeeper who recovered sufficient wit to catch the coin.

"This is for the damage to your room, and this one," Lockstone said flipping the other gold piece, "is for a proper burial for my friend. I want a fine headstone, so spare no expense."

He pulled a wrinkled sheet of parchment and a sharpened piece of charcoal from inside his tunic and scribbled on it. When he thrust it into the innkeeper's hand, he caught a sly glint in his eyes.

The witch hunter pushed his face to within inches of the tavern keeper's nose and growled, "Here's what I want on Emmitt's headstone. I'll be back to pay my respects and if I'm disappointed in any way, I'll put my boot so far up your fat arse you'll be tasting leather for months!"

Blood drained from the innkeeper's face. He nodded then turned and fled down the stairway.

Lockstone grabbed the rucksack and tossed the crossbows in the bag. He cast about and spotted the turtle. It lay closed and he picked it up. Held aloft, he opened it and studied the contents. Inside and coated with fresh blood lay the pieces of razor sharp metal that ended Argatha's life.

He closed the turtle and added it to the tow sack.

With grim purpose, he placed the amulet around his neck and turned to face the fading doorway. Lockstone held up the witch compass, and once again, studied it.

The needle pointed to the magic door.

For a second time, Lockstone put his hands up and tried to push through the gateway.

They passed easily through.

Lockstone took one last look around. *I'm coming for you, Morganna. You're already dead and don't even know it.*

He stepped through the door.

FOURTEEN

BERNICE WALKER WATCHED DR. LUCAS BECKETT HURRY DOWN the wide corridor to the Intensive Care Unit. The big-boned African American woman chuckled at his haste. "Looks like Doctor Beckett is anxious to check on his patient."

Her fellow ICU nurse beside her sighed. "Wow. Why can't all doctors look like him? Tall, handsome, flat stomach, thick wavy brown hair, and best of all, single. Have you ever seen eyes so blue?"

Bernice winked. "Easy, Sofia. What would your fiancée think?"

Sofia pouted. "Always the spoil sport aren't you?"

The two women stood behind a crescent-shaped counter. The ICU patient rooms, arranged in circular fashion like spokes on a wheel, centered around their nurse's station. The familiar smell and sounds of astringents, hums, and beeps filled the air.

Bernice waved the iPad she held at Maria. "Time for you to make your rounds, and *I'll* take care of Dr. Beckett."

Sofia rolled her eyes and picked up the patient roster. With a last look over her shoulder, she began her rounds.

Lucas, his mind still immersed on the wrenching sequence of events the previous night, didn't see the large ICU nurse until he practically ran over her.

A warm smile appeared on her face. "Whoa! What's your hurry, Dr. Beckett?"

Lucas managed a nervous laugh. "Sorry. So, how's my patient?"

"We have her stabilized and her vitals are strong. Say, isn't your 'patient' a little old for a pediatric physician?"

Lucas shuffled from foot to foot, unable to think of a proper response. Finally, he shrugged, aware the ICU nurse was enjoying his discomfort immensely.

Bernice laughed and batted her eyes at him. "What you *really* need is a woman with a little more meat on her bones. If I was just ten years younger, not married, and twenty pounds lighter—"

Lucas interrupted her. "I didn't have a choice, Bernice! I'm watching the Rangers beating the Angels, and hear a knock on the door. I open it and the young lady falls right into my arms. I called 911 right away and did what I could to stabilize her until the ambulance arrived."

The experience was seared into his mind. Had a green-skinned alien greeted him instead when he opened the door, he could not have been more surprised and unnerved. An alien, however, didn't look like the young woman now lying unconscious in the hospital bed. Once past his shock and surprise, even though she lay rain-soaked and bleeding, he could tell she was beautiful.

Bernice pointed her iPad at Lucas' disheveled, blood-stained clothing. "You spend the night here?"

Embarrassed, Lucas looked down. Splotches of crimson stained his Texas Ranger's jersey and Nike jogging pants. He rubbed his face, the abrasive stubble evidence he was long overdue for a shave. He felt as rumpled as he knew he looked.

"Slept on one of the couches in the waiting area. I figured there was no point in going back home…at least not until I found out how the poor woman is doing."

Bernice looked Lucas up and down, a hint of a smile on her face. "Right."

Returning her attention to the iPad, she tapped the touch screen and scrolled through the data that appeared.

"The ulna in her left forearm is broken. A clean break which has already been set and she'll need to wear the cast for six to eight weeks. Most of the ribs on her right side are fractured as well. They have been bound and as long as she refrains from any strenuous activity for a while, they should heal without any complications. No internal bleeding or injuries that we can tell—a miracle if the nature of her injuries are any indication of what happened to her."

Bernice paused. "However, the most serious injury is to her head. She has a severe concussion. We've managed to reduce the pressure and swelling, but the bleeding on her brain was already advanced by the time the ambulance arrived and we were able to get her stabilized."

Lucas closed his eyes in dismay. He knew what *that* meant. "She's in a coma."

Bernice nodded. "It might be days, weeks, or even months before she comes out of it…if she ever does."

The ICU nurse cocked an eye at Lucas. "You sure you don't know her? She's got no driver's license, no credit cards, nothing that would identify her."

Lucas shook his head. "I've already been over this with the police. I never laid eyes on the poor woman until last night. They've made sure to give me the 'don't leave town until we finish our questioning' speech'—"

Frustrated, he stopped.

Bernice laid the iPad down and walked over to the young doctor. She placed a hand on his shoulder. "The strange and unusual happen all the time, Dr. Beckett. Proof of that can be found any given night in the emergency room. Anyone who knows you can vouch for your character. The fact is, you saved this woman's life. If you hadn't acted as quickly as you did, she would have died from the hematoma."

Lucas nodded, although the sense of guilt refused to go away. He squeezed Bernice's hand, grateful for the veteran nurse's attempt to make him feel better. The whole affair was surreal and he kept wishing he would wake up and discover it was all just a dream.

With a sigh, he turned to go and waved at Bernice as he made his way to the elevator. A short time later he found his car and pulled out of the parking garage. His home—located in the rural countryside—was ten miles south of the Longview city limits, a Northeast Texas town of ninety thousand citizens. Fifteen minutes later, he turned off a rural Farm to Market road and followed a graveled track that wound for a quarter mile before ending at a turn-of-the-century farmhouse. The farmhouse, meticulously restored by his late mother, included a large, wrap-around porch. A wicker love seat with colorful cushions hung from chains attached to the porch ceiling, while a pair of comfortable rocking chairs flanked each other next to the carved wooden front door. Twin dormers jutted like gigantic eyes from the second story of the farmhouse.

Rather than park in the adjacent garage, Lucas pulled his black Jeep Wrangler to the circular drive in front of the house. He killed the engine, jumped out, and threw himself into one of the rocking chairs. Brooding, he reviewed the previous night's events. The rainstorm, the knock on the door, the beautiful young woman pitching forward into his arms—

A sudden inspiration struck him. With a snap of his fingers, he leaped from the rocker. Rain meant mud and mud meant the woman could have left a track! Maybe he could follow her footprints to her car or wherever she came from…if the rain hadn't washed all traces of her footsteps away. The whole thing might be a longshot, but right now, it was the best option he was going to get.

He cast about and tried to get a fix on what direction to search first. Open pasture stretched to his right, but a barbed wire fence bisected it and she would have been forced to climb over it—not likely in her condition. The gravel road was in front of him, an easy walk, but again, the distance from the FM Road made this unlikely. She would have collapsed long before reaching the farmhouse. Looking left, he saw a large grove of trees in the distance. It was the beginning of the pecan orchard and a straight shot to the farmhouse. A long walk, to be sure, but the more he thought about it, the more he felt sure this had to be the direction his nighttime visitor came from.

He vaulted off the porch and examined the ground for any telltale sign. After searching for just a few minutes, he stiffened at the sight in front of him.

A bare footprint in the mud.

CFIFTEEN

LIKE A DOG ON THE HUNT, LUCAS FOLLOWED THE MEANDERING
footprints, sometimes losing them, and then picking the trail
back up as a footprint would reappear in the rain-softened
ground. As he suspected, they led straight from the orchard. Soon
he was among the pecan trees. The orchard covered an enormous
area, over two hundred acres, with trees ranging from twenty-
five years to over a hundred years old. This particular grouping of
pecans was around fifty years old, their large trunks and branches
thrusting leafy fingers upward toward the life-giving sun.

Lucas' earlier elation quickly evaporated as he searched the
ground around the trees. Pecan hulls, leaves, and other debris
from the storm were scattered everywhere, obscuring much of
the ground and any muddy tracks the injured woman might have
made. Determined, Lucas continued his search, beginning with the
trees closest to the farmhouse.

After fifteen minutes of fruitless searching, Lucas stopped and
leaned against the trunk of one of the pecans while he considered
whether to continue. Frustrated, he decided he was wasting his

time, and pushing off the tree, turned to make his way back.

Out of the corner of his eye, he caught a glint of reflected sunlight. Twisting, he spotted a small pile of leaves and broken branches lying at the base of one of the trees. A shaft of sunlight penetrated the leafy screen and was now shining like a spotlight on the pile of debris.

There was the reflection again!

His heart beating faster, Lucas trotted over to inspect the debris. Digging around the mound of leaves and branches, his fingers touched cold metal. Triumphant, he pulled a delicate silver chain from the pile. Hanging from the chain was a locket. Inset in the locket was a gemstone of some sort. Holding it up for a better look, Lucas discovered the oval gemstone appeared clear, as if it were a piece of cut glass, or cheap, ornamental jewelry. Stuffing it in his pocket, he continued his search.

Not far from the pile of broken branches was a shoe. Picking it up, Lucas examined it. Made of soft leather, the shoe appeared to be handcrafted, and by its size, almost certainly a woman's shoe. Satisfied he found the origin of where the woman began her journey to his home, this in turn caused another mystery to unfold.

How did she get *here*?

Lucas glanced at the shoe and then back to ground where the mound of leaves and broken branches lay. It couldn't be coincidental they were found together which must mean…

He looked up.

A hole appeared in the canopy, bent and broken branches marking a trail of descent from the crown of the pecan tree.

Lucas stared in disbelief. *The woman fell through the tree!*

What was she doing climbing a tree in the middle of a thunderstorm? Possibilities raced through his mind, each one discarded almost as soon as they appeared.

Maybe she was being chased? But by whom or by what?

His lack of sleep was catching up with him, and weariness began to cover him like a blanket. After a few more moments of searching revealed nothing else, he retraced his steps back to the farmhouse. He needed sleep before his clouded brain could try to make sense of what happened here. Reaching the porch, he made his way through the door and up the stairway to his bedroom.

Collapsing on the bed, he was asleep before he could pull off his muddy shoes.

SIXTEEN

"WHAT CAN I DO FOR YOU, CAROL?"

"You know why I am here, Mason. Don't play coy with me!"

Carol Webster tossed her blonde hair. While middle-age and childbirth had softened her curves, she still retained enough of her former voluptuous figure to cause men to pause and give her a second look. Ruby red lips pursed in irritation as she waited for a response.

Mason Crick, Chief Financial Officer of Good Shepard General Hospital, looked at the attractive woman standing before him with no small amount of amusement. Deciding to ignore her for the moment, he pushed himself away from his desk, turned, and took a few steps to stand in front of a full-length mirror. Mounted on a cherry wood frame, the mirror occupied a space of honor a short distance from where he was seated. He turned one way, then the other and admired his reflection.

A pencil thin mustache adorned his upper lip, his thick, dark hair parted with such knife-sharp precision, the scalp line gleamed in the light. A fitted Brooks Brothers suit covered his trim physique, and he adjusted the red power tie knotted at his neck. A 14 karat gold tie pin completed the ensemble, it's polished surface reflecting a metallic luster.

Carol, arms crossed, tapped her red stilettos. "I don't have all day. Are you going to answer me or not!"

Crick returned to his desk, put his arms behind his head, and leaned back in the custom-made burgundy leather chair he had shipped from Italy. He propped his polished leather shoes on a large mahogany desk—also special ordered—and took his time answering. He was used to dealing with people like Carol Webster. Beautiful, rich, entitled, all paired with the assumption others existed only to serve them—not that she didn't come by her arrogance honestly. Crick crossed paths with her wealthy husband, the President of the Longview Chamber of Commerce, on several occasions at Chamber functions. He considered the man an insufferable prick, whose ambition, rumor had it, included a run for Mayor. The two were made for each other.

Crick, on the other hand, born to a disinterested mother and an alcoholic, often absent father, came from a different economic stratum. Out on the streets at an early age by necessity, *nothing* was given to him, and he earned his current position by climbing over more qualified CFO's, sometimes using brutal means to do so. More than one rival suffered mysterious "accidents" leaving them in the very hospitals they sought to lead. Flies in the ointment like Carol Webster came with the territory, and like flies, needed to be swatted and squashed. Sighing, he smiled.

I'm going to enjoy this.

"Oh sure, Carol. What's it going to be? Oxy's? Xanax? Adderall?"

Crick took a key from his pocket and unlocked a drawer in his desk. He dumped several pill containers into his hand and began to pitch and catch them in the air like a circus juggler.

Carol's eyes followed the pill bottles with a starved, hungry look.

It was all Crick could do to keep from laughing out loud.

Carol's path to addiction began after minor back surgery some ten months before. Oxycodone was prescribed for pain and when her prescription ran out, Crick made sure she got more—for a price.

Opioid addictions were at an all-time high, and for someone as uniquely positioned as Crick, a fortune was there for the taking. Who needed poor street corner junkies, when obscene amounts of money could be made off prescription drug abusers who were middle-class, often wealthy, men and women? The best part was the system *legally* churned out addicts left and right. Crick had more business than he could handle!

Crick stopped juggling. He held a pill bottle aloft as if to scrutinize the contents.

Carol, watching, grew agitated to the point she could stand it no longer. "How much?" she blurted.

Crick took his time. Finally, he said, "A thousand bucks."

Carol's eyes grew wide. "A thousand dollars? I only paid five hundred the last time!"

"Well, the law of supply and demand, you know."

A desperate expression grew on Carol's face. "I-I can't afford a thousand. All I have is five hundred. I can't withdraw any more money from our account without my husband getting suspicious."

"Oh. In that case," Crick took out his key, unlocked the drawer, and began to put the pill bottles back.

"Wait!"

Crick stopped and looked up, a smirk on his face. All arrogance gone, Carol wrung her hands.

"Can't we work something out? Can you give me credit until I can pay you the rest?"

"Sorry. Cash on the barrelhead or no deal." Again, Crick

began to unlock the drawer.

A drop of perspiration formed on her forehead. "Isn't there something…*anything* I can do?" she pleaded.

Crick frowned. "Well, now that you mention it there is something."

Hope sprang into Carol's eyes. "What? What is it?"

"Take off your clothes."

Confused, Carol wasn't sure she heard Crick correctly. "Excuse me?"

"You asked me what you could do and I said take off your clothes."

Her eyes bulged. "You sick bastard! I'll do no such thing!"

"Suit yourself." Crick placed the pills in the drawer, locked it, and returned the key to his pocket.

"You-you can't do that," Carol stammered, "I-I have to have the Oxy's—*NOW!*" Her last words ended in a hysterical shout. A large shadow detached itself from the corner of the room and stood beside Carol.

"Is there a problem?"

Crick held his hand up. "I don't think so, Sam. What do you think, Carol?"

Startled, Carol looked over her shoulder. Fear radiated from her at recognition of the man next to her.

Sam Lunker, listed on the hospital payroll as Crick's "personal assistant", stood at six feet five inches. He weighed almost three hundred pounds of hard muscle, and looked almost as wide as he was tall. Like Crick, he wore an expensive suit and filled every inch of it, the fabric straining to contain his frame. His hair—brown and bristly—grew to a point halfway down his forehead, while bushy eyebrows grew so close together it resembled a unibrow. When large, spade-like hands were added to the mix, Lunker looked more ursine than human.

"No. No problem!" Carol stuttered.

Without further ado, Carol kicked off her shoes and began undressing until she stood before them in only her bra and panties.

Crick rapped the top of the desk. "When I said take your clothes off, I meant *all* your clothes."

"Mason, please. Don't make me do this," Carol pleaded. Tears welled in her eyes.

In reply, Crick held up the bottle of Oxycodone he palmed when he locked up the other drugs. He waved it back and forth, Carol's head swiveling to follow its progress.

She reached behind and unhooked her bra.

Seconds later, Carol stood naked. Face red with humiliation, she tried with limited success to cover herself with her hands and arms. Crick stood up and walked from behind his desk to stand beside Carol. He took his time while he strolled around her as if inspecting a prime heifer at a sale barn. He stopped in front of her, looked down, and chuckled.

"Well, I'll be damned." Reaching into his pocket he took out a fat money clip. Peeling off a twenty, he handed it to Lunker.

"You win the bet. She *is* a natural blonde."

A laugh rumbled from Lunker and the twenty disappeared in his hand. Carol's face flashed a deeper shade of crimson and tears spilled from her eyes.

Crick stepped back and sat on the edge of the desk. "Congratulations, Carol, I think you'll do."

Carol lifted her tear-streaked face and mumbled, "Wh-what?"

"I have a client coming in from Chicago. You're going to meet him and show him a good time. A *very* good time."

Shame and anger put her over the edge, temporarily overcoming her hunger for the Oxy. Carol snatched her clothes off the floor and began dressing.

"Go to hell! I'm not a—a whore! I'm going to tell my husband everything. He's good friends with the Chief of Police and will have you locked up so fast it will make your head spin!"

Unperturbed, Crick asked, "And what will you tell them, Carol? You're an Oxy addict? That you took stock certificates from your joint safe deposit box and sold them to finance your habit? How about those Gold Sovereigns you managed to sneak out as well? I could go on, but, of course, how would you explain this?"

Crick aimed a remote at a large flat screen monitor mounted on the wall, clicked a button, and a video appeared. It was Carol undressing and standing nude in front of Crick and Lunker. With smug satisfaction, he pointed at several locations in the office where tiny security cameras were concealed.

"I'm sure you'll have a logical explanation for *this*, won't you?"

Carol froze at the image of herself naked in front of the two men.

"Isn't that you, Carol? My, I just can't get over the wonders of high definition! Why, you can even see the mole on your—"

"Stop it! Just stop it! I'll do whatever you want," Carol sobbed. Crick watched her begin to convulse and shake, a telltale sign her need for Oxy had reached the point it was almost more than she could stand.

"Good girl." He tossed the pill bottle to her and chuckled, as she rushed to pop the cap and down two of the white, oval pills.

"One last thing, Carol. Sometimes those meds give you more courage than is justified by a person in your situation. You might just grow a backbone between here and your car."

Studying his fingernails, Crick asked, "Your son is a junior in high school isn't he? I wonder how he would react if your strip tease video somehow made its way to the social media sites he and his friends frequent? Why, he might be so upset he could suffer some sort of accident coming home from school one day. Something to keep in mind if your backbone begins to interfere with your common sense."

Carol stiffened, her face drained of color. She finished dressing and stumbled out the door.

"Think she'll talk?" Lunker growled.

"Nah. She's got too much to lose. Besides, as long as she is strung out on Oxy's we've got her by the short hairs. But, just to be on the safe side, have her watched."

Returning to his desk, Crick picked up and studied a report on the hospital's patient population. Although he made his *real* money on illicit prescription drugs, his *real* job required him to keep the hospital profitable and the board of directors happy. With the chaos surrounding Obamacare and cuts to Medicare, the delicate balancing act was becoming more difficult

Seeing an item on the report, he cursed and threw the report down.

"What's wrong?" Lunker asked.

"Doctor Do-Good is at it again. We have a patient in ICU he brought in. No name, no ID, and of course, no insurance. Damn him!"

"Dr. Beckett? I heard about that. Supposedly, a woman showed up at his door in the dead of night with all sorts of injuries. He called an ambulance and had her admitted."

Besides his brawn, Crick valued Lunker for his amazing ability to stay informed on everything which happened in the large hospital. Despite his size, he could be quite amicable and could often be found chatting up various members of the hospital staff from doctors and nurses, to custodians and cafeteria cooks. Very little escaped his attention.

"She should have been transferred to the nearest public hospital, like Parkland in Dallas," Crick spat. "Thanks to Beckett, she's occupying one of the most expensive beds in the hospital!"

"Can't you revoke his hospital privileges?"

Crick shook his head. "We've been over this before, Sam. His mother made a large donation to the Good Shepard Foundation, and he's the darling of a majority on the board. I wouldn't dare try to revoke his rights."

"What if you could prove he was costing the hospital money?"

"I could do that, but I'm supposed to keep Good Shepard profitable. If I'm showing them ways we are losing money instead of making money, then it could be *me* looking for another job! I can't risk it."

Drumming his fingers on the desk, Crick's forehead creased in thought. "Give it a couple of days. If the patient improves to the point she can be moved, have her transferred to Dallas."

"What if Dr. Beckett finds out and objects to the patient being moved?"

Crick smiled. "Then send him to me. I'll deal with Doctor Do-Good."

SEVENTEEN

WET, COLD, AND MISERABLE, LOCKSTONE SAT UNDER A TREE and watched the horizon brighten.

The sun arose a bloody red, its color matching his thoughts. Although the rain stopped hours earlier, his tunic and breeches, still damp from the deluge, clung to his body. This didn't stop him, however, from trying to puzzle out where he was. Having traveled to all parts of the Kingdom and in some cases, beyond, the murky dawn confirmed what he already suspected.

He hadn't fallen into a place unknown to him.

He'd been deposited in a whole new world.

Visions and wonders he never dreamed of appeared before his astonished eyes. Horseless, iron wagons rolled by during the night, bright lights like glowing eyes flashing before them. Buildings, as innumerable as grains of sand and of every conceivable shape and size, surrounded him. Some of these distant structures resembled monstrous trees, and stretched to impossible heights into the sky.

While the sky brightened, the sprawling city awakened, and the hum of activity began to echo in the air. More iron wagons appeared and passed by, and for the first time, Lockstone began to see the citizens of this strange land. Dressed in unfamiliar garb and fashion, they walked briskly by in determined fashion looking neither left or right—as if their destination was right before them. Some were led by animals, dogs by the looks of them, tethered to their arms by leather thongs or chains. Lockstone rubbed his chin.

Strange indeed.

Script appeared everywhere, on buildings, on some of the iron wagons, even on the stone and metal benches that lined the park or garden he found himself dropped into. Although he learned letters from his mother at an early age, it still appeared to be gibberish to him.

Maybe the passage through the portal left him mad.

While he pondered his sanity, a pile of debris rolled out from under one of the benches and sat up. Startled, he reached for his knife. Moments later, he relaxed and shoved the dagger back in its sheath.

It was a man.

A veteran traveler to many a backwater village, tavern, and alley, a smile tugged at his lips at the first familiar sight to present itself to him. Although in a different world, some things, it would seem, were universal.

Like drunkards.

Staggering to his feet, the thin, scrawny sot yawned and stared at the sky with bloodshot eyes. Scratching his crotch, he promptly relieved himself on a nearby bush. Squinting, he spotted Lockstone and limped over to him.

The small man wiped his hands on his greasy shirt, and pointed at the tow sack by Lockstone's feet. Like the script, his speech filled the witch hunter's ears with nonsense. He seemed to think volume would improve Lockstone's understanding, and spoke louder and louder to the point the witch hunter feared he would have to throttle the drunk in order to silence him.

A thought struck Lockstone. The Hunt took him afar and to places within the Kingdom where unfamiliar language was often used. His craft—killing witches—required knowledge of their lore. The witch blood he inherited from his mother allowed him to cast simple spells. This included rudimentary language and communication spells, and he successfully used them in the past to speak and understand unknown tongues.

Closing his eyes, Lockstone chanted.

"—I said, you got any booze in 'yer bag? Are you hard of hearin'? Hey, 'Yo hablo ingles', dude?"

The comprehension of the man's speech was instantaneous. Warmth bloomed on his neck. Lockstone looked down and the amulet glowed a bright amber color. Amplified by its power, the spell worked!

"No. I have no ale," he growled.

"To hell with ale, I'm talkin' the good stuff like Wild Turkey or Johnny Walker."

Lockstone shrugged, wanting nothing more than to be shed of the bedraggled drunk who reeked of piss and cheap beer.

"Name's Jenkins although everybody 'round here just calls me 'Jink'." The drunkard stuck out a grimy paw.

Lockstone stared for a moment, unsure of what sort of greeting ritual he was expected to engage in. Jink settled that for him by grabbing his hand and shaking it.

"Haven't seen you around here." Jink spread his arms wide. "Lots of us hang out here at Griffith Park."

Jink's eyes lit up, and once again, he pointed at Lockstone's bag. "Hey, if you got anything in there worth sellin', I know just the place we can hock it. Then we can go get some booze!"

Jink began to pull on Lockstone's arm. He considered cuffing the troublesome fool, but after a moment's thought, decided against it. He needed supplies and whatever passed for money or barter to pay for it.

By this time, the streets were crowded with people and the iron wagons, many of them blaring and bleating at each other in a cacophony of noise the witch hunter found disconcerting. Following Jink turned out to be more difficult than he imagined, as the small man darted in around every obstacle with practiced ease. His large bulk proved to be less adept at squeezing through the crowd, and more than once when crossing a street, a chorus of angry blaring from the wagons greeted him.

With much relief, he finally caught up with Jink who stopped in front of a shop lined with large windows. Iron bars covered the glass panes, which displayed a variety of merchandise. Most of the wares were a mystery to Lockstone. He looked up and spied a large sign mounted above the door.

Lucky's Pawnshop – Houston's Finest!

Jink winked at Lockstone. "You can pawn anything here. Lucky Eddie is *very* accommodating." He pushed open the door, and the two men entered the store.

A chime sounded as they made their way to a small, thin man who stood behind a counter surrounded by a protective cage. Balding, the shopkeeper's remaining hair lay limp and greasy on his head. He wore a faded blue shirt with the name "Eddie" stitched above the breast pocket.

"Lucky Eddie, this is, um…sorry man, I never caught yer' name."

"Lockstone. Robert Lockstone," the Witch Hunter growled.

"Oh…well, uh, Eddie this is Robert, Robert this is Eddie."

Eddie looked at the men, his mouth twisted in distaste. "Jink, if you've brought me another one of your homeless buddies looking for a handout, you can get the hell out. *Now!*"

Jink held his hands up. "Whoa, Eddie. It ain't nothin' like that. Er, *Robert* here, got some stuff he'd like to sell."

Suspicious, the pawnshop owner studied Lockstone. "My

God, you're big!" Lockstone filled much of the space in front of the counter, and Lucky Eddie was obliged to crane his neck in order to see his face. "I can't decide if you are a washed up professional wrestler or an ex-football player."

He pointed at the witch hunter's clothes. "Where'd you get the shirt and pants? It looks like you just walked here from a casting call of a Clint Eastwood Western."

Lockstone cleared his throat. "I am unfamiliar with what a wrestler or football player is. However, I stand over seven hands tall, and these are the clothes I Hunt in."

Eddie dismissed the comment with a flip of his hand. "Whatever. Look, I'm a busy man, so show me watcha got, Grizzly Adams, or get out!"

Pausing for just a second, Lockstone pitched his sack onto the counter where it landed with a *thump*. Digging through it, Eddie discarded one item after another. Finally, he shook his head in disgust and tossed the bag back to Lockstone.

"What, are you kidding me? Nothing in here but junk. It looks like stuff my grandmother would have thrown away…and she's a hoarder." Eddie's face turned scarlet. "I repeat…*get out!*"

Jink opened his mouth to protest, but stopped when he saw Eddie drag a bat from behind the counter. Scuttling to the door, he ran out leaving Lockstone alone beside the counter.

Eddie scowled, "That means you too, Meatloaf."

Rather than leave, Lockstone reached into a heavy pouch tied to his belt. He pulled out a gold coin and placed it on the scarred wooden surface.

"What about this?"

Eddie gaped at the gold coin.

"You pulling my leg? What, I'm gonna peel the foil off that so I can eat the chocolate?"

"I can assure you it is real. Examine it if you doubt my word."

Eddie snatched the coin and pulled a jeweler's fob at his neck up to his eye. Squinting, he examined it carefully, his doubt melting away. He dropped the fob, opened a pen knife, and scratched the coin's surface. Finally, he took a balance, placed the coin on it, and weighed its mass.

When finished, he looked at Lockstone in wonder.

"There's at least two ounces of gold in this coin. Where did you get it?"

Lockstone flashed a carnivorous smile. "I earned it."

"Yeah, right, seriously—"

Eddie stopped when the door chime announced the arrival of customers. Two young men entered, furtive expressions on their faces, and surveyed the premises. Lockstone studied their movements and recognized another old familiarity—one he and Emmitt were forced to deal with from time to time.

Thieves.

One had the ebony skin so common among the southernmost province of the Kingdom, while the other a pasty-white, as if he never got out into the sun. Both wore clothing so loose, they held on to their pants with one hand so their trousers wouldn't fall to their knees. Dark etchings stained their bare arms in patterns Lockstone did not recognize. They split up and moved about at random examining the items in the shop.

Completing their circuit, they met at the counter flanking Lockstone on either side. Unperturbed, he waited for the thieves to make their move.

"I wouldn't do that…unless you want to be dead," the ebony-skinned thief said pointing a blunt, metal object at Eddie.

The shopkeeper had reached under the counter and held what looked to Lockstone like a larger version of the same weapon brandished by the thief. The little man froze, dropped the weapon, and taking great care, held his hands above his head.

"Not again," Eddie groaned. "This is the second time this month I've been robbed."

"Well, then you ought to know the drill," quipped the white-skinned thief who also held a metal tube pointed at the shopkeeper.

"Let's see...it goes something like *this.*"

Grabbing Eddie by the collar, he pulled him over the counter and ground the point of the tube into his temple. "Give me everything in the cash register and the keys to the cabinet you keep the pawned jewelry in. And if you even *think* about screwing me over, you piece of shit, I'll leave your brains all over the floor!"

Shaking, Eddie was turning to comply when the thief spotted the gold coin lying on the counter.

"What's this?"

Snatching it up, the pale-skinned robber held it up to the light where it glinted with a golden luster. A harsh laugh burst from his lips.

"It's our lucky day, Lamont! Big guy was fixin' to pawn this gold coin." Tossing it to his partner, he turned to Lockstone. "Not so lucky for you, huh?"

A thin smile played across Lockstone's lips. "I generally don't approve of thieves, less so when they attempt to take something which belongs to me. I can't speak for this shopkeeper—he can do as he pleases—but the coin is mine and I'll have it back."

The thief's head spun around. "Hear that, Lamont? Home fries here wants his coin back. Maybe it will be *your* brains on the floor," he snarled swinging the weapon from Eddie to Lockstone.

The brigand's reaction gave Lockstone the opening he patiently waited for. His arm moved in a blur of motion, and with quicksilver speed, he caught the thief's hand holding the metal tube and squeezed. Bones *crunched*, the sound like boots on gravel.

The thief screamed and dropped the weapon.

Before the metal tube even hit the ground, Lockstone pivoted and threw an elbow into the face of the other robber. His elbow met the brigand's nose, breaking it with a loud *crack*. Blood spewed from the fractured nasal cavity, and he dropped like a rock, out cold. Lockstone spun back once again, and his club-like fist met the temple of the pale-skinned robber, still screaming as he clutched his ruined hand.

He joined his partner, unconscious, on the floor.

Lucky Eddie bolted from behind the counter and knelt by the prone bodies of the thieves. "Wha-what, how—how," he babbled at Lockstone. Finally, he stood and stared at the witch hunter. "I've never seen anyone move so fast. Where did you learn to fight like that?"

Lockstone shrugged and bent over to retrieve the gold coin. "You got a back door?"

Eddie nodded and unlocked the door to his cage behind the counter. The witch hunter brushed by the pawnbroker, his mouth still agape, picked up both thieves like loaves of bread, and followed the little man to the back of the store. Lucky Eddie opened the back door while Lockstone peered in both directions. Satisfied no one watched, he tossed the two men in the alley.

After they returned to the front of the store, Eddie scratched his chin while he watched Lockstone turn and prepare to leave

"Hey, just a minute, er, Robert. Got a proposition for you," he said.

The witch hunter paused and looked back at Lucky Eddie.

"I have a small efficiency apartment above my pawnshop. I used to stay there before I got my own place. It ain't much, but you look like, *ah*, like you need someplace to crash. I'll let you stay there for free, maybe even pay you a bit to help about the shop, until you get back on your feet."

Lockstone considered Eddie's offer. Of course, he knew the reason for the shopkeeper's eagerness. He was proof against future banditry. Pulling the witch compass from his neck, he studied it while he mulled over the proposition. The needle point flickered due north, confirming his dearest wish.

Morganna was here.

With few options in this strange, new world, the decision wasn't difficult although it meant the Hunt would have to be delayed. He knew too little about this new Kingdom he found himself in, and without Emmitt to watch his back, the prospect of facing a witch of Morganna's prowess without proper preparation would be suicidal.

Remembering Jink's greeting ritual, he stuck out his hand. "We have a bargain."

Even while the shopkeeper pumped his hand, Lockstone's mind raced ahead to the next stage in the Hunt. The easy part, thanks to Eddie, had been taken care of. The hard part came next—locate Morganna.

Then kill her.

ᴇIGHTEEN

ORGANNA STARED AT THE PLATE OF GRUEL.

The food, tasteless and inedible, lay in a tray atop a small table now swiveled across her lap. The bed she occupied included an upper half cranked to an upright position. This allowed her to sit up and view the same scene she'd observed since she awoke a seven-count of days ago.

A small table and lamp beside the bed.

A window covered with what her attendant referred to as "blinds".

An ugly, green chair with a padded seat.

A privy she puzzled over for so long, she was forced to ask for help.

Various beeping and humming implements whose function and purpose she couldn't even begin to fathom.

Strangest of all, was the flat, metallic square mounted on the wall above her. Like a large eye, it showed scenes of people and places, their visual clarity and speech so crystal clear, more than once she climbed out of the bed and tried to touch them. At first, she thought the object a type of magical door much like the one which dropped her into this new world, but it soon became apparent it was neither door or magic. Later, she noticed tiny versions of the eye carried in the hands of almost all the healers.

Her attendant, a healer with "Anna" on her nametag, called the large eye a TV and the smaller version a cell phone.

Absently, Morganna scratched the puckered wound on her shoulder. Fading now, an ugly black and purple bruise still circled the scar left by the poisoned bolt. By means Morganna did not understand, the healers of this establishment brought her back from the precipice of death. Her recuperation and the slow return of her strength, although a disappointment, gave her time to learn as much as possible about her new environment. Most importantly, this included *where* she was and *who* peopled this land!

Anna proved very helpful, answering all of her many questions when she awoke to find herself in this different and peculiar world. Although she could tell the healer believed her questions proof of an addled mind, Morganna wasn't troubled. Her total lack of understanding of so many things left *her* at times thinking she must be in the grip of fevered visions, not reality.

Morganna preferred to be thought a fool anyway. It worked to her advantage no one suspected her prowess. She needed to test not only her physical recovery, but her witch's strength as well...and she was pleased—*very* pleased—by what she discovered. Her spells, her magic, felt more robust than ever before. Her first attempt at magic—a spell to understand and speak the tongue of those who cared for her—she deemed so successful, she even acquired their accent! The fools considered her harmless, which left her free to plot her escape. Then she would find Tressalayne, and together, they would establish a new coven.

Morganna salivated at the prospect.

From what she gleaned so far, this world knew little of magic, and less of witches. Such virgin territory was rife with opportunity. Best of all, Hunters, such as the cursed Lockstone, appeared to be nonexistent. After all, what need of Hunters with no witches to hunt? Giddy, she couldn't help herself and laughed out loud. Wiping mirthful tears from her eyes, she considered her next move…*escape.*

And she knew *exactly* who would help her.

The stranger whose wagon, or *car*, the doorway dropped her into, was a frequent visitor. This woman, who introduced herself as Karen, appeared to be afraid she might suffer consequences related to Morganna's injuries. Why she would have such a preposterous notion continued to mystify to the coven leader, but her fear served to guarantee Karen's return.

Which was essential to Morganna's plans.

On cue, the door opened and Karen swept into the room. The witch studied her as she pulled a chair up next to the bed. Honey-brown, perfectly coiffed hair fell midway down her neck. Blue eyes with kohl-darkened lashes regarded Morganna with nervous energy. Morganna noted Karen's short skirt, and the generous amount of her tanned legs it showed.

Karen carried a large bag. Reaching in, she removed pants, a blouse, and a lacy bra and panties, and spread them out on the bed.

"I did the best I could to guess your size. Do you feel up to trying them on?"

With a false smile, Morganna purred, "Oh, yes. I appreciate you doing this for me. My clothes from the accident were ruined."

When Morganna mentioned her tattered clothing during her last visit, Karen, eager to accommodate, jumped at the opportunity to replace the lost clothes.

Morganna slid out of bed and allowed Karen to help her dress. The underclothes, panties and bra, constricted her and felt odd. *What purpose did an extra layer of apparel serve?* However, the woman insisted, so Morganna obliged her. The shoes, flat-soled sandals, left her feet bare, a first for her after years of boots and leather bound slippers.

Karen opened the door to the bathroom. A mirror hung above the sink and she motioned for Morganna to look at herself.

The witch gasped. The woman in the reflection was almost unrecognizable! Her face was thinner from weight loss, her figure less full. Her complexion, a pallid white, gave her the look of a dead fish. The clothes—Karen called them a blouse and blue jeans—were a snug, comfortable fit.

A burning anger boiled within her. Lockstone caused this! The witch hunter *almost* succeeded in killing her.

Almost.

A predatory smile played across her face. She was ready to make up for lost time.

Morganna motioned with her finger. "Come here, dearie. I think I have something in my eye."

Karen obeyed and peered in Morganna's eyes.

"I don't see anything. I have some eye drops. Maybe—"

Karen blinked, her eyes becoming heavy. Within moments, they glazed over and became blank.

Morganna stopped the whispered chant, the bewitching spell complete. Pleased, she started to test the bewitching further, when a sudden wave of dizziness came over her. She just managed to make it to the ugly chair, when her legs gave out and she collapsed into the seat. The world spun and swayed. She closed her eyes, and forced herself to take deep, even breaths, while she waited for the vertigo to pass. A stark realization struck her while she waited.

She was still too weak.

Even a simple and uncomplicated bewitching spell cost her dearly. It was clear her road to recovery was far from over.

Despite her weakness, the coven leader was more determined than ever to leave. The *hospital*, as Anna called it, grew to be more like a prison every day, and the constabulary continued to pay her regular visits to ask questions she could not answer.

The dizziness passed, and Morganna motioned to her enthralled victim.

"Retrieve my bag."

Without hesitation, Karen spun and went to a corner of the room where a plastic hospital bag with all the witch's possessions hung from a metal hook on the wall. Returning to Morganna, Karen handed her the bag and stood motionless, hands limp at her side.

Although Morganna lost her grip on Tressalayne when they plunged through the portal to this world, she somehow managed to hang on to the bag with all their magical implements. Of course, the constables searched her bag, but they returned all of its contents, a colossal mistake by them but a boon to a witch of her prowess. Without her tools and implements, Morganna would be hard-pressed to do what she knew must be done to make good on her escape.

Her hand closed around the small vial of *morlaga* potion. Besides youth, the elixir's restorative properties could speed healing. Morganna uncorked the bottle, took a small sip, and then resealed it.

The effect was immediate.

A rush of energy flooded her bloodstream. Strength returned to her limbs, and the dizziness disappeared in an instant. Standing, she made her way back to the privy.

Once again at the mirror, Morganna beheld a different person from just moments before. Her face regained fullness, her cheeks a rosy red with the hollowness gone. Her figure, more voluptuous, caused her clothes to fit tighter. Realizing the effects of the potion was temporary and would not last, Morganna knew she must act *now*.

She pawed through her bag again, and pulled out the small

bottle of changeling powder. She took a risk if she used the powder because it required much stronger magic than the bewitching spell which left her so weak. However, she had little choice. Once out of her room, she might be recognized, the constables sent for, and she would be forced to return. No doubt a closer watch on her would ensue, and the window of opportunity to escape would evaporate.

She couldn't allow that to happen.

Fortunately, all she needed to do was alter her appearance enough to fool those charged with her care. She didn't need a full-blown transformation, and the clothes she now wore went a long way toward modifying her appearance. A subtle change to her face should be enough.

Taking a tiny pinch of powder, Morganna held her hand above her head and let it dribble onto her. The ancient words of the changeling spell whispered from her lips. She closed her eyes and waited.

A bright light enveloped her, followed by the familiar burning sensation. When the feeling passed, Morganna hurried to the bathroom mirror and again, studied her reflection.

Gone was her long, black mane. In its place grew shoulder length, straw-colored hair. Eyes of blue stared at her, with cheekbones higher and sharper than before.

Perfect.

Best of all, the weakness had left her, and the restorative power of the *morlaga* potion continued to hold. She tossed the implements back into the shopping bag her bewitched victim brought her clothes in. Morganna took a last look at her room and smiled.

Time to go.

"We're leaving. If we are stopped, you will introduce me as your friend."

"Yes, Mistress," Karen answered.

"Once we are out of this place, you will take me to the lake house you told me about."

"Yes, Mistress."

"And you're sure it is unoccupied?"

"Yes, Mistress. My husband and I use it only on an occasional basis on weekends."

Morgana rubbed her hands in anticipation.

Time to start her new life.

NINETEEN

L UCAS STUDIED THE IPAD AT THE END OF THE BED.
ICU was practically deserted. Only two other patients occupied beds besides his mysterious woman, with many on the
nursing staff taking advantage of the downtime to grab lunch in
the hospital cafeteria. The soft beeps, hissing, and chirps of various
monitors and instruments were the only disturbances to the silence.

Lucas, on his own lunch break from his practice, used the time
to run over to the hospital to check on the injured woman. Scanning
the data on the iPad, he shook his head. Her vital signs were strong,
but in the most critical area, brain activity, little had changed.

He sighed and took the silver chain and locket from his pocket.
After a moment's hesitation, he placed it on the bedside table. He
knew it to be a foolish act, but besides a muddy shoe, it was the
only material possession of the injured woman he could find. The
symbolic gesture made him feel a little better. Glancing at his watch,
he saw he was going to have to hurry to get something to eat before
returning to his office. Turning to take a last look at the patient, he
froze.

The chain and locket were floating in the air!

As he watched, open-mouthed, the locket slithered through the air, and settled around the woman's neck.

The effect was immediate.

The monitors beeped and chirped with sudden urgency. The woman's heart rate and breathing began to increase, but the most significant change was the EEG readout. Lucas snatched the iPad from its cradle and scanned the data stream. In disbelief, he stared at the sharp spike in electrical activity within her brain. What just happened?

Lucas sank into a bedside chair and looked at the iPad again. There could be no mistake. His mystery woman was coming out of her coma...and it all began with the locket.

The locket!

Lucas jumped up and paced back and forth. He couldn't have seen the piece of jewelry float in mid-air and then place itself around the young woman's neck...could he?

Impossible.

He must have imagined it.

Work and stress must have caused him to see something that couldn't have happened. Yet even as told himself this, the undeniable evidence lay right before his eyes. The locket *was* around the patient's neck, her vitals *were* increasing, her brain activity, negligible up to this point, *was* active and increasing.

Lucas turned and leaned over the bed. His eyes, inches from the locket, searched for any clue to explain what he just witnessed. The patient's warm breath caressed his face, and Lucas found himself distracted by her beauty. Full lips, slightly parted, displayed ivory white teeth, and her complexion, even in the sterile light of the ICU, appeared flawless, a cream-colored hue with a slight hint of pale rose on the cheeks—

"Find anything interesting, Dr. Beckett?"

Startled, Lucas looked up to see Mason Crick observing him,

an amused expression on his face.

"But don't let me stop you, Dr. Beckett. By all means, continue your, ahem, *examination*."

Red-faced, Lucas, stuttered, "Her-her vitals spiked. I-I ju-just…"

His voice trailed off. How was he going to describe what he just saw? He wasn't sure *he* even believed it. Better to be thought some voyeur or creep than to try and explain the unexplainable…especially to a man like Mason Crick.

Lucas returned the iPad to its cradle and faced Crick. "What can I do for you, Mason?"

"Oh, nothing, Dr. Beckett. Like you, I'm here to check on our patient. What great news she is recovering, huh? I've arranged for her to be transferred to Parkland as soon as she is stable. Sounds like it will be soon."

"What? Wait! You can't do that. She is still in a coma!"

"Which according to you, she is well on her way to coming out of."

"Why transfer her to Dallas when we can offer her the medical care she needs here?"

Lucas watched the hospital CFO study his nails, a look of irritation on his face.

"Pardon me, Dr. Beckett, for being blunt, but in my position I deal with imbeciles all the time. I can understand how an ordinary person off the street wouldn't have a clue about the intricacies of hospital finance and medical expenses. It's when I have to explain why water runs downhill to medical professionals with college degrees and acronyms in capital letters I lose patience."

Lucas's face grew warm, the contempt in Crick's voice clearly evident.

"Dr. Beckett, this is a *for-profit* medical institution. You understand the concept of 'for-profit', right? It means to make money, not lose money. And every day we have patients like the

young lady *you* brought us, we are losing money. We have an obligation to our doctors, staff, and *paying* patients to make sure we continue to offer the highest quality of care."

"But not to the poor and indigent," Lucas snapped.

"If the shoe fits, Doctor. Look, I didn't set up the system, but there *are* public hospitals which offer the kind of care this young lady needs."

"And they are chronically overpopulated and understaffed!"

Crick shrugged. "I've made my point, Doctor. A less delicate person than myself might tell you at this point to shove it up your ass if you don't like it." Crick grinned. "Fortunately, I'm not such a person. Is there anything else I can help you with?"

Lucas fought the urge to punch Crick in his smartass face. With great effort, he managed to rein in his temper.

"Okay, once she comes out of the coma, what if I were responsible for her care?"

Crick frowned. "You mean *you* would pay for her medical bills? She's a *Jane Doe*. You don't know anything about her."

"Not a problem. I've got a place I could set her up in, and I could arrange for the medical equipment she would need—"

Lucas stopped at the look Crick was giving him. His cheeks bloomed red with indignation.

"I know several retired nurses who could use a little extra money and stay with the patient while she recovers. I can assure you she would be in good hands!"

"Oh, no doubt, Dr. Beckett, no doubt. Hey, if you want to assume the financial obligation of this patient's medical care, by all means, be my guest."

Smirking, Crick added, "And might I say, it's refreshing there are still Good Samaritans like yourself in the world."

Lucas fought a second battle to quell the overwhelming urge to punch Crick in the nose. The smug bastard knew how to get under his skin. Instead, he checked his watch and saw he would have to forget trying to grab a quick lunch. He would need to fly back to the office for his next appointment. With a curt nod to Crick, he hurried out of the room.

Crick watched Beckett leave, a smile on his face. The idiot was going to assume the Jane Doe's care? Let him! P.T. Barnum had it right. There *is* a sucker born every minute.

Pivoting he was about to leave, when he recalled Beckett's extraordinary interest in examining the young woman so closely. At first he thought it might be some kind of twisted physical attraction for the helpless patient, but upon reflection, with Dr. Do-Good's Boy Scout nature, maybe not. There must be something else. Curious, Crick turned and went back to the bed.

The first thing he noticed was the locket about the woman's neck. Did Beckett put it there? The gem in the locket looked like cheap cut glass, the kind you made costume jewelry from. As he scrutinized it, the gem's surface appeared to ripple and move like water. Astounded, he peered even closer. *It was moving!*

A scratching sound came from beside him. Looking over, Crick's mouth fell open. A pen with the Good Shepard name stenciled on it, furiously wrote on a pad of paper lying on the table beside the bed. The hairs on his neck rose.

No hand held the pen. It moved on its own!

Crick took a step back. A name appeared over and over again on the pad.

Tressalayne

Tressalayne

Tressalayne

Crick's skin tingled as if thousands of ants were crawling all over him. He threw his jacket off, unbuttoned the wrist on his shirtsleeve, and jerked it up. In horror, he saw the same name, *Tressalayne,* appear all over his arm like some grotesque tattoo.

Even as he watched, the name replicated itself over more and more of his skin.

Fear deeper than anything he ever experienced gripped him. Stumbling backward, his feet tangled in his jacket on the floor, and he fell. The itchy, crawly feeling now spread to his legs. Ripping his pants leg up, *Tressalayne* appeared up and down his leg.

Scrambling to his feet, Crick ran out of the room. The nurse manning the ICU station looked up just in time to see the hospital CFO sprint past her.

Unwilling to pause his flight for even a second, Crick skidded past the bank of elevators and fled down the stairs.

Fear followed him with every step.

TWENTY

CRICK'S HAND SHOOK AS HE POURED THREE FINGERS OF MAKERS Mark into a crystal tumbler. He tossed it back in one gulp, then rushed to pour another, spilling some of the premium whiskey onto his desk. Gulping down the second round, his nerves steadied and somewhat fortified, managed to sit back in his chair to review the series of events in his mind one more time.

Once he reached the safety of his office, he stripped off all his clothes and searched every inch of his body. The writing, the name *Tressalayne*, was gone from his skin, disappeared like it never existed.

Except Crick knew better.

Crick knew a thing or two about fear, terror, and even death. His life was a testament to the struggle of climbing to the top of the dog pile by any means necessary. More than once death faced him in the form of a loaded gun pointed at his head, and he had seen and experienced more than his fair share of bizarre and serious shit. Nothing surprised him. Nothing shocked him.

Until today.

The door opened and Lunker walked in. He shut the door, turned, and noticed his boss sitting at his desk dressed in nothing but a pair of boxers. His mouth fell open and he gaped at Crick. "Boss, what—"

"Sit down and shut up. We've got a lot to talk about," Crick snapped.

Crick spent the next ten minutes describing what happened in the ICU room while Lunker listened, his massive brow furrowed.

"Now before you think I've sampled too much of the product, I know what I saw. I *know* what I experienced! Something's not right about that patient, about this…this, *Tressalayne*, and I aim to find out what it is!"

Standing, Crick pulled his pants up. "Here's what you are going to do. First, go back to ICU and get me the pen and pad beside the patient's bed. Then, take a picture of that necklace and locket around Tressalayne's neck with your cell. Finally, Beckett wants us to transfer her care to him. We are going to accommodate him. Whatever he wants, get it for him, no questions asked."

By this time, Crick had his pants on and was working on his shirt buttons. Lunker still sat as if rooted into place.

Irritated, Crick barked, "Why are you still here?"

Lunker jumped up and made his way to the door. Crick called to his back, "And Sam? It goes without saying, this stays between you and me. Until I get this figured out, I don't want anyone, especially Beckett, to know what happened."

Nodding, Lunker disappeared through the door.

Crick finished with the buttons and was tucking in his shirt when his office phone buzzed. Pressing the intercom, he said, "Yes?"

"John Guerra from Nacogdoches Memorial is on the line for you," his secretary stated. "Should I take a message?"

Crick fastened his belt and considered whether or not to take the call. Guerra, his opposite number at Memorial, served with him on several healthcare committees. They often commiserated regarding the complexities of healthcare and the idiots in the profession they had to deal with.

"Put him through."

Sitting, Crick punched the call button. "How's it going, John?"

"About the usual, Mason. Dealing with the same shrinking reimbursements from Medicare, patients with no insurance, and, of course, doctors who want to run every expensive test known to man. We're bleeding money."

Crick chuckled. Guerra could sum up the status quo in the medical profession better than anyone he knew.

"Yeah, I hear you. We've got a doctor who admits patients like they're stray dogs and cats. He should have been a vet instead of a doctor!" Crick filled Guerra in on the latest patient admitted by Beckett…leaving out the mysterious writing that appeared on the pad of paper and on his arms and legs.

"Of course, no insurance, and in fact, no identification period! Beckett knows how to pick'em."

Guerra whistled. "What a clueless idiot. Matter of fact, the same thing happened here about a week ago. Get this, a Jane Doe falls into a BMW—right through the windshield—and she ends up here. No name or ID, and no explanation how she managed to appear from nowhere to fall into the car. Weird shit!"

At this, Crick sat up. *A week ago? Weird shit?* A familiarity nibbled at the back of his brain. Was it possible his Jane Doe and Memorial's were somehow connected?

"Just a minute, John."

Digging through the pile of reports on his desk, Crick pulled the hard copy of the admittance and patient population on the night Tressalyane was brought to Good Shepherd.

"When was your Jane Doe admitted?" he asked

Crick waited while Guerra put him on hold, and searched his

records with the date and time of admittance. A few moments later, he came back on the line.

"The patient was admitted last Monday night at 8:45 pm."

Looking at the report in front of him, Crick found the admittance information on Tressalyne.

Monday night at 9:00 pm.

His eyes widened.

The date and time were almost identical. No believer in coincidences, Crick knew the odds of the two women suffering strange accidents within moments of each other were slim to none. They *had* to be related!

"What's the status of your Jane Doe?"

"Funny you should ask. She disappeared a couple of days ago. Just walked out the best we can tell. No one noticed her leaving, not even the nurses. The police went crazy, demanded our security footage, but even with the security video they couldn't discover how she left. Good riddance I say. One less freeloader affecting our bottom-line."

Crick's mind jumped into overdrive. Something was going on here. Something he didn't have a handle on...yet!

"Look, nice talking to you, John, but I've got an important meeting to get to." After an exchange of pleasantries, Crick clicked off. A familiar feeling crept into his mind.

Opportunity.

Pulling his cell phone from his pocket, he punched a number and waited while it connected.

"Sam. Finish up on everything I asked you to do as quickly as possible, then get back here pronto.

You're going to Nacogdoches."

TWENTY-ONE

LUCAS LISTENED WITH KEEN INTEREST.

"You should have seen Crick. He lit out of here like someone threw firecrackers in his pants!"

Bernice still chuckled at the scene of the CFO making like an Olympic sprinter as he fled the ICU.

"Don't know what spooked that man so, but let me tell you, it was priceless!"

Lucas forced a smile on his face. Normally, he would join Bernice in laughing out loud at the image of Crick fleeing like his pants were on fire, but instead, a chill crept up his spine.

Not after what he saw.

Not after seeing the necklace and locket place itself around the patient's neck.

Crick must have seen something similar after he left. Although Lucas thoroughly disliked the man and knew the feeling was mutual, the hospital CFO didn't strike Lucas as a coward or someone who spooked easily. Whatever Crick saw—whatever happened—it must have unnerved him to the point he rushed out of the room.

After seeing his last patient of the day, Lucas debated whether or not to return to the hospital to check on the young woman. Now, after Bernice's description of Crick's episode, he fought to restrain himself from spinning on his heel and leaving at once.

"Got something for you," Bernice whispered as she leaned forward. "After Crick ran out of the room, I went in to check on the patient. At some point, she must have come out of her coma, because she wrote this."

The nurse thrust a piece of paper in Lucas' hand. He took the note and studied it. From a hospital memo pad, "*Tressalayne*" was written multiple times on the paper in large, flowing print.

"This is her…name?"

"Sure is."

"How do you know?"

Bernice pointed to the room. "Why don't you ask the patient yourself?"

"You mean—"

"Yep. Tressalyane's been out of her coma since shortly after 'Mr. Ants in His Pants' ran out of here."

Lucas stuffed the paper in his pocket and walked into the patient's room. She sat up in the bed and looked up when he appeared, a smile tugging at her mouth. At the sight of her smile, all trepidation melted away from Lucas. He pulled a chair beside her bed and turned it so he could sit facing her.

"Welcome back, Tressalayne. I hope I pronounced your name right. I'm Dr. Beckett, Dr. Lucas Beckett." Lucas reached out his hand.

Tressalayne stared at his hand for a moment before slowly moving her own forward. Lucas gripped her palm and shook it, marveling at the warmth and softness of her touch.

"I-I think you pronounced it correctly, um, Dr. Beckett.

I'm afraid I don't remember much of anything, much less my name."

Lucas noted Tressalayne's slow, deliberate speech, as if she were somehow unfamiliar with the words she mouthed.

"Unfortunately, you took a blow to the head which left you with a severe concussion. Amnesia is not uncommon with such injuries."

"Wh-when will I get my memory back?"

Lucas sighed. "There's no way to predict that. Every case is different. The brain is a delicate organ, and with different people, the brain handles trauma in different ways. It could be days, weeks, months, years, even—"

Lucas stopped himself too late.

"You mean I might not *ever* regain my memory?" Tressalayne whispered, tears spilling from her eyes.

Lucas silently cursed himself. He grabbed a box of tissues from the bedside table, and offered them to the beautiful young woman. She stared at them with confusion, and Lucas cursed himself anew.

She has amnesia, you fool!

Pulling a few from the box, Lucas pantomimed dabbing his eyes, and after a moment, Tressalayne took them and wiped her tears.

Seeking to reassure her, he said, "Its possible, but permanent amnesia is rare, and affects only a handful of patients."

Relief washed over Tressalayne's face. "Truly?"

"Truly," Lucas answered.

Lucas stood and took a clean tissue from the box. "May I?"

Tressalayne looked at Lucas for a moment, then nodded. He used the tissue to gently dab away her remaining tears. Then he took a penlight from his pocket, clicked it on, and examined each eye in turn. The dilation appeared normal.

"Good! Your pupils look great, which means you are well on

your way to recovery." While he said this, he couldn't help noticing her beautiful blue-green eyes.

"The nice lady, Bernice, told me you were responsible for bringing me here and helping me recover from my, my..." Tressalayne stopped, frustrated, as she searched for the word to complete her sentence.

"Injuries?"

"Yes! That's it. Injuries! I don't know why I have so much trouble speaking."

"Don't worry about it," Lucas assured her. "Speech recovery is a common symptom among amnesia patients. Besides," he added with a wink, "for someone who just came out of a coma, your recovery so far is quite remarkable."

"You think so?" The hopeful look on Tressalayne's face appeared like a radiant burst of light to Lucas.

He couldn't help himself and grasped her hand. With a squeeze, Lucas said, "Yes, I *do* think so. You are going to be okay, Tressalayne."

Squeezing back, Tressalayne said, "Thank you, Dr. Beckett."

Tressalayne's touch, soft and warm, was electric, and Lucas struggled to maintain his composure. The scent of her hair, her full lips and pale rose-colored cheeks mesmerized him, his heart doing flip-flops in his chest. A *rap* intruded on his thoughts, and he saw Bernice at the door with several papers in hand.

Grinning, she said, "Big Sam left these for you to sign," then added, "Said something about the transfer of the patient's care to you."

Lucas shot up out of the chair. "What? Ye-yes. Of course," he stammered, red-faced.

He turned back to Tressalayne. "The hospital planned to transfer you to another much larger hospital in Dallas. I told them I would assume your care until you have fully recovered…*if* you agree, and *if* you want me too," he hastily added.

"Why would you do that for me?" Tressalayne asked.

Lucas swallowed hard. "I guess I sort of feel, you know, *responsible* for you."

"But Bernice already told me how you found me and brought me to the hospital. It wasn't your fault."

Lucas didn't know what to say and struggled to formulate a reply.

The ICU nurse saved him further embarrassment. "I'll tell you why, Tressalayne. Dr. Beckett is a good man, and girl, trust me when I tell you, there are damn few good men left in this world. He's trying to do the right thing. In the big hospitals, it's easy to become lost, a number or statistic to be checked off on someone's list. He's wants to spare you of this and make sure you have the best recovery possible."

Bernice hugged Lucas. "I'll take the papers back to my station. Let me know what you decide."

Tressalayne looked at the young doctor, an unfamiliar warmth growing within her over what the nurse said. *He is a good man.* She wasn't quite sure what to make of the statement, but decided she liked the sound of it anyway.

Lucas shifted from one foot to the other. "Bernice kinda exaggerates."

"No, I don't!" a voice called from the nurses' station.

Lucas turned a brighter shade of crimson. "Er, like I said before, you don't have—"

"Okay."

"Um…*what?*"

"Okay. I trust you, Dr. Beckett. After all, good men are *damn* hard to find."

Tressalayne grinned at Lucas, the doctor chuckling in relief.

"Well, okay then. I'll have an ambulance transfer you when I get a place fixed up for you and arrange for a nurse. And please, call me Lucas."

"Thank you...*Lucas*. For everything."

Lucas nodded. "Well, I guess I have some papers to sign. We'll see each other again soon." Turning, he left the room.

Tressalayne watched Lucas leave, the warm feeling inside her blooming ever larger. What is a "good man"?

She looked forward to finding out.

TWENTY-TWO

S AM WATCHED THE TWO WOMEN GET INTO A LATE MODEL BMW and drive off.

He sat in a darkened room looking through a pair of high-powered binoculars. Fastened to a tripod, the binoculars could count the number of moles on the smaller woman's skin should he wish to do so.

He stood and stretched, kicking aside fast food containers and wrappers. Looking around at the place he called home for the past several days, he considered whether or not to try and follow the women. Deciding against it, he instead went to the stack of electronic equipment lying on the marble island in the kitchen. While he went through a mental checklist of all the equipment he would need, he also reviewed the report he would present to Crick.

When Crick first assigned him the task of discovering what happened to some mystery woman in Nacogdoches, he thought his boss had lost it…especially after seeing him seated at his desk and dressed only in briefs.

Now, he wasn't so sure.

From what he observed so far, Crick might be on to something. What that something was exactly, he was still in the process of finding out.

After he arrived in Nacogdoches, he drove straight to Memorial, and posing as a relative, began to ask questions about the nameless woman. While little of the information had been helpful, one particular fact *was*. The mystery woman had one frequent visitor—the owner of the car which struck her and landed her in the hospital. This person, Karen Prescott, made the bizarre claim she fell from the sky and crashed through her windshield. While interesting, it was not as interesting as another fact.

Karen Prescott visited "mystery woman" the very day she disappeared.

After some digging, Lunker discovered Prescott's husband to be a successful oil executive, and a well-known personage about town. Armed with this information, Lunker traced Prescott's residence to a palatial home in the country club district of Nacogdoches. Posing as an interested buyer, Lunker called several real estate companies until he found a house for sale near the Prescott home. In fact, it was just across the street, and Lunker made an appointment to view the house. He arrived early, and waited at the curb in his rental.

While he waited, he saw a silver Beemer meeting the description of Prescott's car parked in the driveway. Noting its shiny new windshield, he got out and pretended to stroll about while taking in the neighborhood. When he walked by the BMW, he placed a transmitter under the rear bumper. Without a break in stride, he continued his stroll and ended up back at his car. The powerful transmitter emitted a tracking signal of several miles, and allowed Lunker to sync the transmitter's signal to the Google maps app on his phone. He could now trace and record every place Prescott's car traveled.

Which led him to the lake house.

Situated on a private one-thousand-acre lake, a number of other cottages and boat docks lay scattered along the shoreline. Ranging from one room cabins to expensive, multi-story homes, most were unoccupied, a clear sign to Lunker they were for weekenders, probably from Houston or Dallas. The house the Beemer parked at was a large structure—easily over two thousand square feet—with a large deck leading to a boat dock, and a detached garage. Somewhat isolated from the other homes, Prescott's nearest neighbor was several wooded acres away.

Perfect.

Lunker checked his tracker and saw the BMW headed south of Nacogdoches, probably to Lufkin. He tailed them the day before to a large mall in Lufkin and figured it a safe bet they were returning there.

That should give him plenty of time.

He stuffed his equipment in a small duffle and went out the back door of his "borrowed" cottage. Although equipped with a standard home security system, by good fortune, it had been de-activated, and was child's play for Lunker to pick the lock and let himself in. He didn't think he would be so lucky a second time with Prescott's home, and came prepared. He double-checked the text message on his phone from the "consultant" he used when faced with similar security systems. The consultant worked for a large, multinational security firm, and for a fee, could supply the alarm code for virtually any private residence or business.

Armed with the code, Lunker set off for the Prescott lake house.

Taking a circuitous route, the big man ended up at the back of the large cottage. He plucked the pick locks from his pocket, and made short work of the lock. Upon opening the door, a *beep, beep, beep* issued from the keypad by the front door. Hurrying, Lunker arrived at the keypad and punched in the series of numbers from the text. The *beeps* stopped, and he sighed in relief. Placing the duffle on the floor, he zipped it open and placed all the electronic equipment on the floor. Then he got to work.

Two hours later, every room contained a hidden spy camera. Placed strategically so the cameras panned each room in its entirety, the tiny spy-cams also supplied an audio feed. He pulled a tablet from the duffle and ran a systems check on his network. Each visual angle from the spy-cams appeared as part of a grid on the tablet. With a tap on the tablet's touchscreen, he could select any camera from the grid or zoom in if need be. Satisfied, Lunker placed the tablet back in the duffle and packed up his remaining equipment.

Pausing, he backtracked to the bedroom Prescott's guest used. On top of a handsome mahogany chest of drawers lay various items and implements. At first, he took them as junk. Now, taking a second look, he wasn't so sure.

One object, an old goblet of brass embossed in odd symbols, reminded him of a trophy cup except it was missing the handles. Next, a number of vials and pouches lay side by side, and looked like they contained dried powder or herbs. Finally, a small, fluid-filled bottle, fluted on one end and bulbous on the other, stood alone and separate from all the rest. Taking out his cell phone, Lunker took pictures of each item. Satisfied, he turned and left.

Arming the alarm, Lunker let himself out the back door. He locked the door and made his way back to the weekender's cabin he was using.

The spy cameras should clear up the odd relationship between Prescott and the woman she befriended. Having observed them both the past several days, Lunker could tell something was off with Prescott. Something wasn't right. When in the presence of the other woman, she stood still and unmoving, like an army private awaiting orders. Studying her face with the powerful binoculars, it appeared to him that Prescott's eyes were unfocused…almost trance-like.

The other woman, the mysterious personage Crick sent Lunker to find, was the complete opposite. She walked about and acted like she owned the place, and when speaking to Prescott, never deigned to even look at her.

Very strange.

He would have given a month's salary to hear the woman's conversation with her "friend". It would answer a lot of questions. Now with the spy equipment in place, he would get his wish.

Live and in living color.

TWENTY-THREE

"WELL, WHAT DO YOU THINK?" LUCAS ASKED. HE AND Tressalayne stood inside a cottage surrounded by a mixture of mature oaks and pine trees.

Tresslayane looked around the cabin. "This is so nice. You really didn't have to go to all this trouble."

Located several hundred yards from the main farmhouse, large picture windows fronted the cabin allowing abundant sunlight to stream in, while giving a picturesque view of a nearby pond. French doors led to a small patio beside the cabin with a table and chairs. A modest kitchen was on the left, while two bedrooms and a bathroom were to the right. A small den was sandwiched in the middle.

"No trouble at all," Lucas replied. "It used to be the where the hired help slept during the pecan harvest, and dates back to the early 1900s. My mother modernized and remodeled the entire cottage, but took great pains to retain as much of the original architecture as possible. She loved it here. This is where she spent her final days before she passed." A troubled look appeared and then quickly flitted away on Lucas' face.

Tressalayne turned and looked at him. "I'm-I'm sorry, Lucas. Are you sure you want me to stay here?"

"Of course," he assured her. "Mama, if she were alive, would have insisted. She liked to make people happy, liked to help people whenever she could. She kept the same attitude till the day she died. She was one in a million."

Lucas' voice cracked at this last comment and Tressalayne placed her hand on his arm.

"You seem to have much of your mother in you."

Her touch, warm on his skin, caused Lucas' thoughts to scatter, and he struggled to reply.

"Th-thank you. Although, trust me, Mama was a far better person than me."

"I guess that's a matter of judgment, isn't it? *You* are the nicest person I have met. You saved my life, a complete stranger, and took care of me, and now…this," she said with a nod at the cabin.

Embarrassed, Lucas shrugged and looked at Tressalayne. Once again, he was struck by her beauty. What he wouldn't have given to have met her under different circumstances.

"What happened to your mother?" Tressalayne asked interrupting his thoughts.

"Breast cancer. By the time she received the diagnosis, she was in stage four. She opted out of chemo and radiation and spent her last days here. We arranged for a hospice nurse to stay with her round the clock, and mercifully, she didn't suffer much. It will be five years ago next month since she passed."

Lucas rubbed his face. "No one's stayed here since, so as you can see, its no trouble at all."

Tressalayne nodded. "I still struggle to understand some of your words, but I am glad your mother didn't suffer."

They spent the next fifteen minutes with Lucas showing Tressalayne around the cabin and putting up her few belongings.

"Well, I guess that's it. Mrs. Garcia will start tomorrow. She's a retired nurse and you'll be in good hands. I've also asked her to take you shopping for some clothes."

Tressalayne looked down at her attire. Her old dress was cut off her and thrown away, and she wore loose blue trousers and a matching top—what her nurse, Bernice, called hospital scrubs. The only original clothing she wore were her muddy, leather slippers.

Lucas continued, "I'll bring you some supper later, and we can talk again if you have any questions."

"Is this really necessary? I mean I feel fine and you're going to a lot of trouble to help me."

"You feel fine now, but it could change in a second. Head trauma is always something to take seriously, and we don't want to take any chances. Plus, you still have a broken arm and cracked ribs."

Tressalayne nodded at the look of concern on Lucas' face.

"Okay." Leaning forward, she pecked him on the cheek. "Thank you…for everything."

Lucas' hand went to his face, his cheek tingling.

"No-no problem. I-I guess I'll see you later."

Stumbling out the door, he got into a golf cart and made his way down the winding dirt track back to the farmhouse.

Tressalayne watched Lucas drive away, her emotions in turmoil. She liked the doctor. In fact, every time they were together, she liked him even more. But the feeling seemed foreign to her as if it were at odds with something inside her, something incompatible with such sentiment. But why would liking someone as caring and kind as Dr. Beckett make her feel so unhinged? For the hundredth time, she wished she could remember something, *anything*, about her past and about who she was.

This uneasy sense of disconnection first came alive when

she awoke from her coma, and it stayed with her ever since. The feeling became heightened whenever she was around the young doctor—almost like she fought against herself.

All she knew for certain was she already missed Lucas.

Frustrated, she turned to go back into the cabin. Lost in her thoughts, she paid no attention to the double doors which opened and then shut behind her as she walked through them.

Her hands never touched the doors.

TWENTY-FOUR

"**D**OCTOR BECKETT, TERESA GARCIA IS ON THE LINE FOR you."

Lucas frowned at Hanna, his receptionist. Normally, Hanna took a message and either he or his nurse called the patient back when time allowed. However, if she took the unusual step of actually coming to the examination area to personally deliver the message, something needed his attention immediately.

Concerned, he asked, "Is something wrong?"

"I-I don't know. I don't think so. However, Teresa insisted on speaking to you *now!*"

"Of course. Transfer the call to my office."

Lucas returned the patient folder to a plastic file holder on the exam room door, and hurried down the short hallway to his office. Why would Mrs. Garcia insist on talking to him on such short notice? Several uneventful days had passed since she began to stay with Tressalayne in the cabin, and the retired nurse mentioned nothing out of the ordinary. Something must have happened. Maybe Tressalayne suffered a relapse?

With these anxious thoughts, he threw himself into his chair and punched the blinking red button on his office phone.

"Mrs. Garcia! Is something wrong?" he asked.

"Well, no, I mean, yes. I mean…you just need to get home as soon as possible! You must see this!" Mrs. Garcia's voice held a tinge of panic, and Lucas' concern ratcheted to new heights.

"Is Tressalayne all right? Has she suffered a relapse?"

"Dr. Beckett, the young woman is okay. In fact, she is more than okay. Things are…happening. Things I can't explain over the phone. You just need to see them yourself!"

Frustrated, Lucas said, "I don't understand. If Tressalayne is okay, why must I drop everything and come home?"

"Doctor Beckett, either come home now, or I'm leaving and you can find another nurse!"

The phone went dead.

Nonplussed, Lucas stared at the phone for several seconds. Then he sprang into action. He glanced at his watch and saw it was almost 11:30. His next patient was scheduled for 2:00. Normally, he would use the lunch break to return phone calls from patients, review medical files and the other minutia that went with his pediatric practice.

Not today.

Calling in his nurse, Sandi, he told her he was leaving early and he wouldn't be back until after lunch. Then he rushed out the door, got into the Jeep, and with a squeal of tires, peeled out of the parking lot.

Thoughts raced through his head as he negotiated through traffic. What could possess Mrs. Garcia to call him in such a panic and demand he come home? Then it hit him.

The locket.

Since he saw the locket rise under its own power and place itself around Tressalayne's neck, he had convinced himself he couldn't have seen it, and that it must have been a figment of his imagination—all the while recognizing he was in denial. However, no unusual activity occurred since then. Other than the loss of memory, nothing about Tressalayne seemed out of the ordinary. Besides, she was fascinating and so...*beautiful*. He *wanted* to believe it was all just his imagination!

Now, maybe Mrs. Garcia saw something too.

The thought caused him to mash even harder on the gas pedal. Careening through traffic, he whizzed by the city limit sign and onto the Farm to Market road. Passing a rancher hauling a hay dolly, the Jeep roared down the highway. He reached the farmhouse, jumped out before the engine even died, and ran to the garage. With a jerk, he unhooked the charger cable from the golf cart, leaped in, and with gravel spitting from the tires, tore out for the cabin.

Minutes later, Lucas pulled up to the cottage and leaped out. He ran through the front door, narrowly avoiding a collision with Mrs. Garcia who sat sipping tea from a mug.

"*Madre Mia*! You startled me!"

Breathless, he asked, "Where is Tressalayne? Is she all right?"

Placing the tea on a coffee table in the den, Mrs. Garcia turned to Lucas and pointed out the window. Tressalayne sat at the end of the dock, her broken arm in a sling and her feet dangling in the cool water of the pond.

"I told you there was nothing the matter with her," she scolded him.

"But, but, you said—"

"I said I wanted you to *see* something."

With a crook of her finger, Mrs. Garcia motioned for Lucas to follow her. She walked into the kitchen, stopped, and turned with arms crossed.

Confused, Lucas said, "Mrs. Garcia, would you please explain what this is all about?"

In response, Mrs. Garcia pointed over Lucas' shoulder.

Turning, his mouth fell open.

A cup and saucer floated motionless in midair.

"It's been like that since mid-morning. I've had to walk around it for fear of hitting my head while cleaning up the kitchen. And that's not all. Doors and windows open and shut as if by invisible hands. Lights turn on and off. Then there's the butterflies."

"The-the butterflies?" Lucas stammered.

"Yes, the butterflies. It seems Tressalayne has taken a liking to them, especially the colorful ones. Every time she goes outside, they appear in droves. They follow her everywhere."

"They-they do?"

"Are you listening, Doctor Beckett? *What's going on here!*"

Lucas was at a loss for words. He *didn't* know either. Helpless, he shrugged.

"I'm sorry, Mrs. Garcia. I-I don't know what's happening. I really don't."

"I see." She tapped her foot. "My shift ends at 4:00, and you have until then to talk to the young lady and offer me an explanation. If not, then consider this my notice." Pivoting on her heel, the nurse returned to the den.

Head spinning, Lucas stumbled out the French doors. Tressalayne remained at the end of the dock, yellow, orange, and blue butterflies swirling around her head while she sat kicking the water. He braced himself.

The time had come for a heart-to-heart.

He walked down the dirt path to the dock. When he reached Tressalayne, he took off his shoes, stuffed his socks in them, and rolled up his pants legs. She looked up and squinted, surprised delight on her face.

"Lucas! What are you doing here? I thought you were healing people today?"

Lucas plunked down on the edge of the dock and thrust his long legs into the pond. The cool water soothed his tired feet as he considered her question. *How did he start this conversation?* Tressalayne learned quickly, her vocabulary and understanding of his profession grew by leaps and bounds every day. However, she still experienced difficulty with some terms and their meaning.

"I am a pediatrician, Tressalayne. That means I specialize in healing *children.*"

"Oh. Of course." Her feet scissored the water into a froth. Beaming, she turned and faced Lucas. "Isn't this delightful? I just love your little sea!"

"Pond, Tressalayne. We call it a pond. Look, we need to talk."

"Okay."

Tressalayne's blue-green eyes, large as saucers, mesmerized him. He shook his head and pointed to the swarm of butterflies above her head.

"How do you explain *that*?"

"The butterflies? Aren't they beautiful? The big yellow ones with the black spots are my favorite."

"Yes, but they follow you and flit around your head like you're the queen butterfly."

"So?"

"*It's not normal!*" Lucas blurted. "Neither are cups and saucers which float, or doors and windows opening and shutting on their own. When you were still in a coma, *I saw your locket unwind, travel through midair, and then fasten around your neck!* How do you explain all of this?"

Tressalayne's hand shot to the amulet about her neck. She stroked it, uncertainty written on her face.

"Ex-explain? You mean butterflies don't follow you if you wish them to?"

"No! Plates and cups don't levitate for me either, and doors don't open and shut unless I physically do it myself! Tressalayne, you've scared Mrs. Garcia to the point she told me this her last day and she is leaving."

Tressalayne's hand went to her mouth, a stricken look on her face. "Mrs. Garcia is leaving?"

Nodding, Lucas was about to say something else, when Tressalayne leaped up. Water scattered from her dripping legs, and she bolted for the cabin. He scrambled to his feet and sprinted after her.

He caught up with Tressalayne in the den where she hugged Mrs. Garcia with her good arm. Tears streamed down her cheeks. "Mrs. Garcia, I won't do it anymore. Please don't leave!"

The nurse put her arms around Tressalayne. "There, there, *mi hija*. What's this talk of me leaving?" Shooting Lucas a venomous look, she continued, "I think Doctor Beckett just misunderstood what I said, *didn't* you, Doctor?"

"Ah, um, *yes*, yes that's right."

"Why don't you go back to the dock while we clear this up?"

"Okay." Tressalayne wiped her eyes with the back of her hands and walked back to the door. She stopped and looked over her shoulder fearful the nurse might still leave.

Mrs. Garcia waved at her. "Go on. *Sera solo un momento*."

"*Esta bien senora Garcia*."

After the door clicked shut behind Tressalayne, Mrs. Garcia turned to Lucas. "Did you realize she speaks Spanish fluently? She heard me talking to my sister on the phone and she asked what her name was—in Spanish! This from a woman who can't even tell us *her* last name."

Lucas shook his head. *Nothing about Tressalayne made sense!* Rubbing his face, he asked, "Why did you change your mind? One minute you give me notice, the next, you tell Tressalayne it's all a misunderstanding. What gives?"

Mrs. Garcia shrugged. "I was upset when I called you. I-I may have overreacted. When she hugged me, I knew I was being a silly, scared old woman." Her face softened. "She is like a lost little sheep. Everything is new to her. Despite all of her obvious confusion, I can tell she is happy, almost like, like…"

The nurse searched for the words before saying, "She is like one of the butterflies she loves so much. They emerge from the cocoon, once an ugly caterpillar, but now a new creature, a beautiful butterfly."

With a hard look at Lucas, Mrs. Garcia added, "And she is eager to please you, Doctor Beckett. She obviously cares for you. The heart is a fragile thing, and you need to be careful with hers."

"Now come on!" Lucas sputtered. "Tressalayne is a patient, and I'm just trying to help her. I never even saw her till a week ago!"

"Nevertheless, I see the way you look at her, and remember, I was a nurse for over thirty-five years. I know what a doctor-patient relationship looks like…and *other* kinds of relationships."

Heat crept up his neck, and Lucas pleaded, "Can we *please* get back to the matter at hand? Namely, what are we going to do about the weird stuff going on with Tressalayne? Also, are you staying or are you going?"

Mrs. Garcia patted Lucas' hand. "Of course I'm going to stay. Tressalayne needs me. *You* need me. As for the strange events concerning our patient, we'll keep this to ourselves for now, don't you think, Doctor Beckett?"

A pent up sigh of relief exploded from Lucas. "Yes! Let's keep this to ourselves until we can, um…figure it out."

Glad to have the strange crisis behind him, Lucas said goodbye to Mrs. Garcia and headed out to the golf cart. He waved to Tressalayne now back to dipping her feet in the water. She stood up, waving back at him.

Her gaze followed him until he crested a knoll and was lost from her sight.

TWENTY-FIVE

Lost in his thoughts, Lockstone lay on the bed and stared at the cobwebs on the ceiling.

His feet hung off the edge of the bed and made it hard to maintain a comfortable position. Comfort, however, ranged far from the most important thing on his mind. Instead, he chaffed over the inability to move forward with the Hunt for Morganna. His new life occupied much of his time—so much of this different world remained a mystery to him. Until he became more acclimated and determined a way to find her, he could do nothing.

The weeks which followed his introduction into this realm were a blur in his mind. True to his word, Eddie set him up in the small loft apartment above the shop. Cramped didn't begin to describe it, with a bed, tiny privy, and kitchen crammed in a space the size of a monk's cell. For a large man like himself, negotiating around and through the loft presented a constant challenge. However, he wasn't complaining.

He'd endured far worse.

One pleasant surprise was the shower. Lockstone considered

himself somewhat more conscientious than most in the Kingdom when it came to personal hygiene, and he tried to take a bath every fortnight…although the goal often eluded him. However, in this world, the quest for cleanliness reached to a new level, and the ripe smell of an unwashed body frowned upon. Hence, Lockstone took to the habit of showering every night.

He soon discovered one didn't have to haul water or heat it in order for the shower to function. You simply turned a knob and water spewed out.

Ingenious.

The shower, tiny like everything else, with the witch hunter barely able to squeeze inside. It took some time to learn how to adjust the water's temperature, and after much cursing brought on by scalding hot or freezing water, Lockstone found an acceptable setting.

A secondhand store a block from Eddie's shop supplied the clothes he wore, a faded pair of blue jeans, and a t-shirt. The shirt displayed a picture of an ale-like drink with script beneath it saying, "Its Five-O'clock Somewhere". A second pair of jeans and t-shirt lay in a small, dusty chest of drawers Eddie dragged from a corner of his shop. He also had an extra pair of what Eddie called underwear. When he asked Eddie if this underwear was optional, the shopkeeper shrugged and said, "Whatever floats your boat, man"

He chose to wear the underwear.

Lockstone learned a few other important things in his short sojourn in the city Eddie called, Houston. This included the small metal tubes the would-be thieves used in their attempted robbery. They were called *guns*…and they were deadly.

Exasperated after repeated questioning from Lockstone concerning these weapons, Eddie, finally drove him in one of the iron wagons to a nearby gun shop. The shop contained a shooting range, and using a pawned gun, Eddie shot at a paper target with the image of a man on it. The weapon's sound, like thunder, caused Lockstone to flinch, and fight the urge to dive on the floor and seek cover.

What the gun *did* to the target grabbed his attention.

The paper image was full of holes.

No crossbow could match the power and accuracy of this weapon. It took little convincing from Eddie for Lockstone to agree he needed a gun, along with the knowledge on how to use one…especially if he continued to work at the pawnshop and discourage thieves.

The witch hunter now went every night to the gun shop and practiced with the gun Eddie called a Glock. He imagined the paper image to be Morganna, the holes he shot through the target, her body. It never failed to leave him with a warm feeling. In short order, Lockstone mastered the gun's use.

The second important thing he learned was the coinage of the Kingdom of the United States was *paper*. Lockstone scarce believed it when Eddie tried to convince him *cash* or little plastic credit cards were what all citizens made purchases with—not gold or silver! At first, he thought the little man lied in an attempt to dupe him out of his gold. However, when day after day, he witnessed customers at the pawnshop paid by Eddie in paper money or redeeming their pawned items with paper money, the witch hunter became convinced he told the truth.

With this veracity established, Lockstone questioned Eddie and learned the cash value of gold to be over one thousand dollars an ounce. Ciphering was another skill his mother taught him before she met her untimely end at the hands of Morganna. After counting the coins in his pouch, at two ounces each, he figured he had the equivalent of over twenty thousand dollars—a fact he planned to keep from the pawnshop owner.

A knock on the door intruded on his thoughts. Rolling into a sitting position, he said, "Come in."

Eddie entered with a flat, metallic object. The image of an apple adorned the surface of the item. "What's up, Big Man?"

Frowning, Lockstone answered, "The ceiling, of course. Is there something amiss with it?"

Eddie hesitated, then shook his head. "It's just a figure of speech, Robert. You may speak the language, but, man, sometimes you act like you're from a whole new world."

The witch hunter stifled a chuckle. *Actually, the old world is where I'm from. The new world is here.*

"Anyway, I brought you a present...you know, to celebrate our, um, arrangement. There hasn't been a single attempt to rob my pawnshop since the day you showed up."

Lockstone nodded while studying the object Lucky Eddie held. "What is it?"

Taken aback, Eddie said, "You're kidding me, right? It's a laptop." Seeing the confusion on Lockstone's face, he added, "You know, a computer!"

The witch hunter shrugged. "I don't know what a *laptop* or a *computer* is."

Eddie looked hard at Lockstone then shook his head. "Okay, I was just trying to be nice, but if you are going to act like a dick, I'll just put it back on the shelf for sale."

Eddie turned to go, when Lockstone called out, "Thank you for the gift. I did not mean to make it sound I was unappreciative. I truly do not know what this—this laptop is. Perhaps you can show me?"

Mollified, the pawnshop owner turned back. "Okay, but, damn, Robert, you must be from so far back in the woods, they still use a horse and buggy. Are you sure you aren't Amish?"

Lockstone shook his head. They'd had this conversation already—along with if he was a Mennonite.

Eddie set the laptop on the small table beside the bed, then powered it up and explained how it worked. After a few minutes, he stopped when he saw the blank expression on Lockstone's face.

"What's the matter?"

"Can you start over...and go more slowly this time?"

Eddie threw up his hands. "A five-year-old has a better understanding of computers than you!"

With a sigh, he leaned forward. "Okay, *listen carefully*. You can use the laptop to look for whatever interests you on the internet. You can search—"

"Wait!"

"Huh?"

"You said *search*!"

"Yeah. So what?"

Lockstone stood and peered over Eddie's shoulder at the laptop's screen. "By 'search', you mean I can find something? Perhaps find *someone*?"

"Of course. People use the internet to do that all the time."

A broad smile spread across the witch hunter's face.

"Then you must teach me how to use this...*internet*"

"Sure." Curious, Eddie looked back at him.

"Do you have someone in mind."

Lockstone's smile crept wider.

"Oh, yes. Yes, I do."

TWENTY-SIX

"**P**LAY IT AGAIN."

Lunker clicked the mouse, and the footage captured by the spy-cams replayed the same scene on the monitor. Lunker had hours of video downloaded, stored on a zip file, and backed up on the cloud. However, he downloaded on the flash drive only those video segments he thought Crick would be most interested in.

That had been a challenging task indeed.

So much of it fell in the category of the unbelievable, even after seeing the same images again and again, Lunker still fought the urge to pinch himself to make sure he wasn't dreaming. Objects moved and floated, manipulated by Morganna, while doors opened and shut—with no hand on them!

The replay showed Morganna in her bedroom. Shoulders slumped in fatigue, her face pale, it was obvious she still had not fully recovered from her injuries. Undressing, she made her way to the bathroom and a short time later, the men heard the shower running. When she emerged twenty minutes later with only a towel wrapped around her, she stood by the bed as if unsure what to do next. Abruptly, she turned and walked to the bedside table, opened the drawer, and took out a small flask. Pulling the stopper, she took a small sip.

"There! See it? She took a hit from that bottle! Now, zoom in!"

Crick leaned forward until his nose rested inches from the computer monitor.

"Look! Do you see her face? It's changed. Her cheeks have color, and are fuller and sharper. Look at the rest of her body and how tight and taunt it's become. Her hair even looks longer and thicker. Sam, *it's like she's grown younger!*"

Lunker nodded. Studying Morganna's body—he learned the mysterious woman's name from Karen Prescott after the first night of studying video—was not an unpleasant experience. She was a looker for sure. However, after scrutinizing the same video many times, he reached the same conclusion as Crick.

Even now, he could scarce believe the evidence before him.

Crick held a blown-up photo he picked up from a series of other photos spread before him like poker chips. "And this is the picture of the bottle she took the hit from?" The pictures were items in the mysterious woman's bedroom Lunker took with his cell.

Eying the photo, Crick noted the flask's fluted shape and bulbous base. It appeared to be made of some sort of amber-colored glass or ceramic material. By his estimation, it could only hold five to six ounces of whatever "Morganna" took a sip of.

Crick waved at the photo spread. "We need to figure out what these things are."

"Already did a Google search, Boss."

"Well?"

Lunker hesitated, an embarrassed look on his face.

Crick, annoyed, glanced at his large assistant. "What are you waiting for? What did you find?"

"It's just…it's crazy. Looney stuff."

Crick pointed at the monitor. "And this isn't?"

"Well…yeah. I guess it is."

"Good! At least we can both agree on that. Now, go get us a couple of beers and then I want to know *everything* your search uncovered."

Lunker retrieved two Bud Lights from the large stainless steel refrigerator in Crick's kitchen. The men sat at a table in the dining room adjacent to the kitchen. The house, a large brick structure, was situated several miles outside of Longview on five wooded acres. Crick picked the location specifically for its remoteness and the lack of any would-be nosy neighbors. The less anyone knew about his business, the better. It was also why they met here instead of Crick's office. He wanted a much less public place to receive Lunker's complete report.

The home's interior was spacious, if utilitarian in regards to furnishings. After two failed marriages and a mountain of alimony, the hospital CFO decided bachelorhood to be both cheaper and easier. In the absence of a woman's touch, like Crick, the furnishings were businesslike, chosen for purpose and function. Not a single painting or picture hung from the walls, nor were there any knickknacks to be found in the entire house.

Handing Crick a beer, Lunker took a long pull from his own, and sat in the chair next to him.

"It took a while, but I finally found out what some of this stuff *might* be used for. Those wax-looking pencils and the black candles are used in, ah…*ceremonies*. The cup-looking thing may be used by certain, ah, groups of people, called *wiccans*, to make what they call 'potions'. I don't know for sure, but those vials and pouches might contain dried powder and herbs—what they make the potions with."

"Wiccans? You mean *witches*?"

"Yeah, but look, Boss, I'm still researching this, and there is probably a better—"

"It makes perfect sense!"

"It does?"

"Of course." Crick gestured at the monitor. "How else do you explain Morganna's sudden transformation? Maybe she or her fellow wiccans discovered a secret herbal formula like some sort of Fountain of Youth concoction. It would be worth its weight in gold!"

Excited, Crick stood and paced.

"Sam, can you imagine what people would pay to grow younger? To reverse the aging process? Whoever controls this formula will be the richest person on the planet! We have to get our hands on it!"

Relieved, Lunker relaxed. "This is weird shit, Boss. But now its beginning to make some sense."

Clearing his throat, Lunker pointed at the monitor. "Boss, there's more. Let me show you the video of Karen Prescott."

Crick, lost in the mental count of his potential billions, paused in his pacing.

"Eh? Who's she?"

"The woman whose car hit Morganna. It's Prescott's lake house she's hiding out in."

Crick returned to his seat and watched Lunker use the mouse to open another video segment. The footage displayed Morganna and Prescott standing in the den of the lake house.

"Get me something to eat," Morganna commanded after seating herself in a comfortable lounger.

"Yes, Mistress," Prescott intoned.

Turning, she walked like a wooden marionette to the kitchen. Taking bread from the cupboard, she removed lunch meat and other condiments from the refrigerator and made a sandwich. Putting it on a plate, she handed it to Morganna

"Get me an ale as well."

"You mean a beer, Mistress?"

Morganna backhanded Prescott across the face. The blow staggered her, the meaty slap clearly audible to the men watching the video.

"Of course, you fool!"

Without hesitation, Prescott retrieved a bottle of beer from the refrigerator and handed it to Morganna. Once done, she stood motionless beside the witch, a trickle of blood leaking from the corner of her mouth.

What the hell?

"Zoom in on her face," Crick ordered.

Lunker zoomed in until Prescott's face filled the screen. She stared unblinking, the blood merging with a thin strand of saliva on the side of her mouth.

"What the hell is wrong with her? Is she drugged?"

Lunker shrugged. "I don't know, Boss. It's like Prescott is in a trance, or hypnotized, or something. All I know is anytime she is with Morganna, she acts just like this."

He displayed more video clips of the interactions between the two women. In each video, Morganna directed Prescott's actions. Not once did Karen Prescott fail to immediately obey, nor did she speak except to acknowledge an order.

Crick chewed his lip, deep in thought. Lunker decided to show him the video he saved for last.

"Boss, I got one more for you. You better hang on to your hat, because I guarantee you won't believe your eyes. It's the craziest shit I've ever seen."

Amazed, Crick snorted. "You're kidding, right? How can it be crazier than what you've already shown me?"

Lunker shrugged. "You just have to see it to believe it."

Crick chugged the rest of his beer. Wiping his hand across his mouth, he belched and nodded at his assistant.

"I'm going to skip the first part of the video, but the upshot is Morganna wants to get out of the lake house. However, she knows the authorities are still looking for her, and she doesn't want to take a chance of being recognized."

"Okay, okay," Crick growled, impatient. "Get on with it."

With a click, the video began to play.

Once more in the den, Morganna ordered Karen Prescott to stay well away from her. From one of the small vials, she took a pinch of powder, held it over her head, and while chanting in a language neither of the men understood, let it sprinkle on her. At first, nothing happened, and as Crick turned to ask what the big deal was, a bright light filled the screen. His gaze shot back to the monitor where Morganna stood enveloped in what looked like a roaring inferno. Almost as quickly as it began, the fire died out.

In the witch's place stood a statuesque blonde who looked nothing like the mysterious woman known to them as Morganna.

Crash.

Crick's chair shot back to fall on the floor. He pointed wide-eyed at the monitor. "What—what happened to Morganna?"

Lunker experienced the same reaction the first time he saw the footage. He knew what must be going through his mind. Doubt, disbelief, then finally, the unsettling feeling your eyes couldn't be deceiving you.

"I wanted to show you the other videos before this one, Boss. I didn't want you to think I'm crazy. The woman standing there now on the video?

That *is* Morganna."

TWENTY-SEVEN

LUCAS PULLED INTO HIS GARAGE AND TURNED OFF THE JEEP. Opening the door, he stood and stretched. It had been a long day, and a steady stream of children paraded through his office with a variety of ear infections, respiratory ailments, and other illnesses while anxious parents waited.

He stepped out into the late afternoon sun, closed his eyes, and enjoyed the warmth on his face. In late spring, such a rare day with cool mornings and warm evenings—the prelude to the long, hot days of summer—was something to be savored.

With great reluctance, he turned and went into the farmhouse. Making his way to his room, he threw his clothes into a hamper and turned on the shower. Ten minutes later he emerged somewhat refreshed, put on khaki shorts and polo shirt, and made his way back to the garage. Getting into the golf cart, he drove to the cabin.

Mrs. Garcia met him at the door, and by the worried look on her face, he could immediately tell something was wrong. A finger to her lips, she led him to Tressalayne's room. Gently pushing the door open, she pointed to the sleeping form of Tressalayne huddled under a blanket on the bed. Slowly, she closed the door and motioned for Lucas to follow her. Leading him to the patio, she sat in one of the chairs.

Lucas grabbed a chair beside her. "What's wrong?"

"The poor girl. She's having nightmares. Tressalayne told me she hasn't slept much at all the past few nights because of them. She's so exhausted, I fixed her some green tea and encouraged her to take a nap. Poor thing's head barely hit the pillow and she was asleep."

Nightmares? Lucas knew it wasn't uncommon for amnesia patients to suddenly recall snippets of memory, and in fact, often proved to be a sign of recovery. But bad dreams were usually not part of this mix.

"Has she described them?"

Mrs. Garcia nodded. "She says people are killed in horrible ways in these nightmares by two evil women. However, that's not the most upsetting part of her dreams."

"What is?" Lucas asked.

"In her nightmares, Tressalayne is *helping* them."

Stunned, Lucas sat back in his chair.

Tressalayne? She wouldn't hurt a fly. Butterflies follow her around for heaven's sake!

Before he could finish another thought, a bloodcurdling scream came from the cabin. Leaping up, Lucas rushed through the patio doors, Mrs. Garcia close behind. Ripping open the bedroom door, Lucas skidded to a stop beside the bed.

Tressalayne sat bolt upright, the blanket held tightly to her breasts. Her face was white as a sheet, her chest heaving. Lucas sat with his arm around her, while Mrs. Garcia did the same on her other side. She shook like a twig in a storm.

As she turned to face him, a chill ran through Lucas. Her eyes, rather than sea green, were dark and brooding.

Dangerous eyes.

The eyes of a predator.

The gem in her locket turned obsidian black, its surface roiling. His unease deepening, Lucas shook her.

"What's wrong? Did you have another bad dream?"

Blinking, Tressalayne's vision cleared, the gem returning to a pearl-white.

"There is so much blood! It's everywhere!" Lips and chin trembling, her voice carried notes of hysteria.

Eying Mrs. Garcia, Lucas shook his head. "I have some sedatives at the farmhouse. You stay with Tressalayne while I go get them."

"No! Don't leave me! Please don't leave me, Lucas!"

Eyes feverish, Tressalayne grabbed Lucas with both arms and held him so tight, he had trouble drawing a breath.

"I'll get them, Dr. Beckett. Are they in the same place you kept the painkillers for your mother?" Nodding, Lucas watched the nurse leave. A moment later, he heard the hum of the golf cart on its way back to the farmhouse.

For several moments, only Tressalayne's weeping broke the silence. Her head lay on his chest, shoulders wracked with sobs. Her heart hammered against his ribs through the thin material of her blouse. Stroking her hair, he pulled her closer. Finally, her breathing returned to normal.

"It's awful, Lucas," Tressalayne whispered. "What's been done to those people. They are being murdered in such horrible ways."

Tressalayne turned tear-stained cheeks toward Lucas. "And I'm there in the middle of it, a part of what's being done to those poor men and women."

Gently, Lucas pushed Tressalayne away so he could look at her face-to-face.

"They are nightmares, nothing more. They have no more basis in reality than the Easter Bunny or the Tooth Fairy. Remember, you suffered severe head trauma. There's no telling what kind of residual effects you'll suffer from because of your injury. These flashbacks are nothing more than symptoms of your continued recovery. Eventually, they will go away."

Hope sprang onto Tressalayne's face. "You think so?"

"I *know* so."

Tressalayne sat silent. Then she asked, "But what if these bad dreams are even a little bit true? What if they are indicators of the person I was before my—my accident? That would make me a monster."

Fresh tears leaked from her eyes at this possibility.

Lucas gripped Tressalayne by both shoulders. "Listen to me. You are reading too much into these fevered dreams of yours. *I* think you are one of the most wonderful people I have ever met. You have a smile that lights up an entire room, and Mrs. Garcia is always telling me how little things like dipping your legs in the pond delight you. She thinks you hung the moon. Does this sound like a monster?"

"Mrs. Garcia likes me?"

"Of course. She loves you!"

A hint of a smile tugged at Tressalayne's mouth at what Lucas said. Then another thought struck her.

"What about you? Do you love me too?"

Lucas opened his mouth and stopped. Tressalayne's blue-green eyes held his, and he floundered in the liquid beauty of her gaze. A warmth blossomed inside him, and he struggled to reply.

"Yes. I love you most of all," he finally whispered. He couldn't help himself. The words left his mouth before he could clamp his lips shut. "I'm sorry. I-I didn't mean to say...I mean that didn't come out right—" Realizing he was only making the hole he created deeper, his voice trailed off.

Tressalayne gazed at Lucas, his face creased with embarrassment. "Say it again. Say the word again."

Lucas squirmed. "You—you mean *love*?"

"Yes…love. When you say it, my heart beats faster, and I feel—I feel *different*. Part of me screams I don't belong here, while another part never wants to leave."

Tressalayne moved closer, her hand on his cheek.

"What is this, Lucas? Why do I feel this way?"

Her nightmares forgotten, she leaned forward, drawn to Lucas. She placed a hesitant kiss on his cheek, then another. Bolder, she moved to his lips.

Lucas, an old hand at kissing girls, was an experienced practitioner since junior high. Through dozens of dates and various relationships, some serious, he lost count of how many women he had wooed, kissed, and in some cases, made love to. However, the kisses from this beautiful woman caused him to forget them all. Her lips were soft and warm, a heady taste of barely realized passion.

Lucas pulled Tressalayne to him, returning her kiss with breathless exuberance. Lowering his head, he buried his face in the sensitive nape of her neck and began to lay a trail of kisses. He worked his way back to her lips, Tressalayne's gasps accompanying his progress. Running her hands through his hair, she urged him on.

She filled his senses to the point of overload, an exotic spice whose smell, taste, and touch he couldn't get enough of.

They fell onto the bed, with Tressalayne beneath him. He unbuttoned her blouse, caressing the soft mounds of her breasts. Marveling at their warmth and firmness, he moved his lips over the pliant flesh. Gasps turned to moans, her back arched in perfect choreography with Lucas's kisses. Impatient, he decided the progress with her blouse wasn't fast enough, and began to pull it over her head. While struggling to remove the stubborn article of clothing, the crunch of golf cart tires interrupted his efforts.

In their sudden passion, they forgot all about Mrs. Garcia.

TWENTY-EIGHT

IKE A DEER CAUGHT IN HEADLIGHTS, LUCAS BOLTED UP, smoothed his hair, and straightened his shirt. Tressalayne, her face flushed, lay with her blouse unfastened to her navel. Her chest still heaved, exposed breasts swaying like a clock pendulum.

"Button your shirt," he hissed.

"But I like it this way," she said with a smile.

"Tressalayne, *please*. Mrs. Garcia will walk in here any minute!"

With a sigh, Tressalayne's fingers fumbled with the buttons.

Lucas paced while he struggled with what do about his beautiful, partially dressed problem on the bed. Reaching a decision, he faced her. "We can't do this anymore."

Tressalayne's face fell. "Did I do something wrong?"

"No, of course not. It's me. What—what we are doing is unethical. I'm a doctor and I'm supposed to be taking care of you."

"But you said it is children you heal." Tresslayne ran her hands up and down her body. "Do I look like a child to you?"

Even with eyes still red and puffy from recent tears, her hair tousled and her blouse rumpled, Tressalayne presented a captivating sight—tight shorts molded to her hips while displaying long, shapely legs. Lucas swallowed hard.

No, she certainly didn't look like a child.

"You don't understand. The perception will be I'm taking advantage of you. Mrs. Garcia already said something to me about it."

Tressalayne sauntered over to Lucas and nuzzled him.

"You said you loved me. Did you mean it?"

"Yes, but—but its not that simple." Frustrated, he threw up his hands. "Can we talk about this after Mrs. Garcia leaves?"

Still nuzzling him, Tressalayne's breath tickled his ear as she mumbled a yes.

Lucas managed to extricate himself from Tressalayne just as Mrs. Garcia walked through the door. He tried not to look guilty, but he could tell from the look on her face she knew something was up. Tressalayne didn't help when she skipped over to her and gave her a warm hug. Seeing her patient go from a sobbing mess to bright-eyed and happy caused Mrs. Garcia to eye Lucas with fresh suspicion.

With a pat on her arm, Mrs. Garcia said, "Doctor Beckett and I are going to go outside and talk. You must be hungry, so I made you a sandwich and put it in the refrigerator. Why don't you eat it while we are out?"

Tressalayne's gaze darted between them for a few moments. Sighing in resignation, she nodded and headed for the kitchen.

Mrs. Garcia pulled Lucas down the dirt path away from the cottage. "Doctor Beckett, I warned you about being mindful of Tressalayne's feelings."

"Mrs. Garcia, I can assure you—"

"But she talks about you all the time. She looks at you the same way you look at her."

Red-faced, Lucas shook his head. "That obvious, huh?"

Mrs. Garcia nodded. "Some things can't be helped. Just be

careful Doctor Beckett. You have a reputation you worked hard to establish, and people *will* talk."

She crossed her arms and continued, "What I really wanted to discuss with you is the awful dreams. You saw firsthand Tressalayne's reaction to them, but there is something more disturbing I didn't get a chance to tell you."

Lucas' eyebrow raised. "More disturbing?"

"During these episodes, *things* happen. The whole cabin shook the first time. It terrified me! I thought it was an earthquake, so I rushed into Tressalayne's room to get her out...but I couldn't get in!"

"You mean she locked the door?"

"No, the door was stood wide open. Something—like an invisible barrier—kept pushing me away. I could see her shake and moan as she tossed and turned on the bed. There was nothing I could do for her. The next episode, I happened to look out the window, and the water in the pond was frothing, heaving, and bubbling. Again, I couldn't get past her door when I attempted to help."

An invisible barrier? An earthquake? The image of the locket sailing through the air to place itself around Tressalayne's neck jumped through Lucas' mind...one of the many unexplained incidents associated with her sudden appearance in his life. He couldn't shake the feeling he was missing something about her— something critical he neither understood nor recognized— which could make clear what to this point strained the boundaries of belief.

"I don't understand. Why is she having these nightmares during the day? Doesn't she sleep at night?"

"After Tressalayne started having the nightmares, she told me she doesn't sleep much at all. She's afraid to for fear of having horrible dreams. My concern, though, is she has no one to stay with her at night. What happens if she injures herself during one of these—these bad dreams? There is no one to help her."

Lucas nodded. He could see the dilemma. Until Tressalayne got past these twisted flashbacks, someone would have to be with her at all times.

Mrs. Garcia chewed on her lip. "Have you noticed she doesn't wear the plastic cast on her arm anymore? I examined her arm and ribs thoroughly, and although an x-ray would be needed to confirm it, I believe they have completely healed. A *normal* person would need at least another six weeks to knit the broken bones."

Mrs. Garcia shook her head. "I know we've avoided talking about the—the *oddness* we see happen with Tressalayne and around her. Maybe we hoped it would just disappear so we could have a laugh and forget about it. But it's not going away, Doctor Beckett, and in fact, it's getting worse. I can't explain it—*any of it*—and I know you can't either. However, there may be someone who can help."

Lucas shot Mrs. Garcia a look. "Really? Who?"

The nurse took a business card from her pocket and handed it to Lucas. The card was red, white, and blue, and embossed with black lettering. Stenciled in bold letters were the words, *Uncommon Antiques & Oddities – The Shop of the Unusual and Unique, Hank Harper – Proprietor,* along with the store's website.

Puzzled, Lucas asked, "How can an antique store owner know anything about what's going on with Tressalayne?"

"I understand the store owner is an expert in antiquities. He moved to Mt. Pleasant a few years ago and opened up his store. A few of the people I know have been helped by him."

"How so?"

Mrs. Garcia shifted uncomfortably. "Well…one was having problems with a ghost, and another with an old chair which moved to a different position every morning."

Lucas couldn't believe his ears. "Oh, come on! You've got to be kidding! Next you'll be telling me this guy conducts nightly séances as well."

Mrs. Garcia tossed her head. "I'm not a fool, Doctor Beckett. I Googled Hank Harper to discover more about his reputation before suggesting he might be of help. He is a guest lecturer at the University of Texas, and has been for a number of years. He also has a PhD in Archeology from Stanford. Does this sound like the resume of a crackpot to you?"

She jabbed a finger at Lucas. "But more to the point, how do *you* explain what's going on, Doctor? It's a long shot, but maybe this Hank Harper knows something we don't."

Chastened, as much as he hated to admit it, Mrs. Garcia might be right. Their options were few to zero, and even grasping at straws was better than nothing at all.

Lucas looked at the card with renewed interest. What did they have to lose? Mt. Pleasant was less than an hour away, and with the store's website supplied on the card, he could check it out tonight. If he saw anything he didn't like, he'd simply toss the card in the trash and forget about it.

"Okay. You win. I'll see what I can do. Now what about the problem of who's going to stay with Tressalayne at night? Do you have anyone in mind?

"As a matter of fact, I do."

"Who?"

"You—my shift is over."

With a crisp pivot, Mrs. Garcia walked back to the cabin.

TWENTY-NINE

"**N**O, I'M NOT INTERESTED IN A LOVE POTION OR ANY OF your t-shirt specials."

Disconnecting, Crick tossed his cell on the desk and rubbed tired eyes. His fingers drummed a staccato on the desk's surface while he considered his shrinking options. Looking around his office in search of inspiration, he racked his brain to avoid the head-on collision with the dead-end he feared rapidly approached.

After the stunning footage of Morganna morphing into a different woman right before his eyes—this on *top* of her age-changing serum—he decided the next step would be to find some sort of wiccan or witch expert who could explain what the implements, potions, and powders used by Morganna were. More importantly, he wanted to know the nuts and bolts of how they worked to reproduce what he witnessed on the video. This would require a certain amount of finesse, for he was certain that not only was the pool of individuals with this expertise small, but their knowledge a closely guarded secret.

For all these reasons, he decided to obtain this information himself. Sam was smart and dependable, but Crick couldn't afford anything going wrong. He learned long ago, when in doubt, to depend on his own instincts.

With the aid of the internet, he surfed for wiccan websites. Most listed phone numbers as part of their contact information along with an email address. Much of his efforts proved to be a waste of time. Many of the so-called *wiccans* he managed to contact tried to interest him in services ranging from fortune-telling to casting curses. Some were downright scary with one demanding a contract signed in blood before any service would be rendered.

Discouraged, Crick looked at the list of websites he compiled. Most were marked through, with only a handful yet to get in touch with. One particular website caught his eye, primarily because of the unusual nature of the product it advertised.

Tea.

When he first came across the website, he almost dismissed it out of hand and left it off his list…until he saw what was displayed in parentheses:

The Tea Emporium & *ATW (All Things Witches).*

It was also one of the few websites to use the word *witch* instead of the more PC term, *wiccan.*

Intrigued, Crick checked his watch and saw it was already after ten o'clock in the evening. He shrugged and decided to take a shot and called anyway. To his surprise, the phone was answered on the third ring.

"Tea Emporium," a deep feminine voice answered. "How may I help you?"

"I'm calling in regard to information concerning certain implements used in wiccan ceremonies."

Silence answered his request, and just as he began to suspect he may have been disconnected, the woman replied.

"I'm afraid you called the wrong number. I don't do gothic or black mass. Now if you'll excuse me—"

"Lady, I'm not calling about any of that," Crick quickly interjected. "All I want is someone to tell me what certain wiccan objects are and what they do."

"I see. And how do you know these 'certain objects' are used by witches?"

"Let's just say I have a good idea."

Crick's heart raced. Since he started the internet search, this was the first person who wasn't spouting weird wiccan shit or trying to sell him a wiccan service or product. Maybe, just maybe, he finally found someone who could help him.

"Look, I can fax pictures of these objects to you, or I can scan them and email them to you. All I ask is for you to look at them and tell me what you think. Needless to say, I'll pay you for your time."

More long silence, and Crick feared he struck out. Then the woman's deep, baritone voice reappeared on the phone.

"I'm not promising anything, but you may send me the pictures along with your cell number. My fax number is on my website. Good evening." The phone clicked off.

Crick located the number adjacent to the business phone number on the website, and faxed the photos taken by Lunker.

Crick yawned, then stood and stretched to work the kinks out of his back and neck. He looked forward to a long, hot shower and then his soft bed. Grabbing his suit jacket, he put it on and was reaching for his cell when it began to trill.

Curious, he looked at the phone and saw an Austin phone number. Snatching it up, he said, "Hello?"

"Where did you get these pictures?"

The woman from the Tea Emporium! Crick's blood pumped faster. He could tell by the tone of her voice he hit the jackpot.

"I'd rather not answer those kinds of questions over the phone. Can we set up a meeting?"

"Yes…and I would say the sooner the better."

Crick looked at his personal calendar lying on the desk. He was booked with meetings the next day, but the day after was relatively free.

"How about the day after tomorrow?"

"Excellent. Can you meet me at my shop?"

Crick glanced at the physical address on the website and saw it was close to downtown Austin.

"Sure. Say about eleven o'clock in the morning? It will take me at least five hours to drive there."

"Of course…might I have your name?"

"Right now you can call me 'anonymous' until we have a chance to meet face-to-face."

"Well, Mr. Anonymous, please take care. Because based on the pictures you sent me, you need to tread carefully.

Very carefully, indeed."

THIRTY

C RICK HIT THE BRAKES AS HE INCHED ALONG IN THE AUSTIN traffic.

To his right, the dome of the Capital Building rose high into the Texas sky, along with The University of Texas Football Stadium. A huge, bowl-shaped structure, the mammoth edifice could seat over one hundred thousand people.

Crick shook his head. Texans and their football. As close to an official state religion as one could get. A born and bred Jersey boy, he like many other Yankees, followed jobs and opportunity to Texas. He didn't get it—not that he cared a whit one way or the other. Hopefully, after his meeting today, he would be well on his way to being so rich, he could buy his own NFL team should he ever feel the need to scratch that itch.

Honking, diesel fumes, and the noise of thousands of cars moving at a snail's pace filled the air. The day, already warm, caused sweat to trickle down Crick's shoulder blades, and he cranked the car's air-conditioner to high.

The address he looked for was downtown, not far off of Congress

Street. Unfortunately, he didn't know enough about the warren of narrow of streets populating downtown Austin to take an alternate route and avoid the gridlock on I-35. Instead, he'd been forced to rely on his GPS which directed him on the shortest route—but also the most congested.

Impatient, he checked his watch. The slow pace of traffic guaranteed he'd be late for his appointment. Drumming his fingers on the steering column, he finally spotted his exit. Like a shaft of sunlight on a cloudy day, a gap appeared in the slow-motion sea of cars. Crick hit his blinker and quickly slid the silver Lexus sedan into the space, the move eliciting a chorus of angry honks. Ignoring them, he sped down the exit ramp to join yet another line of stalled cars.

Fifteen minutes later, he pulled into a gravel parking area adjacent to a craftsman style home. In the near distance, glass and steel skyscrapers rose from downtown Austin, the noise and commotion from the congested area somewhat muted by the quiet, tree-lined street.

Crick exited the Lexus and stretched, stiff after riding in the confines of the sedan for hours. Curious, he studied the house and adjacent area. A white sign with "The Tea Emporium" painted on it in large, flowery, lavender-colored letters, stood in the front yard next to the street. Absent from the sign were any other words, including *witch*.

Crick grabbed his briefcase from the front seat, and followed a flagstone path leading to a quaint porch gracing the front of the house. A pair of rocking chairs flanked the whitewashed front door, while potted red geraniums hung from macramé containers attached to the eaves by brass hooks.

It didn't look like a witch's shop to Crick. In fact, it looked more like a cover photograph on a *Country Living* magazine. An edge of doubt crept into the back of his mind, along with the fear he just wasted a five-hour drive on a fool's errand.

He pushed the door open to the accompaniment of a pleasant *tinkling* from a small brass bell above the door. Tea cozies, doilies, infusers, and a variety of ceramic and metal tea pots of every size and description lined display cases mounted on the walls.

"I'm in the back," a familiar voice called.

Following the sound, Crick passed through another room with a marble counter behind which were row after row of glass containers of coffee beans. On the opposite wall, open shelves held containers of tea. A coffee grinder and scale sat on the counter, and the pungent odor of ground coffee and raw tea filled the air.

Crick crossed into a sun-filled back room, and spotted a spare woman seated in a high-back chair upholstered in a wine-colored print. Black hair, liberally sprinkled with gray, fell past her shoulders, and pale blue eyes appraised him as he entered. The witch wore a blue skirt with a blue and yellow print blouse, and when she stood to greet Crick, he noted she easily matched his six-foot height. Her features retained a Slavic look, with a sharp nose and full lips. Crick guessed her age at somewhere north of sixty, and mused she must have been a real looker in her younger days.

Hand outstretched, the witch greeted him. "It's nice to meet you, Mr. Anonymous."

Seeing no need to carry the subterfuge any further, Crick shook her hand. "Mason Crick."

"Annalise Cousteau. Please take a seat." Annalise gestured to a chair the twin of her own.

An antique silver tea service sat on a table between the chairs, and Annalise poured tea into a bone china tea cup, first for Crick, then for herself. A small bowl of curled lemon rinds lay on the tea service, and with a dainty tong, Annalise placed a rind in Crick's tea and her own.

"Sugar or honey?" she asked.

Crick indicated sugar, and Annalise placed a cube in Crick's tea. She handed him the cup and saucer, then squeezed a generous amount of honey into her cup. Stirring the mixture with a spoon, she added cream from a tiny pitcher beaded with condensation.

"I'd offer you cream, but unlike the Europeans, Americans don't seem to appreciate cream in their tea."

"So, you're from Europe?" Crick asked, his tea untouched.

Annalise took a sip, closing her eyes as she savored the taste. "My parents, actually. I was born in the states. They fled from Romania to avoid capture and imprisonment by the Nazis."

"So your parents were, what? Jews?"

Annalise shook her head. "Gypsies. It seems Hitler viewed us as undesirable as the Jews. Many of my family members were exterminated at Dachau and Auschwitz."

"I see."

Sitting forward, his elbows on his knees, Crick narrowed his gaze. "Pardon me for getting straight to the point, but before we begin, can you tell me what qualifies you to be someone knowledgeable of wiccan ceremonies?"

Annalise placed her cup and saucer on the tea service. "My mother, her mother, her mother's mother and so on are all Romani witches...as am I. Our line stretches unbroken across the centuries."

"Yet you sell tea and coffee, and your sign outside doesn't even mention the word *wiccan*. I find that odd for a self-professed witch."

Annalise laughed, a deep, pleasant rumble.

"First of all, most of the 'wiccans' you refer to are, by and large, frauds. They know no more about witchery than I do about the design of a nuclear reactor. More than a few are disturbed individuals, while the others are out to make a fast buck on impressionable fools. Even the name, wiccan, is an affront for I am a real *witch*, one of the precious few that actually exist."

Annalise reached for her cup and took a delicate sip.

"Down through the centuries, we have learned from unfortunate experience the unreasonable fear the general population holds for witches and the consequences thereof. This fact, Mr. Crick, combined with the small pool of *actual* witches, means there is only an infrequent call for my services. I have to have another means to support myself, hence selling tea and coffee."

With a chuckle, Annalise placed her cup and saucer down.

"As for why you do not see 'witch' anywhere on my sign, you must understand this is Austin. The unofficial motto here is 'Keep Austin Weird'. I have enough trouble with crazies and kooks showing up at my doorstep because of my website without inviting more of the same with my store sign."

Crick nodded. "You've convinced me."

He picked up his briefcase and balanced it on his knees. Opening it, he took out several bundles of cash and placed them on the coffee table.

The witch's eyes widened at the sight of the bundles of one hundred dollar bills. Looking up, her eyes widened further.

Crick held a gun pointed at her.

THIRTY-ONE

Annalise's hand went to her throat. "I-I can assure you there is no need for that."

"No offense, Annalise, but I'll be the judge of what's *needed* and what's not. After all, you *did* tell me to tread carefully."

Paralyzed with fear, Annalise stared at the gun.

"So, what you see pointed at you is a snub-nosed .38. It doesn't shoot for shit much past ten or fifteen feet, but as close as we are, I can't miss. It will blow a hole in you big enough to see daylight on the other side. Got that, girlfriend?"

Annalise, her face as pale as milk, nodded.

"Great. Now that we understand each other, I want you to know if at any time I begin to feel, let's say, strange or woozy in any way, I'll shoot you."

Crick's eyes went dark. "I'll shoot you dead, Annalise. So, if you've slipped a mickey in my tea, you're already living on borrowed time."

The image of Karen Prescott's zombie-like behavior around Morganna lay fresh on Crick's mind. He was taking no chances.

Annalise slumped in relief.

"I put nothing in your tea except sugar."

She reached across for Crick's teacup and took a generous sip.

"See? Would I drink any of your tea if it was tainted in any way?"

Crick smiled, his teeth gleaming, shark-like.

"No, I guess you wouldn't."

Satisfied, Crick placed the gun back in his briefcase. However, he left the briefcase open with the revolver in easy reach.

Crick took one of the hundred dollar bundles and pushed it across the tea service to the witch.

"That's a thousand bucks. There's another four thousand in it for you if I'm dazzled by your information."

Regaining her composure, Annalise picked up the money, the bills crisp in her hand. Next to her lay a valise from which she took a pastel folder. Annalise opened the file, and took out the pictures sent to her by Crick.

She held up the photo of the trophy cup. "I believe this to be a chalice used in mixing and making potions. Although the runes and inscriptions on the chalice are unknown to me, nonetheless, its purpose and function would still be the same."

"What are these runes for?"

"They focus the magic of the chalice which in turn enhances the potency of the potion."

A dry chuckle erupted from Crick.

"Magic? Like pulling a rabbit from a hat? You've got to be kidding."

"You asked for information, Mr. Crick. Whether you choose to believe it or not is up to you."

Crick waved his hand. "No offense intended. Please go on."

Another picture appeared, this one of a small flask surrounded by sealed pouches. "This appears to be a vessel which holds a finished potion. The packets next to it contain the various substances or raw ingredients used in an elixir."

The last photo of the stylus and candles caused the witch's face to grow troubled.

"The stylus is used to draw or trace symbols. Often, they are used to make an outline which can be anything from compass points to boundaries."

Crick frowned. "What would be the point of drawing a boundary?"

"To direct magic or power within a focal point, or to keep something within or without the boundary."

"Okay, so what about the black candles? What purpose do they serve?"

Annalise cleared her throat. "I'm afraid their purpose is evil. Nothing but evil."

Hands shaking slightly, she picked up her cup and sipped the tea while Crick mulled over what she told him.

Coming to a decision, he stacked four more bundles of cash and pushed them to Annalise. Then he took a MacBook Air from his briefcase, powered it up, and turned the laptop to face the Romani witch.

"Watch this."

With a *click*, Crick played a video clip. The footage showed Karen Prescott standing, zombie-like, and ordered about by Morganna.

Annalise's hands began to shake even more.

With another keystroke, Crick transitioned the video to another clip, this one of Morganna sipping from the flask and transforming into a more youthful and robust version of herself.

The teacup now clattered on the saucer.

Finally, Crick played the video of Morganna sprinkling a tiny bit of powder on her head and disappearing into a maelstrom of fire only to reappear moments later as a completely different person.

Crash.

The cup and saucer hit the floor and shattered.

Crick grinned. "Impressive, huh?"

Annalise stumbled to her feet. She took a step back and pointed at the laptop.

"Who—*where did you get that?*"

Crick snapped the laptop shut.

"Remember, I'm the one paying *you* to answer *my* questions, not the other way around."

Amused by her reaction, Crick added, "Seems your *small* pool of witches is a little larger than you thought."

"You-you don't understand. The woman, the *witch* in the video is more powerful than any I have ever seen!"

"I beg to differ. I *do* understand...which is why I'm here."

Crick took five more stacks of cash from the briefcase, and placed them in a tidy pile on the tea service.

"I want to employ your services, and I'm prepared to pay five K up front if you agree. Double that is yours as a bonus if I'm a satisfied customer. Do you agree?"

Annalise eyed the mounting pile of cash, and Crick suppressed a smile. The witch's caution warred with the allure of the money, but he already knew how this act would play out. He'd already given her more money than she probably earned in months—and now he offered her the chance to double the amount.

Greed won out.

"What do you want?"

Crick leaned forward. "First, I want to know what happened in the videos I showed you. Explain it to me."

Annalise, slowly sank into her chair.

"The woman in the first video—"

"—Karen Prescott."

"Yes. She appears to be bewitched."

"And what does it mean to be 'bewitched'?

Annalise, cleared her throat.

"It means she is under a hypnotic spell."

"Which is why she does everything Morganna commands?" Crick asked.

Hearing the name of the witch in the video for the first time gave Annalise pause before she answered.

"Yes, except a true bewitching is both a difficult and rare feat. Most of the time, complete control is impossible. Instead, a suggestion or compulsion is planted in the host's mind which they find irresistible. I have never seen such a total bewitching before."

"What about the stuff Morganna sprinkled on herself which changed her appearance?"

Annalise's mouth opened and closed several times before she could answer.

"In Romani legend, it is said there exists a changeling powder whose magic can transform one into a different person. But, I've always understood it to be a fanciful tale, one told at Gypsy gatherings along with other fables. I never believed it could actually be *true*."

Crick quivered with taunt eagerness, and leaned forward to ask the question he had driven the long distance to have answered.

"What did Morganna drink to cause her to grow younger?"

"It was a potion, probably made in the chalice and stored in the flask," the Romani witch answered.

"Yes!" Crick exclaimed.

He rubbed his hands eagerly. "Can I assume Morganna made the potion and could make more?"

"Of course."

Crick's face split into a wide smile. The pieces were falling into place. Wealth beyond imagining was at his fingertips.

"Is there a way I could approach Morganna safely without the danger of becoming bewitched?"

Annalise nodded. "A warding spell would suffice. I could make a talisman to hang about your neck. It's small and can be worn, unseen, beneath your shirt."

"Is there a way to bewitch Morganna?"

Dead silence greeted this request.

Finally, Annalise said, "You can't be serious. You have no idea how dangerous this witch, Morganna, is."

Crick knew *exactly* how dangerous she was—which meant the odds of her collaboration with him to make the youth potion were slim to none. The only way to get her cooperation was by force.

"What would you need to make a bewitching so I have complete control of Morganna?"

Annalise's eyes bulged. "Didn't you hear me earlier? I've never seen a complete bewitching. To try that on this witch will get us both killed!"

"Fifty thousand dollars."

"It can't be done I tell you!"

"*One hundred thousand dollars.*"

"It can't—"

Crick watched the wheels turn as Annalise stopped, the obscene amount registering in her mind. He took advantage of the pause to leap in.

"Tell me what you need. Just tell me what you need."

Annalise swallowed hard. "One—One hundred thousand dollars?"

"In cash and all yours if you'll help me bewitch Morganna."

Annalise took a deep breath. "A bewitching of Morganna is impossible. However, it may be possible to control her through a binding."

"What's that?"

"It is similar to a bewitching. Once bound, the individual is compelled to obey whatever he or she is commanded to do. The big difference is self-consciousness is never lost in a binding. The person is always aware, which makes the spell chancy. They are compelled to obey, but it is what they are *not* commanded to do which could cause problems."

Intrigued, Crick asked, "Like what?"

"For example a bound person may be directed to make dinner...but not to put rat poison in the food. Or, they may have been commanded to sit, but not to throw a knife at you while seated."

Crick rubbed his chin. A binding complicated things, but it just meant he would have to be careful.

"What do you need?"

"In order for a binding to have any chance, you would have to gather from Morganna, hair, nail clippings, and most important, her blood. I can make the potion, but without these ingredients, it is doomed to fail."

Annalise stared at Crick. "You might somehow be able to get the hair and nails, but how would you ever get her blood? And then, how would you force her to drink the potion?"

"Don't worry, I've got a plan. I'm going to meet with Morganna and persuade her."

Annalise raised an eyebrow. "Why would she ever meet with you?"

"Because I have the perfect bait."

Crick reached into his pocket and took out a notepad. He showed it to Annalise, one word written over and over on all the pages.

Tressalayne

THIRTY-TWO

LUCAS STARED AT THE DARKENED CEILING.

Try as he might, he couldn't sleep. After his conversation with Mrs. Garcia, he moved Tressalayne into the guest bedroom down the hall from his own. She made no objection and appeared relieved to be out of the cottage and in the same house with Lucas. It made him sad to think the cabin, which initially gave her such happiness and joy, now appeared linked to her fears and anxiety.

His own emotions were mixed. Part of him celebrated having her closer, and in fact, wanted her not down the hall in another room, but in the same bed with him. His other half knew Mrs. Garcia was right. People *would* talk, and *would* assume he was taking advantage of a patient. The look in Crick's eyes while Lucas stood over Tressalayne and examined the locket confirmed this fear. Even then, it wouldn't matter to Lucas what others thought, even if it damaged his practice. He knew how much he cared for Tressalayne, despite the strange and inexplicable events associated with her.

Tressalayne's feelings about him though…he just couldn't be sure.

Her passion was real and she made clear her own feelings about him. It *seemed* mutual. But her injuries, specifically her head trauma, could create unstable emotions which appeared genuine at the time, but in reality, were peripheral. Worse, it could induce an unhealthy dependency—a line which unfortunately, some in the medical profession crossed with disastrous consequences. In medical school, he and his fellow med-students studied numerous examples of the cost of such a blunder in their ethics class. Broken relationships, divorce, malpractice lawsuits, even suspension of medical licenses could result from these lapses in judgment.

Still, it would be worth the risk if only he *knew* Tressalayne's affection to be genuine and not somehow related to her post-traumatic recovery.

One thing he had *no* doubt about; he never cared so deeply about anyone before.

He couldn't make it through the day without thoughts of her. Since Tressalayne came into his life with the abruptness of a meteor strike, the highlight of each day was to rocket home, leap into the golf cart, and speed to the cabin to see her smiling face. When, finally, he forced himself to leave, her absence never failed to cause a deep, longing ache to well up within him.

While he pondered his dilemma, a flicker of light caught the corner of his eye. Acclimated to the dark, his eyes were quick to pick up more flashes of light from the den below. Sitting up, he strained to hear, and was rewarded with the muffled sounds of someone moving in stealthy fashion.

He threw off the covers, and on silent feet, padded to the closet. He grabbed a pair of shorts and pulled them on over his boxer briefs, followed by a t-shirt he dragged over his head. Rummaging around, he found his golf clubs and selected a driver. Held before him like a baseball bat, he moved into the hallway. At the staircase landing, he peeked over the rail.

A light bobbed around, held by someone at the fireplace mantel. Pencil-thin, the beam appeared to come from a small, palm-sized flashlight.

An intruder!

Adrenaline coursed through Lucas. The thief, back to Lucas, did not see him glide silently down the stairs. Halfway down the staircase, Lucas realized he left his cell phone in the bedroom. The intruder might be armed, a possibility he should have considered before he foolishly set off to confront him. In fact, he should have called 911 the second he suspected a home invasion.

Frozen with indecision, Lucas finally decided the safe course was to retrace his steps and call the police. Turning, he placed his foot to go back up the steps.

Creak.

Although small, within the dark silence of Lucas' house, the sound echoed like a gunshot.

The flashlight swung toward Lucas.

Before he could take another step, the radiant beam speared him with such brightness and intensity, it blinded him. Crying out, Lucas threw up his hands. His foot slipped on the stair step as he twisted in a futile attempt to avoid the brilliant glare. Arms flailing, the golf club flew out of his hands and he tumbled down the stairs. The painful descent ended when, with a *thump*, Lucas slid onto the hardwood floor.

Groaning in pain from the bruising fall, he shook his head to clear the cobwebs, but before he could make another move, the intruder grabbed him.

Strong arms pulled him up, and in the close embrace, he recognized a familiar soft warmness. Strands of thick hair tickled his nose.

"Lucas! Are you hurt?" the thief's voice asked.

Tressalayne?

The light swung back in his face to blind him anew.

Lucas sputtered, "Tressalayne, get that out of my face!"

The light winked out. Once the spots swimming in his eyes disappeared, he could make out Tressalayne's concerned face in the murky darkness. She supported him easily, no mean feat since Lucas stood six feet, three inches in height, and weighed in at over two hundred pounds.

A glow emanated from her left hand. Puzzled, he grasped the hand and held it up. Like a miniature spotlight, a shaft of bright luminescence erupted from her index finger to pierce the dark.

"Nice trick," he grumbled. Nothing about her surprised him anymore.

He pushed away, and limped over to the wall to flip on the light switch. Light flooded the room. Tressalayne stood at the foot of the stairs dressed only in one of Lucas' t-shirts she used for a nightgown. Almost as tall as Lucas, the t-shirt barely covered her shapely derriere.

"What the hell are you doing?" he demanded.

Tressalayne winced at Lucas' angry question. "I-I couldn't sleep." She pointed at the mantel. "I was looking at your pictures."

"Why didn't you just ask me instead of skulking around? This is East Texas, Tressalayne. *Everyone* owns a gun. You could have been shot!"

Rattled, nerves still on edge, Lucas ran a hand through his hair.

Tressalayne stood frozen, then shook her head. "I'm sorry. I haven't been...*right* since the awful dreams began. I think it's time for me to go."

Lucas' head whipped around. "What? No! You don't even know your last name. You have no place to go *to*!"

Tressalayne walked over to Lucas and put her arms around his waist. "That's true, but I'll have to try and figure something out."

Tears spilled from her eyes as she reached up and caressed Lucas' cheek. "All I know is the only time I feel safe, the only time I feel balanced, is when I'm with you. I wish I could stay here forever. But the nightmares, the dreams—*they mean something*. You say don't worry, but I feel it, Lucas. *I feel it!* I'm evil and I've hurt people, perhaps even murdered them."

Wearing a haunted look, she gazed at Lucas.

"One day I might even hurt you."

Her tears now fell in earnest. Cupping his face, she whispered, "You are such a sweet, kind, and generous man. Just the possibility I might someday be responsible for hurting or injuring you makes me sick to my stomach. Its why I have to leave."

Lucas couldn't believe his ears. But one look at Tressalayne told him she was serious...dead serious. Her eyes looked like they had aged years in just the past twenty-four hours.

He pulled her close. Tressalayne buried her face in his chest and wept. He held her until the sobs subsided, then gently disengaged his arms and took a step back so she could see his face. "Do you love me?"

Tressalayne pushed away. "That's not fair."

Lucas put his hands on her hips and drew her back. "Listen to me. I love you. I love you more than anything in this life, and nothing on earth would ever compel me to harm you in any way. So I know you would never hurt me. You wouldn't!"

"You don't understand!" Tressalayne shrieked. She twisted out of his reach and stood with her hands clenching and unclenching. The house rumbled and shook. A *crash* came from the kitchen as cups fell from the cupboard and shattered.

"Objects float in the air. Buildings shake. Other strange events you and Mrs. Garcia talked about. All caused by *me!*

I don't know how or why I made these things happen. All I know is I can't control them. Maybe you're right and I would never knowingly harm you, but what if I'm in the throes of a nightmare?

What if I *unknowingly* hurt you?"

Thirty-Three

Lucas never considered this possibility. Caught off guard, all he could do was stand helpless, while Tressalayne twisted herself into knots. He refused to believe she could ever injure him, but how could he convince her of that? Desperate for something, *anything*, to convince Tressalayne not to leave, he glanced at the family pictures on the mantel…and stopped. The solution was right there and had been the entire time.

He knew what to do.

He held out his hand. Sniffling, after a moment's hesitation, Tressalayne, took it, her hand folded into his own like a matched pair.

Lucas led her to the fireplace mantel and pointed at the pictures. "You wanted to see my family pictures, so let me show them to you."

He took the first picture off the shelf and handed it to Tressalayne. A man and woman held the hands of a young girl and an even younger boy. The woman and girl each wore a dress, the man and boy, a coat and tie. Broad, happy smiles appeared on each face. The boy was obviously a much younger version of Lucas, the family resemblance apparent in his features.

Looking over Tressalayne's shoulder, Lucas pointed to each person in turn.

"That's Daddy, Mama, and my sister Jennifer, although everyone called her Jen. Of course, the boy is me. We took this picture on Easter right before we went to church."

Lucas then went over each of the pictures in turn on the chimneypiece. Most were similar versions and combinations of Lucas' family, with the last one of Lucas as a young man dressed in a formal robe and cap with his mother. Lucas beamed at the camera, his arm around his mother who also wore a wide smile.

Lucas pointed at the picture. "My med school graduation picture with Mama. She was so proud of me."

Tressalayne noted the absence of Lucas' father and sister in the picture. In fact, none of the pictures showed his father and sister much past the age of the Easter photo.

Puzzled, she asked, "Where is your father and sister?"

Lucas' face darkened. "They're dead. Daddy and Jen were killed when I was 12 years old."

The pain in Lucas' voice was unmistakable. Tressalayne turned and put her arm around his waist. "I'm sorry, Lucas. I shouldn't have asked."

Lucas shook his head. "No, it's okay."

With a sigh, Lucas ran his finger over the Easter photo, touching in turn, the faces of his parents and Jen.

"Jen just turned fifteen. She was a great athlete, you know. She played basketball and volleyball, but she was really good at softball. Daddy would take her to a coach for private batting lessons. On the way back from one of these sessions, an eighteen-wheeler ran headlong into them, killing them instantly."

Lucas took the Easter picture from Tressalayne, and placed the frame back on the chimneypiece.

"I remember when Mama got the phone call. Her face turned

white as a sheet, and she was crying so hard I couldn't understand what she was trying to say. When I finally understood, I didn't believe her. It wasn't until the funeral that it hit home…Daddy and Jen were dead."

"Its so unfair," Lucas whispered in a small voice. "It was a bright day with perfect weather. You could see for miles, yet the semi still crossed the median and hit them. The authorities think the truck driver fell asleep, but we never knew for sure because he was killed as well. He drove for a large transportation company, and they paid a huge settlement to Mama. That's how we were able to buy this place and the pecan orchard."

Lucas' jaw clenched. "But money couldn't bring them back to life. Couldn't fill the hole in our hearts, and couldn't replace the joy and happiness ripped from us." Each word, like a corrosive acid, opened fresh wounds on memories he never wanted to relive.

Tressalayne placed a finger on his lips. "No more. You don't need to tell me anymore."

Lucas took her finger and kissed it. "Thank you, but I want you to know it all. I want you to know everything about me."

Reluctantly, Tressalayne nodded.

Continuing, Lucas said, "Something broke in me the day of the funeral. I was so angry. I just…just couldn't get past it. Every time I closed my eyes, I would see Jen playing catch with Daddy or tickling me when we wrestled. I began to get into fights at school, went from the "A" Honor Roll to flunking, and generally started to behave like an asshole. I barely made it out of junior high, and when I went to high school, I spent more time in the principal's office and detention than I did in the classroom. Eventually I got kicked out, and Mama took me to another high school…which I promptly got kicked out of as well."

Lucas chuckled bitterly. "I lost count of how many private and public schools Mama enrolled me in. When I got expelled from one, she would move me to another. I never cracked a book, and the only thing I did well was raising hell. I fought, drank, did drugs, and generally tried to forget how screwed up life was.

One night I snuck outside to drink a six-pack paid for with money I'd stolen from Mama's purse. It was the week before my eighteenth birthday and one of those moonless nights when the sky is pitch black. Back then I liked the dark. It hid my activities from Mama, and since I didn't like myself too much anyway, I counted it a bonus I was invisible. It was late, probably close to midnight, and I happened to look up. Much to my surprise, I spotted a light shining from a window in our house. I moved closer, and saw the light came from Mama's bedroom. She never stayed up past ten o'clock, so I thought she discovered I'd slipped out of the house.

I snuck back in and went straight to my room. Mama wasn't there, but I noticed her door cracked and light streaming from her room. Curious, I made my way to her door and peeked in. She was on her knees, praying. She must have been at it for hours, her voice so hoarse I could barely understand what she was praying about."

Voice cracking, his eyes filled with tears, Lucas turned to Tressalayne. "But I heard enough. The prayers were for *me*."

Lucas cleared his throat, his emotions making it difficult to talk. "I've seen plenty of pain in my life, Tressalayne, parents who suddenly lose a child, or patients in such physical agony not even the strongest painkillers or sedatives can give them relief. Yet the pain in my mother's voice was far worse than anything I have ever experienced. And all of it—every bit of it—caused by me."

Lucas grabbed the hem of his shirt and wiped his eyes. He took a deep breath and tried to compose himself. "I don't know what kind of monsters you see in your nightmares, but they don't always come with fangs and claws. Sometimes they look just like me, armed with words and actions which cut deeper and cause wounds every bit as deadly."

Tressalayne stared at Lucas, then shook her head. "No, that's not you. I don't believe it!"

"I'm afraid it's true—all of it."

"But you're not—"

"Like that now? No, I'm not. I'm not the same person."

Confused, Tressalayne chewed her lip. "I don't understand. What happened?"

Lucas moved closer to Tressalayne and put his arms around her.

"I fell on my knees next to Mama and started to pray with her. I asked for God's forgiveness. I asked for Mama's forgiveness. It was like scales or blinders were removed from my eyes, and I saw what a heartless shit I'd been. My mother lost her husband and daughter, and all I'd done is pile on even more grief and heartache. Despite all of it, she never gave up on me...and she *never* stopped loving me. It became the most defining moment of my entire life. The anger and rage left me in a rush, and I experienced a peace unlike anything I've ever known before."

Lucas stroked Tressalayne's hair.

"I got my GED and graduated from LeTourneau University in three years. I saw an MCAT announcement on the bulletin board at the university one day, and decided to take it. I scored high enough to be accepted to UT-Galveston Medical School. I've never looked back."

Hands on Lucas' chest, Tressalayne looked up at him. "Why did you tell me this?"

Lucas leaned down and kissed Tressalayne. He leaned his forehead against hers, their faces mere inches apart.

"Because you're not the same person either. Whether real or imagined, whatever you were before, whatever you think you might have done, it's all irrelevant. That person doesn't exist anymore. The Tressalayne I know is a beautiful and wonderful woman. The kind butterflies can't resist."

Lucas heard Tressalayne's breath catch in her throat. Her hand went to her chest. "My heart is turned inside out every time I'm around you, Lucas. I-I can't think straight, and I can barely breathe. You make me feel so different—"

The amulet at her neck flared, the gem erupting in a warm geyser of light.

Startled, Lucas looked down at the locket. "What—"

Tressalayne smothered his lips with her own before he could finish the statement. She caught his hand and pulled him up the stairs. Rounding the top, she led him to his bedroom.

"Uh, what—"

Hand on his mouth, Tressalayne breathed, "*Shh.*"

Peeling off Lucas' shirt, Tressalayne ran her hands over his hard stomach and lingered on the warm flesh of his ribbed muscles. Moving lower, she stripped off his shorts to leave him standing in his briefs.

Lucas swallowed hard. "Look, we can't do this."

"You're talking again. But I know how to make you stop."

Tressalayne took a step back, and slowly raised her own shirt, inch by inch, until it was over her head. She held it in front of her like a matador's cape, and moved it back and forth. Mesmerized, Lucas followed the shirt's progress with the intensity of a starved man watching a steak cook. Finally, she dropped it to the floor. Lucas gulped, unable to take his eyes off her.

Her long, thick hair cascaded past her shoulders. Full breasts jutted toward him, nipples hardened into flint-like peaks. A flat abdomen flared into rounded hips, her waist small enough he could put both his hands around it. Long legs of flawless perfection stretched upward to join her hips.

Tressalayne moved forward with panther-like grace, her hips brushing against Lucas. With a thumb hooked in her panties, she nuzzled Lucas' ear and whispered, "You'll have to take these off."

All of Lucas' ethical concerns about his relationship with Tressalayne flew out of his head in an instant. Without conscious thought, his hands moved of their own volition. Only with great restraint did he manage to slide the panties down when his impulse was to tear them off. To tease him even more, Tressalayne refused to lift either foot which forced Lucas to kneel and pick up each leg in turn in order to slip them off. This put Lucas' head at eye level with her flat stomach and groin. Unable to resist, he cupped her buttocks in both hands. Pulling her toward him, he kissed her navel, burying his lips in the taunt, creamy flesh.

With a groan, Tressalayne placed her hands on Lucas' head. Her fingers ran through his hair, and she urged him on. Coming up for air, Lucas stood and kissed her lips. Marveling at how pliant and moist they were, he moved steadily downward to kiss and knead her breasts.

Her chest heaved in response to his touch, her breath a temperate breeze which caressed his skin with each gasp. Her body trembled and shook within his arms, and his continued assault with hands and lips causing her breathing to mount into a rapid-fire succession of explosive moans.

Tressalayne finally pushed him away. She stood on unsteady legs, mouth parted, her face flushed. After a moment's hesitation, she slipped into Lucas' bed. With one fluid motion, she threw the sheet back and lay down. Smiling, she crooked her finger and beckoned him.

Lucas reacted like a racehorse out of the gate. He tore off his briefs and launched himself beside her. Lying between her legs, her warm flesh further stoked his passion to unbearable heights. Although desire clouded his thinking to the point he could barely restrain himself, he still managed to ask, "Are you sure?"

In response, Tressalayne moved beneath him, positioning her hips. She grabbed Lucas' muscular butt with her hands and pulled, driving him into her. A sharp cry escaped from her lips.

Startled, Lucas saw Tressalayne's face creased in pain.

Astonished, he said, "You mean you're—"

Before he could finish the sentence, Tressalayne pulled again to thrust him even deeper inside her. With preternatural strength, she held him in place and began to rock her hips. Panting, mouth half-open, her eyes never left Lucas' face. When finally, he cried out and spent, collapsed on top of her, she groaned, her arms encircling his broad shoulders to hold him close. Her heart hammered against his skin while his weight covered her like a warm blanket.

After a few moments, exhausted, Lucas rolled off of Tressalayne and they lay side by side.

Recovered, Lucas picked up the sheet and looked underneath it. Spots of blood sprinkled on the mattress cover, and he shook his head.

Mentally, he kicked himself. "I'm sorry. You should have told me."

A finger traced the contour of his jaw. Tressalayne murmured, "I didn't know. Like everything else about my past, I don't remember anything. But it makes no difference anyway. I wanted you...I still want you. There's nothing to be sorry about—unless you have regrets."

Red-faced, Lucas stuttered, "N-No. Of course not."

Tressalayne laughed at his discomfort. Rolling over farther, she kissed him on the nose.

The smile vanished and she searched his face. "I love you, Lucas. My heart burns for you with such intensity, it consumes my every thought. I don't know what I am going to do with myself."

It was Lucas' turn to laugh.

"Why, its simple. You spend the rest of your life with me."

Tressalayne sat up and leaned against the headboard, the movement causing her breasts to hitch and sway. Lucas, hypnotized, followed their movement. Tressalayne rolled her eyes, then grabbed a pillow and covered herself. Lucas groaned in disappointment, and sat up next to her.

"Lucas, *please* listen to me. If our roles were reversed and you loved me as I love you, would you take a chance—any chance—of hurting me?"

"Of course not—"

Lucas stopped. Too late, the verbal trap set by Tressalayne snapped shut.

"Can't you see the dilemma I find myself in? Yes, I may now be a different person, but I still can't control my strange impulses. As long as I'm unable to control them, you're in danger. One nightmare, one bad dream, and I could bring the entire house down on your head."

Lucas gave a stubborn shake of his head. "I don't care. I'll take my chances."

Pulling her knees up, Tressalayne hugged the pillow.

"I *do* care, and I don't know what to do. I can't bear anything happening to you…and I can't bear being separated from you, either."

Frustrated, Lucas rolled out of the bed. He was fresh out of options as well. He snatched his briefs, pulled them on, then ran his hands through his hair and paced trying to think of a solution.

Nothing came to him.

Angry, he slammed his fist into the palm of his hand and collapsed back onto the bed. Out of the corner of his eye, he spotted the business card Mrs. Garcia gave him on the bedside table. An idea inched its way into his brain. Snapping his fingers, he snatched it up and scrutinized it.

He waved the card. "What if there was a way you could learn to control these powers of yours?"

Eager eyes turned to Tressalayne.

"What if someone could show you *how* to use them?"

THIRTY-FOUR

LOCKSTONE GROWLED IN FRUSTRATION.

The glow of the laptop's screen cast a weak illumination on his bearded face. He rubbed his eyes, the dull throb of a headache beating a staccato in his head. With a *click*, he exited from yet another internet news site, then sat back and debated whether or not to call it a night or to continue his internet surfing.

Since learning of the wonder and magic of the information web, he used every free moment to employ it in search of Morganna's whereabouts. It was the most daunting task of his career as a Witch Hunter…and so far a fruitless one.

First, he waited while Eddie removed from the laptop all the previous owner's data. This consisted mostly of pictures and videos of naked and scantily clad women, some of whom were contorted in truly unusual positions. Then, Eddie ran the laptop through an anti-viral program, saying it needed to be de-bugged. Although, he watched closely, Lockstone never saw a single insect flee from the device while Eddie ran the program. However, whatever Eddie did, the speed by which the laptop searched various websites increased dramatically.

Finally, the biggest problem of all presented itself; the mind-numbing volume of information contained within the internet. If every library in the Kingdom combined all its scrolls and books, then multiplied them a thousand times over, it wouldn't represent a drop in the internet sea. For Lockstone, the challenge was to narrow the search parameters so the sheer volume of information didn't make it impossible to study all the results. Once again, Eddie came to the rescue. He showed Lockstone how to use key words in his search and limit the amount of information to sift through. He also suggested Lockstone concentrate on news websites in his search. All good advice except the witch hunter had only a date and a location to use as his key words—with the location, *North*, hardly an exact position.

Regardless, armed with his search words, Lockstone began his unorthodox Hunt.

With the Witch Compass for his directional guide, he started to sift through news websites of cities and communities north of Houston. Although Lockstone's grasp of the technology used to search for Morganna—tenuous at best—he knew enough to realize he needed to look for something reported as unusual or out of the ordinary. Wherever Morganna ended up, Lockstone remained confident her presence guaranteed trouble and commotion. He just hoped it was newsworthy enough to be reported.

Now, two weeks later, he was no closer to finding the murderous coven leader than before.

Cats rescued from trees.

Lost children found.

Couple finds a snake in their privy.

A reported sighting of something called "Bigfoot" in the Davey Crockett National Forest.

Lockstone read and scrutinized hundreds of similar incidents, with none remotely connected to Morganna.

Thick fingers drummed the small desktop, and he decided to give it five more minutes before bed. Scrolling down, his interest became piqued when he came across a news item with the caption, "*Unusual accident lands woman in a local hospital*". With a click of the curser, he discovered it was a news report from a local TV station, complete with the archived video.

"TV"—one of a raft of new and wondrous experiences— was something Lockstone became quickly familiar with. Eddie kept one on in his office, and many of his customers brought them in to be pawned. By necessity, Eddie made sure Lockstone could turn on the TV's, access channels, and generally make sure they were in good working order before he accepted the pawn.

Selecting the video link, the witch hunter watched as two people, a man and woman, sat next to each other behind a long, flat counter. The woman was blonde with impeccably-coiffed hair and make-up, while her partner had wavy brown hair and wore a blue coat and tie. Both shuffled papers, pleasant expressions plastered on their faces.

The female newscaster chuckled. "Well, David, I've heard of UFOs, but you have something which takes this to a whole new level."

With a broad smile, David turned, saying, "Yes, that's right, Allison. Authorities are reporting a woman has been admitted to Nacogdoches Memorial Hospital in critical condition. According to reports, the woman crashed through the windshield of a car driven by local resident, Karen Prescott. Although authorities are still investigating, Prescott claims the accident victim 'fell from the sky' and into her car. The name of the injured woman has not been released pending completion of the inquiry."

Breathing rapidly, Lockstone studied the monitor and noted the TV station, KETV, was located in Nacogdoches. He unfolded and spread a map of Texas on the bed. The witch hunter studied the map's scale and discovered Nacogdoches to be a city approximately one hundred and forty miles north of Houston. He then glanced at the time stamp on the video.

The date was the same night the doorway deposited him into the Houston park.

Lockstone stood and howled in triumph.

He found Morganna.

THIRTY-FIVE

"**W**HAT DO YOU MEAN YOU'RE LEAVING? DO YOU EVEN KNOW how to get to Nacogdoches?" Eddie asked.

They stood by the caged counter in the pawnshop while Eddie counted money from the cash register in preparation for the day's business.

Lockstone gave a curt nod. "I mean to get there as soon as possible."

After watching the video clip several more times, Lockstone searched every news site related to Nacogdoches in the days following the KETV broadcast. He received rock-solid confirmation in a brief byline in *The Nacogdoches Daily Sentinel*, entitled, "Mystery Woman Disappears from Nacogdoches Memorial Hospital".

Authorities report an accident victim admitted to Nacogdoches Memorial Hospital has disappeared from her hospital room. The Jane Doe, involved in a traffic accident seven days prior, has yet to be identified by authorities. Police reports indicate the woman is not fully recovered from injuries sustained when she crashed through the windshield of a car driven by local resident, Karen Prescott, and may need urgent medical attention. Described as a white female in her late thirties to early forties with dark hair and eyes, authorities ask the public to report any information regarding the patient's disappearance or location to the Nacogdoches Police Department. The description erased all doubts for Lockstone.

The "Jane Doe" was Morganna.

Almost a month passed since the witch's disappearance, and the trail grew colder by the minute. The longer Lockstone stayed in Houston, the greater the chances the coven leader had already fled to a place far from Nacogdoches. Two factors, however, worked in his favor.

First, Morganna's protégé, Tressalayne, entered the magic doorway with her. If she came into this world with Morganna, then she couldn't be far off. Morganna would come to the same conclusion and would be loath to flee far from Nacogdoches... not until she located Tressalayne. Second, like Lockstone, the witch faced the same difficult adjustment to this new world. It took time to adapt, and Morganna—too cunning to simply run without a plan—would bide her time, especially if she still needed to recover from her injuries. How she cheated death with a poisoned bolt in her still puzzled Lockstone, but at least it would force her to lay low for a time...and the delay would be her undoing.

As far as the witch hunter was concerned, her death at his hands was assured. He just needed to get to Nacogdoches.

"How do you plan on getting there? You don't know the first thing about driving a car," Eddie persisted.

Lockstone grinned, his teeth gleaming in the early morning light. He pointed with his chin. Eddie followed his lead to a black and silver Harley Davidson parked in front of the store.

"The Hog? You've only been driving it for two weeks, and then just a couple of miles to and from the gun range. You don't even have a license!"

Lockstone shrugged. "I'm competent enough."

It took only one solo trip on the pawned Harley to addict him. He loved the feel of the wind across his face, the rumble of the road and throaty roar of the engine music to his ears. Although the pawnbroker was correct—he'd only been driving a short time—Eddie didn't realize Lockstone never drove straight back to the pawnshop from the gun range. He always took a roundabout route, miles out of his way. Along with prolonging the special kind of freedom he enjoyed when on the bike, he also gained experience and familiarity.

Eddie slammed the cash drawer shut.

"Look, I know you got something going on, some kind of wild hair up your ass you're not telling me. I'm not going to try and talk you out of it. But, there's some things you need to consider before you go off on this big safari of yours."

Ticking off his fingers, Eddie said, "One, you have no license, no ID, nothing! You're what we call an 'illegal alien', and the first time a cop stops you, you'll most likely end up in an INS holding cell. Two, you have no cash. Try pulling those gold coins out of your pocket to pay for something and see what happens. *Nobody* pays for stuff with gold! Its either cash or plastic, which you have neither. Three, my grandmother knows more about technology than you do, and she counts it a good day if she can turn on the TV using the remote. *Everybody* and *everything* uses technology. You didn't even know what a laptop is!"

Agitated, Eddie crossed his arms.

"I know I'm going to regret this, but I'm going to help you out, Big Man, so you don't get yourself killed or arrested."

Lockstone opened his mouth to protest, and Eddie held his palm up. "Don't! You may *think* you know what you're talking about, but I *know* what you need to do before you go out into that great big yonder! I see nothing but disaster, but at least my way you stand a chance to stay out of trouble!"

Lockstone smiled. If Eddie only knew. *Trouble* was precisely what he hunted.

"First thing, the bike ain't street legal. It needs a license plate and some repairs before you can travel any distance without a break down. Then, you need some sort of identification. Even if you are never stopped by a cop, half the places on the planet require a photo ID of some kind. You also need a cell phone for a shitload of reasons I'm not going to bother trying to explain. Finally, you're going to need money, *real* money, not that gold coin shit you're carrying around."

Lockstone's brow creased in concentration. He tried and failed to find holes in Eddie's logic.

Resigned, he raised his hands in surrender. "Okay. What do you suggest?"

Relief washed over Eddie's face. "Now we're talking! What I need, Robert, are two things; time and money. Lucky for you, the pawn business has landed me lots of friends in low places. I know a mechanic who'll fix the bike and 'find' a license. I also got a lead on someone who specializes in fake IDs. Since you can't just walk into a bank to swap your coins for money, I have a buddy who runs a gold and silver exchange and pays cash up front for gold and silver jewelry."

Eddie eyed Lockstone. "And Robert? I don't run a charity here. You're going to pay for it—all of it!"

Lockstone mulled over what Eddie said. The money meant nothing. Since the moment he cradled Emmitt's lifeless head in his lap, gold ceased to have importance to him. It was a means to an end, nothing more. Time, however, was much more precious. Every day spent in Houston meant one day longer he delayed the Hunt for Morganna, one more day she continued to breathe.

"How long?" he growled.

"Two days minimum to get this all together."

Lockstone grit his teeth. "Agreed. But not one moment longer."

Lockstone looked North, Morganna drawing him like an irresistible magnet.

"In two days, ready or not, I'm leaving for Nacogdoches."

THIRTY-SIX

"**O**KAY, WE'LL SEE YOU IN AN ABOUT AN HOUR, AND THANK you, sir, for seeing us on such short notice."

Relieved, Lucas disconnected and pocketed his cell.

Determined to put Tressalayne's fears at ease she could unknowingly hurt him, Lucas emailed Hank Harper—the man suggested to him by Mrs. Garcia—to request a meeting. He replied to Lucas' email later that evening, and they agreed to set up a time on Saturday morning. Lucas called early Saturday to confirm, and told Hank they could be there within the hour.

"Tressalayne!" he called, "Mr. Harper agreed to meet with us at his store, so we need to leave. Are you ready to go?"

Seated in a small reading nook on the second floor between his bedroom and the guest bedrooms, Lucas tapped Harper's business card impatiently on a round, antique table. A Tiffany lamp rested on it, and shimmered and shook in response to Lucas' constant movement.

Tressalayne swept out of Lucas' bedroom—now *their* bedroom—and did a pirouette.

"What do you think?"

Lucas did a double-take. Tressalayne wore a tight denim skirt, her long, supple legs on full display. A white camisole covered her torso like a second skin, her breasts straining against the fabric. An embellished blouse covered the camisole. Tied at her small waist it was unbuttoned to reveal a hint of cleavage.

"Mrs. Garcia thought you might like this."

Ogling, Lucas stifled the impulse to burst out laughing at such a ridiculous understatement. She made even a simple outfit stunning.

In the interim three days before Saturday, Mrs. Garcia showed up at Lucas' door every day, even though he no longer paid for her services. Taking Tressalayne in like a long-lost daughter, the pair embarked on a conquest of Longview to shop, eat at restaurants, receive pedicures and manicures, and finally, topped it off with a trip to a hair salon—all on Lucas' credit card which Mrs. Garcia wielded with reckless abandon.

When handing his well-used card back, Mrs. Garcia winked at him. "I've done my part. Now the rest is up to you."

His bachelor closet, once semi-barren with only scattered clothing, now struggled to hold the fruit of Tressalayne's and Mrs. Garcia's labors. Finding his own clothes became a challenge, but more than worth it to Lucas. Tressalayne now slept beside him every night, shopped with Mrs. Garcia each day, and not once did she mention leaving. Besides, the arrangement came with the benefit of her modeling every new article of clothing—often changing in front of him without hesitation.

Tressalayne took Lucas' hesitation as a sign of disapproval. "You don't like it? Should I change into something different?"

"Huh? What?" Lucas stammered. Sorely tempted to say *yes* for another runway show, he realized they needed to get on the road.

"No, you look great. *Really* great!" he gushed.

Tressalayne sat in his lap and put her arm around his shoulders. Her free hand traced circles on his broad chest.

"Thank you. I know you're doing all of this for me. I wish there were some way I could repay you."

Chuckling, Lucas shook his head. "Wow. So many possibilities come to mind from such a loaded statement. But, I'll have to muzzle myself and say having you in my life is payment enough. I know it sounds like a cliché, but if you're happy, I'm happy."

Threading his fingers through hers, he raised her hand to his lips and kissed it. Her fingers, long, elegant, with glossy nails painted a pastel pink, was smooth and cool in his hand. Beautiful like the rest of her, the only mar to their perfection was the nail on her right forefinger. It looked unnaturally thick, especially when compared to her other fingernails. The manicure succeeded in trimming it to proper size, but couldn't hide its outsized appearance.

Tressalayne nuzzled his neck, her warm breath a feathery caress on his skin. He began to respond and knew once started, they wouldn't be able to stop. Lucas pushed her up off his lap.

"Lets go."

The drive, uneventful except for Tressalayne's keen interest in the passing countryside, was her first trip outside the city besides to Lucas' home. In fact, it was their first trip together, *period*. Lucas regarded it as somewhat of a milestone in their relationship, an *ordinary* activity *normal* couples often engaged in. Unfortunately, ordinary and normal hardly fit Tressalayne. He just hoped Hank Harper could help her. The thought of her absent from his life hovered like a dark shadow he couldn't shake.

Lucas pulled into Mt. Pleasant and followed the business exit to the downtown area. Tressalayne grew more agitated the closer they drew to their destination. She sat straighter, body taunt, her nervousness on open display across her face. Lucas understood how she felt. They had a lot riding on whether or not Hank Harper could be of any help.

Lucas placed his hand on hers and squeezed. "Relax. We're just going to talk to Mr. Harper and see what he has to say."

Tressalayne, her face pale, nodded.

The downtown square, dominated by a large courthouse, was surrounded by boutique shops, niche restaurants, antique stores, and other specialty shops—these businesses having long ago replaced the stores of yesteryear. Brick sidewalks ran alongside concrete planters filled with colorful flowers, the revitalized buildings having acquired an air of freshness belying their century-old architecture.

Hank Harper's store anchored a corner of the downtown square. Rising two stories into the bright Texas sky, a large sign, *Uncommon Antiques & Oddities*, hung affixed to the red brick façade of the structure, and greeted them as they parked in front of the store. Long display windows revealed an assortment of objects. As they got out of the Jeep, Lucas, curious, studied them.

A full-sized mannequin dominated one window. Dressed in the white and black-striped clothing a prisoner would have worn in a bygone era, a rusty manacle with ball and chain clamped to one leg of the figure. On a pedestal not far away, a glass case displayed a shrunken head, its sightless eyes sewn shut. Further down at the next exhibit, a stuffed Grizzly bear reared to a height of more than seven feet. Its mouth, open in a silent roar, revealed gleaming, flesh-tearing canines. At the feet of the grizzly lay a vicious bear trap. Fully three feet in diameter, the trap's steel teeth looked like they could snap a man's leg in half.

Lucas shivered, while Tressalayne looked on with frank curiosity. *Oddities indeed.*

Lucas pushed the door open, the chirp of an electronic chime announcing their presence. A huge piece of limestone greeted them. Perched on a sturdy metal tripod, the bony impression of a birdlike creature was frozen in the rock. A sign fixed above the fossilized remains read, *Ichthyornises – Late Cretaceous*.

The store stretched deeper than wide. Near the back loomed a long wooden counter reminiscent of a saloon bar from the Old West. A staircase behind the bar climbed to the second story and disappeared behind a wall lined with antique Cuckoo clocks. A serenade of *ticks* and *tocks* filled the air.

A few scattered customers browsed about. However, none came across as the owner, and Lucas had no idea what Hank Harper looked like. Shrugging, he motioned to Tressalayne and they walked back to the wooden bar. An old-fashioned metal cash register rested on its surface, a modern credit card machine next to it. In addition, a bell lay on the counter, and after a moment's hesitation, Lucas tapped it a few times with the palm of his hand.

"Ho, there! Be with you in a minute."

The voice appeared out of nowhere, startling Lucas. He leaned over the counter and saw a child struggle to push a heavy box onto a recessed shelf.

Grunting, the adolescent succeeded with a, "Whew!" The boy climbed a set of concealed steps behind the bar to reach the top of the counter.

Lucas' eyes widened.

The "boy" was no child at all.

Thirty-Seven

Hank Harper was a dwarf!

Perhaps four feet tall, the dwarf wore his long, black hair fastened into a ponytail. One ear sported a trio of small red, white, and blue feathered earrings. Laugh lines etched the corners of his mouth to anchor a face of indeterminate middle-age. Twinkling blue eyes apprised Lucas, a ready smile appearing as the dwarf held out his hand.

"You must be Doctor Beckett. I'm Hank Harper."

Lucas gulped and shook Hank's hand. "Pl-Pleased to meet you."

Hank turned and grasped Tressalayne's hand. With a flourish, he brought her hand to his lips. "And you must be Tressalayne. I must say, Doctor Beckett's description doesn't do you justice. You are far more beautiful than I imagined."

Blushing, Tressalayne looked at Lucas.

"And tall! Understand, *everyone* is tall in my eyes, but you seem to stretch to the ceiling." With a wink at Lucas, he added, "Good thing you're tall as well. You two make a fine pair."

Grinning, Lucas took an immediate liking to Hank. He glanced at Tressalayne and could see by her wide smile she was smitten as well. She looked visibly relaxed, her rigid nervousness gone.

Hank pointed to a door behind the bar. "Come into my office, and we'll discuss your problem."

Hank jumped off the steps and waved them in. He waited while Lucas and Tressalayne filed in to take a seat, then closed the door. He settled into a chair behind a desk piled high with papers, documents, and other paraphernalia.

"So, Doctor Beckett, you were a little vague when you called me earlier, but I understand you have a concern regarding Tressalayne?"

"Er...yes."

"Can you be more specific?"

Hank's eyes bored into Lucas, and he fumbled for words. No matter how he presented the problem, the explanation would sound bizarre. Hank would think he was nuts. Suddenly, this didn't seem like such a good idea.

Finally, Lucas said, "Tressalayne...*causes* things to happen."

Hank stroked his chin. "I see. Such as?"

Red-faced, Lucas stammered, "Li-Like solid objects floating, and, and—"

"—The house shakes, water in the small sea beside the cottage froths and boils, *and I can't control any of it!*" Tressalayne blurted.

Continuing to stroke his chin, Hank didn't speak, his gaze bouncing back and forth between Lucas and Tressalayne.

This is where he shows us to the door and recommends a good therapist, Lucas thought bitterly.

Tears appeared in Tressalayne's eyes. "I'm afraid I'll hurt Lucas. Not because I want to, but I have these, these...awful dreams, and when I'm in the throes of the dreams, things happen." Sniffling, she fell silent.

Long, pregnant moments passed. With a sigh, Lucas stood,

his hand held out for Tressalayne, and prepared to leave.

"I'm sorry we wasted your time, Hank. We'll just be—"

"How do you feel about Doctor Beckett?" Hank asked Tressalayne, interrupting him.

Her eyes on Lucas, Tressalayne's face softened. "I love him… very much."

"And you, Doctor Beckett? How do you feel about Tressalayne?"

Lucas sank back onto the chair. In their tender moments together, whether making love, through gentle caresses, whispered conversations, or in a dozen different ways, Tressalayne displayed over and over again, her complete and unreserved love for him. To hear her profess this love to someone they just met, however, touched him an unexpectant way, and at a deeper level than he ever thought possible. A lump rose in his throat. Tearing his eyes from her, he turned to Hank.

"I love her as well. Funny, until this moment I didn't realize how much. I'd do anything for her."

"Then maybe I can help you."

Lucas' mouth dropped. "You mean you believe us? You don't think we're crazy?

Chuckling, Hank waved his arm. "You'd be surprised at what I've heard, what I've personally seen and observed. 'Crazy' doesn't even begin to describe it. The truth is there are many things which occur that have no rational explanation—with the power of the human mind being first and foremost, Exhibit A. Or, as Shakespeare so aptly put it, the 'undiscovered country.'"

Hands clasped in front of him, Hank said, "What I see are two people very much in love, and committed to overcome every obstacle and make it work."

Leaning back in his chair, arms behind his head, a broad smile spread across the dwarf's face. "Now how can I turn *that* down?"

Relief filled Lucas. He leaped up, pumping Hank's hand. "Thank you, Hank, thank you!"

Laughing, Hank managed to disengage his hand. "Now, I'm not promising anything, but I think I know where we can start." He slid off his chair, arm held out for Tressalayne. "Shall we?"

Giggling, Tressalayne threaded her arm through Hank's. Together they made their way past the door, Lucas close behind. Back out into the store, Hank led them to a floor-to-ceiling bookcase which filled an entire corner of the shop. Glass-faced cabinet doors protected volumes, documents, and manuscripts crammed in every nook and cranny. A metal rail curved around the entire length of the bookcase. A wheeled wooden library ladder rested on the rail.

Hank released Tressalayne's arm, and walked back and forth in front of the bookcase muttering to himself.

"Now where did I put it? Hmm…there it is!"

Selecting a key from his pocket, Hank unlocked the cabinet door and slid it aside. He pushed the ladder into position and climbed up until he came to a large volume. With a white binding, it stood out from all the other volumes. With a grunt, Hank lifted the heavy book and cradled it under his arm. Climbing back down, he motioned for Lucas and Tressalayne to follow him. He led them back to the bar, then mounted the steps behind it. With a *whoomp,* he dropped the book, dust flying in all directions.

Turned so the tome faced Lucas and Tressalayne, Hank watched as they studied it. Covered in what appeared to be white calf skin, an intricate pattern of embossed pictures was worked into the leather. The pictures—colorful images of fairies mounted on dragonflies, elfish creatures lounging beneath umbrella-like mushrooms, and dragons soaring on bat-like wings across a backdrop of blue sky—filled the book's cover. Large, flowery script flowed across the top of the volume. Eyebrows furrowed, Lucas quickly determined the words and letters were in a language he had never seen before. Although the leather binding looked fresh and supple, the pictures and images retaining their sharp features, the book exuded an air of antiquity far belying its appearance.

Two studded leather straps disappeared into a pair of brass locks. Discolored with age, they fastened the book firmly shut. *Most* interesting, however, the locks possessed no keyhole—or any opening at all—Lucas could see.

There appeared to be no way to open the book.

Intrigued, Lucas asked, "What is this?"

"An eighth century Celtic book. The language on the book's cover is an ancient form of Gaelic," Hank replied.

Puzzled, Lucas didn't know where Hank was going with this. "So, what's inside?"

"I'm not sure," Hank admitted. "As you can see, the locks are keyless. I haven't discovered a way to release the straps other than to cut them off. I would never damage such a priceless object by forcing it open."

Hank turned to Tressalayne. "In fact, I'm hoping you can help me with my dilemma."

Mystified, Tressalayne looked up. "Me? How can I help?"

"Why, by opening the book of course."

THIRTY-EIGHT

TRESSALAYNE'S GAZE JUMPED BETWEEN LUCAS AND HANK. "I'm sorry, Hank, I don't understand. How do you want me to open it?"

A grin split Hank's face. "I don't know," he answered.

Tressalayne spread her hands. "But…but, if *you* don't know, how do you expect *me* to know?"

Lucas studied Hank. Was the dwarf playing some joke or trick on them? However, he could see no deceit on his face, only earnest concentration. Then it struck him. *Maybe this is a test of some sort, something only Tressalayne can do.*

He leaned over and whispered in her ear, "Just try something, anything."

Tressalayne wiped her hands on her skirt and nodded. She took a deep breath, then approached the book. With absolutely no idea what to do next, her eyes were drawn to the pictures worked into the leather. Then…a curious thing happened. The images appeared to move, the dragonflies' wings *buzzed*, and the dragon's head turned toward her. Voices murmured in the background in celebration.

Tressalayne leaned closer, the voices becoming clearer. A chant repeated over and over again.

"*Blood to blood, bone to bone, a Witch of the White must touch the tome.*"

Tressalayne jerked back and swiveled toward Lucas. "Did you hear that?"

He shook his head. "Hear what?"

Hank watched the proceedings, a wide smile of anticipation on his face.

"Tressalayne, what's going on?" Lucas demanded.

Ignoring him, Tressalayne whipped her head around. With determined purpose, she firmly grasped both sides of the book.

The amulet at her neck flared. A bright incandescence exploded, filling the air. With a yelp, Lucas raised his hands to ward off the piercing light. When it dimmed, his jaw dropped.

The straps within the brass locks wriggled like snakes. Then they receded and disappeared into the leather binding.

The book snapped open.

Sounds of joyous laughter and exultation rang clearly in his ears. A jubilant roar, as if from some beast, reverberated in the air. Lucas moved closer.

His legs buckled at what he witnessed.

With a whir of wings, the dragonflies flitted about. The fairies atop them, their own translucent wings a blur of motion, waved, gleeful smiles on their faces. The golden-scaled dragon trumpeted another bellow while it soared in lazy circles. Jumping, waving, and shouting in a musical timbre, the elves celebrated. Dressed in bright tunics and breeches of blue, green, and yellow, some climbed to the tops of the mushrooms to be better seen. Others engaged in backflips, handstands, and other acrobatic moves.

Tearing his eyes from the amazing spectacle, Lucas glanced at Tressalayne. A look of pure delight shone on her face, and she spoke to the elves and the flying creatures. His shock deepened at her speech.

She used the same mysterious language!

The celebratory sounds rose to a crescendo. Some of the customers in the store looked up, curious. Tressalayne clapped in excitement, grabbed Lucas' arm, and pulled him next to her. Rapid speech in the strange tongue issued from her, and Lucas realized she was introducing him. As one, all the creatures stilled, their eyes fixed on Lucas.

Frozen, he stared at them until Tressalayne gave him a shove.

"He-hello," he croaked. The creatures nodded and waved, their excited speech no more intelligible to him than before.

Tressalayne spoke again. With one arm around Lucas' waist, she planted a soft kiss on his cheek.

Lucas whispered, "What did you say? What are *they* saying?"

"I told the *Daoine Beag* my name, but they already knew it. They expected me, and thanked me for opening the *Leabhar an Chéad Draíocht*. The *Daoine Beag* said they would guide me in its use."

She tightened her arm around him. "They also wanted to know if you were my *Fhéith mo chroí*."

"What's a cu, er, cush, or whatever it is you said?" Lucas asked. "You're using words I don't understand and speaking in some sort of weird language!"

Hank intervened and pointed at the curious stares from his customers. "Let's take this to my office. We need a little more privacy."

"Okay." Tressalayne picked up the book and made her way around the counter to Hank's office. After a moment's hesitation, Lucas followed.

While they seated themselves, the book in Tressalayne's lap, Hank climbed into his own chair and turned to face Lucas. "In ancient Gaelic, *Fhéith mo chroí* means 'vein or pulse of my heart.'"

Lucas' confusion deepened. *What?*

Hank continued, "Taken in its literal sense, *Fhéith mo chroí* roughly translates to 'my darling', or 'my love.'"

Tressalayne blushed, "The *Daoine Beag* know we are lovers. I think they only asked to be polite."

Lucas ran his fingers through his hair. "You know what? Why don't you two clue me in, because I'm tired of having a conversation with myself. *What's going on here?* What are you *both* talking about? Who are these da-dao, or whatever you call them?"

Lucas believed himself prepared for anything. After all, when he'd seen cups and saucers float by, had his entire house shake and move, and experienced all the strange phenomena associated with Tressalayne, what could top that? Yet the surface of the mysterious book turning into a 3-D version of Grimm's Fairy Tales rattled him. The unnerving experience only deepened when Tressalayne began to converse with the creatures in a strange language—*like she'd been speaking it since birth*!

"If I may," Hank said with a nod at Tressalayne. "The *Daoine Beag* or 'Little People', inhabit the *Leabhar an Chéad Draíocht* They are to be Tressalayne's guides, her tutors."

Lucas threw up his hands. "Inhabit what? Tutors for what? You're not making any sense, Hank!"

Hank looked from Tressalayne back to Lucas. "I thought you knew. Isn't this why you sought me out? *Leabhar an Chéad Draíocht* means 'The Book of First Magic.'"

Hank leaned forward, eyes fixed on Lucas.

"Doctor Beckett, Tressalayne is a witch."

THIRTY-NINE

STUNNED SILENCE FOLLOWED.

Lucas couldn't believe his ears. Tressalayne a witch? How the hell could Hank know that? What made him so sure? A dull headache began to pound behind his eyes, and he rubbed his temples. The more he thought about it, however, the more everything made sense. *What other logical explanation could there be?* If, in fact, anything associated with Tressalayne could be considered "logical".

Tressalayne looked at Lucas, a worried frown on her face. "Are you okay? Is being a witch a bad thing?"

Hank glanced sharply at Lucas. "You mean Tressalayne doesn't know she is a witch?"

Lucas shook his head. "She suffered severe head trauma which left her an amnesiac. She has no memory of her previous life."

"I see." Steepling his hands, Hank said, "I'm afraid I'm going to need a fuller explanation, Doctor Beckett."

Sighing, Lucas launched into how he found Tressalayne at his doorstep critically injured, her placement in ICU, and how she came to finish her recovery at his home. While she convalesced, he recounted the strange events he witnessed culminating with the nightmares she was now plagued with.

Long moments of silence followed while Lucas watched Hank digest this new information. Finally, Hank asked, "And your relationship with Tressalayne? That must have developed during her recuperation. Seems to strain the boundaries of your professional ethics don't you think, Doctor?"

Lucas' face flushed red. "Ye-yes, I suppose—"

"Lucas told me the same thing!" Tressalayne blurted. "It's my fault, not his."

Tressalayne reached over and ran her thumb across Lucas' hand. "I don't regret a thing. If I had to do it all over again, suffer the same injuries, I wouldn't hesitate because it brought Lucas to me."

Hugging the heavy volume to her chest, a smile tugged at her lips. "The *Daoine Beag* knew my heart the moment I touched the *Leabhar an Chéad Draíocht*. As far as I'm concerned, my life began the moment I opened my eyes and saw Lucas."

Lucas' heart seemed to expand to twice its normal size. If they weren't seated in the same room with Hank, he would have leaped up and wrapped her in his arms.

The ready grin returned to Hank's face. "I understand. I hope *you* understand I just covered all the bases."

The pressure left the room in an instant, and Lucas' brain gradually re-engaged. While he sorted through the incredible sequence of events, a few questions came immediately to his mind.

"Can I ask you something, Hank?"

"Fire away!"

"How did you know Tressalayne was a witch?"

The diminutive antique dealer chuckled. "The truth is I didn't know for sure. Call it a hunch."

"Why this 'Book of First Magic'? And how is it Tressalayne speaks Gaelic?"

Hank nodded. "Ancient Celtic legend has it only a Witch of the White can open the *Leabhar an Chéad Draíocht*, and only a Witch of the White can learn to use its magic. If true, then the language of this magic would come naturally to Tressalayne— much like the ability of a fish to swim through water."

Lucas chewed his lip. "So, what is a 'Witch of the White'?"

Tressalayne, who followed the conversation closely, moved to the edge of her seat.

"Why, Doctor Beckett, it's a witch who uses white magic."

Lucas stared at Hank. *Was he serious?* Through college and med school, all of his classes and training were grounded in scientific fact, cause and effect, a comfortable blanket of familiarity.

The ground seemed to wobble beneath him. Science and medicine, its foundation shaken and cracked in the earthquake called Tressalayne, were snatched away with breathtaking suddenness.

Lucas tried to collect his wits. "Not to get too much *Wizard of Oz* here, Hank, but do you mean 'white magic' as opposed to 'black magic'? Like Glinda the Good Witch of the South, and her opposite, the Wicked Witch of the West?"

With a laugh, Hank slapped his knee. "A classic! Loved the movie. And not a bad analogy, Doctor Beckett."

Lucas studied the diminutive antique dealer with fresh suspicion. Hank was a veritable fount of information. *How did he know all this? Where did he get all his information?*

"So, how do you come to speak a language you claim is extinct? In fact, you didn't seem shocked at all when all this crazy stuff began to happen. It's almost like you expected it."

A chuckle rumbled from Hank. "Ah, yes. I've seen that look before."

He clasped his hands and placed them in front of him.

"I've been translating Gaelic texts since I was a graduate student at Stanford. I have a talent for ancient languages. They interest me. In fact, the unique and unusual *always* interest me. Where I diverge from many of my colleagues is a willingness to follow paths others consider foolish or flights of fancy. You see, Doctor Beckett, there usually *is* a logical explanation for mysterious events and phenomena...but not always. If I've learned anything in my travels and investigations, it's this; *truth isn't always what we think it is.* Logic and convention can't always be boiled down to convenient facts. The world and the universe as we know it has a depth and complexity we've only begun to scratch. So when you say I *expected* something to happen, a more accurate description would be I wasn't *surprised.*"

Lucas considered what Hank said. Given The Book of First Magic's mystical display, his explanation made as much sense as anything. Besides, the antique store owner may have found the solution to Tressalayne's problem, the entire reason they made this trip.

Tressalayne clutched the *Leabhar an Chéad Draíocht* tighter to her chest. "I just want the nightmares to go away. When I'm gripped by these awful visions, it's like I'm another person, someone who wouldn't hesitate to use violence. I want to live with Lucas and know he is always safe from...from me." She finished in a whisper, hopeful eyes on Hank.

"Can...can the *Daoine Beag* teach me this?"

Hank's expression softened. "Yes. I believe they can."

Pouncing on this, Lucas blurted, "What do we need to do?"

Hank climbed off the chair, walked around the desk and stood in front of them. More or less at eye level while they remained seated, he pointed at the locket around Tressalayne's neck.

"May I?"

Nodding, she stiffened when Hank leaned closer. He studied

the locket's gem, and noted its rippled surface and pearl-white color.

"Fascinating. What a beautiful amulet."

Tressalayne's hand crept up to the locket, fingers closing around it in a protective grip.

"Um, yes. It's all I have left from…from whoever I was before."

Seeing her reaction, the dwarf took a step back and crossed his arms. "I believe Tressalayne's problem may be the latent Talent within her. It seeks an avenue for release. Imagine a balloon filled to bursting. If you release the balloon, air rushes out, the balloon deflates. This pent up magic within her creates a pressure which inevitably seeks a way out. The levitating objects, buildings which shake, these are the result. I believe it will get worse over time unless she can find a way to control and redirect the power within her."

With a gesture at the magical book clutched in Tressalayne's arms, Hank said, "I want you to take the *Leabhar an Chéad Draíocht* with you. Let the Little People help you, tutor you. Practice your craft, become proficient in its use, and when you feel you have been taught all you need to know, return the book to me."

Tressalayne sighed with relief. She leaned forward and kissed Hank on the cheek. "I feel better already."

Lucas stood and clasped Hank's hand. "Thank you. Is there anything else we need to do?"

"Hmm. Yes, well…there *is* one more thing, Doctor Beckett."

Lucas frowned. "Really? What is it?"

"Take two aspirin and call me in the morning." Howling, the diminutive antique dealer doubled over with laughter. Finally, he straightened and wiped the tears from his eyes. "Sorry, Doctor Beckett. I couldn't resist."

Grinning, Lucas slapped Hank on the shoulder. "An oldie,

but a goodie. You got me, Hank…and call me Lucas. 'Doctor Beckett' is too formal among friends."

After a final round of handshakes from Lucas and hugs from Tressalayne, Hank watched them leave the store and drive away.

His smile evaporated to be replaced by one of concern. Difficult times were ahead for the young couple. Perhaps they came to see him in time. Circumstances would soon force the witch to choose. Like a coin balanced on a razor's edge, she could fall either way. It would be a close thing.

A *very* close thing.

FORTY

"**W**EAR THIS WARD AROUND YOUR NECK. IT MUST *NEVER* leave your person while you are around Morganna."

Annalise held up a circular leather patch the size of a medallion. A thin silver chain—looped through the Ward—dangled from the top. Thicker in the middle, the Ward was sewn shut with sturdy thread. A coarse, dry material filled the medallion, and when Annalise fingered the leather, it gave off a scratchy, rustling sound, like sand and dry twigs mixed together.

"In fact, it's better if you wear it beneath your shirt so it lies directly against your skin. This will increase the potency of the warding spell. It should protect you against any attempt to bewitch you."

Crick turned a cold stare at Annalise.

"*Should* sounds less than encouraging, especially for the amount of money I'm paying you."

Annalise returned Crick's look with her own determined gaze. "I've explained how we are dealing with an Alpha witch, the most powerful I've ever come across in my lifetime. Where Morganna is concerned, nothing is guaranteed. However, I'm convinced the Ward will protect you if you wear it the way I have described. Remember, take no chances. Keep it close to your person."

Crick dismissed the comment with a flip of his hand. "You think I'm a fool, Annalise? *I hear you.* I didn't get to where I am in life by taking unnecessary chances, and I *always* have a back-up plan. Trust me, whether this thing works or not, Morganna is going to be taken care of—one way or the other."

Crick's pale blue eyes fixed on Annalise. Devoid of warmth, they drilled into her. "Just like I have a back-up plan if you're tempted to betray me."

Annalise shivered. Crick wore his potential for violence like a second skin. There was no doubt in her mind he meant everything he said. *If only she possessed Morganna's power.* She would fear no one then. Instead, she cowered before Crick like a child.

"Ju-just get me everything I asked for from Morganna, especially the blood," she stammered. "Without it, there is no hope of binding her."

"Got it." Crick glanced at his watch and stood.

"Wait for my call. When you get it, leave immediately. You'll stay at a motel in Longview—I'll take care of the reservation. Then follow the GPS directions to my home and have everything prepared. I'll have Morganna with me, so when I arrive, I want to begin the binding promptly. Any questions?"

Annalise shook her head. Although curious how Crick was going to persuade Morganna to accompany him, she knew better than to ask. Far more important to her was *how* Crick would compel Morganna to being bound. She would kill them all without hesitation the second she sensed a binding spell. However, if the Romani witch learned anything during her short acquaintance with Crick, it was his ruthless nature was matched only by his cunning. He *knew* something, something which convinced him Morganna could successfully be bound.

A cold thread of fear ran down her back. Crick better be right.

Otherwise, none of them would live to see another day.

Lockstone's hair whipped in the wind to the accompaniment of the Harley's growl. The spinning, humming wheels, quickly ate up the miles.

True to his word, Eddie managed to get the bike fixed along with a license for it. A fat roll of cash bulged from the pocket of the black bomber jacket the witch hunter wore. Almost ten thousand dollars, it represented an exchange of over half his gold coins. A newly minted driver's license with Lockstone's bearded face, lay in a leather pouch secured at his waist. A cell phone rested in his shirt pocket, the dangling cord from ear buds plugged into it, while GPS directions in a pleasant female voice broadcast in his ears. Courtesy of Eddie, the directions to Nacogdoches were programmed into the cell's map app. Saddle bags rested on the rear end of the Harley, a change of clothes and what few possessions he owned, including the Glock, packed into them. Although grateful for Eddie's help, the witch hunter knew he had to go it alone from this point on. He refused to give him any more details other than Nacogdoches as his destination.

The image of Eddie wringing his hands while Lockstone readied to leave, appeared in his mind. The pawnshop owner acted like his firstborn was being sent off into the world.

"You have everything?" he asked over and over again. "Remember, my cell number and the shop's number are programmed into your phone. Call me if you need anything."

Lockstone recalled how Eddie stood and waved, his image dwindling in the side mirrors until he disappeared from the witch hunter's sight. The memory caused a lump in his throat. Despite the gruff nature the little pawnshop owner often displayed—particularly when dealing with his clientele of rough and unsavory characters—he possessed an oversized heart. Eddie made Lockstone's successful transition into this world possible, and he owed him everything. With a vow to someday pay him back, the witch hunter gripped the Harley's handles tighter.

First things first, however.

Find Morganna, kill her, and with any luck, survive the encounter. If not, death would be a welcome choice…just so long he took the black-hearted bitch with him!

Hatred clouded his thoughts, and he pictured the coven leader's body, torn and bloodied, lying at his feet. His thirst for revenge, a heady drug, caused a rush of adrenaline to flood into his bloodstream. Goosing the throttle, the Harley leaped forward, Lockstone weaving in and around slower cars. Teeth bared like a madman, he leaned into the wind.

The Hunt was finally afoot.

FORTY-ONE

"WE'RE ALL SET, BOSS," LUNKER SAID.

Crick nodded. They were seated in the same empty lake house the enforcer used for his base of operations since he began to spy on Morganna over a month ago. Since then, he added a fifty-inch flat screen monitor to his equipment, which now sat on the granite kitchen counter. A live feed from each hidden camera streamed on the monitor.

"Good. Call me when Morganna shows up and sees the little surprise we left for her. The second she leaves, call or text me and then get the hell over to the bar. I want you in place before she gets there. Who's the back-up if this turns into a shit storm?"

"Gilbert and Mendoza. They know what to do if it goes bad."

Having used both men for previous jobs, Lunker knew both men well. Leg breakers almost as large as him, but also possessed of good instincts and intelligence. If things went south, he had no doubts they would act accordingly.

"Good. Remember, I want Morganna *alive*, preferably, unhurt. But, if you see me begin to act funny or behave in any way like the

Prescott broad, take her down."

Lunker nodded. Having watched Karen Prescott perform like a robot around Morganna, he knew exactly what Crick feared could happen. The enforcer fingered the Taser on the table beside him. He wouldn't hesitate to light her up like a Christmas tree at the first sign his boss acted goofy. Gilbert and Mendoza each carried fully charged Tasers as well, and while using them for back-up on a single woman appeared to be overkill, he'd seen what Morganna was capable of.

Few things scared Lunker. In the rough neighborhood he grew up in, gunshots were a common occurrence. He learned early to duck and run. Later, as a Marine serving a tour in Afghanistan, he watched crazy jihadists blow themselves and anyone unfortunate to be near them into bloody bits. In his current role as Crick's muscle, he'd been threatened, shot at, even stabbed twice. However, in every case, he knew the score. He knew what he was getting into. Danger and the potential for violence went hand in hand. However, with Morganna, he *didn't* know what to expect.

For the first time in his life, a cold knot of fear twisted inside him.

Crick sensed Lunker's uneasiness. "Just follow the plan, Sam. You got enough juice in the Taser to bring a bull elephant to its knees…if it even comes to that."

The enforcer nodded. "Got it, Boss."

Crick stared hard at Lunker for a moment, then, turned and went out the door. Moments later, the sound of a car engine came to Lunker's ears. He stood and watched Crick drive away. The big enforcer patted the comforting weight of the Beretta in his shoulder holster, then sat back down to await Morganna's appearance in Prescott's cabin.

If the Taser didn't knock the bitch out, despite Crick's instructions, he planned on putting her down.

Permanently.

As he rolled into Nacogdoches, Lockstone spoke to his phone and the GPS directions to Nacogdoches Memorial Hospital flashed on the screen. The pleasant female voice relayed instructions which the big witch hunter followed dutifully.

Having planned how he would proceed once he reached the city, Lockstone knew the hospital would be his initial stop. The first and last people to see Morganna were there. The Hunt would begin by finding out what they knew.

Lockstone fingered Argatha's amulet resting in his pocket. He hated its feel, and always felt soiled after using it. However, his limited magical abilities needed to be amplified to obtain any useful information. Even with the amulet, he couldn't truly bewitch anyone. He *could* plant suggestions and make them so irresistible, the person would be compelled to act on them. He fervently hoped it would be enough.

Lockstone pulled into the hospital parking lot, and spotted the entrance to the emergency room. With a gentle feather to the throttle, the Harley drifted into a nearby slot. He thumbed the ignition off, and the throaty growl of the bike grew silent. Kicking out the bike stand, Lockstone stood, stretched, and went over in his mind once again, how he would proceed.

His most important task would be to find and question anyone who might have had interactions with Morganna before and after her admittance. His next move would be predicated by this information. Having investigated more tragic incidents involving witches than he cared to remember, Lockstone was confident of his ability to ferret out valuable information and point the Hunt in the right direction.

Long strides took him to the emergency room entrance. Glass doors whisked open, the flow of cool air against his skin a pleasant contrast to the heat of the parking lot. He spotted a crescent-shaped counter with several hospital personnel seated behind it. Lockstone made a beeline for them.

The witch hunter stopped at the counter and peered over it.

"Can I help you?"

The woman asking the question wore a name tag with "Susan". Petite, she wore pink scrubs, shoulder length brown hair pulled back into a ponytail.

"Yes, you may have a relative of mine who was admitted here."

With a perfunctory nod, the nurse tapped her keyboard. "Name?"

A friendly smile appeared on Lockstone's face. "Well, *Susan*, that's the problem. I'm not sure. I've got so many kin, they're hard to keep up with."

Facing his first test, Lockstone chanted under his breath, the amulet gripped in his hand. A look of initial confusion appeared on the nurse's face. Then, like a shaft of sunlight through a part in the clouds, a receptive smile flashed across her face.

"I know what you mean! I have so many nieces and nephews, I have to list their names on a Google doc just to remember them all. Let's see if I can help you find your kin."

Eyes fixed on her computer screen, she asked, "The date and time of admittance?" Lockstone told her and watched her peck again on the keyboard.

The nurse wrinkled her nose at the information displayed on the monitor. "We have several patients admitted around that date and time. Two men and a woman listed as a Jane Doe—"

"Wait! It's the Jane Doe!" Lockstone exclaimed.

Eyebrow cocked, Susan looked up. "How can you be so sure? A minute ago, you didn't even have a name to give me."

White teeth flashed as Lockstone's face split into a grin. "Oh, I guess you could say I have a pretty good hunch." He gripped the amulet so tightly it cut into his skin, then resumed his soft chant.

Susan stood. "You look like someone who has good hunches." She licked her lips and traced small circles on the counter. "Tell me, are you married? Do you have a girlfriend?"

With a start, Lockstone realized he might have carried his attempt at bewitching too far…with unintended consequences. His grip on the amulet immediately relaxed.

"Ah, you know, Susan, really all I'd like is any information you could give me about this Jane Doe."

Susan pouted, then slid back into her seat. With a sigh, she peered again at her monitor. "No, I'm sorry. Nothing else. She disappeared about a week after admittance. Caused quite a stir as I recall. The police interviewed everyone on duty at the time we discovered she went missing."

"Can you show me her room?"

"Of course!" Susan sprang to her feet and made her way from behind the counter. She stopped beside Lockstone and looped her arm through his.

"Lets go. The room is on the fourth floor."

While they made their way to a bank of elevators, Susan commented, "My, you have such large muscles. Do you work out?"

A pair of doors slid open just as they reached the elevators, thus sparing Lockstone a reply. Susan punched a button on the control panel. Moments later, with a gentle lurch, the elevator began to rise.

Susan waved a hand back and forth in front of her face. "It is *so* hot in here!"

With a free hand, Susan loosened several buttons on her smock to reveal a smooth expanse of pale cleavage. Lockstone kept his gaze straight ahead.

And prayed for the elevator to rise faster.

FORTY-TWO

THE ELEVATOR TREMBLED, AND WITH A SLIGHT BUMP, CAME to a stop. Moments later, the doors whisked open.

"Ta da! Here we are!"

With a tug on Lockstone's arm, Susan skipped out into a broad foyer. To their left stood the nurse's station. To their right, a wide corridor with patient rooms arranged on either side. She led the witch hunter to a room midway down the long hallway, peeked inside, then swung the door wide open. It was unoccupied.

The witch hunter sniffed the air like a hound on the scent. Then, he closed his eyes and stuck his tongue out as if to taste the atmosphere of the room. Lockstone's senses, hypersensitive to spells and magic, were honed and sharpened over years of tracking and hunting witches. Although weeks passed since Morganna disappeared from the hospital, he knew within moments she had been here. The taint of magic covered everything like a thick blanket, its residue impossible to miss.

But what kind of magic? What spells were cast? If he could determine this, it would go a long way in explaining how she managed to slip out of the hospital unnoticed.

The witch hunter took his time and walked about the room, eyes closed to slits. His hands trailed over the wall, bed, and other furniture, until he found himself in the small bathroom. An especially strong aroma of magic suffused the privy. He took in a great lungful of air, held it, then gradually released it through pursed lips. With a jolt, he realized powerful magic had been worked here, the spell cast, a potent creation.

Familiar with every kind of witchery employed by covens, Lockstone sorted through them in his mind. He knew at once a bewitching occurred, its magical signature unmistakable. A few moments later, he added changeling powder to the mix as well. Even more distinctive than a bewitching, it left a palpable residue. However, the powerful spell whose locus was centered in the bathroom gave him pause. *What is it?* Suddenly, his eyes snapped open.

"Morlaga potion!"

Lockstone spit to rid his mouth of the foul taste the words produced, a growl bubbling from him in an angry eruption.

Susan, near the witch hunter's shoulder, backed up, her hand at her throat. "Wh-what's wrong?"

With great effort, Lockstone reined in his temper. He clutched the amulet and resumed his chant. The fear in the nurse's eyes disappeared, and her features returned to normal.

"Oh, nothing. Nothing to be concerned about," he assured her.

Lockstone paced about the room, his thoughts racing.

One-by-one, the pieces fell into place.

Morganna bewitched someone, someone who helped her escape. Then she used the changeling powder to alter her appearance. No one recognized her, which is why she could walk out of the hospital without being noticed. But, still weak, still not recovered from the poisoned dart, she found herself unable to use magic powerful enough to take advantage of the changeling powder and to cast a bewitching spell. In her weakened state, it forced her to use the *morlaga* potion. Even though the potion's effects were temporary, the elixir would invigorate her long enough to use the magic needed to make good on her escape.

The memory of the corpses lying in the room at the tavern flashed through the witch hunter's mind. Nothing but dry skin and bones, the remains all that was left of the baron's son and his betrothed—the very ones he and Emmitt were sent to save. But they arrived too late, their lives sacrificed to make the potion.

Rage boiled within him. The lads, Emmitt, plus two more innocents *dead* because of his failure to stop Morganna in time. More blood on his hands he could never wash away. Fists clenched, the witch hunter swore under his breath. He noticed Susan becoming agitated again. Forcing himself to take deep breaths, he managed to bring his anger under control.

Lockstone turned to her. "Is it possible to find out who last visited this room the day Mor—I mean the Jane Doe—disappeared?"

"Of course. In fact, I already know because the police asked the same question."

"Who? Who is it?"

"The woman whose car the patient crashed into—Karen Prescott."

They rode down the elevator in silence, Lockstone lost in his thoughts. The admittance nurse stood beside him, quiet and reserved. The witch hunter knew his rage dampened her ardor. While thankful on the one hand, he hoped the successful compulsion he cast on her wasn't compromised because of it.

When they exited the elevator into the emergency room lobby, Lockstone asked, "Do you know where Karen Prescott lives?"

"Patient records are confidential," Susan snapped.

Lockstone sighed, gripped the amulet, and chanted.

"But for you, what's breaking one itty bitty rule?" she gushed.

Susan grasped the witch hunter's arm and ran her hands up and down. She stopped at his bicep to squeeze and knead the muscle. "You are so big, strong, and *hard*."

The emergency room nurse released his arm and waved both hands on her face. Despite the air conditioning, her face was flushed. Fingers fumbled at her scrubs to undo more buttons. She stopped when she discovered how far her smock already gaped open.

Lockstone, fearing the nurse would unclothe herself right there in front of him, blurted, "Karen Prescott! I need to know where she lives."

With a shake of her head, Susan said, "Yes. Okay."

Back to her station, she tapped on her keyboard. A minute later the hum of a printer filled the air. It spit out a sheet of paper with Prescott's address which Susan handed to Lockstone.

"Thank you. Oh…there's no need to mention this to anyone," Lockstone told her. "In fact, you should just forget everything about me."

"Yes…forget everything."

With a look back as he walked out of the emergency room, the witch hunter noticed the nurse upright in her chair, eyes straight ahead. He sighed in relief. *Now, for the next step in the Hunt.*

Find Karen Prescott.

FORTY-THREE

"LUCAS! COME SEE!"

Lucas looked up from his patient notes, and glanced in the direction of the kitchen. *What was Tressalayne up to now?* Since they arrived back home from Hank's store, The Book of First Magic rarely left her side. Every day, something new happened as the "Little People" taught her more magic.

The following Monday, he opened the front door to be greeted by the sight of a school of catfish swimming lazily in midair around the den. He watched open-mouthed while Tressalayne directed their movements like an orchestra conductor, then led them outside to a stock pond in the pasture behind the house. Like fishy torpedoes, they dropped one-by-one to splash back into the water. Later in the evening, they sat on the porch and watched the sun set while a collection of bluebirds, sparrows, and finches settled in the branches of a nearby live oak. From their leafy perch, the feathered chorus serenaded the young couple with chirps and whistles to a Gaelic tune Tressalayne taught them.

Similar incidents filled the rest of the week while

Tressalayne practiced.

Lucas closed the window on his iPad, stood, and walked into the kitchen. He spied a large watermelon on the butcher board countertop. Tressalayne stood nearby wearing an apron, a wooden spoon in her hand. The Book of First Magic lay open before her on an old music stand Lucas rescued from the attic.

She pointed the spoon at the watermelon. "Watch this."

Speaking in words Lucas now recognized as Gaelic, the melon trembled, split open, and ripe, red flesh erupted in a geyser of seeds and pulp. The mess landed on the countertop in sodden *plops*, juice running down to drip onto the floor.

"Oops."

Red-faced, Tressalayne put her ear next to the book. She listened intently, then nodded. The Little People must have found her mistake hilarious, because laughter resonated from the mystical volume.

Tressalayne tapped the spoon and spoke again. The remains of the watermelon swirled upward in a vortex of dripping pulp. The gooey remains spun faster and faster until all Lucas could make out was a blurred image. When the spinning abruptly stopped, a whole watermelon appeared where only seconds before a mushy mess existed. The melon drifted downward until, once again, it rested on the kitchen counter.

With a deep breath, Tressalayne started over. She pointed her wooden utensil and mouthed the words of a spell. Moments later, a small, circular opening appeared in the ripe fruit and black seeds shot out. They formed a cloud above Tressalayne's head, and buzzed in a circle like a swarm of angry hornets. The witch opened the kitchen door, and with a wave of her spoon, the seeds shot out into the sky where they disappeared from sight.

Tressalayne waved her impromptu wand, a triumphant smile on her face. "No more pesky seeds to spit out."

Lucas clapped. "Bravo, bravo! I can't wait to see what you do for an encore."

He grinned and shook his head. The peculiar applications of the magic Tressalayne continued to learn never ceased to amaze him. Who would have thought a spell existed for de-seeding a watermelon? All he really cared about, however, was the effect on Tressalayne. She appeared happier and more secure. Best of all, not once did a nightmarish flashback occur since she gained possession of The Book of First Magic, nor were there any un-controlled demonstrations of her Talent.

He—*they*—owed Hank big time. The diminutive antique store owner really came through for Tressalayne.

Lucas crossed the room and placed his arms around Tressalayne's waist. He pulled her close and kissed her.

"Momentous occasions like this call for a celebration. I mean, it's not every day I get to watch a watermelon spit out its own seeds."

Arms wrapped around Lucas' neck, Tressalayne murmured, "What do you have in mind?"

"I know a fantastic restaurant with great food and a terrific atmosphere. Why don't we go there for dinner tonight?"

Tressalayne stood on her toes to bring herself at eye level with Lucas. "Okay...although I can think of another way we can celebrate right now."

Lucas glanced at his watch. Disappointed, he shook his head.

"Not enough time. I'll need to call and make reservations, and it takes about forty-five minutes to get there. By the time we get dressed, we'll need to be on the road."

With a sigh, Tressalayne trailed her hand down Lucas' chest before exiting the kitchen to change.

Skin tingling from her touch, Lucas pulled a small jewelry box from his pocket. He opened the lid and glanced inside. A romantic dinner tonight would be the perfect occasion.

He needed to ask Tressalayne a question.

CFORTY-CFOUR

"WHAT DO YOU THINK?"
Tressalayne looked around. They were seated in a quiet corner of the Stillwater Inn, surrounded by other couples at tables scattered throughout two spacious rooms. The restaurant—a large, turn-of-the-century house located in the East Texas town of Jefferson—served gourmet fare, and had been converted into an upscale bistro. Starched, white tablecloths covered each table, the muted light assisted by flickering candles. Fresh flowers in quaint vases formed colorful centerpieces, while spotless wineglasses glittered by their elbows. Soft music played from hidden speakers in the ceiling.

Tressalayne leaned forward. "It's wonderful."

Lucas couldn't take his eyes off of her. Dressed in an elegant burgundy-colored cocktail dress, the upper half of her gown was a halter with a hollow back exposing slim arms and shoulders. The mini-length put her long, shapely legs on full display. Amber hair gleamed in the soft light, falling in a thick curtain down her back. Full, ruby-red lips complimented her cream-colored cheeks, blue-green eyes an emerald sea Lucas found himself becoming lost in.

Tressalayne squeezed his leg. "You look so handsome tonight."

Dressed in dark slacks, a blue shirt, coat, and tie, Lucas considered the contrast between himself and the woman across from him. After a short deliberation, he decided he enjoyed the company of the most stunning woman on the planet.

"You are absolutely gorgeous yourself," he replied.

Their waiter appeared and Lucas ordered for both of them. He chose the rack of lamb with mint sauce, rosemary potatoes, and a dinner salad with the house dressing. Because of her head injury, Lucas strictly prevented Tressalayne from any alcohol consumption. However, he decided the time had arrived to waive the prohibition, so he added a red wine. The waiter smiled, tapped his pad, and scooted off to the kitchen. A short time later he returned and uncorked a wine bottle, then poured a small amount in a glass. Lucas sipped then nodded, and the waiter filled their glasses.

It was shaping up to be a magical night.

Happy and relaxed, Lucas viewed the food and wine a compliment to what had to be the most perfect evening of his life. Their conversation flowed in an easy and natural manner, much like they had already spent a lifetime together. He could tell Tressalayne felt the same way. Her eyes glowed, her face a reflection of contentment. When the waiter returned to clear the dishes, he poured the last of the wine in their glasses, and decided it was now or never.

He took a swallow of wine and cleared his throat. "Tressalayne, I have something I need to talk to you about…something I want to ask you."

Curious, Tressalayne looked at him. "Okay. Is something wrong?"

"Oh, no," Lucas said with a nervous laugh. He pushed aside

his wineglass, reached across the table, and held both of her hands in his own.

"I love you. The best day in my life happened when I opened my door and you fell into my arms. Since then, it's been a wild ride and you've turned my life upside down, but I can't imagine any second, minute, or hour where you're not in it. I want to spend the rest of my life with you."

Releasing her hands, he pulled the jewelry box from his pocket and took out a ring. A large diamond formed the centerpiece of the gold band, with smaller diamonds inset in a circular pattern. Sparkling in the light, Lucas held the ring before him.

"Will you marry me?"

Tressalayne's hand went to her mouth at the sight of the beautiful ring. She stared at it before finally looking up. "What does *marry* mean?"

A long silence followed, before Lucas slapped his head. *Of course! Her amnesia!*

Oceans of ink were used writing about marriage, innumerable books published on the subject, even an entire counseling profession established and dedicated solely to the institution of marriage.

And now he had to describe it to a White Witch.

Lucas chewed his lip. *How could he explain the concept of marriage in a condensed, easy to understand fashion?*

"Hmm, well…when people get married, it's because they love each other and want to spend the rest of their lives together. It's a commitment, for better or worse, and usually includes a ceremony called a wedding. The wedding band is symbolic of this love and commitment—which is why I'm offering it to you."

Tressalayne's gaze went back and forth between the ring and Lucas. "And if I take your ring, what happens?"

Suddenly, Lucas didn't like the direction of the conversation.

"It means you feel the same way. You love me and want to

always be with me...*we get married and live happily ever after!*"
The words, sharp and pointed, reflected Lucas' bruised feelings.
He closed his fist on the ring and sat back.

His face, a stony mask, radiated disappointment, and
Tressalayne placed her hand on his arm. "Lucas, this is so sudden. Can't we talk about this when we get home?"

"Sure we can. I'll take that as a no!" Lucas returned the ring to
the box, snapped the lid shut, and shoved it in his pocket.

Lucas, tense and rigid, looked away. Tressalayne squeezed his
hand. "I-I didn't say no."

He jerked away. "You didn't have to."

The evening, which began with such promise, now crumbled
before his eyes.

They rode home in silence.

CFORTY-CFIVE

THE AWKWARDNESS CONTINUED AFTER THEY ARRIVED AT THE farmhouse.

Lucas refused all attempts by Tressalayne to talk. Hurt, confused, and disappointed, he didn't understand what went wrong. How could things have gone from good to bad so fast? Thinking himself a fool, he brushed his teeth and got into bed quickly. When Tressalayne joined him a few minutes later, he turned away from her.

They lay in the dark, the only sound the *tick tock* of the grandfather clock in the hallway.

Abruptly, Tressalayne threw off the covers. She turned on the bedside light, then grabbed Lucas and flipped him on his back. Straddling him, she pinned his arms so he would have to face her. Her crotch ground into his groin, normally a pleasant experience for Lucas, but now used to hold him in place.

"Are we going to arm wrestle too? Because I'll go ahead and cry *uncle*. Now will you get off me so I can get some sleep?"

Angry, Lucas tried to turn back on his side. It would have been easier for him to grow wings and fly for all the good it did him. He didn't budge an inch. With her unnatural strength, Tressalayne could have picked the bed up with him in it.

Her face an inch from Lucas' nose, eyes flashing, Tressalayne said, "You are going to talk to me, and you are not moving until you do!"

"Why? You already made your feelings clear."

Tressalayne went silent, head cocked as if listening to some distant voice. When she turned back to Lucas, a chill ran through him. Her eyes, rather than the emerald-blue which so mesmerized him, appeared clouded and dark, a cruel glint where once a warm liveliness existed.

She wore the eyes of a stranger.

Then, with abrupt suddenness, the dark visage passed. With a shake of her head, Tressalayne sat up and pointed a finger at him. "You can say that after all we have been through? After all the times I've told you how much I love you? Have I not given myself to you and *shown* you what I feel for you? Yet, I ask one question, *one question*, and you act like this!"

Lucas snorted. "You love me, huh? Then why didn't you say *yes* when I asked you to marry me? Instead, you asked questions like we're in a business negotiation. You left me hanging with my heart in my hand!"

Tressalayne wiped away angry tears, and pushed off Lucas. She sat on the edge of the bed, arms crossed. "You don't understand. You *never* gave me a chance to explain."

Lucas sat up and rubbed his arms where Tressalayne held him in an iron grip. Fighting to bring his emotions under control, he finally managed to rein in his temper. He tossed the covers aside and slid beside her.

"Okay. Explain it to me now."

With a deep breath, Tressalayne turned and looked at him. "I'm not who you think I am."

Lucas rolled his eyes.

"Oh, no. Not this again. Since we got back from Hank's store with The Book of First Magic, you've had no incidents. None! In fact, you're happier than I've ever seen you."

Tressalayne struck the mattress causing the entire bed to jump. "Lucas, I am a *witch*. And I have been a different kind of witch far longer than this so-called 'white witch' Hank calls me."

"No...*No!*" Lucas leaped to his feet. "You have no memory. *You suffer from amnesia.* How can you know anything for certain about your previous life? Sure, you've had some bad flashbacks, some uncontrolled demonstrations of magic. Hank said they occurred because you needed a way to release the magic within you. It's why he gave you the Book of First Magic."

"He told you what you wanted to believe."

Glancing sharply at her, Lucas frowned. "Huh? Are you saying Hank lied to me?"

"No, he didn't lie. He just didn't...tell you everything."

Lucas collapsed back onto the bed. "What? Did you two hide something from me?"

"It's not like that! The Little People *are* teaching me use different magic, spells, and potions. But they have also helped me learn to resist my darker nature. So...so I won't return to what I was before. I think Hank knew this. I believe it' the *real* reason he gave me the book."

Lucas couldn't believe his ears. She was describing textbook schizophrenia. *A split personality.* Had he moments earlier viewed a brief glimpse of this alter ego?

"The Little People told you this?"

Tressalayne didn't answer immediately. When she did, her voice contained a hollow sadness.

"No, Lucas. It's me. I've known something's off inside of me ever since I woke up in the hospital. Its clear to me now whoever or *whatever* I was before my accident...its something to be feared, something to avoid at all costs. The nightmares are proof of what I suspected."

She caressed his cheek. "Don't you understand? I *want* to be with you. Until we met Hank and he gave me The Book of First Magic, you were all that kept me from reverting to my old self. Part of me fears if you knew me—the witch I used to be—you could never love me or look at me the same way again. Part of me is afraid this same love blinds you to the possible danger I pose to you."

Surprised at how calm he remained over these revelations, Lucas considered Tressalayne's story. If their roles were reversed, what would he think? *What would he do?* Having told her of his own checkered past, she knew his hands were not clean. He'd had to conquer his own personal demons. Even now, after the passage of years, he still harbored enormous pain for the cruel way he treated his mother, the guilt a stain he could never wash away.

Lucas put his arm around her waist. "You asked me what it means to marry, and I'm afraid I gave you a kind of textbook, cliché answer. If you'll allow me, *now* I'd like to tell you my personal belief, the Lucas Beckett version."

Tressalayne's hand crept to his thigh. "Okay."

"So, first, a disclaimer. I'm kind of old-fashioned when it comes to love and marriage, so I guess I'm not much of a Twenty-First century guy on the subject. See, I believe love, *true* love, to be a rare and precious thing, so whenever a person is fortunate enough to find someone they love, it's readily apparent, a no-doubter. My symptoms included long nights thinking of you. You are always on my mind before I fall asleep, and when I wake, I can't wait to see your face.

I also believe marriage has it risks and rewards, and that it's never, ever going to be a perfect arrangement. Good times, bad times, they come and go. Sometimes it will be hard, so hard, the temptation is to just give up. But through it all, the one constant in a marriage is we have each other. So the question is, who do *you* want by your side to share the successes, the failures, the joy, and the sorrow? Because this is what defines marriage—its what love is all about. And I made my decision.

I choose you."

Lucas twisted, his knees against Tressalayne. "*You* are my true love. I'll never meet anyone again I feel this way about. I don't care about your past, and I don't care about the risks, even if what you believe about yourself is true. I still want to marry you."

Lucas heard Tressalayne's breath catch in her throat. "I don't know if I could live without you," she whispered. "I don't think I could."

Tressalayne shivered and hugged herself. "It terrifies me to realize the only thing I know for certain about my past is that you were not in it. What a bitter life it must have been. Without you I'd be empty and hollow, nothing but a desolate shell."

She pulled Lucas to her. "Go get the ring."

Startled, Lucas asked. "Are you sure?"

"I've never been more certain about anything in my life."

Lucas jumped up and quickly made his way to the closet. Rummaging around in the pocket of his slacks, his hand closed around the jewelry box. He returned, took the ring out, and kneeled in front of Tressalayne.

Lucas took her hand and asked, "Will you marry me?" When she nodded he cried, "*Yes*," and slid the ring on her finger.

Tressalayne held her hand up and studied the ring. The diamonds glittered in the light. She turned to Lucas and kissed him, her soft lips holding his, until finally, she broke, her breath warm on his skin.

"*Bidh mi an-còmhnaidh ga ghràdhachadh riut,*" she murmured in Gaelic. "I will always love you, vein of my heart."

She hesitated, then gently pushed away. "I have something

to ask you."

Lucas, mesmerized by Tressalayne's warm lips, blinked in surprise. "Eh? Um, sure. What is it?"

"You must promise—you must *swear* you'll do something for me."

Sitting straighter, Lucas' eyes narrowed. "What is it?"

"If you ever see me change, if you see hints of my old self emerge, you'll drop whatever you're doing and immediately run.

I want you to run for your life."

FORTY-SIX

LOCKSTONE CRUISED DOWN THE STREET, SHARP EYES TAKING IN every detail.

Large, expensive homes lined the residential street on either side of him. Immaculate lawns, shrubs, and flowers graced each palatial abode. Every house had at least one and sometimes several, of the shiny cars so prevalent in this world. Lockstone dismissed them all, his attention focused on only one home and one car.

Karen Prescott's.

Suspecting a large man on a Harley cruising a neighborhood like this might raise suspicions, he allowed himself only one drive-by of Prescott's house and the silver BMW parked in the drive. Having determined the main entry into and out of the exclusive neighborhood beforehand, he found a location from which he could remain unobtrusive while he watched cars come and go. Only a stone's throw from the entrance, a grove of trees grew next to the road. He parked the motorcycle under the trees, then lounged on the bike, his back against a tree trunk with his feet propped up on the Harley's handles. Anyone who observed him would think he simply found refuge in the shade from the hot Texas sun.

Eyes closed to slits to pantomime dozing, Lockstone sat up when he saw Prescott's car stop and then turn on the road in front of him. A booted foot hit the kick starter, and the motorcycle rumbled to life. He let the BMW get a healthy lead, then released the clutch and followed.

For the next hour, the witch hunter watched Prescott make several stops which included a food store and clothing store. Her last stop came at a large brick building called First Federal Bank. When she returned to the car with her purchases, Lockstone's hopeful anticipation rose to new heights. *Maybe she made these purchases for Morganna.*

When Prescott, apparently finished with her errands, took a route out of town rather than back to her home, the witch hunter's heart threatened to leap from his chest.

She's going to Morganna!

In the rush of excitement, he found it hard to follow at a discrete distance. More than once, he closed the gap with the BMW and had to throttle back. Cursing himself for such an amateur lack of patience, he prayed Prescott wasn't paying close attention.

Fifteen minutes later, the silver car turned onto a tree-lined road. Lockstone stopped at the road and tracked the vehicle's progress. Brake lights appeared in the distance when Prescott slowed and then turned right. He gave the bike gas and rolled after her. Moments later, he arrived at the same turn.

A wide, gated entrance greeted him. An elaborate brick and mortar façade flanked both sides, with a smooth asphalt road in between. Colorful flowers and shrubs grew from the base of the brick facing, and a high metal arch stretched from one side of the entrance to the other. A sign attached to the arch moved gently in the breeze.

Bass Club Lake: Lots available.

The witch hunter returned his attention to Prescott's car. He saw it round a corner and turn into a dense grove of trees. A cottage, barely visible through the thick foliage, sat on the edge of the lake. Prescott stopped beside the cabin, got out, and went inside.

Scanning the area, Lockstone noticed other cottages near the one Prescott entered. Scattered about, there looked to be no rhyme or reason to their location other than proximity to the lake. A broad smile appeared on the witch hunter's lips at the sight of the dense swaths of brush and trees...more than enough cover for someone used to moving with stealth to stalk witches.

He pulled the witch compass from his neck and studied it. The needle stayed fixed and unwavering.

It pointed true, right at Prescott's cabin.

Ferocious joy filled his heart. His hands opened and closed in anticipation of placing them around Morganna's neck. Breath pumped in and out of his lungs like a great bellows, the sharp edge of revenge red-hot within him. Minutes passed before he could bring himself under control and plan Morganna's death.

He spun on his heel to retrieve the Harley, then drove back to the main road beside the gate. There he found a suitable spot, and pushed the bike off the road into a thickly wooded area. He rummaged through the saddlebags on the Harley and removed a small backpack. The witch hunter stuffed it with the equipment he would need, including a pair of binoculars. His last item—the Glock—he checked carefully to make sure the magazine contained a full clip, then shoved it into the back of his pants. He covered the motorcycle with leafy branches and stepped back to observe his work.

Satisfied with the camouflage, Lockstone shouldered the backpack and making his way out of the woods, struck out for the lake.

The vegetation provided abundant cover, but it took him almost an hour to get into position where he could get a clear view of Prescott's cabin. Tempted to move even closer, he decided against it. The trees thinned near the cottage and he risked being seen. Instead, he waited for the cover of darkness to cloak his movements.

Mosquitos and other buzzing insects swarmed around him in the sticky, humid heat. Ignoring them, he looked up at the sky and estimated it would be an hour or more before the sun set.

The witch hunter took the binoculars out of the case and trained them on the cabin. The windows, curtains drawn across them, made it impossible to see any activity inside. It didn't matter. He had time.

All the time in the world.

FORTY-SEVEN

MORGANNA BROODED IN THE DARKENED ROOM.

A single light from a lamp on the table beside her provided the only relief in pushing back at the shadows. Thick drapes covered each window, an effective muzzle on any penetration of sunlight and prying eyes. The murky darkness matched the coven leader's thoughts.

After her escape from the hospital, Morganna thought herself free. Her recovery lingered, however, a direct result of the poison from the bolt fired by the accursed Lockstone. Days stretched to weeks, and now weeks to months. In her mind, she simply switched from one prison to another. While the lake house contained no barred windows or doors, in her weakened condition, it might as well have. Only with the aid of the *morlaga* potion did she have sufficient vigor to cast spells, particularly the one used with the changeling powder to alter her appearance. To stray from the safety of the cabin without disguising her looks created too big a risk of being recognized. Her bewitched victim explained how her countenance had been spread on "social media" by the police. Too many people knew her description.

However, over the past several weeks, her strength and stamina slowly returned. At long last, use of the changeling powder didn't leave her exhausted, and she started to exit the house for short periods of time. Karen Prescott took her on brief outings at first, then increased to longer distances, until finally, they began to frequent a large shopping area called a "mall" in a nearby town. Taking full advantage of Prescott's wealth, Morganna spent the woman's money freely. Clothes, jewelry, eating at restaurants. Morganna purchased whatever struck her fancy.

Her *real* freedom beckoned at last, and the witch eagerly planned for the time she would leave the lake cabin behind. Once she found Tressalayne, they would live like royalty and take whatever they pleased from the fat cattle that passed for humanity on this world. Nothing would be denied them.

This happy dream had been shattered the previous evening—followed by a long and sleepless night.

When she returned from a foray into a nearby town, she discovered a red dress draped across a chair in the cabin's den. A pair of black boots sat on the floor beside the dress, while a black hat rested on the seat of the chair. Pinned to the dress was an unsigned note: *"I have something you want. Meet me at The County Line tomorrow night at 9:00".*

Her first impulse—to flee and go someplace far away—evaporated when she spied the small piece of paper on top of the black hat and the name written on it.

Tressalayne.

One sniff told her the paper reeked of the magical scent of her protégé. There could be no doubt. Someone knew of Tressalayne's whereabouts.

And they knew about Morganna.

How did they find her? *Who* found her? How long had she been watched? More important, what did they want from her—and she had no doubt they wanted something. The fact the authorities weren't already involved was proof of that.

Morganna tapped her talon-like fingernail on the chair's arm. *Karen Prescott must be who led the mystery note-writer to her.* Prescott was her only link to the outside world. The talon scored a deep groove. She should have killed the woman long ago, but then, did she really have a choice? In her weakness, who would have taken care of her?

The sound of an approaching car intruded on her thoughts, and the crunch of tires on gravel came to her ears. A door opened and shut on the vehicle, and moments later, the bright glow of sunlight spilled into the darkened room. Karen Prescott blinked at the door while her eyes adjusted to the gloom. In her arms were several bags of groceries which she placed on the kitchen counter.

She stepped next to Morganna. "Mistress, I—*oof!*"

Prescott flew across the room. Doubled over from the blow to her abdomen, she lay on the ground and fought to breathe. When, finally, she stood on unsteady feet, face white from pain, she moved once again to stand beside the coven leader.

Morganna eyed her with a malignant gaze. "Fool! You led them to me. I told you to make sure no one ever followed you."

"Mistress, I have been very careful—"

Morganna flew out of the chair, and her hand closed around Prescott's throat. Held aloft, the bewitched woman's legs kicked impotently. Shaking her like a rat caught in a terrier's jaws, Morganna's viselike grip choked off all air to her lungs. The kicks became weaker and weaker. With great reluctance, the coven leader realized she still needed Prescott and released her grip. Dropped to the floor, her victim coughed and gagged as she tried to force air through her bruised throat.

Morganna paced the room, deep in thought, while Prescott lay on the floor, her face blue from lack of oxygen.

"Have you heard of a place called 'The County Line'?"

"Ye-yes, Mistress," Prescott answered in a voice raspy from the near strangulation.

"What kind of establishment is it?"

"It is a honky tonk with a large dance floor. Lots of people go there to drink and dance."

Morganna continued to pace while she absorbed this information. That would explain the attire left for her on the chair. *Did she dare show up for this meeting?* Her instincts told her to flee, but the lure of finding Tressalayne proved irresistible. She *needed* her young protégé to form a new coven in this world.

A cruel smile played across her lips. She wanted answers. And whoever discovered her whereabouts was going to provide them…one way or the other. She would play along and meekly go to the bar, certain no one on this world ever dealt with a witch of her prowess before. The fools! Once she determined Tressalayne's location and wrung all useful information from her soon-to-be victims, she would kill them all—along with Prescott. The woman was a liability and outlived her usefulness. However, she needed her for this one last task.

Morganna turned to Prescott still sprawled gasping on the floor. "Be here at eight o'clock tonight."

A cackle escaped her lips. "We are going dancing."

CFORTY-CEIGHT

"**S**HE'S ON THE MOVE."

"Good. Make sure she's on the way to our little rendez-vous and not on the run. You know what to do if she runs. Once you know Morganna is being driven to The County Line, haul ass and get here as soon as possible."

"Understood, Boss."

Lunker clicked off and pocketed his phone. Grabbing his jacket, he checked the Taser again to make sure it was fully charged. Then he checked the Beretta, his fingers brushing the cold steel as it lay snug in his shoulder holster. He hurried to the kitchen table where the enforcer picked up a small black box, a blue LED light blinking on its surface. A red button was mounted on the box next to the LED. Attached to the wiring harness on Prescott's car was another electronic device he placed there the previous evening. When the red button was depressed, it activated the device on the wiring harness and produced a miniature electromagnetic pulse. If Morganna tried to flee, the pulse would fry the car's master controller chip and electronics, thus disabling the engine. The tech expert who provided the gadget claimed it would also scramble all nearby data devices within the car, including cell phones. All the better in Lunker's opinion.

He was taking no chances.

Unable to shake the feeling of impending disaster, he took the unusual avenue of trying to talk Crick out of capturing Morganna. One look from his boss, the kind where men disappeared never to be heard from again, stopped him in his tracks.

He decided in the interest of continued good health to drop the matter.

A momentary spark of hope bloomed within him when, via the spy cams, he watched the witch attack Karen Prescott earlier that morning. After she found the dress and note, Morganna must have deduced the bewitched woman to be the one who unwittingly led someone to her. While Prescott dangled in the air, the witch choking the life out of her, a small amount of compassion for the helpless victim stirred within him. However, her death meant Crick's plan would be blown to hell. The witch would have no one to drive her to The County Line. Those hopes evaporated when Morganna released Prescott.

With a grim sigh, he picked up a tablet and activated an app. The tracker on Prescott's car displayed a strong signal which elicited a satisfied grunt from the enforcer. Everything appeared to be in order. He left the cabin and slid into his car, but didn't start it. He'd let Prescott drive away and get a healthy lead. He knew the route by heart to get to The County Line, and if it looked like they deviated from the route and tried to run, he would blow their electronics. With Gilbert and Mendoza, he would confront the women.

Anything could happen then. A shot gone astray in the struggle could easily occur. Could he help it if the misfortunate bullet ended up in Morganna's heart?

Crick wouldn't believe him of course, but employment

opportunities abounded for men with his skill set. Unfortunately, all potential employers would have the same stringent requirement.

You would have to be *alive* to get the job.

Movement at the cabin stirred Lockstone from his reverie. He reached for the binoculars and watched Karen Prescott emerge and look around. The sun had just set, but the fiery glow in the horizon still provided enough light to see the surroundings clearly. A moment later, Morganna appeared.

Lockstone blinked, his heart tattooing a fierce beat in his chest. It was her! He found her! Relief and emotion washed over him. Angry tears dripped from his cheeks, forcing him to lower the binoculars and rub his eyes. When he looked again, he saw the coven leader in a stunning red dress, a black hat in her hand. She appeared ready for a night on the town.

The two women got in Prescott's car. The faint sound of an engine starting reached the witch hunter's ears, and the vehicle pulled away from the cabin. Throwing all pretense of stealth away, Lockstone jammed the binoculars into his backpack, slung it over his shoulder, and sprinted back to the hidden motorcycle.

Twigs, branches, and leaves slapped his exposed face and arms. Ignoring the stinging pain, the witch hunter charged through the underbrush with reckless abandon. He had to reach the Harley before they disappeared from sight.

Lockstone burst out onto the road and caught sight of Prescott's car turning onto the blacktop. He rushed up the slope to the hidden bike, and wasted a few precious seconds locating the Harley in the faint light. His eyes caught a metallic glint and he leaped to the bike. Large hands swept away the camouflage, and as his booted foot hit the kick starter, the Harley roared to life. Giving the bike full throttle, a rooster tail of pine needles and soil erupted like a geyser as the rear tire bit into the soft loam. Heedless of the trees and branches, Lockstone tore through the forest. When he reached the edge of the trees, the bike went airborne before landing squarely on the road.

With a squeal of tires, the witch hunter roared after Prescott's car.

CFORTY-NINE

SATISFIED MORGANNA WAS HEADED TO THE COUNTY LINE, Lunker started the car and followed.

By design, Crick already reserved a table near the dance floor where the congestion of drinkers and dancers would be the greatest. If extreme measures had to be taken against the witch, the noise and chaos of packed bodies swaying and moving to loud music would make it less likely anyone would notice them take Morganna down.

The other two beefy enforcers, Gilbert and Mendoza, stationed themselves near the bar, and waited for Morganna to enter the honky-tonk. Like Lunker, they wore boot-cut jeans, western shirts, and Stetson hats.

Lunker adjusted his cowboy hat for the hundredth time, distinctly uncomfortable in the unfamiliar clothing. Despite the warm night, he and his men wore light Wrangler jackets to hide the Tasers clipped to their belts and the handguns holstered at their shoulders. Lunker worried less about discovery of the guns than the Tasers. It was Texas after all and a country and western bar to boot. If the bouncers threw out all the patrons with guns, likely they would go out of business in short order. The worse that could happen is they would be asked to leave their guns outside before they would be allowed to reenter.

The Tasers would be harder to explain, so every effort had been taken to conceal them. If things went south with the witch, they would need to be employed to subdue her.

Accelerating, Lunker caught up to Prescott's car and followed at a discreet distance. He noticed a motorcycle between him and Prescott's vehicle. At first he paid it no attention, but when after a series of turns and change of directions the bike still remained behind her, his radar went on high alert.

What the hell?

By this time, full darkness had fallen, and Lunker was forced to study the bike and rider through his headlights and those of passing cars. It looked like an old-style Harley, perhaps from the 60s or 70s, and while he couldn't make out the features of the person on it, he could see it was a man...a *very* large man, one perhaps bigger than Lunker himself.

By now, they were only five minutes from The County Line, and any doubt the Harley was following Prescott's car evaporated.

Morganna had a tail.

Lunker tapped the Bluetooth function on the car's console and moments later, Crick's voice came over the speaker.

"Talk to me."

"We got a problem, Boss. Morganna's being followed by a big guy on a bike."

"What? Are you sure?"

"Positive. He's been following Prescott's Beamer almost from the time it left the lake house."

Silence followed Lunker's bombshell, filled only with Crick's breathing and the faint sound of country and western music blaring in the background.

Crick's voice, cold and flat, reappeared. "Okay, here's what we are going to do. Everything is going to progress according to plan. Have your men on the lookout for this guy. As big as you say he is, he won't be hard to miss. Maybe this is all a mistake or a coincidence, but we are going to take no chances. Get your men ready to intervene at a moment's notice if he or anyone else tries to interfere when we make our move on Morganna."

Lunker closed his eyes in dismay. The situation, already dangerous, became even more complicated.

Teeth gritted, he replied, "Roger, boss. I'll take care of it." The line went dead.

The enforcer punched another number on the screen to call his men and inform them of the change in the situation.

Lunker sat back in his car and gripped the wheel so hard his knuckles turned white. He fought the overwhelming urge to turn the car around and roar away in the opposite direction as fast as possible. Instead, he continued on to the honky-tonk.

When the enforcer arrived at the bar, he noticed the parking lot already full of cars, most of them pick-ups. On cue, he spied Prescott's car roll up and Morganna get out to join the line at the entrance. Then the car pulled away and left.

The Harley sputtered up to a slot big enough for the bike, and for the first time, the lights mounted in the parking lot gave Lunker a good look at the man as he got off the bike.

He did a double-take.

The Harley rider was huge. Close to seven feet tall, barrel-chested, and with tree-trunk sized arms and legs, he looked like a professional wrestler. A thick, black beard sprouted from his face to match unruly black hair falling past his neck. When he made his way to dance hall's entrance, he moved with a smooth grace and efficiency which belied his large size.

Lunker quickly connected with his men inside. "Our mystery man is coming in…and don't worry, you won't be able to miss him. Remember, he is *not* to interfere with our plans."

The enforcer clicked off, found a parking place, and got out of the car. He stood and took a deep breath. The fear and reluctance ebbed from him to be replaced with the cold reality of the action soon to take place.

It was too late to turn back now.

CFIFTY

LOCKSTONE WATCHED MORGANNA DISAPPEAR THROUGH A door and into a large, imposing building. A brightly lit sign with the words, *The County Line*, flashed on and off above the entrance, while music blared from inside the structure.

He'd been in ale halls large and small too numerous to count, but this one was far greater in size than any he had ever frequented. Rather than make his way after her, he studied the line of people who shuffled forward to wait their turn for admittance. Two large men flanked the entrance, and were checking IDs like the fake driver's license Eddie procured for him. Most of the men and women in the line wore a different style of hats and clothes. Eddie took pawns on similar items, especially the hats, so he was not unfamiliar with the style.

The witch hunter looked down at his attire. In no way did he fit in with the patrons of this ale hall…and his size alone would undoubtedly invite extra scrutiny by the gatekeepers at the door. He tapped his lip. He couldn't just wave his hand and make suitable clothes appear. Brow furrowed, he studied the slow-moving line again. The one thing almost everyone had in common were the hats they wore. A smile spread across his face.

Lockstone took off his bomber jacket and stuffed it into one of the Harley's saddle bags. With great reluctance, he removed the Glock from his waist and along with his knife, placed it with the jacket. He rummaged around until he found his other knife, one with a wicked five-inch blade. A gift from Eddie, the blade flicked out from the handle at the press of a button. The pawn-shop owner called it a "switchblade". He pushed it into his boot, straightened, and began to prowl the enormous parking lot for the other essential item he needed.

The huge lot stretched past the reach of the fixed lighting, and dark shadows covered a number of vehicles parked on the periphery. Lockstone started there first. As he walked by each iron wagon, he looked inside. Sure enough, on his third such search, a hat lay in the seat. He tried the door and discovered it locked. Undeterred, he continued his search until he found an unlocked truck with a rack mounted on the rear window. Several hats, along with a weapon—a long-barreled version of his Glock—hung from the rack.

The hats, each a different color of white, brown, and black, appeared scuffed and sweat-stained from hard use. After a moment's hesitation, the witch hunter chose the black one. He tried it on and decided while snug, it would do. With a last look around to make sure no one observed the theft, he stuffed his hair under the hat.

He turned and went to join the line.

Crick nursed a Jack and Coke while he waited for the witch. From the vantage point of his table, he could see everyone who entered the building. Ignoring the blaring music and gyrat-ing bodies, his eyes continually swept the room. They stopped when he spied a tall woman with a black cowboy hat walk in. *Morganna.* Her red dress, distinctive among the hundreds of men and women scattered throughout the honky-tonk, made her easy to spot. She moved with the ease of a lioness approaching a watering hole, and although the place was packed, the crowd parted without hesitation to let her pass.

Crick stood and waved. Morganna, stopped, and her dark eyes bored into him. He waved again, and motioned for her to join him. The witch made her way to his table, her eyes never leaving his face.

Crick pulled out a chair. "Have a seat."

After a moment's hesitation, the witch sat and crossed her legs.

The hospital CFO whistled at the sight of the long, pale legs exposed by her short skirt. "You clean up pretty good, Morganna."

The witch fixed him with a baleful stare. "You appear to have me at a disadvantage. You know my name, but I do not know yours."

Crick laughed. "Yes. I'm sure all this a big surprise to you. By the way, where is Karen Prescott?"

Morganna's eyes narrowed. "You seem to know much about me. I'm very interested in how. But, to answer your question, she left and waits for my call."

"Well, isn't that nice." Crick took a sip from his drink. "Not much use for a bewitched person in a place like this anyway, huh?"

Crick sat back. "But where are my manners? An occasion like this calls for drinks!"

He stood and caught the attention of a waitress. Dressed in a short fringed skirt, cowboy boots, and a tight black t-shirt with *The County Line* stitched in white sequins across the front, the waitress waited while Crick gave her his order.

"Another Jack and Coke for me and my lady friend here." Peeling off two twenty-dollar bills from a money clip, he gave it to the waitress. "Keep the change, sweetheart." Smiling she hurried off to the bar.

"Now, where were we? Oh yeah, my name." Crick extended his hand across the table. "Name's Crick, Mason Crick."

Morganna studied Crick's hand like a snake deciding which part of its prey to strike first. Finally, she slid her hand into his. With an iron grip, she pulled him forward. Her face close to his, the witch began a soft chant. The ward beneath Crick's shirt warmed against his skin.

"Wow. That's some handshake, Morganna." The hospital CFO pushed his face just inches from the witch, then batted his eyes in exaggerated fashion. "Oh, man, what's going on? I feel so funny, like I want to go to sleep or something." Slowly, his head slumped forward.

Suddenly, Crick's head snapped up, and he jerked his hand back. Laughing until his eyes began to water, he leaned back in his chair, and took a handkerchief from his pocket to wipe away the mirthful tears.

Shocked, Morganna stared at him.

Crick composed himself and stuffed the handkerchief back in his pocket. "So-sorry. I couldn't help myself. You should have seen the expression on your face."

"What? How—"

All humor gone, Crick's voice took on steel. "Because that shit doesn't work on me." His expression changed to cold determination. "I know about all your tricks, Morganna, which includes your attempt to bewitch me. So, in the interest of time, I'd advise you not to try any of that bullshit again."

Morganna sat back, stunned, her confidence shaken. *Why hadn't the bewitching worked?* For the first time it occurred to her she might have underestimated the man across from her, and this mistake left her in a precarious position. She would have to be very careful.

In a flat voice, she asked, "What do you want?"

"Atta girl!" Crick gushed. "*That's* the Morganna I wanted to see!"

The waitress appeared at their table, drinks balanced on a tray. Crick stood and took her drink and placed it beside her. Then he grabbed his own and sat in the chair next to Morganna.

"A toast!"

Wary, the witch picked up her drink. "What are we toasting?"

"Why, to you and me." With a *clink*, Crick pushed his glass against hers.

"We're going to do business together."

FIFTY-ONE

ORGANNA, DISPLAYED NO REACTION TO CRICK'S pronouncement. Although outwardly she appeared calm, inside, her nerves were raw and frayed. Not since a young witch, a novice under her own coven leader, had she been so unsure of herself.

The drink in her hand beckoned. She needed something to steady her nerves. Raising it to her lips, she took a swallow, then another, the alcohol burning a slow path to her belly. When she set the glass down, only ice cubes remained. Fortified somewhat, she turned to Crick.

"Explain yourself. What do you mean doing business together?" So many questions needed to be answered, yet she was forced to dance to this man's favor, to answer his questions, not hers. Her confidence began to return, and black anger swelled within her.

With a smack of his lips, Crick put his drink down. "Nothing like good alcohol to seal a deal." With a smirk at her empty glass, he added, "Looks like you could use another."

The glasses jumped and rattled as Morganna's fist struck the table.

"Enough! Answer me!"

Crick raised his hands in surrender. "Sure. No problem." He leaned forward. "You know, we really need to do something about your temper if we are going to work together."

"You fool!" Morganna hissed. "I have ways to kill you that in your worst nightmares you could never imagine."

Crick studied Morganna for a moment, then picked up each fallen glass and placed them upright. When he looked up, he locked eyes with Morganna.

One predator to another.

"Yes, I suppose you could, the operative word being 'could.' But you aren't going to do shit, Morganna. From here on out I'm calling the shots. So, here's how it's going to play out.

You will to take this fountain of youth potion of yours, and make as much as I want, anytime I want. In return, I'll split the profits with you, say seventy percent for me, thirty for you since I'll be taking all the risks. If you cooperate, you'll get rich. If not..." Crick shrugged, "Then I'm prepared to do it the hard way."

Murderous rage exploded inside Morganna. "You worm! How dare you threaten me! Only witches decide the use of the *morlaga* potion, not mortal filth such as you. You are cattle, good only for—for..." A sudden dizziness overtook her and she shook her head to clear it.

Crick placed a sympathetic hand on her arm. "Feel a little woozy? I guess some witches just can't hold their liquor."

Morganna shook off his hand, the effort causing the dizziness to worsen. Through gritted teeth, she spat, "Your death will be slow and agonizing. You cannot force me to do anything, puny man."

Crick slapped his leg. "You got spirit, Morganna, I'll give you that." He threw his arm around her shoulder and pulled the witch close.

"By now things must be a little muddled, and you're probably lightheaded. See, I slipped Rohypnol into your drink, commonly called a date rape drug. In just a few more minutes, I'll have to carry you out of here."

Morganna struggled to speak but found focused thoughts an almost impossible task. Spots began to swim before her eyes.

Crick shook the witch. "Whoa! Not yet." Lips next to her ear, he whispered, "How do you like *my* potion? And you know what? You're not the only witch I know."

Morganna's eyes rolled back in her head and she passed out.

As he suspected, the two men flanked on either side of the door stopped Lockstone and scrutinized him. Each wore snug, black t-shirts from which muscles bulged. Compared to the witch hunter in front of them, however, the bouncers appeared small and insignificant.

"May we see your ID, sir," the gatekeeper on Lockstone's left asked. Blonde, with long hair pulled back into a ponytail, his behavior indicated he was the leader of the two.

Lockstone's bearded face split into a grin. "Of course."

The witch hunter pulled his driver's license from his pocket and prayed it would pass inspection. The ponytailed gatekeeper inspected it and looked at his partner. He shrugged.

The bouncer handed Lockstone his ID back. "Have a good time, sir."

The witch hunter tipped his hat, placed the drivers license back in his pocket, and entered the building.

His senses came under immediate assault from a variety of sources. Music pulsed and twanged, the noise of moving, booted feet and dozens of conversations an eclectic mix that hummed with vibrant energy. Above this wafted the sharp smell of beer.

Moving through couples and throngs of people, Lockstone

spotted Morganna. She was seated, her back to him, with a man, and they appeared deep in conversation. He took an open stool at the bar, then ordered a beer and turned to watch Morganna.

Puzzled, he couldn't begin to guess what the purpose of this dalliance could be. Who was this man? What was the witch doing with him? He directed his attention to Morganna's companion. Middle-aged, fit and muscular, the dark-haired man carried himself with an air of someone who gave orders and expected them to be followed. Dressed in a colorful green shirt, boots, and a white hat, the attire looked ill-suited on him, and the witch hunter suspected it was an attempt to blend in with the patrons of the establishment.

Morganna slammed her fist on the table, which caused Lockstone to drop his beer on the bar and stand. Rather than recoil, the man at the table pressed forward even closer to her. *The idiot! She's going to bewitch him and choke him to death with his own tongue!*

Lockstone's muscles vibrated, ready to jump in before Morganna could claim another victim. His hand slid down to the switchblade in his boot...then stopped. Eyes wide, he watched Morganna totter and sway in her seat, the dark-haired man putting his arm around her for support.

Moments later, the coven leader's hat tumbled onto the table, her head slumped on her shoulders.

The witch hunter stiffened when he spotted Morganna's companion nod at someone in the crowd near the bar. A big man detached himself from the gaggle of drinkers, walked to the table, and together, they half-carried, half-dragged the witch out of the ale hall.

Lockstone tossed a bill on the bar and followed them.

FIFTY-TWO

"MY FRIEND'S HAD TOO MUCH TO DRINK...AGAIN." CRICK shook his head. "Girl just doesn't know when to stop."

The bouncers eyed the woman supported between the two men, grins on their faces at the all too common sight. "Do you need some help, sir?" one of them asked.

"Nah. I'm just going to take her home and let her sleep it off." He peeled some bills from his money clip, and slipped them into the bouncers' hands. "But thanks for asking." The grins grew wider and they wished him goodnight.

Hoisting the witch higher on his shoulder, Crick pivoted, and the two men made their way to his Lexus parked in a corner of the lot.

"Our guy's on the move," Lunker warned.

"Where is he?"

"Right on our heels."

Crick mulled this over, then said, "Wait until we get closer to my car and away from the rednecks at the door. Then have your men take him out."

Lunker nodded. "What do you want done with him?"

Crick's eyes narrowed. "Get rid of him—*permanently*."

Lockstone's long strides took him out the door, and he paused to see where the men took Morganna. After the tumultuous noise from inside the ale hall, the outside appeared calm and serene by comparison. He spotted them headed out into the large lot, the witch's booted feet dragged across the gravel, forming grooves. He pivoted and went after them.

So intent on closing the distance to catch up, he didn't realize he was being followed until something jammed into his ribs. Then, every nerve in his body exploded. His muscles and nerves strummed and fizzled in wild contortions of agony. Although partially paralyzed by the pain, the witch hunter managed to throw a club-like fist backwards. Connecting with a meaty *thud*, he heard a cry, and the paralysis subsided.

Dizzy, he turned to face his attackers. The lights of the parking lot revealed two stocky, muscular men, one black-haired and olive-skinned, and another with wheat-colored hair. The wheat-haired assailant dripped a steady stream of blood from his nose, murderous intent in his eyes. Both men brandished strange weapons with twin prongs, and the witch hunter realized they must be the source of the pain he experienced.

The dark-haired assailant darted in, and Lockstone moved to block the man's thrust with one arm while he hammered at him with his other fist. His movement, however, was slow and clumsy. His muscles refused to work with their normal efficiency. He managed to only partially block the thrust, and while his fist crashed into the side of the man's head, rather than a knockout blow, it only dazed his assailant.

Blinding pain burst again from his side, his other attacker using the distraction to move in. His muscles jerked and twitched.

A *buzz* and *sizzle* came from the weapon jammed in his ribs, and the big witch hunter fought to stay on his feet. The sting of the other weapon erupted from his side, and their energy joined. Agony beyond belief erupted within Lockstone's body, and he shook and undulated.

The witch hunter swayed, and then—like a felled tree— pitched forward, unconscious, onto the ground.

"Okay, Annalise, we'll be there within the hour. Key's under the mat. Let yourself in and have everything ready by the time I get there with Morganna."

Crick clicked off and watched Lunker finish belting Morganna securely onto the front seat. Her head lolled on her shoulders, hair pooled in a black waterfall about her face.

"Clean up here, Sam, and meet me at the house."

With a curt nod, Lunker shut the door and watched Crick drive off. Then he hurried to his men who stood beside the inert body of the Harley rider. He stopped and looked down.

"Damn! The guy's even bigger up close."

"Bastard broke my nose," Gilbert said. Blood still dripped from his face and he aimed a vicious kick at the witch hunter's side.

Lunker looked up to see Mendoza rub a golf ball-sized lump on the side of his head. "You too?"

Eyes creased in pain, Mendoza nodded. "Dude got in a lucky hit. Felt like I'd been kicked by a mule." He shook his head. "Sam, I've never seen anything like it. One Taser should have knocked him out. Instead, all it did was slow him down. It took *both* Tasers sending enough volts in him to cook a Christmas turkey before he finally passed out."

Lunker digested the information, and a chill traveled up his spine. He'd seen up close and personal the special talents wielded by Morganna. Now, a giant of a man with almost superhuman tolerance and strength lay at his feet. Somehow, the two must be connected.

Lunker knelt and went through the witch hunter's pockets. He pulled out a wad of cash and a driver's license, and squinted at it in the poor light.

"Robert Lockstone. Looks like he's got a Houston address."

The enforcer stuffed the license back in the pocket and tossed the cash to his men. "You guys look like you earned a bonus."

Lunker stood and noticed a few people in the line at the door looking in their direction.

"We're out of time. Get this big shithole out of here and make sure no one ever finds the body. Then come back and get rid of the bike."

His men nodded and each took an arm. With loud grunts, they dragged the witch hunter to a nearby black Escalade. Perspiration dripped from their faces as they opened the door and strained to pick up and place the limp body in the back seat. Forced to bend the big man's legs just to get him into the SUV, they finally managed to shut the door. The engine whined to life, the headlights flicked on, and the Escalade rolled out of the parking lot.

Lunker watched the SUV disappear. *One loose end taken care of. Now for the main event.*

Morganna.

CFIFTY-CHREE

A GRAY FOG SWIRLED AROUND LOCKSTONE, AND HE DRIFTED in and out of consciousness.

Fighting to claw his way back to the land of the living, he managed to crack open an eye. The sensation of motion came to him, and he forced the other eye open. Disoriented, he blinked and tried to bring his jumbled thoughts to some semblance of order. The memory of his struggle with the men at the ale hall returned. As the clarity of his mind sharpened, the memory of the strange weapons they wielded also returned.

It was unlike anything he ever experienced. Energy flowed uncontrolled in his body like the raging waters of a burst dam. Every muscle, nerve, and fiber of his body still ached with intense pain.

The witch hunter forced himself to ignore the pain and concentrate on his current predicament. He saw dim silhouettes seated in front of him, and he had no doubt he was now captive of the men who attacked him. Between what his eyes told him and the rumble of movement, he must be in one of the iron wagons. While the destination was unclear, the witch hunter retained no illusions of what waited for him at the end of it. These men were killers on their way to dispose of him.

Carefully, he tested his arms and legs. The last thing he wanted was to alert his captors he was conscious and awake. To his surprise, he discovered he wasn't bound. They must have assumed their strange weapons would leave him incapacitated for a longer period of time.

Teeth gritted to stifle a groan, to his dismay, Lockstone discovered his muscle control tenuous and still weak. He found it difficult to even lift his head, and couldn't overpower a baby in his condition, much less two large men. Unless he came up with something soon, certain death awaited him. The witch hunter racked his brain and tried to think of a way out of his predicament. However, nothing came to mind. Despair, then anger filled his mouth with a bitter bile. Death had been an ever present companion his entire career as a witch hunter. He did not fear it. But, to die, to have his life extinguished without even a struggle, filled him with impotent rage.

Determined to do *something*, Lockstone slowly positioned his body so he could at least get a good kick at whoever reached for him first. His hand brushed against the pouch tied at his belt. His sharp ears picked up the sound of a soft, metallic, *clink*. Puzzled, his eyes widened as he realized the source of the sound.

Argatha's amulet!

A thought floated through his mind, a memory from his childhood. Although possessed of an iron constitution, on those rare occasions he became sick or ill, his mother would hold him and chant a rejuvenation spell. It never failed to leave him refreshed and feeling better. Would it work on a grown man? With no other options, he reached into the pouch, pulled out the amulet, and began to whisper the words of the spell.

The locket warmed in his hand, and with it, strength and vitality flowed to his muscles and limbs. It worked! After a few more moments, he was ready to take on his captors. Although far from recovered, he knew he was now more than a match for the two men who attacked him.

A wolfish grin appeared on his face. A surprise awaited his captors when they opened the door.

A big surprise.

"This looks like a good spot."

Mendoza stopped the SUV and killed the engine. He grabbed a flashlight from the glove compartment and got out. The passenger door opened and slammed shut, and Gilbert joined him. Hands on hips, the two surveyed the moonlit landscape. An open pasture lay before them, thick woods on either side. The surrounding area was rural and sparsely populated—the last house more than a mile back down the blacktop road.

"How you want to do this?" Gilbert asked.

"Cap him twice in the head then bury him. We'll need to save the sod we dig up and place it back on top of the soil. With any luck, it'll rain soon, the grass will grow back, and no one will ever know a body's been buried here."

Gilbert groaned. "Do you know how big a hole we're going to have to dig? The guy's the size of Bigfoot! We need an excavator instead of shovels."

Mendoza's head still throbbed from the blow he received. He was in no mood to listen to his partner complain. "You heard Sam. He said make sure no one ever finds the body. Now stop griping and help me get the stuff we need out of the back."

Resigned, Gilbert joined Mendoza. Together, they pulled two shovels from the back of the SUV. Then they unrolled a length of thick, durable plastic, and spread it on the ground beside the Escalade. By this time, runnels of sweat dripped from both men in the warm, humid night.

Mendoza took off the Wrangler jacket, opened the front door of the SUV, and tossed it on the seat. He returned to the back of the vehicle and wiped the perspiration from his face with the back of his hand.

"Okay, now for the hard part. We have to get the big bastard out of the car and lay him on the tarp. When we double-tap him, let's be careful not to get any blood on the ground. Odds are one in a million, but we don't need anyone to stumble across the blood. Then, we'll dig the hole, wrap him up in the tarp, drop him in, and fill it. When we're finished, we'll smooth the dirt out, lay the sod back, and get the hell out of here."

Gilbert nodded, and the men opened the side door. "I'll grab his legs and pull him out," Mendoza said. "You get his shoulders, and we'll lift him up and drop him on the plastic."

He reached to grab the inert legs while Gilbert positioned himself beside the open door. Without warning, the witch hunter's legs hitched back and then shot forward like pistons. Both booted feet connected solidly with Mendoza's chest, and he catapulted backward through the air. Landing on his back, his head struck the ground hard. Dazed, he fought to draw a breath into his bruised lungs.

With catlike quickness, Lockstone jumped out of the SUV and on Gilbert. The enforcer tried for his gun, but his hand hadn't traveled halfway to the shoulder holster before the witch hunter's hand closed like a vise around his throat. He abandoned the effort and used both hands to try to loosen the iron chokehold.

Bug-eyed, Gilbert's feet left the ground. Desperate, he punched and kicked to no avail. High-pitched squeaks came from his mouth, the airway constricted to a pinpoint.

Through eyes blurred in pain, Mendoza saw his partner dangle from an arm the size of a tree limb. Then, with an effortless heave, Gilbert was flung through the air to land on top of him.

Blackness descended.

FIFTY-FOUR

THE GARAGE DOOR ROLLED UP, AND CRICK QUICKLY PULLED
in. Annalise stood ready by the door, and he nodded with
approval. So far, the plan was going off without a hitch. He hit
a button to shut the garage door, got out of the car, and motioned
for the witch. Together, they got Morganna out of her seat and into
the house.

A large, sturdy chair sat in the middle of the den. Made of walnut,
the heavy antique had an elevated back, arm rests, and thick legs.
They slid the coven leader into the wooden seat, and while Annalise
held her in position, Crick zip-tied her arms and legs to the chair.
After a moment's hesitation, he doubled up on each zip-tie. Then, he
threaded a wide nylon strap around her chest, ran it around to the
back of the chair, and cinched it tight. The strap forced her breasts
upward until they threatened to spill from her dress. However, it
held her upright even though her head lolled on her shoulders.

Crick wiped his hands on his pants. Curious, he looked at
Annalise to see her response at seeing Morganna for the first time.

Fear edged with anticipation lay in her eyes. "What do you

think?" he asked.

"She is…*powerful*. Even unconscious, I can feel the strength of her magic."

The witch turned to Crick. "How…how did you—"

Crick flipped his hand. "Don't worry about it. The ward worked like you said it would, and I took it from there. Now, what do we need to do to get Morganna bound to me?"

"I have all the ingredients except her blood. Once I have that, I can brew the binding potion."

Crick rubbed his hands in anticipation. "Then let's get started. The sooner she's bound, the sooner the money can start rolling in."

Crick noticed Annalise's eyes widen at the statement and chuckled. "What did you expect, Annalise? That this is some grand experiment? Its always been about the money, and Morganna's potions are going to make me wealthy beyond my wildest dreams. Can you imagine what people would pay to look younger or to change their appearance?"

Although the Romani witch nodded, the troubled look on her face remained. Crick's nostrils flared. "Don't tell me using Morganna goes against your witch sensibilities? Are you kidding? You took my money with both eyes open and you're hip-deep in this, so you better deliver!"

Annalise stammered, "Of co-course. I'm prepared to-to see this through."

She opened a leather bag and pulled out a small copper pot and stand. Dented and discolored from age and usage, a tiny pour spout protruded from one side. She placed the pot on the stand, and from the bag, took out several sealed vials. Chanting in Romanian, the witch unsealed each vial and poured a precise amount in the pot. A thin silver swizzle stick appeared in her hand and she stirred the contents.

Crick observed the process with keen interest. The vials'

contents each appeared a different color, green, red, and blue. Wisps of smoke rose from the copper pot even though there was no visible source of heat. An aroma filled the air, which smelled to Crick like an odd combination of cinnamon and cracked pepper.

Annalise reached again into the leather bag and removed a rubber tube and a hollow syringe. With practiced ease, she tied the tubing just above Morganna's elbow. The vein swelled, and inserting the needle, Annalise drew blood into the syringe. When it filled completely, she swabbed the injection site, placed a Band-Aid on it, and untied the tube. Returning the tubing to the bag, she removed an empty vial and injected the blood from the syringe into it.

Annalise faced the pot and took a deep breath. Chanting even louder now, she poured Morganna's blood into the potion.

The reaction was instantaneous.

The pot shook and heaved. A mushroom cloud of crimson smoke, the color of dried blood, billowed from the pot and spewed into the air. It coiled, twisted, and turned. Taking the silver implement from the pot, Annalise barked, "Come!"

The smoke immediately changed direction and flowed to the silver stick the witch held aloft like an orchestra baton. In Pied Piper-like fashion, the cloud followed the Romani witch while she walked to Morganna's limp form. Annalise stopped, and held the silver tip by her mouth and nose, the crimson fog pooling about her face. With each breath, the unconscious witch inhaled more and more of the vaporous cloud until none was left.

She turned to Crick. "I now need your blood."

Taken aback, his eyes narrowed. "You never mentioned that before. Why do you need it?" His gaze burned a smoldering hole in her, and the Romani witch quickly replied.

"To complete the spell! Morganna is ready for the binding, but it is worthless without the blood of the one she is to be bound to. Your blood anchors her will to yours, but we must hurry. The potion loses vitality with the passage of time."

Crick considered her explanation. Annalise could be bullshitting him, but he didn't think so. At this stage of the game, she had a lot to lose—like her life—and little to gain by any double-cross or deception.

He rolled up his sleeve.

Annalise took a fresh syringe, tied off his arm with the rubber tube, and watched his blood fill the syringe. When finished, she injected Crick's blood in another empty vial.

Annalise straightened and cast a glance at Crick. "Next comes the most difficult and important part of the binding spell. Everything must be perfect with no mistakes. Any flaw—any at all—and Morganna will find and exploit it with our deaths the certain outcome of such a disaster."

Crick wore a tight smile. "Then I suggest you do it right the first time." He thrust his chin at the unconscious witch. "Get on with it."

The Romani witch dipped the silver baton in Crick's blood. She touched Morganna's forehead with the tip, leaving a bloody smear. "*I bind you in mind,*" she intoned in a loud, clear voice.

Crick sucked in his breath when he saw the blood disappear into Morganna's skin.

Next, Annalise deposited blood on the coven leader's chest between her breasts. "*I bind you in heart.*" Once again, the blood was absorbed and disappeared.

Finally, the Romani witch dripped Crick's blood on Morganna's arms, legs, and dragging her dress above her hips, on her abdomen. "*I bind you in body.*"

The blood vanished, and a pent up gasp of relief rushed from Annalise's mouth. She staggered to a nearby chair and collapsed into it. Spent, she closed her eyes.

"It is done," she whispered.

"The binding is successful."

FIFTY-FIVE

EVEN THOUGH FATIGUED, ANNALISE ALLOWED HERSELF A small moment of triumph. She did it. *She successfully bound Morganna.* Crick needed only a list of basic compulsions along with a few last minute instructions—then her part in this was through. Once she had her money, she planned to leave at once.

And get as far away as possible.

The Romani witch stirred and looked at Crick. "Once Morganna regains consciousness, you must immediately give her commands which protect you and all associated with you. Do not allow her any time for mischief."

With a weary hand, Annalise pulled a sheet of paper from her valise and handed it to Crick. "I have prepared a list of several commands which should cover most situations. Just remember what I told you earlier. Unlike a bewitching, the binding leaves Morganna fully conscious and aware of everything you will ask or command her to do. If she can find a way to exploit any loophole, she will take it. So be specific in your requests and avoid any generalities."

Crick took the list and read it aloud:

"You will obey me in all things

You will never lie to me or deceive me

You will take no action that harms me or anyone associated with me."

Crick nodded. "Okay. This list seems pretty straight forward." The sound of a car pulling into the driveway interrupted the hospital CFO. He smiled. "That's Sam. Now we can move forward with the next stage of the plan—awaken Morganna and test the binding."

On cue, a knock came at the door, and Crick moved to open it. Sam walked in and spied Morganna secured to the chair. He looked at Crick, eyebrow raised.

"Its done, Sam. Morganna's been successfully bound. You take care of our mystery man?"

The big man shrugged. "I haven't heard from Mendoza yet, but yeah, we took care of it. When I left them, the guy was out cold and they took him for a ride."

The two men took no pains to conceal their conversation from being overheard by Annalise. They were discussing murder. She shivered. *Would she be the next person to 'take a ride'?*

The Romani witch cleared her throat. "I have completed the terms of our agreement. Am I free to go?"

Crick looked at Annalise, his face stretched in a rictus. Her chill deepened. "You did good, Annalise. You came through for me, and I *always* take care of those who give me loyal service."

The hospital CFO walked to the nearby kitchen table and retrieved a briefcase. He picked it up and returned to the chair Annalise sat in. He dragged a nearby chair next to her and sat in it with the briefcase balanced on his knees. The witch's heart raced. The last time she faced this same scenario, Crick pulled a gun on her.

Metallic *clicks* announced the opening of the briefcase. A drop of perspiration slid down Annalise's forehead. After a glance inside, he picked it up and placed it in Annalise's lap.

She pressed her hand to her stomach, and a pent up breath escaped her lips. Inside, lined in neat stacks, were bundles of one hundred dollar bills. "Th-thank you," she stammered. Her hand trembled as she shut the briefcase.

"A hundred thousand dollars as per our agreement." Crick pointed at the money. "Aren't you going to count it?"

"N-no. Th-That's not necessary."

She got up to go, and Crick caught her arm. "Hey, the funs just about to begin. Don't you want to see us bring Morganna around and complete the binding?"

"Oh, no. I'd rather not—"

"But I insist." Crick's grip tightened, and he pulled her back into the chair.

Her face turned ashen. "You don't understand. You don't need me to complete the binding."

"On the contrary. I understand perfectly."

He pointed at Morganna's unconscious form. "I know you're afraid of her. Good! I want you to be afraid. Just like I want to make sure you've done everything possible to make the binding a success. Only way to do that is for you to be here when she wakes up."

"But-but, she'll see me!" Annalise wailed.

"Oh, I'm counting on it. In for a penny, in for a pound, lady. If things go badly, the only question will be who kills you first, me or Morganna."

Crick's fingers dug deeper into her flesh, and she cried out. "So, I better not be disappointed."

Tears sprang into the witch's eyes. Crick released her, and she shrank into the chair. He gave her a last stony look. "So glad we cleared this up."

Crick turned away. "Ready Sam?"

The big enforcer walked up to the unconscious witch and

produced a Taser. With his other hand, he pulled the Beretta from his holster. He held both aimed at the witch in readiness.

Crick approached Morganna. He knelt before her and broke opened a packet of smelling salts. Waving it under her nose, she moaned and her head began to move.

"Come on, Morganna. Wakee, wakee." He patted her cheeks and held the smelling salts under her nose again. With a loud groan, Morganna raised her head, eyes going in and out of focus.

"Here, you go. A little shot of Epinephrine should do the trick." Crick produced a syringe and plunged the needle into her arm. Then he sat back and waited.

He didn't have long to wait. Morganna's head snapped up. She scanned the room, confusion on her face. Then her gaze fell on Crick.

"You!" she hissed.

"Yep. In the flesh."

The coven leader tried to rise and discovered she couldn't move her arms or legs. "Release me or I'll boil you alive in your own blood!"

Crick chuckled, then with a casual motion, backhanded Morganna. The meaty slap rocked her head backwards. "Really? You *still* think you can control the situation? I gave you a chance to partner with me, but you chose the hard way, so the hard way it will be. Sam?"

Annalise watched Lunker stuff a rag in her mouth and stifle the sounds of rage. The sight of the witch, eyes filled with insane hatred spearing the enforcer, gave her even more reason to be gone and as quickly as possible.

Crick pushed his chair next to Morganna. "Hey, see the nice lady over there?" and pointed at Annalise. "She helped prepare the binding spell which I am now going to complete. When I'm finished, you will be bound to me. I'm just full of surprises, huh?"

Morganna's molten gaze fell on Annalise. The Romani witch

huddled in the chair, her body quivering in terror. *Crick deliberately marked her.* Once identified, he knew she could never afford for the coven leader to be free again. The certain knowledge the coven leader would hunt her down guaranteed her continued cooperation.

A sudden realization dawned on her, and Annalise pointed a shaky finger at Morganna. "Complete the binding!" she cried. "There are spells Morganna doesn't need to speak. She can recite them in her mind!"

The grim satisfaction on Crick's face confirmed her worst fears. *Another fly trapped in his web.*

"Of course." With a smirk, he took the list and read it aloud to Morganna.

"You will obey me in all things
You will never lie to me or deceive me
You will take no action that harms me or anyone associated with me."

He tossed the list aside. "Its done."

Crick studied Morganna closely.

A subtle change came over her. The muffled screams of rage stopped. He leaned closer, and while her eyes still held white-hot hate, he saw something else, a look he was very familiar with.

Helpless resignation.

"Yes!" he cried in triumph. "You're mine now," he added in a low voice.

He stood up. "Bingo! Sam, cut her loose. Let's test the binding."

Lunker looked at Crick, his face twisted in apprehension. "You sure, boss? Shouldn't we at least keep her legs tied up?"

Irritated, Crick looked at Lunker. "Just do what I tell you, Sam. You keep her covered and I'll see if she is bound to me."

With great reluctance, the enforcer produced a knife, flicked the blade out, and cut the zip-ties. Then, jumping back, he held the Beretta with both hands, the barrel pointed at the witch's heart.

Morganna slowly rose from her seat and rubbed her wrists where the zip-ties cut into the flesh. The hatred on her face was visceral, and she took a step toward Crick.

"Dog! Spawn of pigs! I'll—"

"Shut up! And stand completely still."

Morganna's mouth closed with an audible *click* of her teeth. Motionless, she stood ramrod straight.

Crick walked around the witch and stopped when he was face-to-face with her. He ran his fingers down her cheek and across her neck and chest. He slid his hand under the top of her dress and traced a circle around her breast. The flesh was warm, and the nipple stiffened at his touch. He retrieved his hand and stepped back. Morganna's face was unreadable, but her eyes radiated seismic outrage and anger.

Crick chuckled. "Whoops! Guess you didn't like *that*. First lesson—When you please me, I'll reward you. When you don't..." his voice trailed off.

Without warning, he punched Morganna in the stomach. With a *whoosh*, the air left her lungs, and she fell to the floor. Strangled gasps came from her lips while she fought to recover her breath.

"On your knees!"

Without hesitation, the witch struggled to her knees. "Kiss my feet!" Bending, Morganna kissed each of Crick's feet.

"Stand! From now on you will refer to me at all times as, 'Master.'"

"Yes, Master," Morganna replied while she pushed herself upright.

Crick looked over at Lunker and grinned. "I could get used to this shit." He waved at Annalise. "Okay, you can go. But, remember, keep your mouth shut. I'll contact you if I need you."

Annalise grabbed the briefcase and scuttled out the door like a scalded cat. Lunker looked at his boss. "You need me anymore?"

"Nah. I've got it all under control." Lunker hastened to follow the Romani witch out of the house, eager to put distance between himself and Morganna.

Crick turned to Morganna and studied her. Then he stepped behind her and unzipped her dress. With a whispery *swish*, it slipped to the floor and she stood clad only in a black bra and panties. Crick whistled at the sight, and noted the puckered scar on her shoulder.

"You know, I bet you have skills other than spells and potions." He began to unbutton his shirt. "And I intend to have you show me in each and every way." Tossing the shirt on the chair, he grabbed her hand and led her to the back of the house.

"I imagine this will take some time…all night long."

CFIFTY-SIX

LOCKSTONE STOOD OVER THE PRONE FIGURES OF THE TWO enforcers, and considered what to do next. Their groans and gasps of pain shuttled to his ears, and he knew he needed to decide quickly before they could recover. The simplest solution was to kill them—no problem in his mind since his execution was what they carried him out here to do. But then an idea surfaced in his mind.

There might be a way he could use them.

Grabbing Argatha's amulet, he kneeled beside the men and chanted. The groans and moans stopped. The enforcers looked up at the witch hunter with warm, friendly eyes.

"Hey, man. Sorry about all this," the olive-skinned man said. "You want to go get a beer?"

"Yeah, we could get a case, come back here, and shoot the shit!" the other enforcer croaked through his bruised throat.

A fierce smile split Lockstone's face. The compulsion spell worked again! He helped both the men up. "What are your names?"

"Jose Mendoza, and this is Jock Gilbert," the dark-skinned man said pointing to his partner. Both men then proceeded to pump the witch hunter's hand.

Lockstone managed to extricate himself, and asked, "Okay, tell me what you know about the woman at the ale hall." He stepped back, chanted, then looked them both in the eye.

"I want to know everything."

The trip back to *The County Line* was far more comfortable the second time around. Instead of lying in pain with jumbled, muddled thoughts, Lockstone sat refreshed and upright in the backseat, while he considered what the two men told him.

The enforcers didn't know much and it soon became apparent they were hired for muscle not brains. They *did* know who hired them, a man named Sam Lunker, who reported to another man, Mason Crick. Crick was some kind of executive at a hospital in Longview, but despite repeated questioning, neither could remember the name of the hospital, nor what exactly Crick did there. However, they claimed Crick was a major figure in the illegal prescription drug trade. Lockstone's grasp of this—sketchy at best—forced him to have the men explain what "prescription drugs" were.

"People pop these drugs to go to happy, happy land, deal with stress, get high, you name it," Mendoza said. "Crick's got the market cornered around here on all the pill mills."

Upon hearing this, the picture cleared for Lockstone. Whether the potions and powders of Apothecaries or these "pills", the differences were scant. People desired them and would pay to acquire them.

By far, his biggest disappointment was their inability to tell him where Morganna had been taken and why. The men were underlings, small cogs in a much bigger web. In the Kingdom, such men were common, and often, expendable. There was no reason to share any more information than necessary to carry out the task. He shook his head, struck again by the similarity of humanity even on different worlds.

The Escalade rolled into *The County Line* parking lot. Even though well after midnight, the lot remained full of cars. The SUV stopped by Lockstone's Harley, and the witch hunter got out.

He went around to the driver's side, knocked on the window and waited while it powered down. "Remember, you killed and buried me," he told the two men. "No one is to know I'm still alive."

"Of course. Mums the word," Mendoza said, a finger to his lips. "Sure you don't want some more money?" When the big witch hunter discovered his cache of money missing, he questioned the two enforcers about it and they immediately returned it to him...along with all their extra cash. Although tempted, he refused to take their currency and gave it back.

"Now, if you find out where the woman in the red dress has been taken, you are to call me right away. But, make sure no one sees or hears you when you call." Lockstone didn't trust the enforcers to remember his number, and watched while they entered his cell's number on their phones.

Mendoza and Gilbert waved while they pulled away and onto the road. Lockstone watched the tail lights disappear into the gloom of the night, then walked to the bike, straddled it, and hit the kick-starter. The engine rumbled to life, and he sat for a moment while it idled.

His next stop was the city of Longview and to locate Crick's hospital. He would find a nearby inn, watch the hospital, and see if he could spot Crick. With any luck, he would be able to follow the man and be led straight to Morganna.

For the first time, the witch hunter regretted his choice for travel. He loved the Harley, but it made it almost impossible for him to remain unobtrusive while he followed another vehicle. The iron wagons were far better at the anonymity needed to keep suspicions from being raised. Maybe the compulsion he placed on the two men sent to kill him would bear fruit.

With a sigh, he engaged the motor, and the bike sputtered off into the dark night.

FIFTY-SEVEN

MORGANNA LAY NAKED, SHEETS TANGLED ABOUT HER LEGS. A hiss of water came from the shower, her Master's cheery whistling an assault on her ears.

Her breasts were sore and chafed, and the muscles in her groin ached from the previous night's vigorous and prolonged activity. But the pain and soreness couldn't match her dark despair.

She was trapped in a cage of her own making.

Arrogance and overconfidence cost her her freedom. Like a fool, she never considered the possibility there might be other witches on this world. She walked right into a binding, and despite her every effort, remained powerless to resist her Master's commands.

She could see no way out.

The Master's cruelty and cunning—more than a match for hers—meant she could never hope he would make a move or give a command which could weaken or dissolve the binding. Her bleak future—to be used over and over at his pleasure—would play out again and again, just like the previous night.

In an abstract way, she held a certain level of respect for her

Master. If circumstances were different and she not bound, his vicious and coldblooded ruthlessness might have made him an equal—a circle populated by precious few. Now, however, all she wanted to do was kill him.

In the cruelest and most painful way possible.

During the night, her Master gave her little time for a respite, but on those few occasions, she used the lull to fashion and turn over in her mind the artful ways she would kill him. Dismemberment, selective organ removal, eyes plucked one-by-one, she fantasized about them all, with the one constant the torture and death would be slow—designed to last for days, perhaps even weeks. These pleasant thoughts were all she had left. It was the only thing which could make her forget the present situation.

The hiss of water stopped, and Crick emerged from the bathroom with a towel around his waist. He rubbed his damp hair with another towel while he leered at Morganna's naked form with frank admiration.

"Damn! You look even better in the morning than you did last night."

He padded to the bed and sat beside her. "I gotta tell you, if I've ever had a better piece of ass, I don't know when it was."

The coven leader remained silent, but her eyes betrayed her true thoughts. Crick laughed. "Yeah, yeah, I know. You want to kill me, scratch out my eyes, boil me in oil, etc., etc. I bet you've already got a list started on how you'll do it."

All humor left his face, and he leaned forward. "But we both know that's never going to happen. So, if it makes you feel better, make your lists, plot all you want, because I'll always be one step ahead of you. Just do what I tell you to do, when I tell you, and be damned sure I'm happy with the results. Remember the demonstration I gave you when I'm disappointed."

Morganna lowered her eyes. *Could he could read her thoughts as well*? Her despair deepened, and for the first time, her iron will waivered.

"The problem you have, Morganna, is we are like twins separated at birth. *I'm just like you, and you can't fool me.* I may not cast spells, make potions or bewitch people, but I know what I want, and I'm not afraid to do what it takes to get it."

Crick pushed himself off the bed. "What I want *now* is the potion which can make someone younger. Can you produce it for me?"

Morganna nodded. "Yes, Master."

"What do you need?"

Morganna considered. "I need everything I brought into this world. All of my implements, potions, and powders."

"Done!"

"Then I must have donors, the younger and more vigorous the better."

Crick studied the witch. "Why? What are you going to do with them?"

A bloodless smile appeared on Morganna's lips. "Drain them of their life essence. It is the essential ingredient in the *morlaga* potion."

Intrigued, Crick asked, "What happens to these 'donors'?"

The witch shrugged. "They are left aged, shriveled husks on death's door."

Crick's mind went into overdrive. The potential pool of "donors" was endless. The homeless, illegal immigrants, drug addicts, even the pipeline human traffickers provided could all be potential sources. And the best part? *No one would miss these forgotten segments of the population*! What's more, the uber-wealthy would pay and pay big for the *morlaga* potion. What was a return to youth worth? A million dollars per dose? Two million? There was so little risk and so much potential for profit, he could scarce constrain himself.

Crick's spectacular rise to gain control of the pill mills resulted from a violent campaign. The scattered bodies of his rivals moldered in shallow graves, food for fish at the bottom of lakes, or rotted in landfills covered by mountains of garbage. His solution to his human problems was as simple as it was ruthless. If someone crossed him, they disappeared. Now, however, he had a better idea, and one far more efficient.

Anyone who caused him problems would become a donor.

The artfulness was so damn slick, Crick even impressed himself. Not only did his problem go away, it earned him a king's ransom. He gestured at Morganna. "Get cleaned up and dressed. We've got work to do."

Morganna stood and went to the bathroom. A few minutes later, the sound of the shower echoed in the bedroom, and Crick grabbed his cell from the bedside table. He punched a number and a few moments later, Lunker answered.

"Sam? You know the issue we've got with Carol Webster and whether she could keep her mouth shut? Well, I've got the perfect solution. I need you to bring me all of Morganna's stuff and then pick up Webster and bring her to the old warehouse. Make up whatever excuse you want, just get her there and make sure no one knows where she is going or why."

Crick tossed the cell on the bed, a cruel smile on his lips. Carol didn't know it yet, but she was about to be transformed from loose cannon to a valuable commodity.

One worth a million dollars.

FIFTY-EIGHT

"**W**HEW! I FEEL LIKE A PACK MULE."

Lucas collapsed on a bench in front of Dillard's. Bags full of clothes, shoes, and other items hung from his arms like ornaments on a Christmas tree. Throngs of shoppers swept by the bench in the crowded mall while he unthreaded the bags from his arms and stacked them beside him.

Tressalayne sat next to Lucas and patted him on the arm. "Poor thing. You want me to send everything to the car?" She raised her hands and started to mouth a spell.

Lucas' eyes widened in horror. "No!" he cried. Some of the packages tottered, then cascaded to the tiled floor, knocked there as he reached in haste to grab Tressalayne's arm. "You can't practice magic in front of all these people! Remember, we talked about this. No one will understand and it could get you in trouble."

Lucas saw Tresslayne smile, and then giggle. Unable to help himself, he chuckled. "Okay, you played me." He extricated himself from the jumble of bags pooled around his feet and stood.

"However, I'm going to get the last laugh. You can clean up this mess while I go get us a couple of soft drinks." He leaned over, kissed her on the head, then pivoted and headed for the food court.

Lucas' back disappeared into the crowd. A happy sigh escaped Tressalayne's lips. She loved him so much she sometimes fought the urge to pinch herself just to make sure it wasn't a dream. She looked at her hand and studied her engagement ring. Even slight movements caused the faceted diamonds to refract light in an array of luminous glitter, the sight a reminder of what the ring represented—marriage with a life and future shared with Lucas. Just the anticipation transformed her heart into a bottomless well of joy and happiness. If she *was* dreaming, she hoped she never awoke.

"Excuse me?"

Startled, Tressalayne looked up to see a statuesque woman standing beside her. Honey-brown hair fell in a glossy wave to the small of her back. Tanned legs extended from a short, white skirt, and a soft blue blouse hugged the woman's small waist, the effect accentuating her full bosom. Expensive jewelry flashed from manicured fingers, while a Saint Laurent leather bag with a Neiman Marcus gold tag hung from the crook of her arm. A face with narrow cheekbones and haughty blue eyes peered at her.

"You must be the pretty young thing Lucas is currently infatuated with." Her mouth twisted when she addressed Tressalayne as if the act left a sour taste in her mouth. "Oh! Where are my manners. I'm Mandi Starkey."

Tressalayne took an immediate dislike to the woman, but forced herself to answer. "I'm Tressalayne."

"Just Tressalayne? No last name like famous soccer players? Oh, how rich. I bet Lucas just ate that up! He's always on the lookout for lost kittens like you."

Anger crept up Tressalayne's neck. "I haven't the slightest idea what you're talking about."

"Why, of course you don't. I heard all about your act at the hospital. Amnesia? Really?" A sarcastic chuckle bubbled from Mandi's lips, and she clapped her hands. "Bravo! How classic. Lucas is so gullible, he couldn't resist your little old helpless self."

Tressalayne's eyes narrowed, and her cheeks grew warm. The woman took a step back and studied her. With a sniff, she said, "Yes, you have the look. Pretty, vulnerable…and *stupid*."

Tressalayne's hands clenched into fists, her knuckles white. "I don't know who you think you are, but I would like you to leave," she snapped.

Mandi dismissed the comment with a wave of her hand. "Well, sweetie, let me clear that up for you. I'm the *last* lost kitten Lucas was with—before you that is.

Her lip twitched. "Lucas is the *only* man to ever leave me— men and commitment, like oil and water you know—but I never understood why. And now I look at you and wonder, *he left me for this*?"

Tressalayne shot up, the rest of the bags and packages tumbling to the floor. "Leave…while you still can," she snarled through clenched teeth.

Mandi laughed. "Oh, my. Is that a threat? Do I need to call the police?" She laughed again. "I think I'll stay right here and wait for Lucas so we can revisit *all* our old times together. What do you think of that?"

Tressalayne's eyes flashed, and the gem in her amulet rippled and turned dark. A growl escaped her lips, and with a jolt, black rage filled her. She pivoted her wrist, and the Saint Laurent bag on Starkey's arm ripped itself free. The purse burst upward, then swooped down to loop over her head. The straps settled around Starkey's neck, and the bag turned and twisted like a pretzel. The leather dug into her flesh, and within moments, she was being garroted by her own bag. With choked gasps, her hands scrabbled at her throat.

Her other arm drew back and Tressalayne swept it in a wide arc. Starkey's body jerked up and flew through the air to slam into a kiosk selling cell phone covers. The kiosk collapsed, the covers skittering in every direction. Not done, Tressalayne swept her hand again, and Starkey cannoned backwards across the floor. Shoppers fell like bowling pins, knocked aside in the densely packed corridor before she fetched up against yet another kiosk, her momentum finally stopped. Panicked screams, shouts, and wails from children filled the air. In the pandemonium, a crowd formed around the woman's motionless form.

Tressalayne's eyes fluttered. She looked around, confused. Then the memory of the woman came to her and she gasped. She looked at her hands still clenched into tight balls, and she forced herself to breathe and relax. When she looked over at the commotion, her cheeks burned. She took a step backward and collapsed onto the bench.

With face buried in her hands, she thought, *what have I done*?

She sat up when she saw Lucas approach, cups with straws in either hand. Neck craned, he walked while looking at the growing knot of people assembled down the mall corridor.

Tressalayne's heart pounded in her chest. *What will he think? What do I do now*? She snapped her fingers, and the scattered boxes, bags and packages, shot up and stacked themselves in neat order on the bench.

Lucas, his attention still on the knot of people, stopped beside Tressalayne and handed her one of the drinks. "What's going on?"

"I-I…" her voice trailed off. She couldn't lie to him, and at the same time, couldn't bring herself to tell him the truth.

Lucas sat his cup beside her. "I'm going to see if they need any help."

"No!"

Surprised, Lucas looked back at Tressalayne. His mouth fell open at the sight of the tears which dripped from her face. Concerned, he wrapped an arm around her shoulders. "What's wrong?"

"I-I don't feel well." The faint sound of sirens came to their ears, and several mall security personnel rushed by. The circle of onlookers parted to let the officers pass.

Lucas, torn, said, "Someone might be hurt. Can you wait here long enough for me to see if they need a doctor?"

"Lucas, *please*! I just want to go home."

The tears turned into a waterfall, and Tressalayne's face blanched white.

Worried, Lucas placed his hand on her forehead, then checked her pulse. "You don't have a fever, but your heart is racing. Let's go." Lucas picked up all the purchases and balanced them on one arm while he curled his other arm around Tressalayne's waist. She rose, unsteady, and clung to him with the desperation of a drowning victim.

Together, they walked to an exit and narrowly avoided the EMT personnel who burst through the doors and raced by with a gurney.

FIFTY-NINE

RESSALAYNE SAT ON THE FARMHOUSE PORCH, THE BOOK OF First Magic balanced on her knees. The sun colored her cheeks as it traveled on its downward descent through a cloudless sky of pastel blue. Although warm, a slight breeze ruffled the sleeves of her cotton blouse and kept the temperature comfortable. Birds chirped and whistled in the trees, a pleasant accompaniment to the peaceful and serene outdoors.

Except Tressalayne's mind was neither at peace nor serene.

The horrific images of what she did to Mandi Starkey kept replaying in her mind; the bag, its leather straps cutting into her neck with each twist and turn, then like a child's doll, jerked off her feet and hurled about as if by some giant unseen hand.

Tressalayne's feared Mandi Starkey could be badly injured or even dead. The hidden malignancy within her erupted with such sudden viciousness, she acted before she could stop it. The woman's arrogance and insults, while they angered her, did not push her over the edge. It's when she continued to talk about Lucas a jealous rage bloomed inside her, one which would not be restrained, and cracked the door for the evil witch hidden in the recesses of her soul.

The attack on Starkey confirmed her worst fears—this witch was alive and well.

Once they arrived at home, she finally found the courage to tell Lucas the truth. This confession—the hardest thing she had ever done—left her wrung out. She didn't know if she could stand to see his look of disappointment, or worse, read judgment on his handsome face. Her heart would surely break in two. Instead, he hugged her and never said a word. It was like he knew she already found herself guilty in the court of her own mind, and needed support, not condemnation.

He left shortly after to go check on Mandi and promised he would be back as soon as possible. Now, well over two hours later, he still hadn't returned. She occupied the time by using The Book of First Magic to practice, not because of her dedication, but because interaction with the Little People always left her with a warm contentment. Even this, however, couldn't improve her morose disposition. The Little People, sensing her mood, tried to lift her spirits. The elves performed acrobatic moves of gravity-defying feats, while the fairies did midair loop-de-loops. They eventually stopped when it became apparent their efforts were fruitless.

Tressalayne heard a car down the road. She leaped up and leaned over the rail. Lucas' Jeep kicked up a cloud of dust as it approached, and he pulled into the circle drive. Apprehension gripped her over the news he brought.

Is Mandy Starkey severely injured? Is she dead? Are the police coming to arrest me?

Hands clasped to her mouth, she watched Lucas exit the Jeep, a weary look on his face. He mounted the steps turned, and collapsed into one of the rocking chairs. He patted the arm of the rocker next to him.

"Have a seat. We need to talk."

Tressalayne swallowed. "Oh, no."

"Now, don't jump to any conclusions. Just sit down and let me explain how things are," Lucas interjected. Body rigid, Tressalayne slid into the rocking chair.

"First, Mandi is going to be okay. She has a bruised trachea and lacerations on parts of her body, but nothing serious. The hospital is going to hold her overnight for observation, and then release her tomorrow."

Tressalayne closed her eyes and released a deep sigh of relief. Although she still carried an enormous sense of guilt, a vast weight lifted off her shoulders. *She hadn't killed anyone.* She could breathe again. "What—what happens now?"

"The best I can tell, nothing. I doubt Mandi is going to press charges, and even if she did, it wouldn't stick. I drove back to the mall and managed to see the head of security. The guy was a fount of information. He told me the witness statements all said the same thing; an out-of-control woman on a rampage. If anything, the mall might press charges on her for the damage she caused. Of course, he checked the security cameras, but some of the cameras were offline for maintenance. The footage of those left showed Mandi crashing into people, which supports what the witnesses said."

Tressalayne accepted the account with a deep sigh. Then a thought struck her, and she sat up. "*Why* isn't Mandi going to tell the police I did this?"

Lucas sighed. "That is a long and sad story. First let me explain my relationship with Mandi Starkey. Before my practice grew and I no longer had the time, I volunteered one day a week at a rehab facility, which in addition, runs a halfway house. Two years ago, I met Mandi, herself a recovered opioid addict, at the halfway house where she also volunteered. Her family is wealthy and established a foundation to support the halfway house, probably in gratitude for her success going through the program.

We started dating, and things got too intense way too fast. We parted ways, and the break-up went badly. Mandi would show up at my office demanding to see me and scaring my patients and staff. She would call at all hours of the night, sometimes going so far I would find her waiting for me when I arrived at home. Once I woke up in the middle of the night and found her lying in bed beside me. Although I took back my key, she must have made a copy, and I was forced to change all the locks. I finally had a restraining order issued and never saw her again…well, until—"

"Today," Tressalayne finished for him.

Lucas glanced at Tressalayne. "Yes. Until today. So, when I arrived at the hospital, she was sedated, but one of the nurses let me look at her chart. Blood tests are often performed on emergency room patients, and when I checked her toxicology report, it indicated morphine in her system."

Lucas shook his head. "She's back on oxys. And that's why she won't press charges. Her family doesn't like their dirty laundry waved around for everyone to see, and once its known she is under the influence, it will be assumed her 'crazy' behavior was drug-induced."

He rubbed his face. "They'll pay off the damages and hope the whole incident goes away."

Tears sprang into Tressalayne's eyes. "I'm sorry, Lucas. She started talking about you. I-I got so jealous…" her voice trailed off, her throat tight with emotion.

"I can't imagine what you must think of me now," she whispered.

Lucas motioned. "Come here."

Tressalayne rose from her seat and stepped over to Lucas. He pulled her into his lap. She rested her head on his broad chest while he caressed her hair, each stroke releasing more of her anxiety. She inhaled his familiar masculinity, the strong beat of his heart audible through the thin fabric of his shirt. For the first time since the altercation with Mandi Starkey, she was at safe harbor.

Lucas traced her chin with his thumb. "I don't want you to ever believe I think less of you because you make a mistake. All it means is you're human, just like me, and I make mistakes all the time."

He put both arms around her and held her tight. "Just promise me if something happens again to upset you, you'll talk to me—immediately—before things get out of hand."

Tressalayne nodded. "I will." She thought how easily the reply rolled off her tongue.

And wondered if she spoke truth or lie.

SIXTY

CRICK PRESSED THE REMOTE AND THE STEEL GATE ROLLED back.

He passed the gate and drove across cracked and fragmented asphalt to a large, abandoned warehouse. Streaks of rust decorated its corrugated siding, while broken and splintered wooden pallets lay in untidy heaps near the base of the building. An eight-foot cyclone fence ran the entire perimeter, rusty barbwire strung across the top. Grass and small shrubs grew in scattered clumps, their hardy roots finding purchase in the broken pavement. The entire area exuded an aura of disuse and abandonment, the only evidence of recent activity the electronic gate and the shiny new padlock on the warehouse door.

Crick dodged the largest potholes, now water-filled puddles from the last rain, and pulled up to the warehouse. He exited the Lexus, stood, and surveyed the entire area. With hawk-like intensity, his sharp eyes searched for anything amiss. He purchased the mothballed building in the old industrial park precisely because of the many abandoned structures. Except for the occasional teenagers looking for a place to hang out while they drank or smoked, the place was deserted.

Satisfied they weren't being observed, he barked, "Coast is clear. Let's go."

Morganna got out of the passenger side and waited for further instructions. Crick motioned and she followed him to the locked door. He fumbled with a set of keys, selected one, and unlocked the padlock. He pushed the door open and walked in, Morganna close on his heels.

The dim interior revealed a large open area. The musty smell of old oil, solvents, and oxidized metal permeated the air. Crick flipped a switch on the wall and a bank of old mercury vapor lights mounted high on the ceiling flickered to life. The cold light displayed stacks of crates and packing material pushed to the back of the structure, while a small office with dusty windows was shoehorned into one corner. Unpainted angle iron and rust-spotted tubular struts rose from the concrete floor, and formed the welded metal skeleton supporting the entire facility.

A single table surrounded by six chairs stood like a desert island in the middle of the empty floor. Made of durable metal and painted an industrial gray, the mothballed furniture represented the few items left within the shuttered facility. Crick made for the table and grabbed a chair. He motioned for Morganna to do the same.

Once they were seated he said, "Sam's going to bring a donor for you to use to make the *morlaga* potion. He also went back to the lake house and got all your stuff. You need anything else?"

Morganna shook her head, then fixed coal-black eyes on him. "You realize the donor will be left near death, their life essence drained away."

Crick shrugged. "Yeah, you told me. That a problem for you?"

A cruel laugh erupted from Morganna. "Hardly. One mortal life is as meaningless to me as another."

Crick cocked his head. "Then why did you ask?"

"To make sure you understand it will take the deaths of many donors to produce even a fraction of the potion you desire."

It was Crick's turn to laugh. "The donors I bring you won't be missed. I got a plan for that too."

A squeal came from the door, and bright sunlight flooded in. Carol Webster stood at the door blinking. A large hand pushed her inside, and Lunker followed after her. She spotted Crick and made a beeline for him. Fuming, with arms crossed, she stopped beside him.

"Why am I meeting you in this godforsaken place? I don't believe the bullshit your goon told me! If this is about the oxys, don't think you can bring me here and bully me for more money!"

Crick looked up, a smile of anticipation on his face. "Carol, I wouldn't dream of it. In fact, I'm going to consider your account paid in full."

Somewhat mollified, she asked, "Okay, then why am I here?"

Crick stood. "Good question, but first, I'd like you to meet a friend of mine. Carol, this is Morganna."

Carol turned, eyes narrowed in suspicion at the woman seated beside the table. After an initial hesitation, she extended her hand. "Good to—"

Morganna's hand gripped hers and pulled her forward, their faces inches apart. Pain registered on Carol's face from the powerful grip. "Ow! What are you doing? Let go of...my... my..." Her voice began to falter, her eyes losing focus in response to Morganna's fierce stare and soft chant. Within moments she stood immobile, and the coven leader released her.

"She is bewitched."

Crick rubbed his hands. "Let's get on with it."

"Yes, Master." She turned to Lunker and he handed over a satchel. She rummaged through the bag and placed the items she needed on the table.

She looked around and chose a suitable spot some distance from the table. A soft mutter came from her while she used the red wax stylus to draw a precise rectangle on the hard, concrete floor. Next, she picked up and moved a chair to each of the four cardinal directions. Then she placed a black candle in the middle of each seat.

Morganna stepped back and studied her work. Satisfied, she turned to Crick. "I need clean water and cloth."

Crick grunted and nodded at Lunker. The big man went to the old office and returned a few minutes later with a scuffed plastic bucket and a handful of paper towels. The bucket, partially filled with water, sloshed when the enforcer put it down.

Morganna eyed the dusty bucket with distaste. Lunker shrugged. "Best I can do on short notice out here in Sticksville."

The witch picked up the bucket and paper towels, then spun on her heel without a reply. "Come!" she commanded and Webster lurched after her.

The coven leader undressed Webster and tossed her purse and clothes into a pile. Naked, she stood like an army private at attention while the witch washed every inch of her body. After more careful scrutiny, Morganna moved away and lit each of the candles.

"Step into the square!"

Without hesitation, Carol Webster marched to the outline on the floor, stepped inside, and turned to face the witch. Morganna grabbed the chalice and moved near Webster, taking care to stand outside the wax outline. Then she began to chant. The harsh, guttural sounds echoed within the empty confines of the warehouse.

Crick and Lunker watched while a vaporous, amber cord rose from within the chalice, then spread into protoplasmic projections which undulated and moved. The vapor sank to the ground, and drawn to the square, crawled along the hard floor. Reaching the wax boundary, the gelatinous cloud paused before it crossed over and onto Webster's feet. Tendrils of the amber fog climbed up her legs and across her torso before they met at her face. Now a single cable again, the tip reared back.

Morganna barked a final harsh command. The vaporous head struck and disappeared into Carol Webster's mouth and down her throat, the invasion spreading to every organ, tissue, and cell. Eyes rolled back into her head, her body shook in silent convulsions. Within moments, the ghostly rope began to retract, its color now a reddish-pink. Low, choked moans came from Webster's throat, her agony apparent in the faint sound. The cloud continued to retreat, crossed back over the wax boundary, and returned to the chalice where it disappeared.

Crick and Lunker followed the entire process with rapt attention. Their eyes tracked the protoplasmic fog and watched it vanish back into the arcane vessel. When they looked back at Carol Webster, they started. An old crone with greasy white hair, rheumy eyes, and liver-spotted skin occupied the square. Bent, she could barely stand.

Lunker took a step back. Minutes before, a vivacious, middle-aged woman stood before him. Now an ancient creature he hardly recognized swayed, ready to collapse, in her place. Bile rose in his throat.

Crick's reaction took a different path. He clapped. "Holy shit! I don't think Carol will be available to attend anymore Chamber functions…not unless they're held in a geriatric center. When's the potion going to be ready?"

Morganna sniffed the chalice. "It must steep, but will be ready to transfer to a flask soon."

"Ha! Good girl, Morganna. When can we make more?"

Morganna sat in one of the remaining chairs. She raised a weary hand and rubbed her eyes.

"I must have some time to recover. The magic used to make the *morlaga* potion is potent. It drains me. Perhaps with some rest I can try again later today."

Crick's fist slammed onto the table. "Bullshit! You're lying to me!"

Morganna scowled. "I am incapable of lying to you, Master." She stabbed a finger at him. "The *truth* is I'm tired. You kept me up most of the night rutting. With a full night's sleep, I would have more stamina."

She added, "If I had my coven, I could produce the potion much faster."

Crick held his anger in check and realized she was right. The binding forced Morganna to tell the truth...which also meant the production of the fountain-of-youth elixir was doomed to continue at a snail's pace. The last part of her statement, however, intrigued him.

"What is a coven?"

Morganna stood and once again, picked up the chalice and drew the aroma of the potion into her lungs. The pungent scent caused her senses to instantly sharpen. "It is almost ready."

She turned to face Crick. "A coven is composed of three witches, an elder, experienced witch or coven leader, and two younger, junior witches. The coven is joined by shared magic. Thus united, the magic they wield is strong and vigorous. Apart, each witch's Talent is weaker with less stamina."

Crick considered. "It sounds like we need more help. What if I could scrounge up more witches so you could form another coven? How about Annalise?"

Morganna chopped her hand. "No! She lacks even minimal skills. With years of tutelage, she might someday be of use, but even then, apprentices are chosen from young girls. Youth is necessary for the malleability needed to absorb and learn. The witch you mention is old, her mind brittle, a waste of time."

Enough skill to bind you, Crick thought. No fool, he knew what Morganna *really* wanted. "What about Tressalayne?"

The coven leader's eyes flashed. "Yes! She is part of my coven. I trained her! Together, we could double, nay, triple, the amount of potion produced! Can you bring her to me?"

Crick chuckled. *Jackpot.*

"I suppose I could arrange it. However, there is one small problem."

Puzzled, Morganna asked, "A problem? What problem?"

"She lost her memory. She doesn't know you from a hole in the ground. Right now she's playing house with the good doctor, Lucas Beckett. I hear nuptials are in the air, a marriage made in heaven and all that. Under those circumstances, what possible use could she be to you?"

Morganna stared at Crick. *Tressalayne lost her memory? Betrothed?* Anger boiled inside her. *No, its not acceptable. Tressalayne was her apprentice, not marriage fodder for some filthy mortal!*

Whether the adrenaline surge caused by her rage or the inhalation of the *morlaga* potion, Morganna's mind focused to a sharp edge, and an idea filtered into her brain….the solution to her problem and Tressalayne's!

She fought to keep a smile of triumph off her face. "Master, I believe I can restore my apprentice's memory and reinstate her to my coven."

Crick's face split into a broad grin. The trickle of millions grew into a roaring river. "Tell me what you need."

Morganna didn't hesitate. "Tressalayne.

All I need is Tressalayne."

SIXTY-ONE

LUCAS RUBBED HIS EYES.

It had been a long day and all of his staff had already gone home. He typed a few more patient notes on his laptop, closed it, then stood and stretched. He grabbed his keys, and exiting the clinic, headed for his car.

The sun appeared low in the horizon, grey-black clouds filtering the fiery light. A low rumble of distant thunder roiled the air. Lucas' Jeep, the lone vehicle left in the parking lot, stood sentinel. He reached the Jeep, unlocked the door, and opened it. A blast of hot, stuffy air struck his face, and he left the door open to let the car's interior cool off.

Suddenly, he felt cold metal press into his back. "Don't move, don't look around, Doc, or you're going to lose a kidney," a rough, male voice whispered in his ear.

His assailant jammed a black bag over his head, then jerked his arms back and zip-tied them. Blind, he was frog-marched to the passenger side of the Jeep. Hands patted him down, removed his keys and cell phone, then shoved him into the car seat. The door slammed and the SUV growled to life.

"Look, you don't need to do this. If you need money, I can—"

"Shut up, Doc. If you know what's good for you, you won't say another word." The voice sounded vaguely familiar and Lucas racked his brain to place it.

The SUV pulled out and rolled out onto the highway.

Tressalayne closed The Book of First Magic and took a sip of ice tea. Today she practiced on temperature—to heat and cool. She placed the glass of iced tea on the kitchen counter, stepped back, and raised the wooden sauce spoon she used for a wand.

In a pleasant, sing-song voice, she chanted and pointed at the tea. Condensation beaded the cold glass, but moments later, steam began to rise from the top, the ice cubes melting. Pleased, Tressalayne paused, pointed the spoon again, and chanted anew. The steam disappeared, and the sides of the glass frosted over.

"Yes!" she cried, arms raised in triumph.

The trill of the cell phone Lucas gave her interrupted the celebration. He often called her when he worked late, and she snatched up the phone, eager to share with him her latest success.

"Lucas, I—"

"This isn't Doctor Beckett," an unfamiliar voice interjected. "If you want to see him alive again and unharmed, you'll listen and do exactly what I say."

Stunned, Tressalayne looked at the phone. *Is this a joke?*

"Hello? Did you hear what I said?" the voice demanded.

Her heart rose to her throat. "Ye-yes. Please don't hurt Lucas. I'll do whatever you want."

"Good, girl. Now listen carefully. Someone will pick you up. Come only with the clothes on your back. No cell phone or any other personal possessions. And lady?"

"Y-Yes?"

"If you contact the police or anyone else, we'll mail your boyfriend back to you…one piece at a time." The connection went dead.

Tressalayne stared at the cell. Moments later, it dropped from her numb fingers to tumble onto the floor. Tears spilled from her eyes. *Please, please don't hurt, Lucas*, she thought over and over again.

She walked out to the porch and collapsed into one of the rocking chairs. Still and humid, the air lay heavy with the scent of rain. Chilled despite the muggy heat, Tressalayne hugged herself. While she waited, thoughts raced through her mind. *Who took Lucas…and what did they want with her?*

She swiped at the angry tears on her face. If they hurt Lucas or harmed one hair on his head, the mysterious caller and all his associates would pay and pay dearly!

She would make certain of it.

Lockstone studied the hospital through the window. The second story room at the inn gave him an excellent view of the front of the facility. He picked up his binoculars and watched an iron wagon with bright flashing lights approach and screech to a stop. "Emergency" in big, red script denoted the entrance. The back doors of the iron wagon banged open, and disgorged an elderly man lying on a small, wheeled bed. Two attendants rushed the man into the hospital, and they disappeared from sight.

Lockstone threw the binoculars on the bed. He observed the same scene many times the past day and night—with Crick and Sam Lunker nowhere to be seen. At some point he would have to press the issue—actually go inside the hospital to search for them—which meant he might have to ask questions about their whereabouts. Either way, it would be taking a risk. They thought him dead and he wanted to keep it that way. With their guard down it would be easier to follow them, and the last thing he wanted was to make them aware inquiries were made.

Even if Crick or Lunker showed up, the witch hunter still didn't have a plan on how to tail them other than with the Harley. The best he could come up with was to shadow them so far behind, they might not notice him.

Might.

Lockstone's gut clenched. He knew from what he'd been told by Mendoza and Gilbert that Crick was no fool. It was unlikely either he or Lunker would miss a large man on a noisy bike, no matter how far away.

With a frustrated sigh, the big witch hunter reached to retrieve the binoculars when his cell rang. Startled, he pawed in his pocket and fumbled for the phone.

"Hello?"

"Hey, big guy! Mendoza here. How ya' doing?" In the background, Lockstone heard Gilbert shout a cheery greeting.

"Anyway, you remember you asked us to tell you anything we found out about the woman Crick and Sam snagged? Well, we think we know where she is."

The witch hunter almost jumped out of his boots. "Yes! Where is she?"

"At an old warehouse south of town. We grabbed and bagged some doctor and took him there. When we delivered the dude, we saw the creepy bitch. Sam's on his way to get the doc's girlfriend. He said Crick's woman wants her for some reason."

Puzzled, Lockstone wondered what possible reason Morganna could have with a healer's mistress. Then it hit him.

"Wait! What is this woman's name, the doctor's girlfriend?"

There was a moment of silence before Mendoza answered. "Don't really know, dude. We heard Sam mention it, but its some weird-ass name—"

"Tressalayne!" Lockstone roared.

"Yeah! Yeah, that's it."

The witch hunter's triumph quickly became tempered by a sobering reality. *The coven is being rebuilt.*

His thoughts raced. A coven on this world would be an unthinkable nightmare. Morganna's death now became even more urgent. Without her, even if Tressalayne survived, the novice witch wouldn't be able to constitute a new coven.

The compulsion spell still held, but he knew it had its limits. *Time to test those limits.*

"Can you take me to this warehouse and get me in unseen?"

A long pregnant pause followed and Lockstone feared he finally breached the boundaries of the spell.

Mendoza's voice crackled in his ear. "Me and Gilbert think we need to wait until dark to sneak you in. That okay?"

A wolfish grin spread on the witch hunter's face.

At long last the end of the Hunt was in sight.

SIXTY-TWO

THE BAG WAS RIPPED OFF LUCAS' HEAD.

Pain stabbed his eyes, and he blinked in the sudden light. He stood motionless while his sight adjusted until a hand shoved him through an open door. Prodded, he stumbled forward until he reached a table with scattered chairs around it. Rough hands pushed him down into a seat, his legs and arms secured to the chair. Trussed like a hog, he looked about and discovered he was in a large, empty building, possibly a storage facility of some sort. The stale air reeked of dust and old, rusty metal.

"Welcome, Doctor Beckett," a voice said, and a man stepped out of the shadows.

Recognition flashed in Lucas' eyes, and his jaw dropped. "Mason! Wh—what's the meaning of this?"

Crick ignored the question and did a slow pirouette. "I admit it doesn't look like much, but the place kinda grows on you. After all, what I start here tonight will make me the richest man on earth."

Lucas stared in disbelief. "Are you crazy? I don't know what you're talking about. What I *do* know is I have been abducted and last I checked, kidnapping is still against the law!"

Crick chuckled. "All in due time, Doctor Beckett—although I must say, kidnapping should be the least of your worries."

Lucas ground his teeth. "Damn you, why am I here? What do you need me for? Stop with the riddles and tell me!"

Crick walked over and stood beside Lucas. "Beckett, you have it all wrong. We don't need *you*. You're just the bait."

Puzzled, Lucas sorted all the possibilities in his head. When the answer finally came, he screamed in rage and struggled against his bonds.

Crick grinned at Lucas' futile attempt to free himself. He squatted beside him. "How's this for an explanation. Your Doctor Do-Good, Boy Scout days are about to come to an abrupt end… and it couldn't happen to a nicer pain in the ass."

With a happy sigh, Crick pulled up a chair and propped his feet on the table. "Now all we have to do is wait for the final piece of my ticket to billionaire-land to arrive."

When the black Yukon SUV pulled up to the farmhouse, Tressalayne didn't wait for it to stop. The heavily tinted windows obscured any individuals inside, but undaunted, she ran up to the passenger side, threw the door open, and leaped inside.

"Let's go—" she started to say before a pair of coarse hands jerked a bag over her head.

"Keep your mouth shut and enjoy the ride," a gruff voice said. "You'll see your boyfriend soon enough, unless you cause trouble. In which case, your tearful reunion is liable to be delayed while I knock you unconscious and dump you at his feet."

Tressalayne fumed, the threat muffled by the thick cloth. Her fear for Lucas' safety fueled a cold edge of rage within her, and she struggled to contain it. Like a wild animal, it fought to escape the cage within her mind. She knew for his sake, she couldn't lose control, she had to hang on and see this through. But, once she found Lucas, she would protect him at all costs.

Even if it meant unleashing what she fought so hard to restrain.

Night had fallen when the two enforcers picked up Lockstone in the same black Escalade which days earlier they abducted him in. The dark sky, aided by fat rain clouds, was pervasive, relieved only by brief flashes of lightning. Impatient, the witch hunter chewed his lip while riding in the backseat. After what seemed like an eternity, the big SUV drove through an area with abandoned, dilapidated buildings, and rolled to a stop.

Mendoza pointed to a large structure some two hundred yards down the street. "That's the place. Can't get any closer or someone might see us and get suspicious."

Lockstone's sharp eyes studied the building. The roof's pitch rose to an impressive height, and a tall fence encircled the facility and adjacent lot. The immediate area around the edifice was illuminated by only two lights mounted on the roof. Directed at the flat landscape below, this left large areas swathed in shadow. A smile tugged at the corners of his mouth.

Perfect.

He got out of the iron wagon just as the first drops of rain spattered on his head and shoulders. He grabbed his backpack and slung it over his shoulder, then started to make his way to the warehouse. Mendoza's voice stopped him.

"Wait!" The enforcer jumped out and popped the tailgate on the Escalade. He took out an implement and handed it to the witch hunter.

"You'll need the bolt-cutters to cut the fence and get in. Also, we remember an office stuck in the corner of the building. It might have an exterior door or window. I'd try there first if your goal is to sneak in unseen."

Rain began to fall in earnest and Mendoza hurried back into the car. "Good luck!" he called over his shoulder. The SUV pulled away and left Lockstone alone in the storm.

He leaned into the downpour and trotted toward the final confrontation with Morganna.

SIXTY-THREE

LUCAS SLUMPED, EXHAUSTED.

The wild attempt to free himself did nothing but produce angry, red welts on his wrists and ankles. Even though he knew his efforts were useless, he couldn't help himself.

He was being used by Crick to trap Tressalayne!

When he realized Crick's plan, blind rage consumed him. All he could focus on was to free himself so he could place his hands around the hospital CFO's neck and throttle him. Once those frenzied efforts proved futile, he managed to rein in his runaway emotions and think with a clear mind.

Why did Crick want Tressalayne? He always suspected something amiss about the man, that behind his façade, something else lurked. Nurses and colleagues at Good Shepard sometimes whispered rumors about him, but he never took the time to inquire further—none of which explained Crick's current interest in Tressalayne, anyway.

Helpless to do anything else, he studied his "prison". *Definitely a warehouse of some sort,* he thought, as evidenced by the large open area, pallets, and packing material. The bank of industrial grade light fixtures mounted on the ceiling high above provided an uneven illumination. Some worked fine, some barely glowed, while others remained dark and didn't work at all. This created a patchwork of pools of light. The quirky light made it difficult to see clearly, and with a start, Lucas realized Crick was not alone.

A woman stood in a dimly lit corner and watched him. Tall, she wore blue jeans and a red blouse, with hair the color of the shadows. Even at a distance, Lucas could feel her eyes bore into him. Violence and evil dripped from her, and he quickly averted his gaze.

Not far from the woman, movement caught his attention. At first, he thought his eyes played tricks on him, because a lump of packing material moved, swaying to and fro. His mouth fell open when he realized the "lump" was an elderly woman. Clothes draped from her emaciated body like bedsheets, while she tottered and struggled to remain upright.

Crick laughed at the expression on Lucas' face. He motioned to the two women. "Doctor Beckett, let me introduce you to my associate, Morganna. I can't wait for you to see her in action." The witch stepped forward, while the old crone floundered after her.

Up close, Crick's associate appeared even more intimidating. Voluptuous, she possessed a cold, terrible beauty, her eyes bottomless wells of stygian black. She observed him with a raptor-like intensity, a predator regarding its prey. A chill spread deep in his bones.

Crick nudged his chin at the ancient woman. "Oh, and this is Carol Webster, a client, or should I say, *former* client, of mine. Unfortunately, Carol's a little indisposed." He sniggered. "Seems she caught a bug earlier today and it just *drained* her."

In the stronger light, Webster looked like a cadaver. Pallid, paper-thin skin stretched across a brittle skeleton, and her breathing came in hoarse gasps. Lucas suspected she suffered from respiratory failure and needed to be hospitalized at once.

"Mason, this woman needs immediate medical care. She's liable to go into cardiac arrest at any time!"

"Still the Good Samaritan, huh?" Crick grabbed Lucas' hair, jerked his head back, and leaned close. "Well, guess what?" he snarled. "You ain't seen nothing yet! You and Carol are soon to become a matched set!"

With a harsh laugh, he released Lucas' hair and stepped back. Crick wiped his hands on his shirt. "You're a fool, Beckett. A minnow swimming in a sea of sharks. Why, I bet you still leave milk and cookies for Santa Claus. Dumb shits like you are why people like me exist—to take, and take, until you've nothing more to give."

He jerked a thumb at the old woman. "Take this idiot. Tell me, *Doctor* Beckett, in your medical opinion, would you say good old Carol has given just about everything she's got?"

Lucas stared in horror at Carol Webster, the implications of what Crick said dawning on him.

"No," he whispered.

"What's that? No?" Crick squatted to be at eye level with Lucas. "I can assure you what we have here is a definite *yes*. Now listen, because the next part is so delicious, I can't wait anymore to tell you. Your girlfriend, pardon me—fiancée—is going to help turn you into *that*!" Crick stood and pointed at Webster.

"No!" Lucas shouted. "You filthy bastard. You leave Tressalayne alone! The chair shook and rocked, while Lucas redoubled his struggle to free himself. Face red, he strained against his bonds, cords of muscle on his arms etched in sharp relief.

"I'll kill you, I'll kill you!"

Crick laughed while Morganna watched motionless, her expression a frozen mask.

The warehouse door banged open, caught by the wind and rain. Lucas stopped struggling, and he, Crick, and Morganna, all turned to look.

In walked Tressalayne.

SIXTY-FOUR

TRESSALAYNE ENTERED THE WAREHOUSE WHILE LUNKER, GUN drawn, maintained a firm grasp on her arm. When she spotted Lucas, she shook off his hand, and oblivious to the weapon, ran to him.

Breathless, Tressalayne fell at his feet. "Are you okay? Have they hurt you?" Her hands ran over his body searching for bruises and abrasions.

"What? What's this? Your wrists are bleeding!"

She stood and chanted in Gaelic, and his bonds snapped and fell away. She helped him up and put an arm around his waist, her strength easily supporting him.

Tressalayne watched Lucas rub his numb wrists, and furious, turned to face his captors. "You'll pay for this!" she hissed. Lunker joined Crick, and both men held guns pointed at the young couple.

Crick snorted, his steely gaze on the witch. "Smart girl. *Payment* is why you're here."

He swung the barrel of his Beretta at Lucas. "Now, here's another important detail you need to know. I'll put a bullet in Doctor

Beckett at the first sign you don't cooperate fully with me. Maybe I'll kneecap him first so you can hear him scream. Or, hell, maybe I'll just put one through his brain and get it over with. Either way, you're going to do what I tell you to do."

Lucas could feel Tressalayne shake with anger and rage. If she lost control like she did with Mandi, a violent confrontation was inevitable—with one or both of their deaths the end result. No matter how practiced she had become with the aid of the Book of First Magic and the tutelage of the "Little People", she couldn't cast a spell faster than Crick could pull a trigger.

He needed to calm her down.

"Tressalayne, I'm okay. Other than sore wrists and ankles, they haven't harmed me. *Don't* let them provoke you!"

"Listen to the good doctor, sweetheart…for both your sakes," Crick said, menace dripping from his voice.

"Tressalayne, *please!*" Lucas pleaded. "They have guns." With relief, he felt her agitation begin to ebb.

"Enough!"

Lucas' head snapped around to see Morganna step forward and point a finger at Tressalayne. "You *will* do what you are told!"

She looked at Lucas, revulsion on her face. "This…*toad* will be taken care of soon enough. He is no longer your concern!"

Her gaze caused Lucas' blood to run cold. Death, terrible death was in those eyes.

"How dare you! Don't you threaten Lucas!" Tressalyne spat. The rigid tension returned with a vengeance, and Lucas felt a burst of energy course through her like a breached dam. He tightened his grip on her and prepared for the worst.

Morganna ignored her protégé's outburst, her face equal parts anger and sorrow. "So, its true. You have no memory of me." The coven leader quickly regained her composure. "No matter. Every problem has a solution...yours included."

Morganna glanced at Crick. "Master, may I proceed?"

Crick stepped back and performed an exaggerated bow. "By all means."

Lucas followed the exchange, his eyes darting back and forth between them. "What—what are you going to do?"

Morganna sneered at Lucas and turned to Tressalayne. "Soon all things will be returned to their rightful order. Your eyes will once again see clearly."

Lucas heard Tressalayne growl, a low, guttural, bestial sound he'd never heard from her lips before. She forced him behind her so that her body shielded him from Morganna. Kinetic energy crackled about her, raising the hair on Lucas' neck.

Morganna raised her arms and chanted. The harsh syllables grated on Lucas' nerves, and his ears itched in pain. The air shifted, motes of dust danced and swirled, and a sound, like a distant rush of wind, echoed faintly, then grew stronger and stronger. Cobalt blue sparks of intense radiance appeared and darted about. Morganna manipulated her fingers and drew them toward her until they formed a ball of brilliant midnight blue. The fierce glow forced Lucas to hold his hands up to protect his eyes from the blinding light.

The growl he heard earlier from Tressalayne grew louder. Through the cracks of his fingers, he squinted and saw her back arched and her feet spread as though prepared for an assault. Above the maelstrom caused by the explosion of magical energy in the room, he heard a final cry issue from Morganna.

With both hands, she threw the crackling ball at Tressalayne. It exploded in a shock wave of heat and energy, and even partially shielded by Tressalayne, the blast of magic picked up Lucas and hurled him backwards.

Temporarily blinded, he lay stunned and helpless.

Lockstone studied the fence, grateful for the tool given him by Mendoza. He eyed the barbed wire stretched across the top and concluded in short order going *through* the fence was far preferable to climbing *over* it.

Rain dripped from his beard while he snipped the fence until he had an opening big enough to slide through. He took a quick look around to get his bearings and headed for the warehouse.

He found the main entrance easily enough. Light leaked around the door's edge, and in the rain-swept darkness, it flared like a beacon. The witch hunter avoided it, however, aware he would be spotted the second he stepped inside. Instead, he slipped along the side of the building and looked for the door or window Mendoza said could be part of an interior office.

The murky night and driving rain made it hard to see. The lights fixed on the roof and pointed at the ground below offered little help. Their weak illumination barely pierced the sheets of rain and darkness. Lockstone, forced to reckon by feel, ran his hands along the corrugated metal, its surface rough, cold, and wet beneath his fingers. Progress was slow, the witch hunter loath to hurry on the chance he might miss the possible entry into the office.

His hand brushed against a smooth, metallic surface. He stopped, wiped the rainwater out of his eyes, and peered closer. His sharp vision detected a dim outline, and when a flash of lightning briefly illuminated the entire area, he smiled in triumph.

He found the door.

The lightning flash also revealed a knob with a hasp and padlock above it. The witch hunter groped and closed his hand on the lock. Coarse with rust and age, the bolt cutter made short work of it. However, when he attempted to turn the knob, he discovered it too was locked.

Lockstone sat back on his heels. If he attempted to batter the door open, even in the storm, the noise would likely alert those inside. Instead, he took his knife from its sheath and wedged the stout blade into the doorframe next to the knob. Teeth gritted, he levered the blade back and forth, muscles bunched in effort. Squeals and groans from tortured metal filled the wet air, and the witch hunter prayed the fury of the storm would cover the sound. Suddenly, with a *pop*, the tongue sprang free and the door swung open.

Lockstone swept inside, the knife held before him. Crouched, water dripped and pooled at his feet while his eyes and ears strained to detect any sound or motion. He held his position until satisfied no alarm had been raised. Finally, his head swiveled right then left. Dark shapes indicating furniture of some kind surrounded him. Dusty windows lined the front of the office, and he could see dim light filter through from the warehouse's interior.

He crab-walked back to the exterior door and pulled it shut, then slid along the floor until he reached the office windows. With great care, he raised his head until his eyes were just above the window frame. A strange sight immediately presented itself. A group of people stood near the center of the cavernous floor. Two men he recognized from the ale hall, Crick and Lunker. They held guns on a young man and woman. The woman's back was turned to him, but she looked vaguely familiar. Nearby an ancient crone stood swaying like a sapling in a breeze. Then another woman stepped into the light, and his breath caught in his throat.

Morganna!

SIXTY-FIVE

THE SPOTS DISSIPATED, AND LUCAS' VISION CLEARED. WITH A groan, he sat up and reached for Tressalayne.

Her hands covered her face and she shook her head over and over again as if dazed or confused. Despite Crick's threat to shoot him, he staggered to his feet and rushed to her side.

"What's wrong? Are you okay?" he cried.

Tressalayne's hands fell to her side, and she raised her head. When she looked at Lucas, her gaze was alien and distant. Her eyes, instead of the warm blue-green, were now cold, shards of ice filled with malice. The amulet at her throat squirmed and writhed, the gem a midnight black.

"You promised you would run. You broke your oath," she said. "Now its too late."

Her voice, flat and without emotion, carried no weight of accusation. To Lucas's stunned ears, it rang like a statement of fact much like a judge passing sentence.

He turned to Morganna and shouted, "What did you do to her? What did you do, you—"

His voice stopped abruptly and he gagged. An invisible hand held his windpipe in a viselike grip. He scrabbled and tore at his throat in an impotent effort to relieve the pressure. He sank to his knees, eyes bulging.

Crick knelt beside Lucas, and chuckled. "I think the message here is you talk too much." With a smirk he stood and motioned to Morganna. Disappointed, she flicked her hand, and the pressure on Lucas' airway disappeared. On hands and knees, he drew hoarse breaths into his oxygen-starved lungs.

"Now let's see. Where were we? Oh yeah, can I assume you have restored Tressalayne's memory?" Crick asked Morganna.

Morganna's smile revealed sharp white teeth which gleamed in the light. "Yes, Master. But let's be certain."

The coven leader walked over to Tressalayne and stood in front of her. "Do you remember, and if so, do you understand the current situation?"

Tressalayne nodded. She began to chant, her hands and fingers moving in perfect choreography with the spell.

Lucas's ears itched and burned. Shocked, he realized she was using the same language spoken earlier by Morganna. "Tressalayne, stop," he croaked.

She ignored him and continued.

Lunker, his gun trained on the younger witch said, "I don't like this, Boss. What's she doing?"

Crick shrugged. "I guess its part of the process of restoring her memory." He threw a sharp look at the enforcer. "What the hell difference does it make, Sam? If it means I have two witches to make potion instead of one, then it's money in the bank. So, for the last time, let me do all the thinking and keep your mouth shut!"

Tressalayne, oblivious to the exchange, stopped and looked at Morganna. "I am ready."

Morganna clasped her hands and closed her eyes, a look of

pure euphoria on her face.

"Then you know what to do. Proceed."

Lockstone eased the backpack onto the hard floor. He dug through it to check and recheck his inventory. Satisfied, he closed it and secured the pack on his back. Next, he pulled the Glock from his waist, popped the clip to make sure it carried a full load, then pushed it back in place. Finally, he pulled the slide back and loaded a bullet in the chamber.

He closed his eyes and prepared himself. The countless hours spent at the gun range with the new weapon ran through his mind. He was confident he could put a bullet through Morganna's black heart if he could just get a clear shot. If for some reason the gun failed him, he had other options. He reached behind him and patted the backpack.

His Kingdom weapons would kill a witch just as dead.

He tested the door leading from the office onto the main floor. The last thing he needed was loud squeals or screeches to give him away. Thankfully, it opened with a minimum of noise, and he cracked it ajar.

The witch hunter took a deep breath. *Time to bring the Hunt to an end.*

He pushed the door open and scuttled out onto the warehouse floor.

SIXTY-SIX

LUCAS, STILL ON HIS HANDS AND KNEES, WATCHED TRESSALAYNE turn to Crick and Lunker. Alarm covered Crick's face at Morganna's comment, and his eyes narrowed to slits.

He gestured at Tressalayne. "Shoot her, Sam!"

The big enforcer, gun already pointed and aimed, needed no further encouragement. He pulled the trigger. The gun bucked in his hand, the noise of the shot magnified like the explosion of a stick of dynamite within the confines of the warehouse walls.

"*No!*" Lucas screamed. Tears in his eyes, his mouth dropped at the sight of Tressalayne still on her feet. Crick's goon couldn't have missed at such close range!

Lunker, a look of disbelief on his face, fired again and again. The *ping* of spent shells bouncing off the floor and the harsh smell of cordite filled the air.

And still, Tressalayne stood.

She opened her hand and spent bullets dropped to the floor one-by-one.

Plink, plink, plink.

Crick reacted quickly. He trained his own gun on the witch, but before he could pull the trigger, Tressalayne barked a command and the gun was ripped from his hand.

Crick screamed in pain, his fingers twisted and bent like pretzels. "You bitch! You whore! Sam, do something!"

Mouth slack, Lucas saw the big man hesitate. Fear oozed from him. "You don't pay me enough for this shit!" He dropped the handgun and ran.

He made it only halfway to the door before Tressalayne chanted and closed her fist. A shimmer appeared in the air in front of the enforcer, and he collided with it, bounced backwards, and lay on the floor stunned. To Lucas' astonished eyes, it looked like he ran headlong into an invisible wall.

Tressalayne leaped on Crick in the blink of an eye. She tore his shirt off to expose the Ward on his chest, ripped it from his neck, and threw it away. Next, she opened her mouth wide and placed it inches from Crick's. He struggled in a vain attempt to pull away from her grip.

Face ashen, Lucas watched wisps of vapor arise from the hospital CFO's mouth. Crimson, they condensed into droplets, which in turn, formed a ball of blood which roiled and rotated. Finished, Tressalayne hurled Crick away from her. The hospital CFO slammed onto the floor, rolled, and slid to a stop.

Tressalayne turned to Morganna and led the crimson sphere to the coven leader's lips. There, it transformed back into the blood-red vapor. With shuddering breaths, she inhaled until none was left.

Arms raised in exultation, Morganna screamed, "Free!"

With catlike quickness, Morganna pounced on Crick who picked himself up off the hard concrete and attempted to scramble away. With an effortless heave, she lifted him to his feet, his toes barely touching the floor.

A purple bruise blossomed on Crick's cheek, along with other scratches and abrasions. "Put me down," he snarled. "I *order* you to put me down!"

"Fool!" Morganna hissed. "The binding is undone. You are mine!"

Crick's face underwent several transformations from anger, to fear, and finally, cold resignation. "How?" he asked.

Morganna stroked his neck with her talon. A cruel smile spread across her face.

"Don't you remember? You gave me permission me to 'plot all I want'. Even then, I could think of no way to undo the binding. It was unbreakable. But when you forced me to make the *morlaga* potion, it revealed your weakness, the *one* way I could unravel the binding."

Beads of sweat appeared on Crick's forehead. "Bullshit," he growled. "The plan was perfect."

Morganna laughed. The deep rumble rang in the air, filled with violence and bloodlust.

"*Greed.* Your lust for riches became your undoing. You weren't satisfied with only me and the wealth the *morlaga* potion could bring you. No, you wanted more, another witch to increase the production of potion. When you mentioned Tressalayne and her memory loss, the trap was set. I knew you couldn't resist the temptation of restoring her memory."

A trickle of blood ran from a gash on Crick's head. Morganna stuck a long, limber tongue out and slowly followed the trace of blood. This brought her lips within inches of Crick's eyes, her breath hot on his skin.

"Did it ever occur to you to wonder how a member of my coven would react once she regained her memory and full control of her faculties? That perhaps she would immediately detect the Ward and Binding and attempt to undo them? Even then, with one word you could have forced me to stop her and ordered me to bind my own apprentice. But your blind greed numbed you to any danger your rash decision could bring."

Crick shrugged, a difficult feat when held in Morganna's steel grip. "Okay, you got me. Now let's get down to business. There's no reason we can't both get rich off your potion. I have a distribution system second to none. We can be full partners, and I guarantee you won't be disappointed. Hell, I'll even agree to a split where you get sixty percent of the profits."

Morganna released Crick and walked a slow circle around him. The hospital CFO remained hanging in midair, his feet pumping without success to regain purchase with the ground.

Morganna stopped in front of Crick. "But I can have it all. Isn't that what true greed is all about? A lesson I well and truly learned from you. Besides, no amount of gold would ever be worth my revenge."

Her eyes narrowed. "You treated me like a brood mare, rutted with me as if I was a common tavern whore, and used me for your own ends. No one does that and lives!"

Morganna steepled her hands, and a deep sigh escaped from her lips. "The hours I spent on creating a truly unique death for you, my only escape from the bondage you put me under. More's the pity it won't nearly be prolonged enough, but I have plans which need to be put in motion and I can't take the time to draw out your agony."

Crick spat, the bloody phlegm landing at Morganna's feet. "Think I'm scared? You'll have to do better than that, *witch*! Enemies worse than you have tried to kill me for years, and by rights, I should have been dead a dozen times over. See, I always have a backup plan, and it includes you. So, if I don't walk out of here in the pink of health, my personal lawyer has instructions to put a million-dollar contract on your head."

Crick barked a harsh laugh. "You'll be looking over your

shoulder the rest of your life…and good luck with the potion. The second you try to peddle it, every hit man on four continents will be drawn to your trail like flies to a carcass."

Morganna chuckled. Her mirth grew until her body shook with uncontrolled laughter. Finally, she wiped her eyes and once again faced Crick.

"So, I would be hunted?" A fresh peal of laughter escaped her lips. Recovering, her eyes turned hard and she ripped her blouse, the buttons popping. Her shoulder was displayed, the pale flesh revealing a puckered, purple scar.

"You who took advantage of me in every conceivable way, saw me naked and exposed, never once asked about *this!*" she said pointing at the angry wound.

"Being hunted is the way of life for witches on my world, and I've survived every Hunt and every Hunter ever sent after my coven."

Morganna raised her talon and placed it on the center of Crick's forehead. A grunt of pain escaped his lips as the sharp nail pricked his skin.

"How do you think I ended up on your world? I escaped from the greatest Hunter ever produced, the same one who wounded me. Your threats are empty, no more substantial than wind whistling by my ears.

Now, prepare to accept your fate."

SIXTY-SEVEN

LOCKSTONE FLITTED FROM ONE POOL OF SHADOW TO THE NEXT. Rain hammered the roof, the *rat-a-tat* sound magnified within the walls and abetted by loud rumbles of thunder. The witch hunter knew his fear of being overheard was a needless concern. An army could have breached entry into the warehouse and never been heard over the fury of the storm.

Large metal pillars, spaced at intervals, supported the ceiling and were arranged down the middle of the floor. Although not wide enough to conceal his large frame, they provided partial cover, and he used them to draw closer to Morganna.

He peered around a steel beam and spied Morganna in front of another woman which, he assumed, must be Tressalayne. During their previous battle at the inn, he'd been too busy dodging explosive balls of magic to have gotten a good look at the junior witch. However, she looked very familiar.

Her apprentice appeared angry, and she held a young man—her paramour, the doctor, according to Mendoza. Crick and Lunker stood nearby, guns drawn, and the sight drew a hiss of dismay from his lips. *That* complicated things.

Two more killers to deal with.

Lockstone noticed another individual, and his eyes narrowed at the sight. An ancient crone wobbled not far from Morganna. His gut clenched at the sight of the abomination, evidence of a *morlaga* spell and the introduction of the coven leader's black magic into this world.

She has to be stopped!

He closed his eyes and leaned back against the metal post. There was a good chance Crick and Lunker would turn their guns on him once he began to fire at Morganna. The men were hardened killers used to violence. He couldn't depend on them hesitating once they identified him as the shooter.

Lockstone swallowed. The picture of destroyed families—husbands and wives, daughters and sons, all slaughtered for Morganna's ends—flashed through his mind. Last came the image of Emmitt, his closest friend's head cradled in his lap as he drew one last rattling breath.

The witch hunter's jaw clenched in anger and he recalled his vow. Morganna's must die...even if it meant his own death as well. Time to make good on his pledge.

He edged his eyes around the post once again. Although difficult to hear above the tumult of the storm, he could tell an angry exchange was taking place between Tressalayne and her mentor. Puzzled, he watched Tressalayne force the young doctor behind her.

He puffed out his cheeks. Tressalayne tried to kill both he and Emmitt with the same ruthless abandon as Argatha and Morganna—she was part of the same murderous coven! Yet now she shielded the doctor from Morganna. It went against the grain, and displayed an emotion foreign to every witch he ever hunted.

He rubbed his chin. *Could it be possible she loved him?*

If time allowed—provided he survived the gunfire sure to come his way from Crick and Lunker—he planned on killing Tressalayne once he disposed of Morganna. Now he wasn't so sure.

He shook his head. All that mattered was Morganna's death. Once he cut off the head of the snake, the coven would be destroyed.

Suddenly, his inherited witch blood began to tingle. He risked another look and his jaw dropped. Magic boiled from Morganna, her spell raising goose bumps on his skin. Bluish light crackled and sparked all around her, while Tressalayne took a defensive crouch.

His thoughts raced. He needed to act now while this distraction drew all the attention. He stilled his heart, counted to three, and leaped out.

Legs spread, he held his gun with both hands, the sights centered on Morganna's chest. Before he could pull the trigger, the coven leader completed the spell and hurled a sphere of magic at Tressalayne.

The world exploded around Lockstone.

The force of the sorcerous blast catapulted him backwards into a mound of wooden packing material. A sharp pain pierced his side, and his head struck something solid.

The witch hunter blacked out.

SIXTY-EIGHT

ORGANNA HELD THE TALON CENTERED ON CRICK'S forehead and mumbled a spell. Suddenly, a gunshot rang out, and a chip from the concrete floor at the witch's feet flew into the air. Another shot roared, followed by the *spang* of a ricochet.

The coven leader's head snapped around to face the source of gunfire. Lunker staggered to his feet and held a gun pulled from an ankle holster in an unsteady hand. He blinked to clear his vision, and before Morganna could react, fired another shot at her. The bullet flew wide, striking Carol Webster in the chest.

A red stain bloomed from the wound. She coughed once and collapsed to the floor with a brittle thud.

Hope sprang into Crick's eyes at the sight of his enforcer shooting at Morganna. "Kill her, Sam! Put the bitch down!"

Morganna barked a spell. The harsh words reverberated off the walls, and the coven leader manipulated her free hand. With the other, she pulled Crick along. His feet brushed the floor as Morganna walked straight toward the enforcer. Lunker tracked the witch's approach, took careful aim, and squeezed the trigger.

Nothing happened.

He looked at his gun. Try as he might, he couldn't pull the trigger. Beads of sweat formed on his lip and he redoubled his efforts...all to no avail. The fingers on his gun hand wouldn't move.

By this time Morganna reached Lunker and stood in front of him, the barrel of the revolver inches from her chest. Her eyes mocked him.

"Having trouble? Let's see if I can help you."

Morganna rotated her wrist. Lunker's hand moved, and the barrel swiveled away from the coven leader. With slow but steady motion, it turned toward the enforcer. Lunker grabbed the pistol with his other hand, the corded tendons in his neck distended in the struggle to stop the gun's progress. Teeth gritted, the big man's body shook with herculean effort, but still the gun moved.

The barrel stopped when centered on Lunker's chest. He looked at Crick, a grim look of resignation on his face. "You should have let me kill her when I had the chance." Morganna closed her fist.

The enforcer's finger pulled the trigger. The roar of the automatic filled the air and Lunker emptied the clip at point blank range into his heart and lungs. His body jerked with each bullet, the impact causing him to stagger backwards. He managed to remain upright, the revolver still pointed at his chest, while blood gushed from his mouth and poured from multiple wounds. The air carried a coppery tang, and a crimson puddle formed at his feet.

The gun dropped from Lunker's nerveless hand, and he fell backwards to lay still, lifeless eyes fixed on the ceiling.

Morganna stared at the body. Then she turned, her hard eyes on Crick. "A quick and painless death, not something my coven is noted for. Your soldier forced my hand and compelled me to take immediate action. Your death, fortunately, will make up for my disappointment."

Morganna once again placed her talon on Crick's forehead. The sharp tip pricked the skin, and a drop of blood oozed from the wound. She chanted a spell, her voice rising higher and higher.

Crick panicked, eyes wide at the sight of Lunker lying dead on the floor. His breath erupted in ragged gasps. "Wa-wait! We can still make a deal!"

Morganna ignored Crick, withdrew her talon and stepped away. Her chanting continued, while the hospital CFO, suspended in midair, struggled wildly, unable to gain any purchase in which to escape.

"Morganna, you're making a mistake! Look, you can name your price, any price, and I'll—"

Morganna ended the spell with a sharp cry, and Crick's body went rigid. A crimson slash began to crawl on the CFO's skin from the tiny prick on his head. Thin, the "line" leaked blood while it traversed down his nose, chin, neck, chest, and then down his torso. It continued past his groin, up his back and spine, before meeting again at the point on his forehead.

The striation completely bisected Crick's body into two equal halves.

Morganna placed both hands in front of her, and pulled them apart as if she were parting a curtain. The demarcation on Crick's skin grew wider, and a wet, sodden sound, like damp fabric being torn, floated in the air. Crick screamed. The coven leader laughed and manipulated her hands even farther apart.

The striation now became a bloody crevasse which revealed muscle and white connective tissue. Crick's screams rose to new heights, a raw unrestrained crescendo, which competed with Morganna's wild peals of laughter. The CFO's skin inched farther and farther apart, drops of crimson ichor spattering the floor. Morganna jerked her hands apart, and with a moist *rip*, the skin flew off Crick's body to flop on the floor in two oozing lumps.

Crick hung in the air, bare tissue, tendons, and muscle glistening in the light. His lidless eyes rolled in frenzied abandon while he writhed in agony. The screams from his denuded lips grew weaker and weaker, his frantic convulsions less vigorous. Finally, his head drooped and he stopped moving.

Morganna frowned. "A pity. I hoped to enjoy his pain for a bit longer."

She turned to Tressalayne who stood silently off to the side. "Bring the healer to me. Tonight, we establish our coven on this world."

A savage cackle escaped her lips.

"And what better way to start our sojourn than with the perfect *morlaga* donor."

SIXTY-NINE

FACE ASHEN, LUCAS COULDN'T TAKE HIS EYES OFF THE CARCASS of what had once been Mason Crick. Like a side of beef straight from the slaughterhouse, his body hung in the air while blood and other fluids dripped to the floor. Numb, his senses barely registered Tressalayne grabbing him to take him to Morganna.

Once he stood before the coven leader, he finally found his tongue. "You're a murderer, a monster! Not one, but *two* men killed in the most twisted ways possible. No one deserves to die like that!"

Merciless eyes appraised Lucas. With a chuckle, Morganna pointed at Carol Webster's crumpled form on the floor. "I long ago lost count of all my victims, but I believe you missed one. She makes three."

The coven leader stepped closer to Lucas and gripped his face with both hands. "With you soon to become number four," she breathed.

Her eyes bored into his and Lucas grew drowsy. He struggled to stay alert, but moments later, unable to help himself, his eyes closed and he fell into a dreamless sleep.

Lucas groaned and came to. Dizzy, he raised his head and looked around. His senses slowly returned, and with a start, he realized he was naked. The cold cement tickled his bare feet, and he looked down to discover he stood like a soldier at attention within a red square drawn on the floor. Legs straight, knees locked, his arms lay rigid by his side.

He gasped and tried to move, only to realize his limbs refused to obey. His head and neck were the only parts of his anatomy to respond. Morganna and Tressalayne stood before him, and odd-shaped cup in the coven leader's hand.

"Wha-what's going on," he croaked.

Morganna stepped forward. "A fair question, and one I'm eager to answer. You are the next donor for the *morlaga* potion, which I plan to sell to the highest bidder. With the gold, excuse me, *money* from the sale, I will establish my coven on your world."

A chuckle escaped her lips. "Although in truth, with so many doe-eyed cattle to choose from, I fear my skill may suffer from ensorcelling such easy prey."

The witch paced in front of Lucas. "*You*, however, pose a special challenge. You defiled my apprentice, an insult which demands punishment. I could torture you, of course, but then what's left would be of little use for the potion. I decided, therefore, to have it *both* ways. You will be conscious throughout the entire spell. Your pain and agony will be exquisite while your life's essence is torn from you. True, the potion will still lose some potency, but the fools on this world won't know the difference."

Cold fear crept up Lucas' spine. He turned to Tressalayne. "Don't let this happen. You aren't like her. *You are not a murderer!*"

Tressalayne remained motionless.

Morganna cackled. "Enough!" Chanting, she mouthed the *morlaga* spell, the harsh words echoing off the walls of the cavernous warehouse.

A chill sweat beaded Lucas' skin at the sight of a vaporous coil rising from the receptacle held by Morganna. It drifted to the floor, and snakelike, undulated and slithered toward him. It crossed the red outline and moved to his feet. Cold tendrils crawled up his legs and onto his torso. He willed himself to keep his fear under control, and redoubled his efforts to free himself.

It was useless. His limbs wouldn't obey.

By this time, fingers of vapor caressed his neck and Lucas knew he didn't have much longer.

It was no use.

A calmness settled on him and he turned his head to Tressalayne. "Its not your fault. *She* did this to you. Our love is real and no amount of lies from Morganna will ever change that. I know who you are, who you *really* are…and deep inside, you know too."

Lucas swallowed and turned away. The protoplasmic fog now hovered suspended before his face, the tendrils merging.

"I love you, Tressalayne. You'll always be my *Fhéith mo chroí*." Eyes closed, he added, "You're my love, *the vein of my heart*." Tressalayne blinked and her lip quivered. Then the amber cord struck.

SEVENTY

FHÉITH MO CHROÍ.

The word reverberated in Tressalayne's mind. Her heart clenched, and a familiar ache budded inside her. The amulet at her neck jumped and wriggled, the gem partially black, partially white, the colors pulsing back and forth as if at war with one another.

A hoarse scream of agony tore from the lips of the donor.

The sound pricked her heart and something wet rolled down her cheeks. Her hand crept up and she touched her face. She held her hand before her and stared in wonder at the warm moisture on her fingertips.

Tears.

Another scream ripped the air.

She looked at the donor, his handsome face contorted in pain. The sight caused her to clutch her chest, her emotions unraveling.

"*No,*" she whispered.

The tears, uncontrolled, cascaded from her eyes.

"*Noooooooooo!*" she howled.

She leaped forward and snatched the chalice from Morganna's startled grip. She backhanded the coven leader, and Morganna flew through the air to land, stunned, on the floor.

Tressalayne held the chalice and squeezed. A high-pitched keen issued from the magical implement, and the amorphous fog withdrew from Lucas to flee back into its depths.

The cup crumpled in Tressalayne's hand.

She hurled the ruined vessel away and crossed the red rectangle to catch Lucas who had fallen to his knees.

She held him to her chest. "I'm sorry, my love."

"Kn-knew you would come back to me," he coughed.

Tressalayne motioned and one of the metal chairs slid across the floor and came to a stop at their feet. She helped Lucas into the chair, and caressed his cheek.

"I must go now."

"Wha-What? What are you going to do?" Lucas asked.

Tressalayne stood and looked back at Lucas, her expression hard.

"I'm going to kill a witch."

Lockstone groaned and lifted his head. His vision swam before him for several moments before it cleared. Groggy, he looked around. His body rested in a dark corner surrounded by a jumble of wooden planks. When he tried to move, a sharp pain stabbed his side. He looked down.

A jagged section of one of the planks protruded from his side. The splintered end, coated dark with his blood, exited far enough from his body he could grip it with his hands. He ripped his tunic to examine the wound and sighed with relief. The broken plank pierced him just above and to the side of his waist, narrowly missing vital organs.

He shifted and a wave of agony gripped him. Through gritted

teeth, the witch hunter weighed his options, and quickly determined they were few with none of them good. If he lingered, the blood loss would weaken him to the point he might not be able to extricate himself. If he attempted to free himself, he would have to pull the jagged wood from his body and find a way to staunch the wound before he bled out.

His reverie was interrupted when shots rang out followed by a long period of silence. Then multiple gunshots followed. Lockstone struggled to locate the source of gunfire, but he had a poor vantage point from where he lay impaled. Distance, the support columns, and uneven lighting made it hard to see anything. Worse, the storm assaulting the warehouse made it difficult to hear.

A scream rose above the tumult of the storm. After a beat or two, a succession of screams continued unabated. Filled with hysterical notes of torment and agony, the sound galvanized the witch hunter into action.

He snatched the knife at his belt and placed the leather wrapped hilt between his teeth. Then he pushed himself up and forward. The action pulled the splintered plank backwards through his body. Choked sounds of pain escaped through his clenched teeth on the handle. With a final heave, Lockstone propelled himself forward and free of his impalement.

The knife dropped from his mouth, and the big witch hunter pitched forward. Spots swam before his eyes, and he feared he might swoon. He fought to keep his consciousness, aware if he passed out, he would bleed to death.

Lockstone struggled to his hands and knees, then crawled to the pile of wooden debris. Mounds of packing material lay scattered on the floor. He grabbed handfuls of the straw-like material and with a hiss of pain, stuffed it into the gaping wound at his side. The packing quickly turned red, saturated with Lockstone's blood. However, it staunched the flow to a slow seep.

The witch hunter scrabbled to his feet and looked around. The Glock was nowhere to be seen and he didn't have time to look for it. The howls of torment had weakened and stopped, an ominous sign.

He picked up the backpack, its weight a comforting reassurance. *The old ways were the best anyway.* But then a thought struck him and he hesitated. He dug Argatha's amulet from his pocket and dropped the backpack. Zipping it open, he pushed his hand inside, and grabbed a crossbow. He made sure the amulet rested on the bottom, and then rearranged the other implements on top of it. Standing, he shrugged the pack back onto his shoulders.

He turned and staggered toward Morganna.

SEVENTY-ONE

THE TWO WITCHES CIRCLED EACH OTHER, EYES LOCKED ON one another like wrestlers seeking an advantage.

Lucas twice tried to stand to get a better vantage point, and both times he collapsed back into the chair, still weak from the debilitative effects of the aborted *morlaga* spell. He could feel his strength returning, but not nearly fast enough. Finally, he regained enough stamina to locate his pile of clothes near his feet. With as much speed his weakened condition allowed, he pulled his clothes back on.

He eyed Crick's handgun on the floor not far from where his skinned body still hung suspended in mid-air. If he could just get to it while Morganna was distracted, he might be able to shoot her.

The fact he could so easily entertain the thought of taking a life, shook him. He became a doctor to save lives, not end them. However, the malicious evil which dripped from the witch had already led to the deaths of multiple people…he would have become the coven leader's next victim without Tressalayne's intervention. Morganna *had* to die before she hurt anyone else, especially Tressalayne.

The last look she gave him before going after Morganna chilled him. Her eyes, hard as steel, contained no warmth, no compassion.

The eyes of someone used to violence.

Worse, when she turned away, he caught a glimpse of her amulet…the gem's color was now an obsidian black.

He shook his head. It didn't matter. *Nothing* mattered anymore except to protect Tressalayne. He couldn't let Morganna harm her. If he couldn't stand, he'd move another way. Falling on his hands and knees, he crawled toward Crick's gun.

"You fool! You destroyed the chalice, and for what? The love of a mortal man!" Morganna snarled.

A thin smile appeared on Tressalayne's lips. "Yes, the same man you tried to use the *morlaga* spell on. For that, I'm going to kill you."

A harsh laugh erupted from Morganna. "A mere apprentice challenge me? Your fate is sealed! While you lay broken at my feet, your lover will be torn and ripped to pieces before your eyes. The last sight you will see are his lips writhing in agony."

With a quick flip of her hand, a pulse of green fire shot from her palm at her apprentice. Tressalayne didn't try to dodge the fiery ball, but instead, raised her hand, caught it, and in one smooth motion, hurled it back at Morganna. The coven leader barely had time to raise her arm and block the sizzling sphere. The explosion of heat and energy staggered Morganna.

Her eyes narrowed. "Learned a trick or two, eh? Good! I haven't faced a decent challenge in ages."

Morganna chanted and the air turned bitterly cold, her breath billowing in white clouds. Crystals of frost appeared and formed jagged shards. The coven leader barked a final word, and the spears of ice shot forward at Tressalayne.

Tressalayne twitched a finger, and a circle of fire roared to life before her, the intense heat driving Morganna back. The ice shards passed through the fire and melted, turned into harmless mist. The coven leader, arms raised to shield her eyes from the red-hot glare, gaped at the ease which her apprentice defended herself.

She snapped her fingers, and with a blur of motion, one of the heavy metal chairs flew toward Tressalayne. Without taking her eyes off the coven leader, Tressalayne reached out and caught the chair in midair. It quivered and shook in her grip, the sorcerous power of each witch straining to overcome the other. Finally, Tressalayne wrenched the chair free and launched it at Morganna. It slid along the floor, sparks flying and metal squealing. Unable to react in time, the chair bowled over the coven leader, and she crashed to the concrete.

Hissing in pain, Morganna leaped up. Fear and uncertainty filled her eyes. "Where-how—"

"You taught me well." Tressalayne stepped toward Morganna, her tread light and confident.

"For example, the most important lesson I learned was to conceal my true abilities. Better to be thought a green apprentice than an ambitious one…and a threat to your leadership of the coven."

Morganna backed up. Her eyes darted back and forth. "Your dalliance with the mortal has driven you mad. I mentored you, nurtured you, kept you from harm. *I saved your life from Lockstone!*"

"Did you? I wonder what poor Argatha would have to say about that? You sacrificed her so *you* could escape. Only opportunity and circumstance prevented my life from being given as well!"

Tressalayne stopped, lips set in a hard line. "Once, like me, you were an apprentice witch. What happened to *your* mistress, *your* coven leader? Did you conceal your talent and bide your time? Did you nurture your mistress's trust and when the time was right, betray her?"

Tressalayne leaped forward. The sudden movement caught Morganna off guard. Her arm shot forward and caught Morganna by the throat. She lifted her into the air while Morganna squirmed and fought. Sparks flew, the air thick with ozone, their magic's competing for supremacy.

"You see, I know the answers to all those questions. In your haste to return my memory, you made a mistake. Only a small one to be sure, but enough to make things clear to me. Your spell restored my memory, *but included parts of yours as well.* I saw the sleep draught you slipped your mistress, and heard the *crack* of her neck, broken by your own hands. I saw faces of apprentice witches who came before me, killed because you feared their skill might one day challenge your supremacy."

Tressalayne shook Morganna and tightened her grip. "And I saw my own face in your memories, the next apprentice to be disposed of. Seems I didn't conceal my Talent nearly well enough."

Tressalayne released Morganna, and she fell to the floor. The coven leader coughed and gagged, her breath wheezing gasps.

Tressalayne stood over her. "Despite all the blood and betrayal, your worst offense was to deny me any opportunity to experience love, to never know the feel of being held and cherished. *You withheld from me the most precious of all life's gifts!* But I'll take solace when I kill you. They'll be no one to mourn your death, no one to carry on your memory. You will be forgotten, your remains turned to dust and scattered in the wind. It will be like you never existed. A fitting end don't you think?"

"Weakness!" Morganna spat. "Love makes you weak! Do you think I care one shit about legacy? To survive, a witch must be merciless and strong. We take what we need, kill those who oppose us, and use the mortals as we see fit. It is a grand life spoiled only by emotion. WE DON'T NEED LOVE!"

Morganna rolled away and jumped to her feet. A dagger appeared in her hand and she flipped it at Tressalayne. It sped toward her throat in a blur of motion.

And passed harmlessly through the apprentice witch.

Morganna, mouth agape, watched Tressalayne's image waver and disappear. Strong hands suddenly appeared at her back, lifted the coven leader, and tossed her through the air. With a *crunch*, she struck the wall, bounced off, and slid to the ground. Stunned, she watched Tressalayne approach.

"Dissipation spell. Don't you remember? You said only a witch of great power and experience could cast the spell."

Tressalayne looked down at Morganna. "I mastered dissipation long ago…not that I care about my prowess any more." She looked back at Lucas, and her eyes softened. "My witching days are over…but not before your life ends."

Morganna began to sob and crawl away. "No, don't kill me! I'll submit, do anything you ask. Please don't kill me!"

The last thing she expected to hear was the implacable coven leader beg for her life. Distracted, Tressalayne missed Morganna turn away and palm an object. With a furtive sleight of hand, she raised a vial to her lips, and with a fluid motion, downed the contents. Moments later, her body rippled and swelled, the flesh pink and vibrant. Triumphant, Morganna leaped to her feet, younger and more vigorous.

The coven leader flipped the empty vial so it landed at Tressalayne's feet. "The last of the *morlaga* potion. You should have just killed me, but instead you droned on about love."

Morganna laced her fingers together and cracked her knuckles. "Now, dearie, where were we?"

SEVENTY-TWO

WITH A SCREECH, MORGANNA ATTACKED TRESSALAYNE. Another ball of energy appeared in her hand, and the coven leader launched it at her apprentice. This time, it was Tressalayne's turn to throw her arms up to ward off the explosive magic. The impact with Morganna's magic jerked her off her feet and blasted her backwards. She landed with a painful *thud* on the hard floor, her breath driven out of her.

Morganna was on her before she could get to her feet. Revitalized and strengthened by the potion, the coven leader's magic easily overcame Tressalayne's resistance. She barked a command and Tressalayne rose in the air to hover before the coven leader. Lips pulled back in a rictus, Morganna pummeled her apprentice. Helpless to stop her, Tressalayne's head pitched side to side from the force of the blows. Tiring of her apprentice's face, Morganna switched to her torso. The *crack* of ribs breaking filled the air while Morganna landed one vicious blow after another.

Blood poured from Tressalayne's mouth, her breath hoarse gasps of pain. Barely conscious, her head lolled on her shoulders.

"*No!*" a voice cried.

Enjoying herself immensely, Morganna debated which arm to break first, when the shout interrupted her pleasant thoughts. She turned and saw Tressalayne's mortal love with Crick's weapon pointed at her. The gun hiccupped, smoke and fire spewing from the barrel.

Blam, blam, blam.

Lucas, reached Crick's handgun about the time Morganna drank from the hidden vial. He looked up in horror to see Tressalayne hanging helpless before the coven leader, a punching bag for the enraged witch. Meaty *thuds* resounded in the air, his beautiful Tressalayne absorbing blows which would have staggered a heavyweight champion.

Desperate, he snatched the gun up. The cold steel lay unfamiliar in his palm, and he could count on one hand all the times he fired a weapon. Nevertheless, he pointed the gun and fired. The gun bucked, the shots wild, and he realized he would never hit the witch unless he moved closer.

Lucas staggered to his feet, and stumbled toward Morganna, the handgun held before him in shaky hands. He saw the coven leader's mouth move, a spell on her lips. He managed to miss with two more shots before he heard a rumble behind him. He glanced over his shoulder and his mouth fell open. Part of the floor of the warehouse cracked and broke into chunks of rubble, the concrete sections wedging themselves together like pieces of a jigsaw puzzle. Within moments, the grey hunks took on the rough parody of a human shape complete with arms and legs.

On feet fashioned from broken sections of cement, the creature pounded the floor in pursuit of Lucas. Pieces of rebar reformed into hands and fingers, and before Lucas could escape, Morganna's sorcerous creation had him in its grip. Arms wrenched backwards, he cried out, his shoulder dislocated. The gun dropped from his hand, and the creature spun him around to face the witch.

Tressalayne, one eye swollen shut, moaned at the sight.

Morganna clapped her hands in delight. She barked a command, and the chair which earlier knocked her over, spun upright and sped toward Tressalayne. It stopped and positioned beneath her. Morganna snapped her fingers, and the apprentice witch dropped into the seat. With a *squeal* of bending metal, the arms of the chair looped around Tressalayne's arms to hold her tight, then slid backwards to seat her beside Lucas.

Morganna paced before them, a frown of concentration on her face. She stopped and faced her captives.

"Now *who* do I torture and kill first?"

Lockstone staggered toward the sounds of battle, crimson drops marking his passage like breadcrumbs. Weak from blood loss, he reached a nearby support pillar and leaned on it to watch the sight unfolding before him.

The two witches battled back and forth, and astonished, he saw Tressalayne quickly get the upper hand. Before she could finish the coven leader, however, Lockstone's sharp eyes spotted Morganna drink a philter of some sort. The transformation, instantaneous, caused him to groan in dismay.

Morlaga potion!

The one-sided battle turned in the blink of an eye, and the coven leader proceeded to beat her apprentice senseless.

The roar of multiple shots from a handgun startled Lockstone, and he spun to see the doctor advance on Morganna. None of the shots came anywhere close. His witch senses crawled at the powerful spell cast by Morganna in response. The floor cracked and shook. Then, a bizarre creature rose from the rubble to grab the doctor and hold him captive.

Within moments, it was over and Morganna stood victorious.

Lockstone raised the crossbow and tried to center it on Morganna. No matter how hard he concentrated, he couldn't keep his hands from shaking. The loss of blood cost him dearly, and he would be lucky to hit the wall with the bolt much less Morganna. He briefly considered trying the rejuvenation spell again, but quickly discarded the idea. Morganna would detect the use of magic and be on him before it would do any good.

Time for his backup plan…the one which would probably cost his life. He dropped the crossbow, took a deep breath, and stepped into the light.

He headed straight for Morganna.

SEVENTY-THREE

ORGANNA CAUGHT MOVEMENT OUT OF THE CORNER OF HER eye. She turned in a crouch, hands held high ready to defend herself. Her mouth fell open at the sight of a bloodied, bedraggled, Robert Lockstone stagger toward her. A ragged wound gaped at his side, a bright crimson stain on his tunic and breeches. He swayed on his feet.

Morganna stifled the impulse to immediately attack. The witch hunter didn't look like he could defend himself against a rabbit. Suspicious, she watched him wobble over to one of the support pillars and slide slowly down until he rested on the floor. A long smear of blood coated the metal stanchion, and gleamed in the light.

A cruel smile spread on her lips. "Why, Robert, you look like you've seen better days. The last time we met, I seem to recall you put a poisoned bolt in me."

Lockstone grimaced as he shifted his position against the hard metal beam. "Yes, I believe you're right. One of the highlights of my career, although I'm disappointed you somehow managed to cheat death."

Morganna approached the witch hunter, vigilant for any weapon or sign he might attack her. "Your wound looks grievous. Oh, I do hope the pain is excruciating."

Lockstone nodded. "In your battle with Tressalayne, I got caught up in a blast of magic."

Morganna threw back her head in exultation. "This *is* a propitious night! My traitorous apprentice and her lover, and now my most implacable foe at my mercy!"

Morganna's eyes narrowed in suspicion and she pointed her talon at Lockstone. "*Hmm.* This is too easy. Why would you walk to certain death? A trap?" Her eyes darted and looked in the dark corners for an accomplice. "Where is the other witch hunter?"

Lockstone's lip curled. "Dead, thanks to you! There is no one to help me!"

Morganna knelt beside Lockstone, her dark eyes boring into him. "Then I'll ask again. Why?"

The witch hunter shifted and grimaced from the effort. "A better question would be *how* I managed to follow you to this world."

Morganna tapped her lips. "I am rather curious. How *did* you accomplish this feat?"

"Simple really. I used the same gateway you created and came after you."

Anger crossed the coven leader's face. "Impossible! Only a member of my coven would be allowed passage. You lie!"

Lockstone chuckled. "Yet, here I am."

The witch hunter spat, the bloody phlegm landing at Morganna's feet. "But, to answer your original question, why would I risk my life and approach you?" Lockstone pointed at his wound, streaks of blood leaking from it. "Thanks to you, I'm dying, so while I can't kill you, I can at least goad you one last time. I'll have to be satisfied with the look on your murderous face before I die."

Ignoring the pain, the witch hunter leaned forward, teeth bared. "I took the amulet from Argatha's dead body. You should have seen her. Full of holes and bled out like a hog dressed for slaughter. There it lay on her gray, dead neck, so I took the locket and was allowed entry through the gate. Think about it, Morganna. I used an amulet from your coven and it led me here. I used your own vaunted magic to follow you. The great Morganna couldn't protect her own coven, and even allowed a Hunter to corrupt an amulet and use it against her. Wait until all your sister witches hear about this." Lockstone shook with laughter.

Morganna rose to her feet, skin flushed. Her hands clenched and unclenched. "Where is the amulet?"

The witch hunter wiped his eyes and looked up. "Amulet? What amulet?"

Spittle bubbled at the corner of the coven leader's mouth. "WHERE IS IT?" she screamed.

She leaped forward, grabbed Lockstone, and stabbed stiffened fingers into his ragged gash. A howl of agony tore from Lockstone's lips. Morganna released him and he slumped forward onto the floor.

Face ashen, the witch hunter pushed himself upright, fresh blood pumping from his wound. Voice hoarse with pain, he said, "Okay. N-no more."

Lockstone pulled the backpack from his shoulders. "Its in my pack." He began to pull open the zipper. "I'll get it for—"

Morganna barked a command and the backpack was torn from the witch hunter's grasp to fly into her hands. "You think me a fool? *I'll* search for the amulet!"

The witch upended the pack and shook it. A crossbow, fell out to land with a *thump* on the floor, followed by clumps of packing material. The witch shook harder.

A smile grew on Lockstone's face, and a chuckle escaped from his lips. Morganna shot him a venomous glance then returned her attention to the knapsack. Impatient, with a rip of fabric, she tore it in two. The entire contents spilled to the floor. A heavy object struck the floor with a *clunk*, and a knobby sphere bounced out of the straw packing and rolled to a stop…at Morganna's feet.

All mirth left Lockstone's face. Eyes cold, he said, "Give my regards to Argatha in hell, you black-hearted bitch."

Click.

The turtle snapped open.

SEVENTY-FOUR

MORGANNA STARED AT THE ROUND OBJECT, HORROR spreading across her face at the realization she had been duped. Terror filled her veins with ice. She pivoted and raced for the door.

Razor-sharp wafers of metal rose into the air from within the turtle. They turned and twisted like miniature weathervanes, before finally orienting themselves.

Straight at Morganna.

The cloud of shrapnel streaked toward the witch, the whisper of its passage, a *whisk* in the air. Morganna punched the air before her and the warehouse door blew backwards, torn off its hinges. The coven leader plunged through the opening and out into the black, storm-wracked night, the flotilla of sharp iron in hot pursuit.

Silence abruptly descended within the building, the steady drumbeat of rain and the occasional roll of thunder the only sounds to break the quietude. The dank, warm smell of rain wafted through the ruined doorway, while the wind moaned as it whistled by.

Suddenly, an image appeared at the door-less entrance.

Morganna stumbled back into the warehouse, rain-slicked hair plastered to her scalp. She staggered forward, a dazed look on her face. The coven leader opened her mouth to speak, but instead of words, a gurgle of crimson spewed from her lips. Water dripped from the witch's sodden clothes and mixed with blood gushing from multiple wounds. Morganna listed from side-to-side, her eyes dimmed…then became vacant.

She pitched forward, dead before her body hit the floor.

Lucas, his shoulder afire in a throb of pain, watched Morganna fall, a red pool spreading beneath her inert form. The turn of events happened with such breathtaking speed, he could scarcely comprehend what happened. Moments earlier their demise appeared so certain he could feel death's icy presence, and the next, Morganna's lifeless body lay on the floor. A snippet from The Wizard of Oz ran through his mind, and a hysteria-fueled giggle escaped his lips.

Ding-dong, the wicked witch is dead.

The concrete creature holding him shuddered and collapsed into a pile of broken rubble. Next to him, the chair Tressalayne was manacled to announced its return to original form with a screech of metal. Released, she stood on unsteady feet and rushed to Lucas. He cried out in pain at her desperate embrace.

"Hold on," he grimaced, and stepped away. He gripped his injured shoulder with his good arm and twisted. With a *pop*, it slid back in place. Face pale with relief, he turned back to Tressalayne.

"Now where were we?" His arms encircled her and pulled her tight. When he attempted to kiss her, Tressalayne's own yelp of pain appeared in his ear from the pressure on her bruised lips.

"*Ahem.*"

Lucas looked up to see the giant of a man responsible for

Morganna's death. Tressalayne stiffened in his arms at the sight of him.

"Who-who are you?" Lucas asked.

"Robert Lockstone," the big man answered. "I'd greet you properly, but as you can see, I'm somewhat indisposed."

Tressalayne wrenched herself from Lucas' embrace. "Witch Hunter!" she spat.

Lockstone held his hands up. "Now, now, Lass. I admit I hunt witches, but you seem...*different*. You have nothing to fear from me."

Lucas placed a hand on Tressalayne's shoulder. It trembled with tension. "Look at him. Even if he is lying, he couldn't hurt a flea in his current condition. In fact, we need to get him to a hospital as soon—"

A *buzz* like a swarm of bees filled the air. Lucas looked over his shoulder and spotted the shrapnel rising from Morganna. Her body jerked like a marionette, each jagged piece tearing itself from her flesh to join the swirl of bloodstained metal.

A cry of dismay escaped Lockstone's lips. "Get back, Lad. Get out of the way!"

"Wh-what?" Lucas pointed at the cloud. "What's it doing?"

Lockstone grabbed the metal pillar and with a groan, pulled himself upright. "There's a witch still alive...*Tressalayne!*"

The horrible implication dawned on Lucas. "No! You have to stop it!"

"Can't, Lad. Only the wizard which placed the enchantment on the turtle can undo it...and he is back on my world." Lockstone's voice cracked, tears in his eyes. "I'm sorry, Lad."

The buzz rose to a crescendo, the swarm of shrapnel speeding toward Tressalayne. "No!" Lucas screamed.

He leaped in front of Tressalayne to shield her. With both arms, he grabbed her and turned so his back faced the sharp metal. Every time the deadly cloud moved, so did Lucas. The hum of the swarm was deafening.

"*You're going to get yourself killed!*" Lockstone cried above the angry noise. "The enchantment won't hold the swarm much longer. Let her go, Lad!"

Lucas, his face inches from Tressalayne, shook his head and whispered, "I don't care. I'll die before I let you go."

Tressalayne placed her hands on Lucas' face. Softly, she said, "I see now how you filled her heart with such joy and yearning. But the witch you love is no longer here. Only her shadow remains a part of me…Morganna saw to that."

Tressalayne smiled, a wistful look on her face. "I wish we had more time. I've only begun to taste the love you shared. But…it is enough. I know what she would do."

Tressalayne pulled him forward and kissed him. "You are my beloved, my first and only. I will always love you."

With sudden movement, Tressalayne's hands slid down to Lucas' hips. Before he could react, she lifted him and tossed him away from her. The cloud immediately attacked. Tressalayne, her eyes on Lucas, shook from the impact of the shrapnel. She stood for a moment, then with arms outstretched, fell forward. The sharp iron rose from her lifeless body and swirled above her. With a soft *hum*, it moved to the turtle, and one-by-one, the pieces dropped back into the turtle. With a *click*, the lid snapped shut.

Lucas howled and crawled toward Tressalayne. He reached her and cradled her head in his lap. Rocking back and forth, tears spilled from his eyes. "*No, no, no, no, no!*"

His body wracked by sobs, he held her tighter and hugged her body to his chest.

The doctor's raw cries of anguish pierced Lockstone's heart like a knife. How many times had he experienced the same scene, the loss of loved ones, the inconsolable grief of those left behind? He became a witch hunter to prevent such events.

Didn't he?

Lockstone looked at his hands. Tressalayne didn't deserve to die. Her perversion was due solely because of Morganna. When given a chance, she changed. She found love. Another witch in another time and place made the same choice.

His own mother.

He shook his head. *Revenge? Anger? Hatred?* Is this what drove him now instead of justice? If so, he was no better than Morganna.

Then his own tears came, along with a singular desire he thought he would never feel.

He wished he never became a Witch Hunter.

SEVENTY-FIVE

Lucas stroked Tressalayne's hair. Numb with grief, he couldn't focus, his mind a gray cloud of anguish. *How could he live without her?*

A groan interrupted his thoughts. He looked up and saw the witch hunter, Robert Lockstone, sink back to the floor. Fierce joy filled him at the sight of his suffering, the man responsible for Tressalayne's death! After a moment, however, he recalled the look on his face and the sound of regret in his voice. He realized the witch hunter never wanted her death—only Morganna's.

Gently, he laid Tressalayne's head on the cold floor, stood, and made his way to Lockstone.

The big man looked up at him, his face edged with guilt. "Just leave me be, Lad. I'll eventually bleed out, sooner if I pull this wadding out of my wound."

Lockstone leaned back and closed his eyes. A tired sigh escaped from his lips. "I expect you would like that. I know I would. I've seen too many people I care about die because of my mistakes. Your Tressalayne is just one more on my growing list."

Lucas knelt and pulled Lockstone's shirt away from his wound. Ragged, torn skin circled the gash. Blood continued to seep as he studied the wound.

"We need to get you to a hospital." Lucas cast about and spotted clumps of the straw packing from Lockstone's knapsack strewn on the concrete. He grabbed a large handful and firmly held it to the gash. He pulled the witch hunter's hand over and pushed it on the wound. "Hold this in place. It will slow the bleeding until we can get you to the emergency room."

Lockstone shook his head. "Why are you helping me?"

Lucas stood and wiped his hands on his pants. "Morganna would have killed us anyway. You tried to stop her." He paused, pain in his eyes. "Besides, the Tressalayne I knew—the one I fell in love with—would have wanted me to help you."

He dragged a chair over and helped Lockstone into the seat. As he straightened, a *whoosh* erupted from where Morganna lay. Both men turned, looks of astonishment on their faces.

Her body floated in the air covered in flames. Ash dripped from her remains, the fire growing hotter. Suddenly, Tressalayne's body ignited as well. Lucas and Lockstone were forced to scramble away from the intense heat. A raging inferno covered the remains of both witches, smoke and flames licking high toward the ceiling.

Then with an audible, *pop*, the fire snuffed out.

Instead of the witches' bodies, all that remained was a gray pile of ashes.

Lucas pointed a shaking finger. "What—what happened?"

Dumbfounded, the witch hunter shook his head. "I don't know, Lad. I've never seen anything like it. Witches don't conflagrate when they die. It must have something to do with how the magic of the Kingdom interacts with the magic here."

The howl of the wind picked up and the building began to rattle. Lockstone cocked his head and listened. The storm's intensity was growing.

Alarm on his face, the witch hunter limped over to Lucas. "We have to get out of here, Lad. It's not finished!"

The words no sooner left his lips when a section of the roof blew away. Rain and wind poured inside. A sound like a runaway diesel locomotive grew louder and louder.

Lockstone grabbed Lucas' arm. "C'mon, Lad!" he shouted over the maelstrom.

Out of the corner of his eye, Lucas caught a glint within Tressalayne's ash remains. He jerked his arm from the witch hunter and ran to the gray mound. Desperately, he dug through it and closed his hand on cold metal. He pulled it out.

Her amulet.

More frenzied digging proved fruitless. He couldn't find the engagement ring he gave her. By this time, the roar of the storm's fury reached an earsplitting decimal level. Objects within the warehouse became deadly missiles picked up and hurled against the walls.

Lucas stuffed the locket in his pocket and raced toward Lockstone. He put his arm around the big man and helped him through the blasted ruin of the doorway. Once outside, rain and wind lashed them, the howl of the storm even more intense. Lucas, frantic, looked for Crick and Lunker's vehicles. He spotted dark shapes not far away alongside the building. They struggled to reach them, the gale threatening to pick them up off their feet.

The first vehicle, a Lexus, was unlocked but after yanking the door open for a look, Lucas saw no keys. Heads and shoulders pitched forward against the wind, the two men checked the SUV next to the Lexus. Lucas jerked the door open.

A set of keys dangled from the ignition.

Lucas helped Lockstone into the passenger side, then ran around and leaped into the driver's seat. The big SUV started on the first crank, and he rammed it in reverse. The car jumped and screeched, the headlights revealing rain and debris whizzing by horizontally. He put the vehicle in drive, and with a squeal of tires, headed for the gate. Accelerator floored, he didn't pause, and the SUV plowed through the gate with barely a tremor.

They barreled down the rain slick road. Lucas spared a glance in the rearview mirror. A flash of lightning revealed a long, black funnel snake down from the sky...centered directly over the warehouse. Another lightning bolt traveled down the funnel to strike the rapidly disintegrating building. Whole pieces, ripped from the foundation, spiraled into the air to join the debris field. Face grim, he tore his eyes away and pushed the accelerator harder.

They sped faster into the wet night.

SEVENTY-SIX

Lucas ran after Tressalayne.
Wildflowers in a riot of colors grew ankle high at his feet, the sun bright in the sky. A warm breeze caressed his cheek. He stopped and looked around.

Now where is she?

The tinkle of laughter, the sound so familiar to him, came from his left. He looked and caught a glimpse of movement. A smile spilt his face and he resumed the pursuit. A sound like thunder reverberated in the air and he looked up. He saw only clear blue, and puzzled, wondered how there could be thunder with no clouds. The sound persisted and became louder and louder. The sky turned dark, and the picturesque meadow fragmented and disappeared. Worse, he couldn't hear Tressalayne's laughter any more.

Come back! Come back!

Lucas awoke with a start. He sat up, empty beer cans cascading from his lap to scatter at his feet. A sharp pain pierced his head like someone attempting to drive a nail through his skull. He moaned and held his face with both hands.

Knock, knock, knock.

The sound came from the door, and he looked up with dull, bloodshot eyes. His mouth tasted rancid like something crawled up into it and died. A month-long growth of beard, stained with dried food and vomit, itched incessantly. He ignored the knocking and scratched the scraggly growth while he searched for something to drink. He brought one discarded beer can after another to his mouth and shook out the tepid remains. Disappointed, he hurled the last one across the room.

The knocks now progressed to a steady banging. Irritated, Lucas yelled, "Go 'way. Leave me alone!" The effort caused the drums in his head to pound anew, and with a groan, he sank back into the chair.

"Dr. Beckett, its Hank Harper!" a voice cried from the other side of the door. "I've been trying to reach you for weeks. I really need to speak with you!"

Lucas looked at the table beside him. He pushed aside a sea of empty take-out containers, and found his cell. He held it up and squinted.

Dead battery.

His mind slowly processed the fact he hadn't charged the phone in weeks. It took too much effort to recall if this was by accident or design, and he dropped it back on the table.

"Go away, Hank. We've got nothing to talk about," he called out in a hoarse voice.

"But, Dr. Beckett, you still have my book! You promised to return it when you finished with it."

The Book of First Magic. The name brought back a flood of memories, and tears filled his eyes. It still lay on the music stand in the kitchen. The one and only time he attempted to enter the kitchen, he spied the book and completely unraveled. He bolted outside and collapsed on the ground. For hours, all he could do was lie in a fetal curl and weep. He hadn't entered the room since.

Lucas rubbed his face. If Hank took the book, he could at least use the kitchen again…although given his lack of appetite, it wasn't high on his list of priorities.

Decision made, he stood and stumbled to the door. When he opened it, bright sunlight streamed in and stabbed his eyes. He staggered back and blinked. When his vison cleared, he saw a large individual beside Hank's diminutive form.

Lockstone.

"Hello, Lucas," the witch hunter said extending a ham-sized hand.

"What—what are you doing here?"

Hank stepped forward. "I realize you are going through some difficult times, Dr. Beckett. Robert informed me of what happened to…to Tressalayne. I can't begin to imagine the pain you are going through."

Hank motioned with his hand. "May we?"

After a moment's hesitation, Lucas nodded, and they stepped inside. Dirty clothes, beer bottles, and pizza boxes littered a nearby couch, and Lucas swept them on the floor to clear a space.

"Guess I need to hire another cleaning lady," he quipped and then collapsed back into his chair.

The two men sat down and Hank cleared his throat. "Grief can affect the way the brain functions—profoundly at times. I mention this because you seem to have forgotten the phone call to me from the hospital. If I may, let me sum it up for you. In our conversation, you said a grievously injured friend would need my help once he was released from the hospital's care. Then you disconnected and I haven't heard from you since."

Lockstone spoke up. "Hank took me in and let me stay with him during my convalescence. An act of kindness for which I am indebted." The witch hunter shifted his weight and pointed at Lucas. "But it was *you* who saved my life, Lad. You could have left me to die and no one would have been the wiser. I'm forever grateful to you."

Hank patted the big man's knee. "After Robert sufficiently recovered, I drove him to the building where the, er, unfortunate events occurred. The place was scoured clean, with not even a loose nail or screw to be found. Nothing is left except the foundation. Its like a structure never existed there."

Except a warehouse once did once exist and Tressalayne died there, Lucas' bitter thoughts shouted in his mind.

Weary, he waved his hand. "Thanks for the update, Hank, but I'm not really interested in hearing more." He sat up and pointed toward the kitchen. "The book's in there. You'll do me a great favor if you just take it and leave."

The two men looked at each other. Saddened, Hank nodded and stood. "Of course. Be back in a moment." He turned and disappeared through the door.

After a few minutes, he came back out empty-handed. "I seem to have a problem."

Irritated, Lucas asked, "What is it now?"

"I can't move the book."

Lucas rolled his eyes. "Oh, come on. Get Lockstone to help you if its too heavy!"

Helpless, Hank shrugged. "Go see for yourself. It won't budge an inch."

SEVENTY-SEVEN

LUCAS BOLTED UPRIGHT, HIS DULL HEADACHE AN INSISTENT throb. He just wanted to be left alone!

"Okay, okay, I'll get your damn book for you! Then I want you both to get the hell out!"

He stalked to the kitchen door and kicked it open. The odor of stale food and old coffee grounds assaulted his nose. He spotted The Book of First Magic perched on the black music stand in the corner. Bile rose in his throat and his breath came in choked gasps. He turned to run out, but then stopped. Hands clenched, body shaking, Lucas pivoted and forced himself to move until he stood above the music stand.

He put his hand in his pocket and fumbled about. His fingers touched cold metal, the reassuring feel a balm on his tattered emotions, and he pulled out Tressalayne's amulet. He held it up to his nose, nostrils flaring to catch the faint remnants of her scent.

"Miss you. I miss you so much," he whispered.

The Book of First Magic lay closed. The embossed images of the mythical creatures—frozen on the white leather—stirred familiar memories. He recalled the look of delight on Tressalayne's face the first time the Little People spoke to her, and a faint smile came to his lips.

Happy times.

He couldn't help himself, and reached out and touched the cover.

A ball of light burst from within the book. Its incandescence so dazzling, Lucas yelped and stumbled back, hands up to shield his eyes. It whizzed about the kitchen like a crazed firefly until it stopped and settled before Lucas. The sphere of light grew larger and became translucent. He could detect movement within its crystal walls, the image becoming clearer and clearer. Then the light faded, and the sphere disappeared.

Tressalayne stood before Lucas.

"Hello, my love. I've missed you too."

Stunned, Lucas' mouth dropped open. He barely registered the commotion of Hank and Lockstone bursting into the room.

"You—you're alive? Are you real? *Dear God please tell me I'm not hallucinating!*" The last came out in a hysterical shout.

Tressalayne ran forward and launched herself into his arms. "Yes, I'm alive, I'm real, and I'll never leave you again!"

Lucas held Tressalayne in a desperate embrace, afraid if he let go she would disappear from his life again. He buried his face in her hair, the thick tresses warm with clean scents of water, wind, and sky. His body shook with sobs and he pulled her tighter.

Hank and Lockstone watched the scene in stupefied amazement. The big witch hunter, in particular, couldn't believe his eyes, and rubbed them over and over again as if to clear his vision.

Tressalayne stretched upward on her toes and kissed Lucas. One kiss led to another, and soon he was covering her face and neck with his lips.

Breathless, Tressalayne pushed herself away and looked Lucas up and down. Her face fell. "You've lost weight." Concerned she ran her hands up and down his chest and back. "I can feel your ribs through your shirt!"

Tressalayne pulled a small flask from the sleeve of the long cream-colored dress she wore. She handed it to Lucas. "Here. Drink this."

Obediently, he raised the vial to his lips and downed it with one gulp. His headache disappeared, and energized, he felt better than he had in weeks.

Tressalayne brushed his hair and beard with her fingers. She *tisked* and wrinkled her nose. "You need a shave and a bath. I'm not getting married while you look and smell like yesterday's garbage."

"Ma—married?" Lucas stuttered.

"Of course." She held her hand up to display the engagement ring on her finger, diamonds glittering in the light. "Isn't that why you gave me this?"

"Yes, but I couldn't find it in your—"

He stopped and held her by the shoulders. "I saw you die. I—I saw your remains…" He couldn't continue. The memory, even with Tressalayne alive and right before him was too painful to relive.

Finally, he said, "I don't understand."

Tressalayne sighed and stepped away. "It is difficult to explain, but you did see me die…at least part of me. My old self— the dark witch—died, while the white witch survived to become part of the world of The Book of First Magic. There is much even now which still remains a mystery to me. One moment I'm with you facing an evil witch, the next, the Little People are singing to me, your ring still on my finger."

She smiled. "I'm a creature of magic now, my love. The transformation started the day you brought me to the *Leabhar an Chéad Draíocht* and introduced me to the Faerie domain within.

I can only stay here for short periods of time, a day and a night at the most before I must return. *But I can bring you with me*! Two worlds, yet we never have to be apart!"

Tressalayne turned and rubbed her thumb softly against Lucas' cheek. "I've been waiting impatiently ever since for you to touch the book and summon me."

Tressalayne grabbed his ear lobe and gave it a painful yank. "What took you so long!"

Without waiting for an answer, she whirled and faced Hank. "I believe among your many talents you are authorized to perform marriage ceremonies?"

"Why, yes, but how—"

"We want to get married…now!"

Hank raised his hands. "Of course, but I don't have the proper documents with me which need to be signed and—"

The music stand slid with a *screech* to rest before Hank. The Book of First Magic took flight and fluttered over to the granite countertop where it landed with a *plop*. Tressalayne snapped her fingers and several pieces of paper issued from the book. They knifed through the air to settle in neat order, side-by-side, on the music stand.

After a moment's hesitation, Hank picked them up and studied them. He nodded, a broad smile on his face.

"Everything seems to be in order. Now, if the bride and groom to be will step forward, we'll begin. Robert, you'll be the witness, so please stand next to me."

"Wait!" Tressalayne cried. She turned to Lucas. "Do you have my amulet?"

Lucas nodded and handed it to her. She closed her fist on the locket and murmured. When she opened her hand, a band of gold lay in her palm. She placed it on Lucas' finger.

"I don't need this any longer. I've got something far better. *I've got you*."

With a sweep of her hand, a shower of golden sparks rained on Lucas. He experienced a brief but overwhelming urge to itch, and then it was gone. He looked down and saw he was dressed in a coat, tie, and slacks...the same clothes he wore the night he proposed to Tressalayne. He rubbed his face and discovered he was clean-shaven, his hair neatly groomed.

Tressalayne looped her arm through Lucas'. *"Now* we are ready."

Face radiant, Lucas turned with Tressalayne toward Hank, a thought percolating in his mind.

Sometimes...dreams can come true.

EPILOGUE

ANK AND LOCKSTONE WATCHED THE HAPPY COUPLE JUMP into Lucas' golf cart and head for the cabin, the first stop on their honeymoon. Tressalayne wanted to kick off her shoes and dip her feet into the pond. The cart disappeared from sight and a short time later, they heard splashing and shrieks of laughter.

Hank smiled. "And they lived happily ever after."

Lockstone shook his head, a puzzled look on his face. "How can two witches occupy the same body, the same soul? And why would the Tressalayne of my world save the Lad's life? Its baffled me ever since I saw her die. Her heart beat just as darkly as Morganna's!"

Hank clapped Lockstone on the arm. "You, my friend, of all people should understand the vagaries of magic. One size *does not* fit all, with all sorts of fluctuations and ripples of unintended consequences. Tressalayne landed in a different world with no memory, a blank slate. She met Lucas, fell in love, and nothing was the same. She became a Janus Witch."

Lockstone cocked his head. "Eh? What's that?"

Hank chuckled. "Janus is a god depicted in ancient mythology with having two faces or two minds. One face is turned to look at the past, the other face to the future. An apt description of Tressalayne, don't you think? Her past died in the warehouse along with Morganna. And her future? It just arrived in a golf cart at Dr. Beckett's cottage."

Lockstone frowned. "But that still doesn't explain why the *past* Tressalayne sacrificed her own life for the Lad's!"

Hank sighed. "You're right. But for just a moment, put yourself in her shoes. In your entire life, all you have known is the conflict of the Hunt, kill or be killed. There's no room for any emotion except self-preservation and survival. Then one day, you feel something different. Its new and wonderful, a ray of sunshine in an otherwise drab existence. *Love!* The schism in Tressalayne's personality cracked the door just wide enough for her dark side to receive a taste of what love is like."

Hank turned thoughtful. "'Greater love has no one than this: to lay down one's life for one's friends.'" He pointed at the witch hunter. "A quote from a Book I highly recommend."

Lockstone scratched his beard and nodded. "Aye. You know, for a small man, you have big thoughts."

Hank laughed. "I guess I'll take that as a compliment." He rubbed his hands briskly. "Well, I think we're done here. What will you do now?"

Lockstone looked south. "Got a friend in Houston who owns a pawnshop. Doesn't seem to be much demand for witch hunters on this world…at least not anymore. I think I'll give it a try helping him out. What about you?"

Hank said, "I'll go back to my store in Mt. Pleasant. Opportunities have a way of coming to me from time to time." He paused and grinned at the big witch hunter.

"I can't wait to see what the next one brings."

Annalise closed her laptop and sighed.

For days she searched the internet for news on the disappearance of Mason Crick and his assistant, Sam Lunker. The police had no leads. The men just dropped from sight. In the course of her search, she came across another news account of a freak storm which produced a small, but powerful tornado on the outskirts of Longview. The tornado, oddly enough, destroyed only an old warehouse leaving the surrounding area untouched. What drew her interest, however, was the tornado struck the very night the police reported Crick and Lunker vanished.

How coincidental.

Except, she knew no coincidence existed. The men undoubtedly died at Morganna's hands. But something must have gone wrong, because Morganna died with them.

She picked up the velvet covered object she placed earlier on the table. She pulled off the slip cover to reveal a glass tube partially filled with a dull red liquid.

Morganna's blood.

Unbeknownst to Crick, Annalise only used part of her blood in the binding spell. She saved the rest and managed to slip it in her pocket without him any the wiser. Up until the night the two men disappeared and the tornado struck, the blood glowed, a testament to the power of the coven leader's magic even when separated from her body.

Then, the same evening the hospital CFO and his assistant vanished, the ambience disappeared, proof Morganna perished.

She stood and shouted. "*Yes!*"

Free! Free from Crick's criminal web, free from retaliation from Morganna! She grabbed the sealed tube and hurried to her bedroom at the back of of her store. A framed print of an ocean scene hung from a wall. Annalise pitched the print aside to reveal a wall safe. She spun the dial until, with a *click*, the lock released and she pulled open the door. In the back of the safe lay a battered jewelry box, and the Romani witch reached inside and grabbed it.

Anticipation gripped her, and she hurried to a small, windowless room she kept locked at all times. She entered the room and secured it behind her.

She could take no chance she would be interrupted.

A small, but sturdy, table occupied the center of the room, a single chair beside it. Open shelving lined the walls, filled with dried herbs, unguents, and vials of liquids. Larger glass containers held preserved toads, lizards, snakes, birds, and insects.

With a steady hand, Annalise drew a rectangle on the table's surface in red wax. She placed black candles at each precise corner of the rectangle and lit them. Lastly, she placed the glass tube with Morganna's blood in the center.

Annalise closed her eyes and chanted. The air stirred, a whisper of sound like the slither of a snake across dry leaves. A faint glow appeared in the blood and grew brighter and brighter. Annalise cracked an eyelid and spied the glow. Trembling with excitement, she stopped her chant.

The Romani witch placed the jewelry case in front of her and opened it. With great reverence, she took out a silver chain tarnished with age. Attached to the chain was a dull, gray gem, cracked and fissured. She laid it on the table and retrieved the tube of blood.

She broke the seal and poured Morganna's blood on the shattered jewel. It flowed into the broken cracks and crevices. Not a single drop escaped to spill onto the table.

The chain wriggled and undulated, the silver glinting with a shiny new sheen. The stone roiled and rattled against the table. Then…it stopped.

An amulet lay before Annalise. The color of the gem, whole again, took her breath away.

Midnight black.

THE CONQUEST OF THE VEIL
(Book I)
By
MICHAEL SCOTT CLIFTON

PROLOGUE

The Empire of Meredith: One Thousand Years Ago

TENDRILS OF BLACK SMOKE ROSE IN THE EARLY MORNING air.

Huddled within a thicket of vegetation, Larson Crump watched, his heart in his throat, while the manor house slowly burned to the ground. Greedy, licking flames consumed the once grand structure and with a groan of tortured wood, the southeastern corner of the manor collapsed in a shower of flame and sparks.

Above the noise and tumult of the raging fire, a scream rang out and Crump jammed a fist in his mouth to stifle a whimpering cry. His hands shook with tremors as he parted the thick screen of leaves. Despite his need for caution, a moan escaped his lips at the sight he beheld. There, against the backdrop of the burning manor, Lady Sonja stood stripped naked and struggled in the grasp of...*creatures* straight from his worst nightmares! Beneath a set of small piggish eyes, the brutish beasts possessed wicked, yellow tusks which jutted from their lower jaws. Waddles of pinkish-gray flesh framed their necks, the boar-like heads attached to a squat torso of powerful arms and legs.

Crump returned his attention to Lady Sonja, and groaned at the sight of the long, bloody slashes which marred her breasts, the streaks of crimson painting her ribs and abdomen. His eyes widened when Lady Sonja's husband, Lord Will, was brought forward and forced to stand beside his wife. Face battered and bruised, he fought with the nightmarish creatures to assist his wife. Amused grunts and squeals erupted from the beasts, and they rained blow after blow until fresh blood ran down his face and head.

There was a stir among the throng of manlike beasts, and they parted to provide passage for two figures. From his vantage point, Crump could see a couple, a man and woman, strut through the brutish creatures and up to the manor's veranda. Ink-black hair fell to the woman's waist, and even from a distance, he could see she possessed a terrible beauty. The man, slightly taller than the woman, wore sharp features and a cruel smile.

When the couple turned to face the grunting man-beasts, Crump saw their eyes for the first time. Black as a bottomless pit, they oozed a malevolency so potent, Crump's legs trembled and his hair stood on end.

Sorcery! The dark magic filled the air to such an extent Crump felt it assault his senses, like some ill breeze portending disaster.

From the veranda, the sorceress turned and held a small, round object high above her head for all the assembled creatures to see. Loud squeals and grunts boiled into the air until the enchantress held up her hand for silence.

"The Orb is ours! It is now *our* time and *our* destiny! We shall be the Masters and they," she said, a slender finger pointed at Will and Sonja, "shall be the ones who serve us! We will kill all who oppose us!"

Lowering the Orb to cradle it in her hands, the sorceress

turned to Sonja. "Before you die, I want you to know *your* Artifact, *your* creation made our ascension to power possible." Lady Sonja flinched at the words as if struck by a hammer. Fresh despair spread across her tear-streaked face.

Laughing, the sorceress pointed and Lord Will was thrown into the mass of man-beasts. Raw screams tore from Lady Sonja's throat at the sight of her husband torn to bloody pieces.

The violent sight and sound overwhelmed Crump's senses. Gorge rose in his throat and what little remained in his stomach spewed out. Mercifully, the screams came to an abrupt end. Crump sank to the ground and wept, his thin shoulders shaking.

He wiped his eyes and tried to make sense of what happened. His friends, the Lord of the Manor...*all dead!* He alone survived and only because he spent half the night in the bushes with a belly flux. When the creatures attacked, there had been no outcry, no alarm raised—almost as if the entire staff was drugged or ensorcelled by some dark magic.

All but Crump.

Fresh shrieks bruised the air when Lady Sonja, in turn, was given to the creatures. Her desperate cries reverberated into the early morning and pierced Crump's soul like a dagger.

He turned and fled.

PART ONE:
EAST TEXAS
(PRESENT DAY)

CHAPTER 1

BRRRRING!

Even before the last notes of the lunch bell faded, class-room doors flew open and students exploded into the hallways of Spring Hill High School. Mona Parker found herself carried along like a leaf in a river as she unsuccessfully tried to navigate a course to her locker. Finally, she reached the intersection of two hallways and found a quiet eddy while students rushed past her to the cafeteria. Once the flow abated somewhat, she backtracked to her locker. Opening it, she removed a brown paper bag containing her lunch along with a large, hardbound book. She stuffed her backpack into the cubbyhole, closed the door, and hurried to her favorite location to eat lunch.

Bursting out of the glass doors leading from the high school, Mona turned a corner leading to the student commons area. With a sigh of relief, she spied her coveted table still unoccupied. Her eyes darted left and right to see if anyone else might beat her to it. No other students were in sight, and Mona rushed to the table and breathlessly threw her book and bagged lunch down.

Success!

At first glance, the outdoor picnic table didn't seem to have any visible attributes that would lend itself as a desirable lunch location. Covered in a crisscross veneer of ugly blue polyure-thane, it was uncomfortable to sit in, and depending on the season—fall, winter, or spring—it either never seemed to get enough sunlight or too much. However, this particular table possessed one thing Mona found valuable above all else.

A location with a perfect view.

On cue, a slender boy with a lunch tray in hand walked up to another of the picnic tables directly across the commons area from Mona. Setting the tray down, several friends joined him moments later.

With a happy sigh, Mona arranged her book, a large illustrated edition on antique clocks, in front of her. She found the book in the nonfiction section of the school library, and while she had absolutely no interest in antique clocks, the book with its oversize, large-print format, propped up perfectly on a table. Moving the spine of the book like a gun sight to zero in on a target, Mona finally positioned it perfectly so when she looked up above the spine of the book, there he was.

Brock Stanton.

Brock's blue eyes flashed while he chatted with his friends, and Mona felt her heart beat faster when he smiled at some comment. She "met" him over a month ago when they accidentally bumped into each other. Coming from different directions in the always crowded hallways, Mona turned a corner and ran right into Brock. Mona dropped her books and he picked them up and apologized. Best of all, he displayed the same dazzling smile before he turned and left.

Mona had a crush on him ever since.

Quite by accident, she discovered later that Brock and his friends often frequented the same table and location at lunch. Since then, she and her trusty antique clock book were fixtures at the picnic table across from him. The last time she checked out her book (for the 3rd time), the librarian gave her an odd look and asked if she was doing a research paper. Mona mumbled something about liking the pictures, then stumbled out and made a mental note to start searching for another similar-sized book.

Although they had not spoken or even crossed paths again, Mona loved to peek at Brock over her book and fantasize about being his girlfriend. In her happy dreams, they traveled to exotic and romantic locations with breathtaking backdrops from which to kiss and hold each other.

Walking hand-in-hand on the dazzling white sand of a secluded Bermuda beach just as the sun is setting. Check!

A Colorado ski lodge with the gorgeous snowcapped Rocky Mountains in the background. With arms wrapped around each other, they watch their breath billow out to comingle in white clouds. Check!

An intimate Paris bistro sipping an espresso together while a white aproned maître d' hovers nearby smiling at the lovely couple. Check!

Sharing a delicious chilled shrimp cocktail, their—

"Well, well, what do we have here?" a voice intruded on Mona's dreamy meanderings.

Startled, Mona looked up. Eyes shaded with her hand in the bright December sunlight, Mona's pleasant fantasies came to an abrupt halt. Her heart sank and despite the unusually mild day, she felt a chill run down her spine.

Lady Anne Golightly stood beside her with hands on slim hips, a predatory smile on her face like that of a cat preparing to pounce on a mouse. Silky blonde hair cascaded past her shoulders, while glacial blue eyes regarded Mona with no small amount of contempt.

Mona gulped, a cold knot of fear growing in her stomach. As a freshman four years earlier, Mona had been in the snack bar line at lunch, a rare thing for her since she usually had no money for such things. As usual, a long, conga-like line of students had formed and moved at a snail's pace. When Lady Anne and a coterie of her friends breezed into the snack bar, they simply stepped in front of Mona. With laughs and snorts, they acted like Mona's place was theirs for the taking with her no more substantial than a ghost or a vapor. When Mona objected, loudly enough it seemed to attract one of the coaches on cafeteria duty, he made Lady Anne and her friends go to the end of the line. When she walked by Mona, Lady Anne fixed her with cold, hate-filled eyes.

It was the last day of "normal" high school life for Mona. Since then, Lady Anne had made Mona her special project.

Dead rats found in her locker.

Photo-shopped images of her face on a naked, grotesquely obese woman, which Lady Anne shared via all social media sites.

Humiliating text messages sent to Mona describing various parts of Mona's anatomy.

Opening her P.E. locker and discovering her P.E. clothes had been urinated on.

At first, Mona tried to fight back by going to the Principal, Mr. Garrett, but no proof could ever be found directly tying Lady Anne to the harassment. In fact, it served no purpose other than to make the acts worse and more frequent. Because Lady Anne's father was president of the largest bank in Longview and a member of some standing in the community, Mr. Garrett was reluctant to pursue the matter vigorously, and soon quietly dropped the matter.

Mona finally turned to her foster parents, Bud and Elaine Baker (something she would only do if absolutely *desperate*!), and tearfully asked for help. With feet propped up on a scarred and stained coffee table, Bud looked at her for a moment before draining the last of his Coors Light, belched, and told her to stop being a pantywaist whiner and to suck it up. Elaine dismissed Mona's problems with a wave of her hand, and the Bakers promptly turned their attention back to the cage-fighting event on TV.

Mona never mentioned it to them again.

Since then, Mona avoided Lady Anne and kept as low a profile as possible. It didn't stop the harassment, but Mona found it lessened somewhat. Now, Lady Anne's acts of cruelty came in ebbs and flows.

Today was a flow day.

Hand trailing over the top of Mona's propped up book, Lady Anne made a leisurely circuit of the table before coming to a stop behind Mona. She bent and peered over Mona's shoulder—which put her gaze directly on Brock.

"Something tells me you aren't reading your book, Mona," Lady Anne breathed in her ear. "What's the matter? The pictures not big enough for you?"

Tittering erupted from several of Lady Anne's friends. Like sharks sensing blood in the water, they arrived suddenly and formed a semicircle around Lady Anne, their eyes aglow in eager anticipation.

Lady Anne straightened and made a show of tapping her forefinger on her lips as if deep in thought. She paced back and forth, then moved in front of Mona to block her vision of Brock. With a sudden movement, Lady Anne whirled around, placed both hands on the table, and leaned in toward Mona.

"I think you are studying something other than your pathetic book." With a glance over her shoulder, a twisted sneer appeared on Lady Anne's face. "I think you are looking at those boys over there." Mona's breath froze in her throat.

No, no, no, oh please God, no! Please don't—

"The problem is…which one are you *really* looking at," Lady Anne purred interrupting Mona's silent pleading.

Wearing skin-tight leggings and a short skirt, Lady Anne's shapely posterior jutted directly at Brock and his friends while she spoke to Mona. It made quite an impression, and the boys' attention riveted on Lady Anne.

"Eeny meeny miny moe," Lady Anne intoned while she pointed her finger at each boy in turn. "I think it is...*you!*" With a dramatic sweep of her hand, she gestured at Brock.

All color drained from Mona's face and she found it hard to breathe. This reaction sealed her fate, and Lady Anne gleefully skipped across the space between the tables and returned moments later, arm-in-arm with Brock.

Her head spinning at the sudden turn of events, Mona couldn't believe the nightmare unfolding before her eyes.

Lady Anne pointed a slim, manicured finger at Mona. "Brock, I believe you have a secret admirer." Hoots and snorts erupted from all sides as Brock's friends joined the crowd surrounding Mona.

Seeing his friends laugh at him, Brock reacted like he'd been scalded. His face turned red and he took a step back from Mona.

"That's a bunch of crap! I don't even know who she is!" Brock's protest served only to make the howls of laugh louder.

Mona felt hot tears come to her eyes at Brock's reaction.

"Why, Brock, I think you are mistaken," Lady Anne exclaimed with a puzzled look. "Why else would Mona spend the past month looking at you every day over this book?" She knocked the book over, the multicolored pictures of old clocks flapping in the breeze.

Inwardly, Mona groaned. Lady Anne knew...had *known* for at least a month she was secretly gazing at Brock. The she waited to spring her trap until the perfect moment arrived.

Her fingernails dug her into her hands, and Mona desperately tried to stem the tears that threatened to erupt at any moment.

How could I have been so stupid, stupid, stupid not to notice!

"I think the *only* proper thing to do would be to ask Mona out right here and right now, Brock!"

Lady Anne leaped on top of the table and waved her arms like a carnival barker, crying out to the dozen or so students around the table, "Don't you agree? Brock needs to ask Mona out!"

Turning to face Mona and Brock, Lady Anne chanted, *"Ask Mona out! Ask Mona out!"* Within seconds, the assembled students picked up the chant and soon it echoed throughout the commons area.

Brock's face turned purple with embarrassment and rage. He whirled on Mona and spat, "Look, you dirty little bitch! Stop spying on me and leave me alone!"

Spinning, he pushed his way through the knot of students and stalked off. The show over, students began to drift away in ones and twos while they giggled and pointed at Mona. Soon, only Lady Anne remained. Like a devastated area in the aftermath of the storm, a ragged silence filled the air. Mona stared dully at the pages of her book fluttering in the light breeze.

She felt nothing.

She felt empty.

She felt *dead*.

Lady Anne moved and seated herself next to Mona. She whispered in her ear, "You *are* a dirty little bitch, but I would add an *ugly* little bitch as well".

Numb, Lady Anne's words barely registered with Mona. Finally, she mumbled, "Please leave me alone. Why won't you leave me alone?" This elicited a derisive snort from Lady Anne.

"Oh, Mona. Leave you alone? Of course not. What would be the fun in that?"

"Why? Why not?" Mona pleaded. "You have everything and I'm…I'm a nobody. Why can't you just leave me alone?"

Lady Anne stood and smoothed her skirt. Picking at a piece of lint on her blouse, she looked down at Mona, her expression hard.

"Because people like *me* are supposed to pick on people like *you*. You're the garbage in the garbage disposal, Mona. All you're good for is to be ground up and flushed down the drain. That's all your miserable life means to me."

With a smirk, Lady Anne added, "Well, I'd love to stay and chat some more with you *girlfriend*, but speaking of life, I have to get back to mine. *Ta!*" Blowing her a kiss, Lady Anne skipped off.

Moments passed before Mona finally stirred. The tears which earlier threatened to gush from her eyes were gone. Instead, she felt nothing but helpless futility. Cornered like a rabbit, she had no way to escape, no way to stop Lady Anne's predacious bullying.

She stood and picked up her lunch and book. Her mouth tasted like ashes, and she dropped her lunch in the nearest trash. Moving like a robot on autopilot, Mona walked to the media center, turned in her library book, and after a few minutes of aimless wandering, found herself alone in the girl's bathroom.

Running water in the sink, Mona cupped some of it into her hands and splashed it on her face. The shock of the cold water brought her mind back into focus, and she looked at herself in the mirror above the lavatory.

Frizzy brown hair spread out like foam around a narrow face. Her cheekbones were shallow, angular planes, giving her a pinched expression like she wore shoes too small for her feet. Her raptor-shaped nose, long and slightly hooked, had a pair of black-frame glasses perched on it. Brown eyes, puffy and red, stared back at Mona from behind the glasses. Mona's complexion, pasty-white, resembled a minefield littered with angry red spots indicative of recent acne flare-ups. Mona stepped a few paces back, and as she did so, the rest of her body came into view.

She wore blue jeans and a long-sleeved blouse and sweater, which covered skinny, birdlike arms and legs. Her bra size, 32A, hadn't changed since her 7th grade year, and even now, at almost 18 years of age, Mona more closely resembled an adolescent girl than a woman.

She was unremarkable.

She was plain and colorless as water.

She was a nobody.

"I hate my life," Mona whispered to the image in the mirror.

"Do you hear me? I HATE MY LIFE!" she screeched.

The tears she earlier successfully banished, now came back with a vengeance. Stumbling into a stall, Mona shut and bolted the door. Hugging herself, she leaned against the wall and sobbed.

Mona's misery so completely consumed her, she lost all sense of time. When at last she stopped crying and looked at her phone, she realized lunch was over—she was already fifteen minutes late to her next class!

Mona unlocked the door and staggered out of the stall. Unable to bear seeing herself again in the mirror, Mona averted her gaze to the gray, concrete floor while she splashed water for a second time on her face. Patting her face dry with paper towels, she couldn't help recalling how happy she had been when enmeshed in her daydreams of Brock…and how quickly Lady Anne turned her happiness into humiliation. There was a lesson to be learned here.

Dreams were a dangerous thing.

ABOUT THE AUTHOR

Mike Clifton has been involved in public education for over 38 years as a teacher, coach, and administrator, and currently lives in Mount Pleasant, Texas with his wife, Melanie. He enjoys all kinds of book and movie genre's, especially action/adventure, fantasy, urban fantasy, paranormal fantasy, paranormal romance, thrillers, and sci-fi. He has been a finalist in numerous short story contests, is an East Texas Writers Guild First Chapter Finalist for the fantasy novel, *The Conquest of the Veil*, and has professional articles published in the Texas Study of Secondary Education magazine. His books contain aspects of all the genres he enjoys…fast-paced action, adventure, mystery, fantasy, and romance/relationships.

You can follow Michael Scott Clifton at:

www.michaelscottclifton.com
www.facebook.com/michaelscottclifton
www.twitter.com/michaelsclifton
www.instagram.com/clifton4688
www.linkedin.com/in/mike-clifton-42875063